Love
Arrested

Doris Vilk

This is a work of fiction, and the characters, places, and events are the creation of the author. Resemblance to any person, living or dead, is entirely coincidental.

Coming Soon in the Chatham Series:

Love Attempted

Love Avenged

Website: www.DorisVilk.com

DEDICATION

For Sharon, a superb dental hygienist and my friend, who heard my story and encouraged me to write it.

CONTENTS

	Prologue	1
1	Lynchfield Prison	5
2	The Good Life	14
3	A Hollywood Romance	19
4	Life on the Inside	24
5	Not All Screws Fit the Mold	34
6	At Death's Door	46
7	I Feel Pretty?	53
8	Life is a Mess Hall	57
9	Master Manipulator	63
10	An Interesting Proposition	71
11	Franklin L. Lomegistro, M. D.	80
12	The Encounter	88
13	Reward or Torture	95
14	A Broken Woman	104
15	Back to Lynchfield	108
16	The First Time Ever I Saw Your Face	110
17	PR Disaster	133
18	A Second Chance	137
19	Beach Getaway	145

20 Essential Oils   154

21 Name That Tune   160

22 Just Another Night Out With the Gang   173

23 Love is in the Air   179

24 Back in Orange   183

25 Inpatient   187

26 The Prisoner's dilemma   198

27 The Show Must Go On   204

28 The Road to Freedom   219

29 Refuge   229

30 Afternoon Delight   232

31 Latin Love   236

32 Games People Play   238

33 Pornogate   242

34 Another Verdict   275

35 Freedom and Franklin   282

    Epilogue   290

    About the Author   295

ACKNOWLEDGMENTS

With sincerest gratitude I wish to thank all the interesting and wonderful people I met along life's journey that have inspired me to create the characters and circumstances that formed in my mind's eye and that I have finally put down on paper for others to enjoy.

My greatest thanks to my editor Patricia Nolan of "About The Words" who took my story and transformed it into something greater than I could have imagined. Thank you also to Gregg E. Brickman--I couldn't have self-published without your prompt help and mentor's guidance. And to Victoria Landis from Landis Design Resource, your creativity for the cover design surpassed my expectations and brought Love Arrested to visual life.

To Sharon Kotler, Judy Lehman and Joyce Z. Hunter, my confidants, thanks for lending me your ears as I constantly bounced story ideas off of you.

Lastly, I give my greatest appreciation and thanks to my family, my mom, my husband Larry, and my son Jordan who put up with my collage storyboards, my endless reading out loud, and the continuous clicks from my laptop keys, not to mention late meal preparations. I wholeheartedly appreciate the time you lent me to convey the world of Susan Chatham.

PROLOGUE

"GUILTY." The jury foreman read the verdict clearly, but Susan Chatham couldn't believe her ears. Throughout her trial she had sat quietly and tried carefully to rein in her emotions. Today, in a navy blue suit with a pleated skirt, pink-laced blouse and matching navy pumps, she looked beautiful, but tired. Each day her outfit had been selected carefully. Nothing "showy" or fancy was allowed. Nothing to reveal what her life had been like prior to this God-awful trial. Her long black hair was styled conservatively and her makeup was minimal. She was a natural beauty. Even with a freshly washed face she turned heads. But the stress was showing. She was thin. The twinkle in her blue eyes was dimming ever so slightly. Her fair porcelain skin had taken an unfortunate turn toward pale. She was worn out. While the judge and jury had shuffled into the courtroom to take their seats, she had tried to make eye contact. No one would look at her. When asked to stand as the verdict was read, she did so. She had never experienced such silent anguish, such profound fear. All she could hear was her heartbeat pounding inside her head. When she heard that horrible word, "guilty," she felt her knees give out. She caught herself with the edge of the table and tried to stay steady. She struggled to breathe. And then the tears came. Loud sobs she simply couldn't control.

Her attorneys had coached her somewhat, tried to prepare her for every possible outcome. But there was no way to prepare her for this. Especially when she was on trial for a crime she had not committed.

The trial itself had been surreal. The judge had been difficult and many things weren't allowed into evidence. The best of her attorneys had been in a car accident two days before the trial began, and he was in the hospital. The law firm had replaced him with a less experienced attorney, since the remaining partners were already committed to other trials. Susan had wanted to go with another firm altogether, but her husband Dale McCraven had refused to spend the extra money, already upset about her expenditures. Susan had no idea what he was talking about. She hadn't been spending any more than usual. As a matter of fact, she had been so busy recently with her hit TV show she barely had time to get her nails done. But their bank accounts told a different story. And she certainly had not gone to Kane's Jewelers and stolen those diamonds. It was absurd. She felt as though she were losing her mind. The store's video footage was clear. It looked like Susan, in an outfit she owned, at Kane's trying on the expensive and exquisite diamonds she had previously admired. It also showed her putting some diamond earrings and other pieces in her pockets and walking out of the store without paying. But how could that be? She wasn't there that day! Could Kane's have gotten the dates mixed up? But then, how could she explain the identical diamond earrings found in her home, in a jewelry box she kept partially hidden? They had been discovered by a police search warrant that left her home ransacked. She couldn't explain any of it and that's why she was here today.

Everyone she cared about had turned on her. Her close friend and body double Allison Cray had even testified against her. Allison had also recommended Susan's current law firm and had advised her to plead innocent and go to trial instead of taking a plea deal. Susan knew of course she was innocent of all charges, but she had considered the plea deal because it meant so much less jail time. With a short prison sentence, as soon as she got out, she would have spent every waking moment clearing her good name. But now, with this guilty verdict, her sentence would be much harsher.

Susan had gone over with her attorneys, her father Richard, her husband Dale, her twin brother Tommie, everyone she knew in fact, her timeline on the morning in question. She had started the day meeting Allison for coffee. She had gone shopping for some necessities at the mall. She had run to the bank. Her day had been hectic because she had tried to cram so much into some rare time off. After her arrest, she had berated herself for using cash and throwing away her receipts. But she knew there would be a bank statement. It would show the ATM transaction with a date/time stamp. She begged her lawyers to track down the evidence. No one would listen and no one seemed to care about a cash withdrawal. They all focused on that video footage and Allison's testimony.

For Susan, Allison's testimony was difficult to swallow.

"I was on the L bus."

"Yes, my car had trouble and Dale McCraven, my employer, was expecting me at work."

"I was on the L bus as it passed by Kane's jewelers."

"Yes, I know Susan Chatham."

"Yes, I am her body double and we work together on the television show CSI."

"Yes, Susan Chatham is my close friend, but I won't lie for her."

"Yes, I saw Susan Chatham in front of Kane's that afternoon. I saw her from the window of the L bus."

Everything Allison had said was a lie, but the video footage backed up her story. And so did Dale. He seemed to be under Allison's spell. They had been inseparable the months prior to Susan's arrest, but she had been too busy and too trusting to take real notice.

"What is wrong with him?" thought Susan. "Why is he behaving like this? Is he having an affair with Allison? Is that all it took for him to turn his back on me and our seven year marriage?" There were no answers, only more questions.

She knew her father thought she was guilty as well. In middle school, she and her best friend Jenny Cavilieri had gone into a department store and while they were messing around, Jenny had decided she wanted to steal something. Susan didn't want any part in it, but she stood by her friend instead of walking away. That was a big mistake. Her father hadn't believed her then, and he didn't believe her now. He had been humiliated by that incident and swore he would disown her if even so much as a hint of impropriety reared its ugly head ever again. It was all just too much. Susan was a skilled actress and performer, but she was no liar and no thief. This whole experience was a complete nightmare. She wished her mom were alive. Gloria Chatham would know what to do.

The judge's stern voice jolted her back into horrible reality. "Susan Jordyn Chatham McCraven you are hereby remanded to Lynchfield prison for a term of incarceration of five years with the possibility of parole in no less than three years."

She was quickly handcuffed and shackled. The sobs were reduced to a steady stream of tears pouring out of her bloodshot eyes. She saw Dale, her father and Tommie leave the courtroom without even a glance in her direction. It hurt so much to see them walk away. It felt as though they were walking out of her life for good.

No one was smiling in the courtroom except Allison Cray. She stared at Susan with a smirk on her lips. Susan looked in disbelief as Allison mouthed the words "you're fucked," turned on her heels and left the room. Susan left the courtroom too, but through a different exit, escorted by three officers, in handcuffs and shackles. Her empty stomach was aching as the tears kept coming. She bowed her head and stared at the ground. Her entire body, including her brain, was numb.

CHAPTER 1
LYNCHFIELD PRISON

Sometimes it's better to just remain silent and smile.
~ Unknown. ~

The moments after her removal from the courtroom were a blur. Susan remembered being ushered into a room, her attorneys meeting briefly with her about motions for an appeal. The guards removed her handcuffs and shackles just long enough for her to change into a pair of jeans and a tee. Her sharp courtroom dress clothes were taken away. While putting on her sneakers, no socks, she was quickly approached by the police guards again and returned to handcuffs and shackles.

"Umm, they are a bit too tight." Susan's voice sounded strained and meek. Her complaint fell on deaf ears. She went along without putting up a fight, but they were still so rough with her. She wanted to cry, but her tears ducts had finally gone dry. Her head pounded, and her heart beat abnormally fast, with intermittent skips. Was this a panic attack or a heart attack? She almost wished she would drop dead.

When Susan was pushed into a prison van with bars on the windows, she tried to pretend for a moment that this was just another television or movie scene. She had starred in many police dramas. She had always admired their realism. Now, she acknowledged to herself that there was no way to properly convey the horror of being led off to prison. The look of the vehicle, the other convicts and the officers were nothing like on TV. The smells made her want to wretch, despite her empty stomach. She sat motionless, not wanting to look at anyone or anything around her. As the van sped off, she bounced like a rag doll on the bench seat. This was a far cry from the soft leather seats and smooth suspension of her blue Porsche.

Susan wasn't sure if she had closed her eyes in prayer and had fallen asleep, if she had passed out, or if she had been in a trance, but she didn't remember the rest of the ride to Lynchfield. Her next recollection was being grabbed to get up on her feet, and pushed to get into line and enter the prison for new inmate registration. She saw the brick exterior and barbed wire fencing and felt a chill in her bones, despite the heat of the day.

She was commanded to remove any jewelry and valuables, and was fingerprinted again. It wasn't any easier getting fingerprinted in prison than it had been after she was arrested the first time. Her photo was taken and she was weighed. She was then led into a room along with the other inmates and ordered to strip naked. Susan had done some partial nudity for acting, and she enjoyed getting nude for sex, but this didn't even vaguely resemble any kind of safe or erotic environment. This was brutal and violating. She was forced to bend over and cough at one point. Her mouth was inspected, as were her genitals and anus. It was humiliating. She was sprayed with delousing powder as if she were an animal. Susan had showered just that morning before court. Now instead of her expensive Italian hair products, she smelled like lawn fertilizer and disinfectant. She was pushed into another room to take a cold shower. She was instructed to urinate in full view of everyone. She was sprayed with delousing powder a second time and handed orange scrubs to wear. The plain loafers she was issued were a half size too big for her feet and her heel came out of the back with each miserable step. "What about underpants and a bra?" she asked. No answer. She was handed what would barely pass for a pillow, worn-out linens and a rough burlap-like gray blanket, and told to carry these things to her bunk assignment.

Susan arrived woozy and disoriented to Cell Block D. Cream-colored cinderblock walls with bunk beds and a metal storage locker and desk below. In the bottom bunk lay a woman with caramel skin she later found out was Puerto Rican. The woman's orange scrub top was pulled taut by her large breasts, her pants tight from her ample backside. Her hair was combed in ringlets but kinky. Susan looked at her cautiously out of the corner of her eye, not knowing what to expect from this cellmate. The woman in turn looked at Susan with a smile in her eyes, as if to say, "Relax kiddo, everything will be okay." Susan was put at ease for just a few seconds, but she didn't believe for one minute that everything would be ok. She burst into tears as she prepared her bed. She was so disoriented and miserable, she couldn't even figure out the simplest of tasks. Roberta Jimenez, her cellmate, quickly took over and showed her what to do as gently as she could. Miraculously, Susan fell asleep, not hungry, even though she hadn't eaten anything at all that day. It was a fitful sleep, the kind of sleep that an exhausted body succumbs to, even when the mind cannot believe what it is processing.

It was still dark when roll call took place the next morning. Roberta Jimenez shook Susan. "Get up quick, quick, stand up straight, tuck in your shirt, tie your hair back, make your bed tightly, and stand up and don't say a word, don't blink, don't smile, don't look. Here they come!" Susan moved as rapidly as she could, her pulse racing, her face flushed. In that split second when she opened her eyes, she forgot where she was and what had happened to her. That blissful split second brought her to tears again. Among the women at Lynchfield penitentiary, she stuck out like the "Newbie" she was, like the "College" she was, like the "Beauty" she was.

George Ferguson was the guard on duty that first roll call. He walked near Jimenez and Chatham saying their names out loud and walking closely enough that his hands brushed near both women's breasts and buttocks. He counted them and moved on, but his head turned back to acknowledge Susan. "Nice," he whispered lasciviously and loud enough for her to hear. Whatever he meant, Susan was sure it couldn't be good. She began to tremble and hyperventilate. She didn't even want to think about having to avoid or defend herself against a horny guard. She forced herself to put it out of her mind and try to calm down. Were all the guards like this one? They certainly couldn't all be that gorgeous, but they might all be that menacing.

After the count, it was time for breakfast. Roberta looked at Susan and shook her head. Her face betrayed pity and concern. She tried to say Chatham but couldn't with her Puerto Rican accent. She settled on "Chatty." It would have been funny to Susan under any other circumstances. Instead, she barely took notice of her kind-hearted cellmate's attempts to put her at ease and make small talk. She just tried to focus on what she could learn and how it might help her survive.

"Chatty, you are too pretty, girl. It will get you into trouble. The lesbians will be all over you, and if they don't get you, George Ferguson or another guard will. Make yourself ugly girl."

"How do I do that?" Susan asked in barely a whisper, her voice betrayed her panic.

"Shit girl, ain't you ever been homely in your whole life?"

"No," Susan said, slightly embarrassed. "I've been a model since I was a toddler and now I'm on TV. Well, I was on TV." Fresh tears welled up in her eyes.

"Don't cry Chatty. Okay, yes, maybe crying will make your eyes less blue and your nose red and less perfect. Let's mess up your hair, wrinkle that scrub top some." It was no use. Trying to make Susan unattractive was like turning the swan back into the ugly duckling. Impossible.

Prison breakfast was as discouraging as her prospects for survival in this unbearably foreign environment.

"This isn't oatmeal," Susan said. "It's wallpaper paste."

Someone at the table laughed, then a second later, she felt the "oatmeal" still it its bowl, hit her in the face. She winced from the pain. A guard approached, "Is there a problem here?"

Roberta quickly stepped in. "No problem officer, just an accident."

"Thanks Roberta," Susan said.

"Everyone goes by last names here," said Roberta. "It's Jimenez."

Seeing the worried look on Susan's face coupled with an already forming welt on her cheek and the remnants of food dripping down her chin, Roberta turned to her and whispered in her ear. "You can call me Bert."

The first weeks were an unmitigated disaster. Susan could barely choke down the "food" she was served. What she did manage to swallow was awful. The food was plain, too salty or no flavor at all, mostly canned, lots of sandwiches and cold cuts, too many salty soups, barely any vegetables, salads, or fruits. Any vegetables or fruits that did appear on the menu were canned, overripe, or spoiled. Susan's stomach ached constantly. She was losing weight quickly.

Sleeping was difficult. The cots were too narrow and thin and the springs banged at your bones. With every toss or turn, a loud creaking noise echoed through the concrete jungle. Other noises could be heard all night as well, bodily noises, grunts, the occasional shout or cry. The sheets and blanket were rough and itchy and Susan was cold every night to the point of shivering. She often cried herself to a fitful sleep. Sporadic at best, she rarely got more than four hours of rest. She existed in an exhausted state.

The other inmates started calling her "College Snot" early on in her sentence. Mostly because they thought she was a university smart ass, but also because her incessant crying meant her nose ran constantly. They had no idea where she had come from and what her life had been like prior to Lynchfield. If they had, they would have cried along with her.

At night, when it was time for lights out, Bert did her best to coach and support Susan. She was the only source of comfort and Susan was beyond grateful that she had landed her as a cellmate. She would have had a complete nervous breakdown otherwise. Bert taught her how to make the bed. What and how to eat. She taught her how to stay safe in the showers, how to manage to pee and take a shit when you had no privacy. She taught her who the "nice" girls were, who it was safe to talk to, and who to avoid. The main gang was known as the "The Bitch Warriors," run by an inmate named Beulah. Beulah had murdered more than one person in cold blood and should have been sent to death row. She was a violent psychopath. She had plea-bargained into Lynchfield. "No matter what, stay clear of Beulah, Chatty," warned Bert. The thought of walking the same halls as a convicted murderer and violent inmate would have been laughable to Susan just weeks prior. Now it terrified her.

Bert also had a mental spreadsheet on the guards that she shared with Susan. Who was safe and who to avoid. She taught Susan little tricks to help her maintain her sanity. Staying upbeat was particularly challenging. None of it was easy, happy, or hopeful, but all of it was meant to keep Susan as safe as possible, and help her do her time.

Susan followed rules and order despite her weakened state. She was assigned to work duty, mostly cleaning. She mopped and swept and cleaned the bathrooms. The toilets were disgusting all the time. The smell often made her ill. There were no other finishing school graduates at Lynchfield. Susan soon began to smell permanently of pine oil cleaning fluid and her hands began to roughen and crack from the harsh, toxic liquids.

The first several visiting days, Susan allowed herself to feel hopeful. That proved to be a mistake. She received no visitors, ever. She would periodically check her commissary account, but only the funds she earned during her work detail were there. That amount was not enough to buy anything. Her collect calls to Dale, Allison, her Dad and Tommie all went unanswered and unreturned. No one in her life communicated with her. No one wanted anything to do with her; at least no one on the outside.

George Ferguson began to hit on her within weeks of her arrival. George was actually quite good looking, tall, dark and handsome for sure. He was muscular with deep brown eyes and wavy dark hair. In another life, Susan would have found him attractive. In the state she was in, however, both married and completely despondent, returning his advances was out of the question. Her husband Dale's behavior during and since the trial had been awful, but still she couldn't bring herself to even contemplate infidelity. Somewhere in the back of her mind, she believed that after her release, she would start fresh with Dale. Her old life could somehow be rebuilt. She explained this to Correctional Officer Ferguson, but it only seemed to annoy him. His annoyance turned to anger as she repeatedly refused his sexual attention or his offers of contraband.

"I'm married. I won't cheat on my husband. I don't do drugs. I don't want anything from you. Please leave me alone." Susan would be as gracious as possible. He persisted and she resisted. Finally, he threatened her with demerits and swore he would make a lot of trouble for her if she didn't "play nice." He made good on his threats.

When Susan was first called into Warden Michael Ramsey's office, she was too naïve and too new to know that was never a good thing.

"How are you making out Chatham?" Warden Ramsey was tall, thin, with a black mustache, and salt and pepper hair. He seemed to have a permanent five o'clock shadow. If he noticed that Susan looked like death warmed over, he didn't show it. Susan assumed he was used to seeing shattered women. She just stood there looking at her feet as Bert had coached her. It was all she could think to do. "Less is more at Lynchfield," Bert would say.

"Cat got your tongue Chatham? Or is it that actresses have nothing to say when no one is providing them with a script?"

Susan realized he knew who she was, but still she said nothing. No one else had seemed to acknowledge her celebrity status. This was not what she had in mind when she would complain to Dale that she wished she were anonymous sometimes.

"Officer Ferguson keeps giving you shots."

"Shots sir, I don't understand? No one is shooting at me."

"Ahh, so you do have a voice. Shots don't come from a gun Chatham, they are demerits, infractions."

"What did I do?" Susan asked sulking.

"Nothing from what I can see on the video footage," Warden Ramsey responded.

Susan felt as though the wind had been knocked out of her. "Oh no, not more video footage of me. Now what will I be accused of that I haven't done? Now what will happen to me?"

She hoped the Warden hadn't noticed her knocking knees.

"Okay Chatham, I don't know what's up between you and Ferguson and all of these demerits/shots. He is one of the best guards here. Keep your nose clean and out of trouble. I will dismiss these. At least I will dismiss any I don't see evidence for. You got that Chatham?"

"Yes." She breathed a sigh.

"It's yes, sir, Chatham."

"Yes, yes, sir, Warden Ramsey, sir."

"Much better Chatham. Okay now get out of here."

"Thank you."

"Christ Chatham, thank you, sir."

"Thank you, sir."

The Warden smiled at her and opened the door so Susan Chatham could leave. She did so promptly. He watched her walk down the hall, and thought, "That girl is just too pretty for her own good. Our little celebrity won't last long. Let's see if she can handle herself."

CHAPTER 2
THE GOOD LIFE

Sometimes you have to accept the fact
that there are things that will never
go back to how they used to be.
~ Curiano.com ~

During the first few months of her incarceration, Susan reminisced often on how life used to be. Even though it was agonizing to look back, she forced herself to do so, because between the tears, the happy memories would provide comfort. The happiness was fleeting, but it fortified her. In her memories she felt safe.

She had come from a happy upper middle class home, growing up with her father Richard and her mother Gloria. She was a twin, so her brother Tommie and she had always had a special bond. As far back as she could remember she had been in front of a camera. Her mother told her that when she and Tommie were toddlers, her close friend had suggested modeling. Gloria had decided to give it a try and sent in a few photos to various parenting magazines and cute kid contests. It didn't take long for the twins to be discovered. Susan first appeared on the cover of "Parenting" magazine at age four. Tommie hated every second in front of the camera. It was so boring for him to get dressed up and sit there for hours waiting. All he wanted to do was play. For Susan it was love at first sight, she was a natural on camera. She would grace the covers of many more magazines and be featured in several articles on everything to do with little girls. She had found her calling.

At home, Susan and Tommie's parents tried hard to make sure their lives were as normal as possible. Their lifestyle was comfortable, but they were assigned chores and taught gratitude and humility. It was so hard for Susan to conjure up gratitude at Lynchfield. Humility was easy. More like humiliation.

Susan had an enriched childhood, and enjoyed many hobbies. She especially loved cooking with her mother. They would prepare delicious meals from all over the world and Gloria, a classically trained chef, taught Susan real culinary school techniques. By the time she reached middle school, Susan was creating her own recipes and could compete with the best. The food at Lynchfield, however, was unsalvageable. Julia Child couldn't have made that slop taste good or put a positive spin on any aspect of those ghastly meals. She was used to gourmet. This food was garbage. It was so offensive to Susan to have to put that crap into her body. She was used to elegance and refinement. She prided herself in her healthy lifestyle. She had gone from the best of everything to the absolute worst.

Eventually, after many years as a child model, Susan became interested in other aspects of performance. She was a naturally talented singer and took not only voice lessons but also studied every form of dance. Every member of the Chatham family was an avid athlete and loved all sports. Susan excelled at swimming. She juggled these myriad activities for as long as she could, but by high school, acting was number one. Tommie took a more traditional path, sticking with academics and sports, particularly soccer.

Socially, both Susan and Tommie were popular, but

Richard and Gloria Chatham weren't at all fond of Susan's best friend, Jenny Cavilieri. It was hard to know what drew Susan to Jenny, but they were inseparable in grade school and middle school. Jenny was a wild child. She talked back to her parents and to her teachers. She was frequently in trouble, but Susan would try to see the best in her. They spent many Saturdays at the mall, shopping and boy-watching. When Jenny suggested they steal a shirt from a department store they were browsing in, Susan told her she was foolish.

"Come on, scaredy cat, just one top," taunted Jenny.

"Jenny, whatever you want, I can buy it for you. I don't want you to get in trouble and I am certainly not going to steal anything. That would be the end of me."

"Let's just see if we can get away with it. It'll just be a one time thing, I promise."

"I'm sorry, Jenny. I can't do it. I don't want to do it. It's stupid and I'm out."

"Ok, forget it then," said Jenny.

Susan should have known better, but she carried a naiveté that always made her vulnerable. As they walked through the department store to get to the mall exit, Jenny made a detour in the "juniors" section. Before Susan knew it, Jenny had stuffed items into her knapsack and put a lacy bra in Susan's open satchel. What happened next would forever haunt Susan and put a permanent rift between the girls. They were caught and Jenny did nothing to steer blame away from her closest friend, who was entirely innocent. It was a low point in Susan's young life and the backlash from her father was heartbreaking. If not for Gloria Chatham, that stupid incident would have ruined Susan's relationship with her father forever. As it was, several months passed before Richard and Susan's relationship approached back to normal.

Susan thought now, "Isn't it ironic that I am the one who ended up in jail." She had heard through the grapevine that Jenny, the working class girl from a broken home, had made it big as an attorney in New York. Maybe Susan should have called her when she was arrested. Would Jenny have even taken her call? They hadn't spoken since that fateful day.

When Susan reached high school, she went from pretty to gorgeous. Her body, while model thin, had hints of curves. She filled out a B-cup and from behind, there was no question she was a woman. Swimming had kept her muscles toned and genetics had given her a nuclear metabolism. Her long black hair was the envy of every teenage girl, not only in her high school, but also in the nation. By the time she was a sophomore, Susan was starring in a popular teen TV show. Even though she was a "star" and was making millions, her parents insisted she continue regular high school and graduate with her class. Looking back now, Susan was glad they did. If her parents hadn't been so focused on keeping her "normal" she would have been even less able to handle Lynchfield.

With her brother Tommie as the star of the soccer team, Susan made a point of going to as many of his games as she could manage with her busy teen-star schedule. She was happy to support her brother, yes, but boy were his teammates cute.

There was so much eye candy at the games; she brought popcorn to watch the show. There was one player in particular who gave Susan butterflies. Dale McCraven was tall with curly sandy hair and olive skin. He always had a dark tan, belying his Irish ancestry. His eyes were a dark gray and his teeth a bright white. He was, in a word, dreamy. Susan always had her eye on him, but he was much more interested in sport. At least that is what Susan thought. Dale did indeed notice his good friend Tommie Chatham's sister. He was just too shy to do anything about it. He didn't realize how appealing he was and he never thought he had a chance with a girl like Susan. She was a famous teen actress and model. He thought there was no way. He was interested in going into show business himself, but behind the camera. His ambition was to become a producer. Maybe he would hire Susan one day. Maybe he would be so famous she would want to be in one of his movies. Dale didn't realize Susan would have done anything for him, beginning at age 16. Susan, Tommie and Dale were separated during their college years. But fate brought them together again.

Susan forced herself to continue her trip down memory lane. In between crying fits and silent despair, she needed to dissect every year, every hour, every minute of her life. It was the only way she could keep her sanity and at the same time, figure out exactly how she had ended up here. In the dead of night, every night in her cell, long after Bert had fallen asleep, Susan thought of Dale McCraven. A man she had loved since high school. A man she thought would be with her forever and stand by her through thick and thin. "Wasn't he her for better or for worse?" Fame is fickle and every actress fades, but she believed in the love she shared with Dale. She never thought anything, or anyone, could come between them.

CHAPTER 3
A HOLLYWOOD ROMANCE

Lots of people want to ride with you in the limo,
but what you want is someone who will take the
bus with you when the limo breaks down.
~ Oprah Winfrey ~

When Susan left Los Angeles to go to college on the east
coast, it was with excitement tinged with sadness. Dale was at
UCLA film school during her last two years in high school,
and it was a difficult decision to leave home. She and Dale
had connected romantically her senior year and decided to try
a long distance relationship. Finishing college was something
Gloria Chatham had wanted Susan to do, and she had hoped
Susan would attend her alma mater. It was a priority in
Susan's family, despite her modeling and acting success, and
she wasn't going to let her parents down. Dale worried that as
soon as Susan walked on campus, she would be swarmed
with suitors and whisked away from him, even before he had
a chance to marry her and give her the glamorous life he was
working toward. He expressed his concern to Susan, and she
showed him how she felt about him in ways that left little
doubt that she was devoted.

Susan did indeed have many admirers at college, but Dale was the man of her heart. She couldn't put her finger on it, but she just knew she was destined to marry him. It didn't matter if they were in different states or different coasts.

When Dale graduated with a degree from UCLA, he went right to work. Hollywood welcomed him with open arms, thanks to some school connections and a knack for picking winning scripts. Susan came back to LA at every opportunity and by the time she graduated two years later, Dale was well on his way to establishing himself as an award winning director and producer. His youth wasn't an issue, his talent shone through. He asked Susan to marry him on a Malibu beach at sunset and she answered exactly as she had in her mind so many times.

Dale and Susan McCraven became the ultimate Hollywood couple. He was so handsome, and she, so beautiful. He had the abs, legs, and ass of a soccer player, which he still enjoyed and would play on weekends in various leagues. Susan's cascading black hair, fair skin and piercing blue eyes made her the toast of Tinseltown. She had no trouble transitioning from teen star to female lead. Her swimming and dancing became more like hobbies, but both kept her toned and fit. She also still loved to sing, although now it was more at home or in the shower, and not professionally, although her voice was lovely just the same.

Dale and Susan enjoyed each other's company and were always active and on the run. Their sex life was equally active.

When they tied the knot, their wedding was featured in every magazine. Susan looked stunning in her Versace gown, with Dale by her side looking gorgeous in a black Hugo Boss tux with white shirt and silver bow tie and vest. Everyone in the family looked radiant that day. Well, almost everyone. If someone had paid closer attention to the "mother of the bride", they would have noticed that Gloria Chatham appeared quite pale and stick thin. Richard Chatham had noticed and was concerned by his wife's recently inexplicable weight loss. She ate normally, they had every meal together, but she still kept shedding pounds. He wondered if perhaps she was just overcome by emotion. Gloria was so proud of Susan. They were so close. Richard was proud of her too, but he couldn't shake a sense of doom and gloom. He would sometimes think back on that horrible shoplifting episode and become instantly nauseous. Gloria never looked back on that, and if he mentioned it, she would shut him down immediately. He just felt that something would happen to his only daughter, and he wouldn't be able to protect or counsel her. On this special day, he glimpsed away from his wife and back to his daughter, and decided to focus on the festivities.

The Veuve Clicquot Ponsardin Brut champagne flowed, the gourmet meal was to die for and the 7-tiered wedding cake was a showstopper. The best caterers in LA had been hired and supervised by Gloria Chatham. They did not disappoint. A well-known local band played live and a DJ was hired to run the turntable when the band took breaks. The guests danced until the wee hours of the morning, with no one more exhausted than Dale and Susan by the end of the reception.

The morning after their wedding, Susan and Dale left to go on a Caribbean honeymoon to St. Maarten. They ate, and drank, and sunbathed nude on China Beach. They enjoyed every activity and Watersport the five-star resort had to offer. Their energy was endless, and at night they had wild, hot sex, often into the wee hours of daybreak, until they were spent and unable to carry on. It was a wonderful time.

Tragically, their honeymoon had to be cut short a mere five days into their planned ten-day getaway. Susan received a call from Tommie to come home if she could, Mom was quite ill, and Dad very distraught. Susan felt instant panic and told Dale, whom she affectionately called Dilly, that they needed to get back to LA. Something was wrong with Mom.

Gloria Chatham lived a mere two months from diagnosis to funeral. She passed away from uterine, endometrial adenocarcinoma. By the time it was caught, it was labeled stage IV and had metastasized all over her body. Her oncologists tried chemotherapy, but it was too little, too late, and just added to her considerable suffering. There just wasn't anything doctors could do. Susan was with her mom through those final, horrible two months. She regretted leaving Dale, but her family needed her, and she wouldn't dream of being anywhere but by her mother's side. She took care of things around the house and tried to comfort her depressed dad. She felt bad leaving Dilly, but of course he understood.

Gloria's passing was difficult on everyone and changed the family dynamics. Every member of the Chatham family handled their grief differently. They drifted apart as a result. Susan stepped up and tried to maintain her dad's schedule the way her mom had, making his appointments, seeing to household chores and everyday matters. But she noticed a change in her father. He was just never the same after Gloria died. Also, Susan was supposed to be a newlywed. She needed to get back to her husband and her career commitments. She sensed that Richard Chatham wanted her to stay longer, and resented her when she didn't. Or was it just her imagination? Perhaps his depression was clouding his judgment. Susan was right in getting back to her husband. She would just need to be there for her father as much as her schedule permitted.

Susan went back to her Hollywood life and Richard Chatham buried himself in his work. Tommie Chatham returned to his life as a successful financial planner and delved into his active social life, and rarely saw his dad or his twin sister.

Dale and Susan both had hectic demanding schedules. He was producing several projects at a time and had become quite the Hollywood Mogul. She starred in several CSI episodes, and other TV shows and made many popular Lifetime TV movies. She often traveled around the world with various modeling projects, mostly for cosmetics and sometimes for jewelry.

The couple loved each other dearly but simply couldn't

spend a lot of time together because of their careers. When they did come together, they made wild passionate love, so their sex life never suffered the distance. They tried to have a date night once a month to visit their favorite restaurant, Mrs. Chen's Dim Sum. They would join their Hollywood friends, actors, writers, directors, and have a great night out. Dale and Susan McCraven appreciated the quality time they enjoyed together even though they didn't have the quantity they desired. They weren't fully aware that the time spent apart created a unique opportunity for someone who wanted Susan's life and would do anything to get it. That someone was Allison Cray.

CHAPTER 4
LIFE ON THE INSIDE

Do you ever feel like Cinderella?
I don't mean the happily ever after,
I mean like when she's doing everything for
everyone else and still isn't good enough.
~ Unknown ~

Susan woke up, startled from another bad dream, breathing hard, in her bunk bed in Cell Block D. She must have dozed off while reminiscing. She blinked away her sleepy eyes several times and swallowed hard, but her throat stayed dry and raw. She tried to lick at her dry lips but there was no saliva. Susan looked over at Bert who was fast asleep. She was still here, in this wretched prison, cut off from her life and those she loved. The nightmare was real, it wasn't a sick dream or a movie set. She was a year into her sentence and she still couldn't get used to this obscene travesty of "justice." She couldn't figure out how Bert managed to sleep so soundly here at Lynchfield? She wondered if Bert had simply stopped going over the past in her mind, a hundred times a day, like Susan did. Dissecting every interaction she had ever had, analyzing and reading into every single life event. What was she searching for? She didn't really know, maybe a clue as to how she ended up here. It was dark, well almost dark. By now she knew emergency lights were always on, so "lights out" didn't really mean what it would mean anyplace else. She rolled over trying to close her eyes, tears running down her now salty face. She tried to wipe them away with the back of her hand. Her previously soft conditioned skin felt dry, rough and cracked now. It ached like the rest of her body. She wondered if Allison Cray was using up her expensive hand creams, night serums, and moisturizers at the home she shared with Dale. Wasn't Allison shacking up with Dale now? She had heard that on TV of all places. The nasty inmates at Lynchfield had gotten a snickering chuckle out of that bit of breaking news. Now her Hollywood past was common knowledge. Finding out about Dilly felt like the final blow to her already broken heart. But Susan and Dale weren't divorced yet. Were they really separated - by more than just a barbed wired prison fence?

Even after all this time, Susan still missed her master bedroom and the bed she shared with Dale. The room had been about the size of the entire Cell Block D where Roberta and Susan lived. Her bed had been an extra-large and deep California King with a soft pillow top mattress and satin sheets in beautiful jewel toned colors. Her comforter had been heavy weight goose down with a duvet of 1000 count Egyptian cotton, its extra softness worlds away from the rough Burlap blanket she wrapped herself in now. This prison issued blanket, if could you even call it that, was grossly inadequate. She often slept in her orange scrubs, and sometimes even in the prison sweatshirt, although it offered little additional warmth. Susan missed the softness of her silk pajamas. Her feet missed having spa pedicures and relaxing in her padded, memory foam Vionic slippers.

She was also always hungry. Going to bed hungry was the worst. She hated everything that was served at Lynchfield. Many times a Bitch Warrior stole her food, or they would spit into it and she wouldn't get to eat at all. "Starving out" was what they called it. Even when they weren't actively starving her out she could barely manage to swallow most meals. Her stomach hurt, and she was either constipated because she hadn't eaten enough or had diarrhea from scarfing down something horrid that hadn't agreed with her.

The Hollywood mansion she had shared with Dale had eight bedrooms and nine baths. Now she had to use public prison toilets with no doors. She would have to wait to be handed toilet paper by the guards. Many ogled her as she relieved herself. It was all too humiliating and she found she couldn't relieve herself properly. Her body just refused to cooperate, except when she had the runs, and then she was so embarrassed. And the smells were so nasty in those dingy bathrooms. There was little ventilation and no air fresheners. Not only did she have to do her business under those circumstances, she also had to clean the filthy bathrooms during her work detail.

Susan would remember frequently all of her trips to Pier One. She remembered casually lingering in the store, smelling all the wonderful air fresheners before deciding on the Citrus Sage for her master bathroom with Dale. She had taken something so ordinary and trivial for granted. She realized that now. Her whole life was full of reminders of everyday things and situations she had not valued in the least.

In addition to insomnia, Susan was plagued by nightmares. Her terrifying dreams would wake her up in a cold sweat, or screaming, and Bert would "shush" her and tell her to stop. Bert reminded Susan that if she didn't stay quiet she would get herself beaten up or thrown in the Shoe. The Shoe was the dreaded, lunacy inducing solitary confinement segregation section of Lynchfield. This scared Susan further and gave her worse dreams. Some of the night terrors were about getting arrested, some about her trial, how her Dad had yelled at her and disowned her, her abandonment by Tommie too. Some of the nightmares involved Dale. He hated her now. He accused her of stealing their money, the jewelry, of cheating on him. Susan knew she hadn't done any of these things. Her nightmares reflected the fact that she had no friends, other than her cellmate Roberta Jimenez. Where had all her Hollywood friends gone? All those fellow actors and actresses that had danced, and drank, and eaten her gourmet food, and fucked at parties in her home?

Susan realized that most of her nightmares actually came from remembering the sweet and privileged life that she had lived before Lynchfield, remembering the beautiful house, the wonderful vacations, the fancy cars, and swank Hollywood parties. The new reality of waking up at Lynchfield Women's Correctional Facility was consistently unbearable. That terrible cot, those springs, that burlap blanket, the cold, the hunger, the nasty odors, the cold showers, the loneliness, the embarrassment of being in prison. And so she woke up several times during the night. But there was no privacy, and she found no relief, no comfort.

One of the guards would look in on her frequently. He was a regular on the night shift. Susan thought he was ruggedly handsome, if a bit rough looking. This guard had gentle green eyes and a square stubbly chin, and Susan liked that he had strong shoulders and arms. His very dark almost black hair, which he spiked towards the side with some type of gel, made his tanned face look quite distinguished. He smelled about as nice as anyone could here at Lynchfield too, clean and soapy. His uniform read Sterling. Officer Sterling, but she had overheard one of the other guards refer to him as Paul.

Officer Sterling would come to her bedside several times during his patrol. He would see she was wide-awake, and acknowledge her scared eyes with his handsome green ones. He wouldn't say a word. He would just give her a nod. Susan also noticed him looking at Bert while she slept. He looked at her with longing, but also in a protective way.

Paul Sterling had noticed this new inmate in Cell Block D. He agreed with George Ferguson that this one was a looker. He was amazed however, that someone so pretty, like Chatham, could look like a scene from a horror movie every time he looked in on her. She wasn't sleeping. She had had more trouble than most adjusting to this life. It was taking so long. He was worried she would never adjust, and those were the ones who ended up dead, or worse. Yes there were worse things than death in prison.

At one point several months into her sentence, Officer Sterling approached Susan. "Chatham, you need to get some sleep. You aren't supposed to be awake. If you aren't going to sleep then at least close your eyes and rest. Stop crying. Please don't make me have to write you up. I don't want to have to give you a Shot."

She looked at Officer Sterling and nodded, not knowing what to say. Bert had taught her not to look at anyone, and not to talk. Not to the other inmates, and especially not to the guards. But Susan was usually a people person, and bubbly and talkative and easily made eye contact and conversation with anyone. It was an intrinsic part of her personality. It was difficult to turn off, even in her present circumstances and despondent state. Everything about prison life was so strange and foreign. Everything about prison life was shitty.

She lay there breathing hard, actually gasping, after one of her nightmares and she was hungry and cold and she opened her tear filled, terrified eyes just as Paul Sterling walked by.

"Chatham," he said sternly. Paul Sterling had had enough of her nightly shenanigans.

His voice scared her more. Susan startled, and being too close to the edge of the narrow bed, lost her balance and fell, hitting the floor with a thump. She quickly stood up, rubbing her now sore knees, with uncontrolled tears flowing down her face. Bert didn't even stir. She could sleep through a hurricane.

"Jesus Chatham, are you all right?" he said grabbing her arm. But not in any way that hurt her as she had imagined, but rather more helpful and caring. "I've had enough of you Chatham, come with me."

Susan stood trembling, and used the bottom of her

orange scrub top to dry her face. Where was he taking her? Was he going to rape her, beat her or worse? The rumors around prison life were awful, and they were true. Susan thought her time had finally come, she was going to receive the full prison treatment.

"Please sir, I have to pee," she said hoping to stall whatever sentence he had in mind for her.

Sterling said nothing to her as he walked her over to the open door toilet, handing her some toilet paper, he turned his back to her, to actually give her some privacy. This wasn't what Susan had expected. Susan hadn't really had to pee. "Shit," she thought, "now I have to make myself pee."

She envisioned when she was a little girl and her mom Gloria would run the water so Susan would pee before getting in the car on the eve of a road trip. What made her think about that now? She assumed it was symptomatic of her months in prison. Vivid memories flooding back during waking hours and sleep time.

Sterling waited until she flushed then placed some hand sanitizer in her hands. The alcohol burned in the cracks of her skin. She winced. He looked at her, shaking his head, but not in response to the stinging of the hand sanitizer.

"That didn't sound like someone peeing Chatham. Are you dehydrated? When did you last have something to drink?"

Susan just looked into his green eyes with her beautiful blue ones. She didn't dare speak directly to a guard. Bert had taught her that much. He thought she had the most beautiful blue eyes, but she was looking way too skinny.

"You look too thin Chatham," he said next.

Susan shrugged her shoulders. "No shit, Sherlock," she thought to herself. She almost cracked her first smile in months at the thought of issuing that sarcastic remark. She quickly came back to reality.

"When did you last eat?"

She didn't answer. "Are you being starved out?"

Susan just looked at him feeling the emptiness in her

belly and wondering if he could see straight through her orange scrub pants to her empty stomach underneath.

"Jesus Chatham, you aren't drinking, you aren't eating and you aren't sleeping. You won't make it this way. How long are you in here for?"

But Susan didn't know what to say. She couldn't bear to admit that she had to serve at least two more years before being eligible for parole. He grabbed her arm again and continued with her down the hall. Her panic returned.

Paul Sterling was thinking he had to get this girl something to eat and drink, and somehow after that coax her into getting some sleep or she wasn't going to make it. He would have to speak with the Warden and see what could be done to help this inmate. He couldn't deny the fact that it had reached crisis point.

He led her to the guard station.

Susan was shocked when he walked her down a long hallway and into a yellow painted tiny but well lit office and motioned for her to sit on a wooden chair. He reached down into a large white cooler behind the desk and handed her what?

A strawberry flavored cold yogurt and a plastic spoon.

"Chatham," he said to her in that stern voice again.

"Eat it," he commanded looking at her with a puzzled expression. Why was she just holding the yogurt he had just handed her? She hadn't had decent food in months. He could tell this inmate was starving. He knew that look only too well from his experience working at Lynchfield. He then asked her, "Do you like yogurt?"

Susan nodded her head yes then ate the yogurt quickly. She surprised herself when she had finished it with the spoon. She proceeded to stick her tongue into the cup to lick every little bit of it off without even thinking. What had happened to her finishing school manners? Extreme hunger had taken over any rules of etiquette.

Officer Sterling stared at her shaking his head again.

"Do you want some coffee?" he asked her, pouring a cup

of black coffee from the pot on the shelf. It smelled wonderful but coffee really wasn't Susan's preferred drink.

"No thank you," Susan spoke up. She knew this wasn't the time for a beggar to be a chooser, but she had suffered so much eating and drinking what repulsed her, she just wasn't going to choke down a cup of coffee. There would be many more sacrifices to come. Coffee always smelled better than it tasted, she would just enjoy the aroma. A respite from shit stained toilets and BO.

"Ah, you do have a voice."

"Tea drinker?" he assumed.

"Yes, Sir," Susan answered softly and slowly, as if the slower she answered the softer her punishment would be.

"Stay here." He left her sitting there as he walked out of the room. Susan sat motionless on the hard wooden chair, not daring to move, not daring to look into the cooler to see if there were any more delicious yogurts, which she really wanted to do. She was still famished. It took all of her self-control not to look in there and help herself to one, two or six more if she found any. But he had told her to sit there.

Paul Sterling returned and smiled when he saw that she had obeyed. Susan hadn't thought that the guards knew how to smile before she saw him do this. Most always looked like they would eat you alive and spit you out along with barbed wire. He handed her a Styrofoam cup with hot water then bent down to retrieve a tea bag from the desk drawer.

"Lemon Ginger?" Paul Sterling raised his eyebrows, not being familiar with this flavor and wondering if she would like that.

"Have some tea, Chatham. Sugar?"

"Thank you, Officer Sterling, Sir," she nodded.

Susan put the tea bag in the cup and began to dunk it in and out. Her hands trembling in fear, was this it? Eat a yogurt and sip tea with a guard or did he have something sinister in mind? She couldn't let herself believe this was as innocent as it seemed. Letting down your guard in Lynchfield was dangerous.

He noticed her shaking and the terror in her eyes.

"Chatham?"

Susan looked up at him taking a sip, trying to steady her shaking hands and lips. He thought she looked like the deer on the highway when the car lights would flash into their unsuspecting eyes.

"Chatham," he said this time more softly and gently, "relax, please." He felt pity for this beautiful girl, who seemed so out of place in this prison. He wondered what her crime had been. She seemed like a goody two shoes to him and he couldn't imagine she had done anything to end up here, being guarded by him and the others. He stared at her pretty yet scared and sad face. He wouldn't pepper her with questions; he would just let her rest for a few minutes and enjoy her tea.

"Drink your tea, are you sure you don't want any sugar? Take some deep breaths, then go lay down, close your eyes, and try harder to get some sleep girl."

He lectured her.

"I am serious Chatham. You won't survive here. You have to try. Dig deep. It's the only way you will make it."

But Susan was so frightened, and blue, and full of woeful emotions and his gentleness only reminded her of the real world she had left behind and the scary one she now inhabited. She couldn't control and hold back the tears that rolled down her pale face. She picked up the yogurt container that was empty on the desk to give it just one last lick in case she had forgotten any yogurt that was still left in that empty cup.

He looked at her sadly shaking his head.

She wondered what he thought of her, but she was so tired by now, she welcomed when he grabbed her arm and led her back to bed. Covering her with that burlap coverlet, he told her, "Go to sleep Chatham. I have my rounds to finish." All the times he had passed by her cell, they had never spoken. He had never stopped to look at her, although she had noticed he looked at Bert. She was grateful he had shown her kindness. He and Bert were the only ones in this shitty place who had. She watched him walk away and finally fell into an exhaustive sleep.

CHAPTER 5
NOT ALL SCREWS FIT THE MOLD

Nothing ever goes away until it
teaches us what we need to know.
~ Pema Chodron ~

Waking up in the morning was even more terrifying than trying to sleep with nightmares. All prisoners had to jump out of bed, make their beds tightly, with square corners, get into their oranges, if not wearing them already, tuck in their shirts, put on their shoes, and tidy their hair. They had to stand straight by their bunks, and look straight ahead or down but never at another inmate or into the guard's eyes.

The mornings when Guard George Ferguson was on duty were the worst. George always made Susan uncomfortable. He was relentless in his advances and seemed to grow more and more annoyed with her as the months passed. She felt he would strike hard if given the opportunity. He was so good looking but he would always brush against her in inappropriate ways, touching her breasts, or her ass, and once he stood really close and she could feel his hardness between her legs. He was a loose cannon. She worried constantly that he would take her somewhere and rape her. But so far, he hadn't. She couldn't understand why not. He just looked at her every time he passed her in the hall, biting his lower lip suggestively at her. She found herself oddly attracted to him, but afraid of him at the same time.

The female guard, Officer Jackie Somners, was usually on duty in the shower room. Officer Somners was about Susan's height, but had a bigger bone structure. She had fair skin and freckles and very pretty hazel green eyes. She had long blond hair with highlights and she wore it in a tight ponytail, with bobby pins to hold down the sides. Her lips were pink and although she didn't wear much makeup, Susan always thought of how pretty she could be if one of the makeup artists from one of her TV movies could give her a makeover. Susan stood at attention each morning, not making any eye contact as her bunk was inspected.

One particular morning, Officer Somners was on duty for roll call. "Open your locker Chatham," she barked.

Susan did as she was told. But the truth was no one from home had visited Susan. No one had brought her the items she had listed on the form that she had filled out of toiletries and other items that she would need. She didn't have enough money in her commissary account and so all she had in her locker was anything the prison had issued her or stuff that Bert had given her. A lot of trading went on in prison and she had stuff that others didn't want, like dental floss. Was she the only one that flossed her teeth around here? She had three packs of sample size Oral B floss.

So when Officer Jackie Somners opened Susan's bunk locker on that morning, that's what she found: three packs of Oral B dental floss, one prison issued tooth brush, a half squeezed tube of minty paste, one prison issued shampoo and soap, a small pack of tampons, half a box of sanitary pads, two hair ties, a comb, a brush, and her half used roll of toilet paper, and one very dog eared, and dirty paperback book, that she had checked out from the Lynchfield library. Nothing else, just empty shelves.

"Where's your stash, Chatham?"

Susan didn't know what to answer. She had no stash of

anything.

"Do you speak Chatham? Where's your stash? Your stuff?"

Susan spoke softly, not knowing where to put her eyes, "This is my locker, Ma'am? Sir? Officer?" not knowing how to address the female officer directly.

"Chatham!" Somners said angrily.

Jackie Somners assumed this inmate was hiding contraband somewhere. Most inmates' lockers were overflowing. Where was this girl keeping her belongings?

"Umm . . . I don't know what stash you're talking about. I don't have any stuff, I swear."

The other inmates overheard and were laughing at Susan.

"Silence," Somners yelled.

Susan felt her knees quiver, this hadn't happened before, in the dozens of other locker checks. What was happening?

"Chatham, you've been here long enough to know. Don't play innocent or stupid. Stash, your stuff, your things, where are you keeping everything?"

"I am sorry Sir," Susan finally decided to use that. "I . . . this is all I have here, I don't have my other belongings here, they are at home."

The inmates laughed again.

With that Officer Somners shook her head and moved onto the next inmate. Susan felt her heartbeat exploding in her chest. What is it with guards shaking their heads at her? She didn't know or understand all of the rules here, nor the current lingo. Her learning curve was triple that of the typical Lynchfield inmate who had spent most of her life living on the wrong side of the law. The world and everyone in it didn't believe any answer she gave them about anything, even though she was being truthful. Their worlds had been full of lies and abuse; even the guards. There were no well-adjusted do-gooders here.

Susan moped along when it was time to go to breakfast. The undercooked eggs appeared as runny and slimy as always. Despite her hunger, she couldn't stand to get diarrhea again, so she decided against eating them. The bacon was overdone but she crunched on it for protein and she managed to eat half a piece of her dry toast before Beulah, one of the Bitch Warrior gang members, stole the rest of it. She drank the 4 oz. container of apple juice way too quickly before Beulah could steal that away too and choked on it, coughing until her face was red and more tears streamed down. As usual, she left the mess hall hungry.

On her Cell Block's shower day, Susan would retrieve her shampoo and soap, thinking the sliver was too small and not sure it would be enough to bathe with.

She walked into the shower room taking off her orange scrubs and the panties and bra, a nude color and very plain. Oh how she missed her lovely lace thongs and sexy Demi bras. She wondered if Dale would find her sexy in these. Doubtful. Dale didn't want her in any manner of dress now.

She walked nude into the room which had multiple shower-heads all lined up against the white tiled walls. There were no privacy curtains and therefore no room for modesty. She watched as everyone showered, embarrassed by those who had their periods with blood washing down and grossed out by the way most peed right in the shower. She wondered who was looking at her body, and also wary because Bert had told her that the showers were where most of the lesbian rapes took place. She couldn't imagine how that could happen as the guard seemed to be staring at their naked bodies. Did the guards look away? Did they participate in the rapes? Was Bert just telling her stories to frighten her? She couldn't believe she had avoided that trauma for as many months as she had. How long would her "luck" continue?

Susan felt the water on her back and down her hair. The shower pressure was adequate but the water was cold or tepid at best. Susan turned forward and closed her eyes and for a moment imagined she was back home in her Hollywood Hills spa bathroom with the modern white subway tiles and green and blue glass tile accents. She could almost feel the massage jets and hear the music through the Bose speakers. She could see the steam rise from the hot water and smell the scent of her luxury soaps, shampoos and body washes. She pictured Dilly, his chiseled abs glistening with drops, his cock long and hard, rubbing up against her thighs. His strong arms wrapped around her waist, his hands lustfully cupped her tits.

"Chatham!" Officer Jackie Somners called out to her, harshly yanking her out of her daydream. Susan realized she hadn't washed herself at all, and had just stood daydreaming in the cool stream of water.

"Out Chatham, now! Now! Do you want a shot?"

Somners handed her a towel. Susan toweled off and put on the new clean oranges she was issued, and new underpants that happily fit her better, shoes more her size, but no bra.

"Officer Somners, please sir, I am missing my bra," Susan said.

Somners looked at her. There was that head shake again, "Sorry Chatham. That's all that arrived for today. You'll have to do without."

Susan felt lucky that her breasts were still upright and perky and maybe she could get away with no bra like she did the first day she had arrived and not been issued any underwear.

She dressed herself in her oranges and brushed her long now unconditioned hair and put it in a high ponytail. She looked in the mirror. They didn't allow glass so it was just a shiny piece of metal that had been scratched and marred over the years. You could barely make out your reflection. With what Susan could see, she noticed her cheeks and eyes more sunken in. She looked sad, more like when she played the dead CSI character than like the Susan Chatham that was nominated for an Emmy for that role. Somners pulled her away.

"You are the day dreamer aren't you?" asked Somners.

Susan turned around and looked her in the eyes, quickly realizing that was a no, no. Her eyes filled with terror. Susan felt faint.

Somners noticed her growing pale skin because she

grabbed her arm and sat her down on the floor. She instructed Susan to sit there until she got all the other inmates out of the showers, dry, dressed and out to their work duty rotations.

Somners bent down and looked at Susan and said, "Chatham. What is wrong with you?"

Susan didn't know what to say. She wanted to say, "I am innocent, I was convicted of a crime I didn't commit and sent here to this fucking hell hole. I am used to being wealthy and living in a beautiful multi-million dollar home with luxury bedding, spa bathrooms, maids and servants, driving a luxury car and fucking my rich gorgeous husband. I am a Hollywood star wearing beautiful expensive designer outfits. I eat gourmet foods which I either prepare myself or have world famous chefs prepare for me, and I shit and pee where I want, when I want, and in privacy. And now I live here. What the fuck do you think is wrong with me?" What could she say?

"I am okay Sir, Ma'am, thank you. I will get up and go to my job duty now, thank you."

"Chatham, you can just call me Officer Somners."

As Susan started to stand up she was wobbly on her feet.

Officer Somners grabbed her arm and led her out of the shower and down the hall, where they ran into Officer Paul Sterling who was just arriving for his double shift.

"Hey Jackie," said Paul.

"Hi Paul," responded Jackie as the two friends greeted each other.

Then Paul questioned Jackie, "Chatham giving you a hard time?"

Susan looked down blushing, "Chatham's having a rough day. A rough year really," Jackie answered.

"Well, she doesn't eat, doesn't drink, doesn't sleep, she isn't going to make it," said Paul.

"She doesn't take her shower or get dressed properly either," added Jackie.

"Paul, you think it's time for a bail out?"

"Yes, Jackie good idea," Paul answered.

Susan felt as though she were on a different planet. Her head was spinning. She didn't feel well at all, and didn't understand what the Guards were talking about. She was frightened and as usual, wanted to cry and go home. Sadly, that wasn't an option. She wished Bert were around to ask what to do next. Feeling faint, she quickly plopped down on the floor and wondered if the guards would take out their baton sticks and hit her, fire her with pepper spray, or worse shoot her with the guns they carried in their belts.

"Bail out!" Paul said to Jackie seeing how poorly Chatham looked.

Paul grabbed one arm and Jackie took the other and they walked her unsteady feet back to the Guard's office where Paul had taken her that one night.

They sat her on the wooden seat again.

Susan didn't know what to do, so she looked up at them and said over and over again, "I'm sorry."

Officer Paul Sterling spoke sternly but with a hint of kindness. "Chatham, I told you the other night, you need to eat and drink and sleep, and take care of yourself. You are making yourself sick."

Jackie sat with Susan and Paul left, but to Susan's surprise, came back with a sandwich and a bottle of water and handed it to Susan. Susan took a bite and it tasted like Heaven. Peanut butter and jelly never tasted so gourmet. She drank the water down like it was the best drink she had ever had, even better than her favorite Mojito cocktail. She felt much better and almost instantly the color returned to her face.

Jackie Somners walked her back to the showers and handed her a new soap and shampoo and waited for Susan to really wash, then handed her another clean dry towel. While Susan was showering Jackie found a bra to go with the rest of Susan's oranges. Then she handed her a pass.

Susan looked down. "What is this?" she asked.

"It's a sick leave pass Chatham."

"Go to your Cell Block, lie down in your bed and take a nap."

Officer Somners looked at her with pity.

"Chatham, you've been bailed out, now just say thank you and go do as you're told."

Susan thanked them through tears and fell asleep. She slept until the next morning.

"Damn, Chatty," Bert said as she woke her the next morning a few minutes before morning countdown. "What the hell happened yesterday? Where were you?" Susan told her about the guards and asked about the bail out.

"Damn Chatty, no one ever gets bail out. That's when the guards think an inmate is in trouble and they actually come to your rescue. Honestly I thought it was just some myth or rumor made up by some inmate bitch. I guess being "nice" and being a "looker" has its privileges."

"I think they feel sorry for me," Susan said despondently.

"You are pretty, but pretty hopeless in here Chatty. One thing, just because they bailed you out, you have to go right back to the way things were. You won't get no more special privileges. Still don't look at them, don't expect nothing, got it? Otherwise you will be given shots or sent to the Shoe. Don't let your guard down ever here Chatty."

"Got it." Susan acknowledged. As usual, Bert was right. She got no more special treatment from Paul Sterling or Jackie Somners, and knew better than to expect any.

As time went on Susan was able to cope for the most part, but she still rode the emotional roller coaster of prison life. Things took another turn for the worse the week of her birthday. The previous year, her birthday week had been spent on a Caribbean Cruise with Dale. They had enjoyed the best time. The weather had been spectacular, warm, sunny days, crystal clear and calm aqua Caribbean waters. During the day they enjoyed various excursions at the ports of call. In Grand Cayman they went snorkeling and swimming with the stingrays at Sting Ray City, enjoyed a beach BBQ at Labadee in Haiti, and swam with dolphins in Cozumel. Susan's favorite experience had been after climbing Dunn's River Falls in Ocho Rios, Jamaica, Dale had arranged for cooking lessons with a Jamaican chef, and Susan had private lessons in making Jamaican beans and rice, Jerk chicken, and traditional BBQ. Afterwards, she and Dilly had shared an intimate birthday dinner that she had prepared with the Chef's help. Dale and Susan's sex life on the cruise was as varied as their activities and ports of call. Rocking in the ocean had a different flavor for Suze and Dilly. This birthday was a fucking nightmare.

Roberta Jimenez walked into her cell compartment to find Susan crying, a bruise already developing on her cheek.

"What happened now Chatty? What's wrong?" Bert asked.

Susan was sobbing so hard, she could barely catch her breath, and her voice came out like hiccups.

"It happened Bert. I went to take my shower, I got jumped," Susan wept pitifully. "Shamara and Cheyenne were waiting for me. I didn't see them Bert, I should have been more cautious but I just let my guard down for a minute. The Blacks and Whites had taken a bet on who would rape me first Bert. Who does that Bert?"

"Oh, Chatty, I'm so sorry. I can't say that I am surprised though. Your looks and all, it wasn't a question of if or how, it was only a question of when. I am only surprised that you lasted this long before they did you in. Tell me more."

"I went to take my shower, and I was just lathering up, when I closed my eyes to keep the shampoo out, they ganged up on me and grabbed me from behind. I called for the guard but no one came. I couldn't see exactly who very well, but there was a group of them, one knocked me down and someone slapped my face and one went down on me and later another had a vibrating dildo," Susan explained through her tears.

"Happy Easter!" Bert said.

"WHAT? What are you talking about Bert?" Susan yelled angrily at her, thinking her friend was being so nonchalant and mean about what had happened to her, as if it was expected, her prison rite of passage. It wasn't Easter. It wasn't even fucking spring.

"Happy Easter Chatty, the "Rabbit" vibrator. Was it pink or purple?"

"What the fuck, Bert, I didn't see or care what color it was!"

"Pink means this will be a one time thing. Purple means one of the Lesbians wants you to be their new gal Chatty. You better pray it was pink."

"What the fuck Bert!" Susan stopped crying and became furious.

"You know Chatty, it isn't always a bad thing in here. Are you hurt badly?"

"No, not really, my face stings, and I think I may have hit my head, I have a lump forming."

"It gets very lonely in here, when you are lonely and horny, lesbian sex isn't so bad Chatty."

"I'm not gay Bert!"

"I prefer men too Chatty, but some action once in a while calms the pussy itch."

"You leave me speechless Bert really." Susan rolled over in her bed and tried to go to sleep, wondering if she would feel like Roberta Jimenez does about sex with the passage of time, and if the "Rabbit" was pink or purple and who might be wanting her sex next? Susan was also worried about the fact that she had reached orgasm during her assault. What if anything did that mean? Everything in prison was tinged with violence and rage. Nothing seemed to follow a normal course. Everything was ass backwards and confusing. She decided to continue to take life one day at a time and be grateful she wasn't hurt worse.

The icing on the birthday cake came on visiting day. Dale was coming. Susan was ecstatic. Despite being angry with him and his horrible behavior, he remained her husband and her link to the outside world. He had remembered her birthday. Susan lit up. She had her first real live visitor.

"Help me look better Bert, please," Susan begged.

Susan couldn't deny she was losing some of her hotness. She had grown pallid from lack of outdoor activities, and her lost sleep had created dark bags under her eyes. She had a golf size lump on her forehead from her shower attack, and a deep purple and yellow bruise on her cheek. Most of all her weight loss was striking. Between the "starve outs" and her not liking the food choices at Lynchfield, the lack of commissary money with which to buy snacks or supplemental food, she appeared almost emaciated.

Bert helped her fix her hair, she used some contraband blush to try to add some color to Susan's cheeks, but it did little good.

Susan had a knot in her stomach all day in anticipation of seeing Dilly. She tucked her orange top in and tied her orange scrub pants tighter. Susan smiled broadly and went into the visitation hall to see Dale.

He looked so handsome in his blue and white striped oxford collared shirt, khaki pants and Sperry loafers. His hair was combed back with gel, and he had a wonderful smelling aftershave on, Susan's favorite. The sight of Dilly took her breath away, her heart fluttered, her panties wetted. But as Susan approached him to plant a kiss, he pulled away. Dale frowned and he had that certain expression on his face that he always had when he was going to deliver bad news. She had come to know this facial expression almost too well, having seen it almost daily during her trial.

Susan tried to smile back and be cheerful. "You remembered my birthday Dilly! Thank you for coming!"

"Crap, Suze, it's your birthday? I wouldn't have come today if I remembered it was your birthday, I would have picked another day." He then sighed, "Better to get this over with anyway."

Susan's heart sank into the ground. He hadn't remembered her birthday? He appeared angry at her still.

Why was he here? Before she could think any further, he got a dig in.

"You look like shit, Suze." She wasn't sure how he even noticed since it seemed as though he was looking right through her, dismissing her.

Susan looked down, her smile now long faded, feeling embarrassed, sad, hurt, dejected, feeling like hell had opened its gates to swallow her in. Her voice was barely a whisper now, "Why are you here Dilly? Why did you come today?"

"You know it's been over for some time Susan. I don't know what got into you. The money decisions you made, the stealing, and your incessant lying. Suze, I just can't, I can't take it anymore. I don't trust you anymore. I don't feel . . . I don't love you anymore. I'm seeing someone else and I want a divorce."

He passed the forms to her, and asked one of the guards for a pen.

Susan's lips trembled and tears welled up in her eyes. She wanted to cry out loud. She wanted to yell and scream and defend herself. "I didn't do anything. I didn't mess with the bank accounts. I wasn't at Kane's. I didn't steal any jewelry. I am not cheating on you Dilly, even though if I did, it would make my life here with the guards, especially Ferguson, much easier." But she said none of this out loud. Instead, in the softest of voices she replied, "I understand."

All was now lost for sure. She took the pen, swallowed hard and signed the divorce papers. Happy Fucking Birthday.

CHAPTER 6
AT DEATH'S DOOR

Life has knocked me down a few times.
It has shown me things I never wanted to see.
I have experienced sadness and failures.
But one thing is for sure . . . I always get up!
~ Unknown ~

Bert woke up in the middle of the night several weeks later to
a foul smell and the awful sound of Susan retching. It would
have taken something severe to wake Bert up, and this was it.
She looked over and Susan was up, sitting on the floor
violently throwing up into the waste can.

"Chatty? What's wrong?" Bert got down from her bunk
and went to Susan.

Susan was throwing up too much and didn't answer her.
Her face was ashen. Bert walked over to her and held her hair
back so it didn't fall into the vomit-filled can. She felt that
Susan's face and neck were hot. She was burning up.

"Shit, Chatty are you sick?"

Bert felt Susan's forehead again and then her arms.

Susan was hot and covered with a clammy sweat.

"You ARE sick! Oh My God Chatty, you are burning

up."

Bert handed her a small hand towel so she could wipe the vomit from her face.

"I'll be right back, I'm going for some help." Bert left their bunk area to fetch one of the guards.

Susan felt terrible, worse than usual. Her head was throbbing and her whole body ached. She felt like her arms and legs were made of concrete. She was afraid she was getting Bert into trouble. Despite her agony, she was frightened that she would be given a shot or thrown in the Shoe because she was up in the middle of the night. She had soiled her bed and was hurling into the waste can. The stench was worse than the toilets she scrubbed during work detail. Her heart was beating so fast she felt it would jump out of her chest, but instead she heaved into the waste can again.

By the time Bert returned with one of the guards, Susan was laying on the cold, hard floor in a fetal position. Her body was spooned against the smelly waste can.

The guard was tall and lean and Latin. Gomez, Officer Juan Carlos Gomez was his name. He had dark caramel skin, short black spiked hair and thick dark eyebrows with a huge wide mouth full of large white teeth. He looked like he should be in a cologne ad with his shirt off, but instead he was bending down and feeling Susan's forehead. He slipped his hand in between her scrub top and back and felt her clammy moist skin.

"How long has she been like this?" Officer Gomez asked Roberta Jimenez.

"She's been sick all night," Bert told Officer Gomez.

"Did she take anything?" he asked.

"No, I don't think so. We don't do drugs," Bert responded.

"Food poisoning?" Gomez asked. "Or some type of stomach flu?"

"I don't know, she needs some help, she is not herself, and she is too sick, she doesn't stop vomiting and she soiled the bed and she seems very lethargic and I am very worried about her. Please help." Bert ranted on, making her plea to the Guard.

Officer Gomez quieted Bert and turned his attention to Susan.

"Chatham, get up, sit up girl. Chatham, now!"

But Susan wasn't able to move. She was so sick and so weak. She closed her eyes to the spinning room.

Officer Gomez could see this inmate was very ill. She wasn't faking it and she wasn't playing games. He looked in her bunk and noted the dirty sheets. He looked in the waste can, wondering how one human could vomit that much. Especially one human who was that stick thin. He put in a call to Medical on his walkie-talkie but didn't wait for them to arrive. Instead he lifted Susan Chatham up in his strong arms and carried her to the Medical Department himself.

He arrived with her and was greeted by nurse practitioner Sally Icasa. Sally Icasa had a short black bob, pulled back over one ear. She had on a regular Guard uniform but with a white lab coat over it. Her shoes were black and sneaker-like with rubber soles and lace tie-ups. They were sensible shoes, but quite manly looking. She had thick natural eyebrows and no make-up. In her haze, Susan thought she looked a bit butch.

"Hi Sally, I have a present for you. Inmate Susan Chatham. Food poisoning, stomach flu?" announced Guard Gomez.

"Hi Juan Carlos." Sally retrieved a medical history form.

"Dr. Lomegistro is out, but I'll tend to her."

"Chatham, I need to ask you some questions."

Susan was really out of it and offered no response.

Juan Carlos answered what he could for her.

"Chatham, Susan Chatham, Cell Block D, Bed 2, fever one day. Vomiting. Diarrhea. Lethargy. Unresponsive."

Sally found a bed for her. Susan vomited again before they could get her into bed, then passed out.

When Susan woke up she saw she was in the Medical Department and she was in a comfortable bed with clean white sheets. She too was clean, someone had given her a bath, and her hair was clean too, tied back with a soft tie. She saw she had an IV in her arm. Her orange scrubs were gone and she was wearing a medical gown and no undies.

She felt like she was burning up and her head was throbbing. Although she still felt nauseous and queasy, she didn't think she would vomit again. Her arms and legs ached and were still heavy but at least not like concrete, maybe just like heavy books. Was she hungry? No, she had no appetite at all. But she had to pee very badly.

She looked around for a guard, or a nurse?

She didn't want to wet the bed.

She tried to stand up but even sitting on the side of the bed made her dizzy.

Before she got any further, she noticed the cute Latin guard coming towards her again. It was Officer Gomez.

"Chatham, wait! Don't get out of bed yourself girl. You have been very sick. Here, let me help. Where do you think you are going?" He spoke very matter of fact.

"Please, I need to pee sir," she managed to utter.

Juan Carlos Gomez steadied her and took her to the bathroom just to the side of the room she was in.

Susan's legs were wobbly and he had to steady her and help her sit on the toilet, but like Paul had done before, Juan Carlos also turned his back so she could pee in some sort of privacy. The door remained open and he was right there, but with his back turned, it made all the difference.

He handed her some toilet paper but Susan was so weak. So much for privacy, she allowed him to wipe her clean like a child. He lifted her up and marched her back to the bed and after helping her climb in, walked over to wash his hands and grabbed a chair to sit by her bedside.

Susan whispered, "Thank you."

He smiled at her. Another guard who knows how to smile, she thought. He surprised her with his conversation.

"You are a rare breed, Susan Chatham. You are the only one around here that has any manners. I have also never seen anyone that sick ask me for dental floss," he laughed heartily.

Susan had no recollection of any of the conversations that he was telling her about. She had talked to him at length but she didn't remember any of it. She hoped that she didn't say anything inappropriate or anything that would land her in the Shoe.

"You are quite funny; when you are sick anyways," he laughed again.

Sally walked in and she laughed too. "Is our little clown up?" she asked.

Susan was confused and a bit embarrassed. She had been delirious with fever, and she had no idea what she had said. Obviously she had been very entertaining.

"How do you feel Chatham?" Sally Icasa asked, taking her blood pressure, pulse and respiration. "Flip Chatham, lay on your stomach."

Susan did as instructed.

Icasa lifted off the covers, opened Susan's hospital gown and inserted a Vaseline covered anal thermometer into her.

Susan was ashamed. Why were they using an anal thermometer in this day and age? Is that how they had been taking her temperature? She was mortified and with both guards here, the door open and the Medical Department enclosed all in glass. Anyone walking by could have seen her there naked with a thermometer sticking out of her ass. There was simply no dignity at Lynchfield Prison.

Susan quickly became angry and humiliated. In her mind this was bullshit. Couldn't they use a forehead or ear thermometer that would give a temperature in seconds? Or even one under the tongue. But no, here in Lynchfield an inmate's temperature was taken in the ass to remind them that they were nothing.

She swallowed hard against the growing lump in her throat.

It felt like an eternity before that thermometer was pulled out, wiped clean and read.

"101.3, you still have a fever Chatham," said Nurse

Practitioner Icasa. She then reached for a syringe and gave Susan an injection of some medication, also in her ass. After, she closed her gown and covered her with the blanket.

"Sleep Chatham." She turned off the light and she and Juan Carlos walked out of the room.

Susan woke up hours later and her fever had broken. She was soaking wet but feeling quite hungry now. Sally Icasa came into the room and without saying anything, removed Susan's bedding and clothes, and put clean linens on the bed. She gave Susan a sponge bath, dressed her in a clean gown, and returned with a meal tray.

Susan stared intently at the tray but couldn't seem to feed herself. Her arms felt weak and shaky and unsteady, but she was starving. Sally sat next to her.

"Here, Chatham, let me help you."

She picked up the spoon and handed it to Susan. She gently helped her eat some chopped meat and whipped potatoes. Susan didn't know if the food was better down in Medical or if she was just so hungry, it tasted halfway decent. Or, Heaven forbid, she had been in Lynchfield so long she was beginning to like their cuisine. Doubtful, but whatever the reason, she welcomed every bite and ate all her dinner.

"Our staff doctor, Dr. Lomegistro is on vacation this week. I didn't want to bother him, but if you hadn't recovered on your own, I would have had to. You were close to the edge, Chatham." Susan wanted to scream to Sally Icasa, "I'm fucking innocent, don't you see? I'm over the fucking edge!" But she couldn't release her frustration. She knew that would make everything so much worse. She decided to be grateful that the doctor hadn't been called in from vacation and she had survived another day. "Hope you had a swell vacation, Dr. Lomegistro," Susan thought bitterly, but refocused on the current comfort of her infirmary bed and her full stomach.

Officer Gomez returned soon after dinner and brought with him a dog-eared library book.

Susan thanked him for doing that. It was a simple but profound gesture of kindness after months of torture. Susan

51

would think about that. She would think about Bert and Officer Sterling. She would think about her bail out with Officer Somners and the treatment she had received from Officer Gomez and Nurse Practitioner Icasa. She would refocus and get through this somehow.

Susan felt much better and read several pages of the novel. She dozed off again, slept through the night and woke up to Juan Carlos waiting to take her back to Cell Block D and back to her Lynchfield "normal" inmate life. She needed to muster up all of her inner strength to face the coming months. Like Officer Sterling had suggested, she needed to "dig deep." He was right.

CHAPTER 7
I FEEL PRETTY?

Change is mandatory for extraordinary results.
~ Unknown ~

"Bert, I really need to get my hair trimmed, what do I do?" Susan asked.

"Chatty, you know we have a Salon."

"Really?"

"Yes, really. How long have you been here now? Get a clue! Jaleesa cuts and colors hair. She even has rollers and relaxants. But, Chatty, your hair is beautiful why would you want to touch it?"

"Bert if you don't get the ends trimmed it won't stay looking good, plus I need conditioning. My hair is fried from being in here."

"I'm not sure about them having your fancy-schmancy conditioners, Chatty, but I am sure she can trim you up. Sign up outside of Cell Block C."

"Okay thanks I will," Susan replied.

Susan headed over to Cell Block C and saw the sign-up sheet. She put her name and inmate number - #24682 - on the next available line and took a seat. There was so much she still didn't know about Lynchfield. She had spent so many months just surviving. She had fixated on the shitty food, the crassness of her fellow inmates and the guards, her constant humiliation and the injustice of her sentence. She had focused only on her misery and her daydreams.

It was a small waiting room with three wooden chairs that resembled the same ones that she had seen in the guard station. Inside there were two black vinyl salon chairs. Susan noticed a sink by the wall and above it shelving holding lots of plastic bottles. The room was painted yellow and orange. She briefly thought about her salon at home. She remembered sipping on Champagne or fruit infused waters and enjoying a canapé with caviar. Jean Pierre would greet her by name and shampoo her hair with the most amazing shampoos and conditioners. He would massage her scalp and trim her hair, or put in any foils she desired. Getting your hair trimmed was a sensual experience with Jean Pierre at Salon Miku. She had to stop doing that. Her life in Hollywood was over. There was no point spending her hours lost in daydreams. This was her life now and she had to figure out a way to make the best of it, so that when she got out, she could focus on figuring out what the hell had happened to land her here in the first place. Better to plot revenge and play the prison game while she did her time.

Susan sat in her oranges on the wooden seat and watched a tall, big breasted African-American woman applying chemicals to another inmate's hair while a second inmate, a butchy tattooed redhead sat in the second chair waiting for half her head to be shaved.

Susan counted her money to pay for her trim. She was making very little money through the prison work duty. It had taken her months to save up anything. No one from home had sent the commissary money she requested dozens of times. She had resorted to doing odd jobs for other inmates to earn a little extra cash. She was on her own. Starvation and the flu had nearly killed her, now she would make an effort to survive. This would be her most challenging role.

The odd jobs had piled up. She made beds, did some of the inmates' homework assignments, cleaned and organized lockers for inspections, anything to earn a few cents or dollars here and there. She looked at the dollars and cents she had with her and couldn't believe that her entire funds fit in the palm of one hand. This wouldn't have even paid for parking outside of Salon Miku. Again, she was back to her old life. She forced herself to come into the present-day.

Finally it was her turn and she took a seat.

Jaleesa felt Susan's hair.

"Girl, why do you want to do anything with this? This is the most gorgeous hair I have ever seen in Lynchfield!"

Susan thought she was nuts. If only Jaleesa had seen her hair prior to prison. She would have passed out. "I just want a trim, please, just an inch off to get rid of split ends." She showed Jaleesa her money.

"Fine, can I wash your hair? I just want to touch it," Jaleesa asked her.

Susan found this so odd, but agreed.

Jaleesa washed her hair and put some conditioner on it.

"I really love your white girl movie star hair," Jaleesa commented.

"Thank you," Susan responded. She chuckled inside but instantly became nervous.

Susan stared in the mirror as Jaleesa trimmed her hair. Her stomach dropped thinking that her hair might be ruined, and that this inmate had sharp scissors near her head. It wasn't smart to be vulnerable in prison. Ever. Could she trust her? She was having second thoughts about this. Who really gave a shit at this point what her hair looked like? Who was she trying to impress? She should have just forgotten about her fucking hair and kept to herself.

Jaleesa's hands were dry and rough, her fingers pulled at Susan's scalp during the wash and again during her application of the conditioner. It didn't smell very good either. Susan's heartbeat began to race and she almost bolted out of the chair.

There was constant anxiety in prison. Susan scoped out the exit, kept her eyes on Jaleesa and those scissors. Jaleesa began to trim her hair with great care. Susan relaxed just a bit, but not entirely. She watched how Jaleesa measured twice before she would cut even once. Surprisingly Susan's haircut came out terrific, and the conditioner really improved the texture of Susan's hair, almost back to her "Hollywood" healthiness. Susan could hardly believe it. She sighed with relief.

"Thank you Jaleesa." Susan paid and gave her a 50% tip.

"Chatham, you overpaid me," Jaleesa responded.

"No, no I didn't. You did a marvelous job and you made me feel great. I needed this Jaleesa. Thank you again."

She smiled her broad white Hollywood smile and walked back to her cell.

Jaleesa and the other inmates at the Salon just gawked after her.

"That girl is crazy! She thinks she's still in Hollywood and rich, but she's just a dumb ass loser like the rest of us here," said inmate Hilary Dugan.

Jaleesa defended Susan. "Say what you want about her Dugan. That girl is special. You are just jealous."

"Jealous of that College Snot. Never. Beat the shit out of that tiny sorry ass of hers when I get the chance."

CHAPTER 8
LIFE IS A MESS HALL

Every guy thinks that every girl's dream
is to find the perfect guy . . . please,
every girl's dream is to eat without getting fat!
~ Unknown ~

The cafeteria at Lynchfield was a large noisy room with grey
and green vinyl tile floors and white tiled walls with a green
tile stripe running horizontally along the walls and large
windows with metal grates. There were long rectangular
tables lined up in a horizontal pattern with blue plastic and
metal frame chairs that were too narrow for comfort and
resulted in the plus size inmates' asses spilling over when they
sat. Up front was a typical metal and glass-enclosed buffet. In
the back of the room were trashcans for disposables and
racks where empty trays were to be placed after meals were
eaten.

The cafeteria had been a source of high-level stress for
Susan since she first arrived at Lynchfield. Where you sat and
with who was a political game in prison. Sitting in the wrong
seat, looking at the wrong person, eating food in the wrong
order, there were so many made up rules that governed

meals. Susan could barely remember them all even though Bert had tried to coach her.

In the early days Susan was often "starved out" or had her food stolen, spit on, and even thrown out. One day Susan had accidentally knocked over her drink on Lorelei Summer. That night she found feces in her bed. A guard had prevented Lorelei from stabbing Susan with a fork, but no sleight, whether accidental or intentioned went unanswered.

Hilary Dugan made good on her threat to Chatham after the visit to the salon. She didn't beat Susan's ass but she did stick her foot out on purpose when Susan was coming out of the cafeteria line with her food tray. Susan should have known to always watch where she was going. The foot trip was so common it was a joke. Dugan's foot sent Susan flying over the tile floors, spilling her food and drink over herself and the floor. She ended up without dinner again. Her knee hurt for about two weeks afterwards, making her mopping duty difficult and painful.

The inmates often hung out in the recreation room playing cards, board games, or watching TV. There were books to read and coloring books and crayons to color or draw with. Susan enjoyed coloring, reading and watching the cooking shows.

After she had been inside for a while, she would comment on the chef's techniques and the other inmates looked at her like she was crazy. Susan would instantly remember that she didn't belong there. She was so out of place. She would withdraw further.

She couldn't talk to the guards honestly, or to most of the other inmates. She conversed with Bert and a few other inmates that Bert had told her were "safe." There was Dottie the seamstress, who had stolen tips, Pam the purse thief and Katie the art thief. That was the "nice" gang. Was she in a gang now? Would they ever really "accept" her, this gang of misfits? Who could she really trust? The answer was no one. Susan, who was once giggly and bubbly and full of energy and passion, became depressed and withdrawn. She was frightened of everything: the other inmates, the Guards, of getting shots, of the Shoe, of getting raped, beaten or worse. She was lonely and never had any visitors. Visiting day would come and go and after several months, she stopped checking her list or going to see if someone was there for her.

She remembered when she had first arrived she would stand in the long lines to use the hall phones. There were six phones but the lines were still so long. Everyone had three minutes to make collect calls. Susan would stand in the long line to wait her turn. No one would accept her calls. She had tried Dale, her dad Richard, her brother Tommie, Allison, (especially at the beginning when she still thought she was her friend), many of her Hollywood friends and co-stars. Not one would accept her calls. At first this made Susan cry too. Now she just stopped going to the phones at all. And she never had any incoming calls either. Her mother would have taken her call, she was sure of it. Why had she lost the only person who had given her unconditional love? Many of the inmates in Lynchfield had lost their mothers as well, but in different circumstances. They had lost them to drugs or to violence, even murder. These girls who would grow up to be inmates had been raped by relatives and ostracized. They had been left to fend for themselves. They had taken up with the wrong man, 100% of the time, and ended up serving time. It was the same old cliché, and it was true. They were lost and they were angry. Susan understood them more each day, but was still terrified of most of them. These women didn't want understanding. They wanted revenge.

No visitors, no calls, no letters, no e-mails, no contact whatsoever with her former life. How had she survived this long? Human resiliency. She had played resilient characters many times and had been self-righteous and flippant in her attitude toward these fictitious creations. Now she knew that resiliency was something to be admired and never taken lightly. It was hard won and it was precious. It had kept her alive when she should have died. Susan wanted revenge now too. Susan wanted to stay alive.

The other inmates were as diverse as the general population of any society. There were whites, and white supremacists, and blacks. There were Asians and Latinos and all religions too: Catholics, Protestants, Lutherans, Evangelical Christians, Jews, Muslims, Buddhists and Atheists. Some were "nice" and some were "Bitch Warriors," with many other gangs and groups in between. Some would help you like Roberta Jimenez and Susan Chatham, and some would love to kill you like Beulah Walcott. What they all had in common was damage. They were all damaged, broken by the circumstances of their lives. They lived with varying degrees of rage and depression, rage turned inward.

There was substance abuse everywhere in the prison. Some inmates were on hard drugs, and some were alcoholics. It existed here for them just as they had been on the outside. Drugs came in via contraband through diapers, sewn into clothing, stuck on the back of mail or taped to the bottom of shoes. Guards facilitated the exchanges. Alcohol was equally snuck in or some of the inmates made their own moonshine with fermented fruits, honey and other foods. Guard George Ferguson was heavily involved in contraband and the drug trade, aided by other guards on the take.

Money was as big a commodity on the inside as it was on the outside. Inmates and guards stole, they cheated, they did jobs for each other. There was gang activity both within the prison and contacts with the gangs on the outside. Some wrote to outside sources for money, making up lies. The hardened criminals became harder and the petty criminals also changed. Everyone changed in prison. Roberta Jimenez could see that even Susan Chatham was changing.

"Chatty are you okay?" Bert would whisper at night when they had time to talk. At first, Susan had shared with Bert stories about her life, her husband, and about Hollywood. But later Susan became quieter and withdrew. She sat in her bed staring into space, speaking little. Her expression grew harder.

The guards began to notice her increasing quietness too.

The "edge" she was forming. Susan Chatham had quickly set the record for the best-behaved inmate at Lynchfield and she managed to have a record free of shots and free of visits to the Shoe. But, it also was noticed that the Susan Chatham before them now was not the same Susan Chatham that had arrived at Lynchfield a year prior.

At one point, Warden Ramsey called her into his office again. He hadn't had any contact with her since their first meeting.

"Chatham. How are you holding up?"

Susan knew the memorized answers to give.

"I am fine, thank you Warden Ramsey, sir."

"Are you eating? Drinking? Sleeping?"

"Yes, sir, thank you sir, all is good."

"Well several of the guards are concerned about you."

"Thank you for your concern sir, I am well, all is good."

Susan nodded her head knowing inside that everything was actually terrible and that more often than not she wished she were dead. She was trying to survive and digging deep to do so. The digging had formed a hard shell. The surviving had made her angry. The injustice had made her quiet.

How would Susan have described her current state if she were sitting in a psychiatrist's office? "It was as if you were behind glass and you could see the world around you but you couldn't be a part of it, you couldn't touch it and you couldn't let it in." On top of the numbness there were layers of anxiety and rage. There were panic attacks that came constantly but were based on actual and not perceived threats. It was a deadly psychic combination.

Deep down, Susan missed loving and being loved. She missed touching someone and having someone touch her. She missed kindness. It was so rare here. The loneliness hurt more than any sore knee, any beating, and hurt more than cold showers or being starved out.

Was she lonely, depressed, dejected, angry, or all of the above? It really didn't matter. She was existing without interaction or meaning. Susan Chatham was changing as a result of her being sent to Lynchfield, and she would never be the same as her former self. She would come back again and again in her mind to the person who was ultimately responsible for her conviction and imprisonment. It was furiously maddening and so unbelievable that this woman had managed to destroy her life so completely. But she had. In the depths of despair Susan would find strength in her desire to survive and to find vindication. She had lost the battle, but she would not lose the war.

CHAPTER 9
MASTER MANIPULATOR

Have you ever just stopped and realized
that if you hadn't met a certain person,
your entire life would be completely different?
~ AwesomeQuotes4Eva ~

Dale and Susan had been married more than six years by the time they became close with Susan's body double Allison Cray. Dale had already developed a close relationship with her as his administrative assistant. She had managed to become his right arm and with her physical appearance resembling Susan's, Dale found he was attracted to her. It was a strange sensation, because he was so in love with Susan. But Allison was so like Susan. Over time the attraction grew and when Allison knew she was close, she pounced.

By Hollywood standards Susan and Dale were happily married. Looking amazing, lots of money in the bank, swanky parties, sweet wheels, and plenty of hot sex between the sheets. Aren't those the things that make for a successful marriage? They had had so many good years. It wasn't the approaching seven-year itch that proved the demise of this love story. Instead it was the carefully formulated plan of a psychopath.

The plan came to fruition and life came crashing down one day when two police officers showed up on the CSI set. The cast and crew were in the middle of filming when the police arrived. They were shocked at first. A few laughed thinking it was some kind of prank reality TV show. This was no show: Susan Chatham was read her Miranda rights, handcuffed and forced into the back of a real police car. They drove her away in tears without as much as an explanation. That day, Dale watched in horror, as did most of the crew.

Allison Cray was lurking in the background, dressed like Susan for her role as her body double. She was also wearing a slight smirk on her lips and an evil look in her eye. In her mind she thought, "Gotcha! Got your husband, got your job, gonna get your life. Bye-bye Susan."

Susan was out on bail soon after her arrest. Dale listened closely to what Susan had to say, but none of it made any sense to him. Allison Cray had been systematically poisoning Dale's thoughts. Quickly, conversations between Dale, Allison, and even Richard Chatham turned against Susan. The evidence was so overwhelming. Susan had been stealing money and moving it into accounts Dale didn't know about. Susan had gone into Kane's and tried on very expensive jewelry like she had on many occasions, especially before red carpet events. But this time she walked out with several valuable pieces without paying. The store clerks had testified that it was Susan. The video footage showed that it was Susan and Allison Cray had seen her from the bus. Allison volunteered to the police that she had had car trouble and didn't want to be late for her meeting with Dale. That was the reason she was riding the bus that day. No one ever bothered to check out her story.

Dale began to pull away from Susan. He didn't even want to be in the same room with her. Susan Chatham was immediately black balled in Hollywood, and the CSI team quickly had Allison Cray take over Susan's role. Allison had made sure she flirted with Dale from the beginning of her acquaintance with him. She also made sure the flirting seemed innocent and playful, but it was anything but. As soon as Susan was arrested, Allison came on to Dale. After slipping Ecstasy into his drink one night, she went home with him, seduced him and they had sex. It was the perfect ambush. She got him at his most vulnerable and months of planning had worked like a charm. Dale and Susan's marriage had begun to fall apart even before the trial began.

During trial prep, Susan spent all of her time with the attorneys. She began to lose sleep and lose weight with worry. Dale rejected any attempts she made to connect with him and to have sex with her husband. He was all over Allison, but Susan was unaware of this latest development. She wept all the time. She waffled between disbelief and wretched sadness. Dale was acting like a dick and her dad was callous over the phone. It was a total nightmare.

"I thought you were over all this after your escapades with Jenny Cavilieri, Susan! What the hell Susan? You had it all, you could have bought those jewelry pieces! Is it a high for you? A cry for attention? What is it Susan?" Richard Chatham would scream at his daughter, then not believe any of her answers.

"Over what dad? What are you taking about? I DIDN'T DO THIS! I am being set up. How can my own father not believe me? I know I could have bought those pieces. I wasn't in that fucking store on that fucking day. Don't you understand?" Susan was beside herself. She couldn't get the crime and the accusations out of her mind. "Why won't anyone believe me?"

She thought about the day of the crime. She had met Allison Cray for coffee that morning, she had gone shopping for errands for Dale, and she had gone to the bank. She hadn't been at Kane's jewelers. But there was video footage and testimony that she was there. That she was guilty. The police had found one of the diamond earrings in her jewelry box at her home. How? What? Her attorneys had told her to worry because it didn't look good. Did she want to take a plea deal?

Susan, still not suspecting Allison Cray, had met with her for coffee after her attorneys broke the news.

"Allison, they want me to take a plea deal. If I don't and they find me guilty, my sentence will be longer. What should I do?"

Allison knew exactly what Susan should do. Susan needed to be gone for as long as possible so Allison would have time to finish her work on Dale, to audition for parts that Susan would have been up for, to live life in Susan's place. She encouraged Susan not to take the plea deal, and not to go for a second opinion when Susan thought her attorneys didn't have her best interests at heart. Allison smiled at Susan knowing how this would go down, if she had anything to do with it.

Susan hadn't a clue how this could be happening to her, but Allison Cray knew. She had planned it all along hadn't she? She had access to the couples' bank accounts, their house keys, and it didn't hurt that she was a dead-ringer for Susan and had the same clothes, and even the same hairdresser. She learned to mimic her mannerisms to perfection.

The trial was in a few months, but it was already as if Susan was in prison. Allison was taking over Susan's life, and Dale, although distraught about his wife, had long ago lost faith in her, and was already enjoying even hotter sex with this ex-stripper, Allison. She was a clone of his wife anyway, especially when he was drunk or high. Allison had gotten very good at fixing Dale's coffee, light on the cream with an extra dose of drugs, which he didn't suspect.

Life hadn't always been easy for Allison Cray. Allison had been born in the rough part of Los Angeles, on the wrong side of the tracks. On top of that she was a bad seed. She never cared much about anyone but herself. She learned to manipulate and take advantage of anyone she needed from an early age. If you had something Allison Cray wanted, you had better look out. She stole, she dealt in drugs, she lied and betrayed. Her saving grace had always been her beauty and athleticism, but she had always used those attributes to be even more cold and evil.

She liked to spend more money than she could earn and was always hustling. Unbelievably, she was discovered one day by a talent scout while dancing at a strip club. She would laugh when she looked back on that fateful day. She was a lying, cheating bitch and she had been given a golden opportunity just because she was hot.

The next thing she knew, she was a modeling star, but she looked too much like another well-known model Susan Chatham. Susan Chatham was famous, the real star. She had been a child model, had been in that stupid teen show and had grown up to be a beautiful and accomplished actress. Allison's agent knew there was no competition, so she decided to use Allison's athleticism to their advantage. She suggested Allison try to become a body double for Susan. They would pursue projects for which Susan Chatham had already been cast. They would approach the producer, usually Susan's husband Dale, and offer Allison's services as a body double. It was genius and it worked. When Allison had forced herself into Dale and Susan's life and was deep in their good graces, Allison dumped the agent that had made it possible and cheated her out of her cut. She didn't bat an eyelash before or after. She had done the same to the talent scout who had discovered her and to every person who had been unfortunate enough to cross her path.

Allison Cray was a true con artist and could manipulate her way into anyone's heart and mind. She soon became very friendly with Susan Chatham, and in addition to being her go-to body double, she also began to moonlight as Dale McCraven's assistant. With Susan's demanding schedule, Dale was often alone. Allison began her attack in subtle yet carefully planned ways. She gained Susan and Dale's trust. Men were so stupid and Susan was so trusting.

"Dale, would you like me to get your coffee?"

"Dale, would you like me to take your bank deposit for

you?"

"Dale, would you like me to buy Susan's gift for you?"

"Dale would you like me to drop that off at your home for you?"

Allison was spending more and more time around Dale. She was learning Dale and Susan's mannerisms, their habits, and their schedules.

Once, when Susan was away on a modeling shoot, Dale asked Allison to join him and Susan's brother, Tommie Chatham for drinks after work. The three got drunk, and Allison took out some pot and got them stoned too. She made sure she stayed sober. Allison took advantage and asked Tommie to tell them funny childhood stories about Susan.

Tommie shared and they all laughed.

Then Allison, her greed all consuming, went in for what she wanted. "So is she really Miss Perfect? She must be human. Any flaws? Tommie? Spill it. What's the worst thing Susan did? Did she ever get into trouble?"

"Hell yes," Tommie squealed.

"She got caught shoplifting with her kleptomaniac friend Jennifer Cavilieri in middle school. My Dad went ballistic!"

Tommie put on his best Richard Chatham impression.

"Susan Chatham, what were you thinking? Stealing? Do you want to end your modeling and acting career, just as it is beginning? Why would you and Jennifer steal anything? Was it a high? A dare? I should ground you for a year!"

Tommie laughed thinking back. There had always been a little envy in him against his sister. Then, acting like his dad, "Susan, if you ever, if I ever hear that you steal anything ever again, I will have nothing to do with you. I will not tolerate that ever!" That was all the information Allison needed.

Dale trusted Allison implicitly as his administrative assistant, and soon without Susan's knowledge, she was moving Dale's money into accounts she had opened, and was an authorized user on his credit card.

Her plan was almost ready for execution.

When Dale asked Allison to pick up a top and shorts as a

gift for Susan, Allison bought two of the same. One set for Susan, and one identical set for herself.

She used Dale's credit card to buy herself a red Corvette. The GM sales manager wrongly assumed it was Susan buying the car and paying for it with her husband's credit card. Everyone in town knew them and no one thought to question the purchase. After all, Dale drove a Jaguar, and Susan a Porsche, the Corvette, they assumed, was for "auto cross" car racing fun. It was just another extravagant purchase in a town known for its excess.

When moving money around for Dale, Allison moved other money around. She made it look like Susan was overspending and using the money irresponsibly.

Allison Cray was preparing to go in for the kill. She formulated the final phase of her plan. Meet Susan for coffee and confirm that she was wearing "the outfit." She would make sure Susan was going on the shopping errand for Dale and to the bank to get her out of the way. She would go to Kane's Jewelers. She knew that was Dale and Susan's favorite store and that Susan often went there. She would dress like Susan and ask to try on expensive diamonds. She would steal the jewels and make it look like Susan did it. She would let herself into the McCraven's home and make sure she planted one of the stolen items into Susan's jewelry box. Everyone would think Susan's kleptomaniac tendencies were back. She studied the bus schedule, and she would say she was on the L bus and that she saw Susan exiting Kane's at the time of the crime. She would make sure Susan got caught, and frame her for the crime. With Susan out of the way, she would continue to turn Dale against Susan. She would slam home thoughts that Susan was a thief, or a kleptomaniac. She was misusing his money, even when she had plenty of her own. She was doing things behind Dale's back, how awful. Allison also came on to another man, one of her strip club regulars, and made it look like Susan was cheating on Dale. She made sure that Dale turned on Susan and then she would fuck him to seal the deal. Allison would steal Susan's life and career completely. Greed was her powerful motivator.

"By the time Susan Chatham gets out of jail, I, Allison Cray will be the fucking star. That bitch can live in my shadow for a change, like I have lived in hers my whole life."

Everything had worked like a charm. It had almost been too easy. Allison was amazed at how stupid and gullible people were. The happiest day of her life, besides the day she finally bedded Dale, was when the Jury foreman uttered that beautiful word. "Guilty". Allison had almost laughed out loud. She had to bite her lip until it bled to keep from giggling. She went over that day in the months that followed and it excited her almost to the point of orgasm. Speaking of orgasm, it was time to find Dale. She could use one and that poor sucker was always ready to please. Ah, life was good.

CHAPTER 10
AN INTERESTING PROPOSITION

A strong woman doesn't give up even though
her heart may feel heavy. She courageously takes
one more step, then another, and another.
~ WomenWorking.com ~

George Ferguson strutted down the hallway at Lynchfield prison assertive and confident in his good looks. He was always on the prowl. His swagger was exaggerated and behind it was the story of his childhood. As a young boy, George had been severely abused by his single mother. Instead of showering her only child with love and affection, she had showered him with beatings and humiliation. She had instilled in him a deep hatred of all things feminine. He left home the day after high school graduation and had never looked back. After a series of dead end jobs he decided to try to become a correctional officer at a women's prison. He had found his calling. Brutality against the female inmates became his sport of choice. He reveled in it. To have incarcerated women at his beck and call was exactly what his damaged psyche needed. He took full advantage of the position he had been placed in. If the hiring committee had looked further than the pages of his application, they would never have considered hiring him. But since they hadn't bothered to read between the lines, Guard Ferguson took his post and began his reign of terror. He barked orders and threatened at will. He ogled at them in the showers and while they relieved themselves. He wasn't supposed to fuck them but he often did. He wasn't supposed to hit them but he often did. He wasn't supposed to sell them drugs or sneak in contraband but he often did. He loved his job.

Susan Chatham, that hot bitch, had him fixated. He wanted to lose himself in every one of her orifices. He wanted to feel those pouty full lips of hers on his dick. He wanted to bite her nipples and suck on her hooters. He wanted to watch her choke on his cum, pee in her mouth and shit on her. Vile ways his mother had abused him, he was consumed by wanting to do to others. Things that once tormented him, now made him horny. He was a sick son of a bitch, just the way he wanted to be.

"Where is she?" he wondered. He paced the hallways, searching for her, knowing all of the places she might be, where she would be sweeping, or mopping, or in the bathroom cleaning the toilets.

Then he spotted her, mopping the floors near the utility closet. How convenient, a nice quiet and private place to fuck her brains out. He lusted after her fiercely. Damn that girl was hot, even with her hair tied back, and dressed in oranges, and with a wet mop in her hands. He wished she held on to his hard cock like she did that mop handle. He wanted to take that handle and fuck her ass with it.

"Hey Chatham! Stop," He barked at Susan.

Susan froze in her tracks, placing the mop back into the bucket, and standing at attention.

"Oh, no shit, Ferguson." She was attracted to him and terrified of him at the same time. He was always brushing up against her breasts or reaching for her ass, and Bert had warned her that he had fucked more inmates than anyone at Lynchfield. He was always coming on to Susan but her divorce, although in motion, was not finalized. Plus Susan was so miserable at Lynchfield, for the first time in her life, sex was the last thing on her mind.

She kept her eyes downcast as Ferguson spoke, "Mopping again Chatham?"

"Yes, sir, Officer Ferguson sir," she replied, standing at attention, looking down, her fingers nervously twisting in front of her.

He lifted her chin so she couldn't help but look into his sexy eyes, his gorgeous face. Her blue eyes now fixated on his.

"You know Chatham, if you would just give me what I want, I would get you a better job duty assignment and make your life easier around here." He bent close and licked her cheek from the corner of her mouth up to her brow. Susan took a deep breath in before responding.

"Thank you for your offer sir. I know you have offered to take care of me several times, but as I have said before, I am still married to my husband, and I won't cheat on him. Please sir. I will do anything you ask of me as an inmate but I cannot have sex with you."

"Oh, Chatham, you have no idea what I would and wouldn't do to you."

Susan thought he was talking about how he would make her come but he had more sinister ideas in mind.

He showed her some crack wrapped up in a balloon.

"Want some? Sell some? Trade some?"

"Thank you, but no. I don't do drugs. I don't want them, won't sell them and won't trade for them."

"Oh Chatham, why do you force me to write you up?"

"But sir, I haven't done anything wrong."

"Sometimes it isn't about what you do, but what you aren't willing to do." He pulled on her ponytail, but playfully.

"I am so sorry Officer Ferguson. Please sir. I just want to do my job duty, serve my time," Susan pleaded.

"No Chatham, it's not that simple."

He pushed her against the wall, controlling her body, and

before she could react he had his hand down her pants and grabbed her sex.

"I could make you feel really good Chatham. I see the way you look at me. I know you know I'm hot. One day Chatham soon enough, I'll make your pussy come."

With that he inserted his fingers deep into her, then promptly pulled them back out. Handed her back the mop without even looking at her further, and promptly went to Warden Mike Ramsey's office.

Susan stared after him, nervous but ever so slightly turned on. For a brief moment, a spark of desire ignited in her. But George Ferguson was not to be toyed with. He was to be avoided. He was hot but dangerous.

George headed to Warden Ramsey's office with an idea he had been turning over in his mind for months. It had come to him shortly after that sexy bitch Chatham had come to Lynchfield. He wanted her to himself so desperately. But he needed to find a way to solve a problem for the prison. What could he do? Then a light bulb came on. He had a solution to the overcrowding problem. He had a plan he would present to the Warden that would give him the chance to get into Chatham's pants.

"Warden Ramsey sir, may I have a word with you?" George got away with what he did, because he knew how to play the game well, like every psychopath. He knew how to win. Brown nose your superior's ass, so you could fuck an inmate's ass. It was a simple formula, and he had it down pat.

"Sure, Ferguson, what's up?" Mike Ramsey motioned for him to sit down.

"Sir, last week at the "State of Lynchfield" staff meeting you asked for brainstorming ideas and suggestions on how to deal with some of the problems here at Lynchfield."

"Yes, Ferguson, I am getting a lot of pressure from above. The overcrowding has surpassed all legal limits. The last warden got fired over those last two rapes and inmate pregnancies. We are over budget and out of funds. Expansion isn't an option, hiring more guards isn't an option, and yet every day the number of new inmate registrations goes up. Where the hell will we put them all? How will we feed them? Clothe them?"

"Yes, sir, I get it, sir," Ferguson acknowledged. "I have a suggestion, a plan," he continued. "House arrest sir. Affix the prisoner with an ankle bracelet with a GPS tracker. You will know where they are at all times. If the inmate tries to escape or misbehaves . . . zap them with a built-in TASER in their tracks."

Mike Ramsey sat up and leaned forward. "That is a very interesting concept. I am sure that the house arrest anklets could be modified in that way. Go on, tell me more."

Ferguson continued, adding his twist.

"But, some of these inmate's crimes are too severe to just put them in their own homes for house arrest right?"

"Well yes, of course, that's why they have been sentenced to incarceration and not just house arrest in the first place," Mike clarified.

Ferguson went in for the kill. "House arrest for those types needs more supervision, therefore, house arrest with a guard, sir."

"What? What are you saying Ferguson?" Mike asked with his eyebrows raised and his mustache twitching.

"Sir, we can't keep them here, and we can't just put them on house arrest in their own homes, unsupervised, but what if the house arrest was in the guard's home, beta test it, pick one of your best guards and pick one of your most rule following inmates."

Ferguson saw that Warden Ramsey was actually considering this as a potential solution. Would the public allow it? Would the "Powers That Be" approve it?

Before Mike could over think it, Ferguson took control. He was very good at getting what he wanted.

"Who is your best inmate sir?"

"Best inmate Ferguson? What do you mean?"

"Best, you know, never been in the Shoe, no demerits or at least the fewest demerits (shots); would be able to get letters of recommendation from other guards?" Ferguson knew the answer of course.

Mike Ramsey smiled, "Ha! That would probably be Chatham, Susan Chatham. Jesus, that girl even flosses!" Then Mike continued. "You know, she hasn't had any shots. Actually the only one that ever gives her shots is you Ferguson?"

He looked at him suspiciously and continued, "What is it with you and her anyway, George? You give her shots and I just dismiss them because there is no evidence on the video footage of any wrongdoing on her part."

Ferguson needed to cover his tracks. He couldn't very well say he gave her shots because she refused to fuck him. Or could he?

"Oh, well you know, I keep inmates in line with the threat of shots. Maybe that's why she has done so well?"

He paused, letting everything sink into the Warden's mind.

"I would do it Warden Ramsey sir. I would offer my services as a Correctional Officer to host an inmate, hell, give me inmate Susan Chatham, house arrest with me, put a GPS/TASER anklet on her, house arrest with a guard, and call it a furlough. Beta test it sir, I won't let you down. I'll take her during my "leave" week, so it isn't like you are reducing the number of guards here, I would be gone that week anyway."

He watched Mike Ramsey carefully. Then slowly persisted.

"One week, maybe two at most, modify the program how you see fit. One to two weeks gets one inmate out and opens up that bed. If it works, and is a success, then you can expand, modify, it will let you rotate inmates in and out, help the overcrowding." George was getting a hard-on just thinking about his plan.

"Get the inmate to give written consent. It may, no, actually I guarantee, that it would reduce the rape and improper sexual advances that are going on around here."

George smirked knowing that he was the number one offender in rapes and sexual advances, but knowing Warden Ramsey's ignorance of these facts.

"I see Ferguson, you have really given this a lot of thought."

"Yes, sir, I have, Warden Ramsey, sir." Had he ever.

Mike rubbed his chin, seriously intrigued by this bizarre but possible suggestion. He trusted George Ferguson. He naively thought he was one of his best correctional officers. George made very sure to cover all tracks of his improper conduct. His mom had taught him well. He had learned both how to play the part of a goody two shoes, and how to control, dominate, and get what he wanted, even how to use sabotage when necessary.

Goody two shoes? Susan Chatham was a goody two shoes. That girl would probably jump at any chance of getting out of prison, even if only for one or two weeks furlough.

"Okay, Ferguson, nice work. I will give this some serious thought, and take it up the chain of command to see if it will be approved. It will take some time. Work out the kinks and legal aspects of this. Are you sure you would be willing to serve as the beta testing host?"

"Yes, sir, Warden Ramsey, sir," George responded.

"And if Susan Chatham can get the recommendations and she gives her consent, you would take her, even though you have wanted to write her up on so many occasions?"

"Oh yes, sir." George tried to control his smirking grin. "Furlough, a reward. Get inmates to behave with a promise of furlough, like a dangling carrot in front of a horse, promising convicted inmates a chance to get away from prison, if only for a little while. Encouraging better behavior and reducing overcrowding at the same time."

"Okay then Ferguson, I get it. I will keep you posted on the progress. Write it up formally like we have discussed it here today."

"Yes, sir, I will have it for you by tomorrow. Will that be soon enough sir?"

"Yes, Ferguson."

Mike stood up, offered his hand and said, "Thanks, George, really, good idea, nice job."

George Ferguson stood and shook the hand of Warden Ramsey. He left the office thinking of only one thing. Susan Chatham. "You'll be my bitch soon enough. I am gonna have a great time with you." He could feel an erection forming in his pants, a twitch in his palm.

After George Ferguson had left his office, Warden Ramsey gave his idea further thought. It might just work. Mike Ramsey had always been a believer in rehabilitation. He knew these women had had many setbacks and had been victims of circumstance as much as bad decision-making. He had tried throughout his career to be the best leader he could be, stern but fair. Of course there were some inmates that were beyond help. Beulah was one. What a piece of work she was, a sociopath by anyone's definition. But there were others in the system that could be saved, who deserved a break. He picked up the phone and rang the Medical Department.

Nurse Practitioner Icasa answered. "Sally this is Mike, is Frank around?"

"Yes, Warden Ramsey, he is. One moment please."

"Dr. Lomegistro, Warden Ramsey is on the phone for you."

"Hey Mike, what's up?" Frank Lomegistro was always happy to speak with his old friend. They had known each other since college. They had been roommates in fact. It was Mike who had given him the job as staff physician at Lynchfield, at a time when Frank needed a change.

"I just finished a meeting with a guard, and he had an interesting proposal."

"Oh, really? What was that?"

"He thought we should try out a unique new furlough program. House arrest with a guard for some of our best behaved prisoners, a test to help with overcrowding and offered as a reward. He said he would be willing to take the first one as a test. What do you think?"

"Well, Mike, it sounds like an interesting idea," said Frank. "Is this a guard you can trust?"

"He can be a bit of a hothead sometimes, but he's an excellent guard and has never been in any trouble here. He seemed genuinely interested in coming up with something useful." Mike Ramsey had been completely fooled by George Ferguson.

"Well then give it a chance. If it works out, maybe I'll volunteer as well."

"I don't know Frank. Remember, these are prisoners. You're a doctor, not a corrections officer."

"I'll bet I can handle it."

Mike put the phone back in the receiver. He had always trusted Frank Lomegistro's opinion. He considered him a close friend and wise in his counsel. As soon as he received George Ferguson's finalized plan, he would complete the necessary paperwork and get the ball rolling on the cutting edge program.

CHAPTER 11
FRANKLIN L. LOMEGISTRO, M.D.

At any given moment you have the power
to say this is not how the story is going to end.
~ Unknown ~

Franklin Lawrence Lomegistro had never imagined that his
medical career would include a stint as the staff physician of a
women's prison. A series of unfortunate events had led him
here, but he was grateful nonetheless to have a job that he felt
was worthwhile and a life that was relatively peaceful. Prior to
Lynchfield he had been a surgeon at a prestigious hospital,
happily married to his precious Evangeline. His life had been
a success and he had been happy. He allowed himself to
reminisce.

Evangeline had been five years younger than Frank.
They had met in Key West, Florida at Sloppy Joes. She had
just finished her certification as a massage therapist and Frank
was on spring break during his second year of medical school.
He had come on this trip with a dozen other young guys,
mostly other medical school classmates. He had even brought
his roommate from undergrad, Mike Ramsey. Both men were
enjoying the sun, the boating, the snorkeling, and especially

the bars. Frank, like his friends, was on the prowl. They were typical guys on vacation, horny and searching for an escape from the pressures of their studies.

Frank's hair was dark back then. Now his sideburns were sprinkled with salt and pepper. Evangeline had caught sight of him at a local watering hole and she thought he was adorable in his preppie plaid shorts, polo shirt and Sperry shoes. His hair was slicked back and on the longer side. When she got to know him, she had fallen in love with his intelligence and humor. His broad shoulders didn't hurt either. He loved her wavy long blond hair, which she loved to pin back in unusual folk art barrettes or hair ties, and those big gray eyes like saucers. Evangeline had a medium build with fair freckled skin, and tall, almost reaching his 6 ft. 2 in. height. She dressed in tropical print summer dresses with her big straw bag looking every bit the Texan tourist. Frank had not been looking for love. He was looking for a hot babe for a quickie. But he fell head over heels for this serious, hard working gentle woman with a heart of gold. Frank thought he would get the business from his macho guy friends because he had met someone, but they were all supportive. Mike especially encouraged Frank to go for it. Frank was the marrying kind and Mike knew it.

Frank and Evangeline became instantly inseparable after their first long walk on the beach. They spoke effortlessly for hours. Maybe it was the margaritas or the frozen rum punches with the little umbrellas. Maybe it was too many conch fritters or too much key lime pie, but they fell in love hard and fast. At first they maintained a long distance relationship, but as soon as she could, Evangeline left her suburban Dallas home to join Frank in Los Angeles. Wedding plans soon followed.

Evangeline's dad was the minister who married them, and Mike Ramsey served as best man. They married in Texas in a barn style wedding and honeymooned in the most logical place, Key West of course.

When they returned to Los Angeles, Evangeline worked

as a masseuse in a chiropractor's office by day, but often came home to an empty apartment. Frank was either studying, and after medical school, spent what seemed like 24 hours a day at the hospital during his internship and residency. When he was home, he was exhausted. She was a typical doctor's wife, sometimes feeling like a widow. Instead of complaining or wallowing, Evangeline took on private clients at night and earned extra income. The extra money in those early years helped pay back Frank's medical school loans. She never missed a day of work.

When Frank finally completed his medical training, he joined the staff of Regional Memorial Hospital. There, he worked equally as hard, often taking the shifts others didn't want like holidays and evenings. He was a shoo-in for Chief of Staff in the Emergency Department when that position opened up.

Evangeline was so proud of her husband, and he loved her with all his heart, appreciating her equal hard work and dedication. They made good money and had a wonderful life together and soon they longed for a family. Together they left their apartment and bought a large suburban home with the mandatory large family room and loft they hoped to make a playroom someday for their kids. Unfortunately those bedrooms were destined to remain empty.

Frank and Evangeline had a good if not successful love life. After her third miscarriage, infertility became an issue. Evangeline felt disappointed and grew distraught. Their love was still there but the romance part waned. Sex became a chore. It was all about ovulation timetables and basal temperatures and discussions about whether they would consider in-vitro fertilization. Infertility and all of its accompanying stress reared its ugly head. But through it all they loved each other. Spontaneous intercourse had been put on the back burner, but they found small ways to be intimate. Evangeline often gave Frank incredible massages using all her training and he would rub her feet at the end of her day. They were content.

They both felt their marriage was a happy one and there was no doubt they loved each other deeply.

The week before one of Frank's many medical conferences, Evangeline began to complain of nausea and headaches.

"Maybe you are pregnant Evangeline," Frank thought, but didn't say out loud. He prescribed some meds for her nausea and for the headaches, suspecting migraines.

"Honey when I get home from the conference we will get these headaches checked out if you still have them. Maybe a CAT Scan or even an MRI?" Frank suggested.

"Oh Frank, always the doctor and assuming the worst! I am sure it is nothing. Maybe I have some type of food poisoning. That chicken salad I ate a few days ago tasted funny. I should have known. Dr. Bernstein took us all out for lunch for Alice's birthday." Evangeline lay down and dismissed both him, and her pain.

She seemed much better the next day, and again the following day when Frank left for San Francisco for his conference on the "State of Emergency Medicine in California." They kissed each other goodbye after Frank reminded her of some dry cleaning that needed picking up and asked if she would please schedule his next dental cleaning. Evangeline agreed, and went to work as normal. Dr. Bernstein had a full schedule of massage clients for her in the office. The nausea soon returned as did the headache, but still she went to work.

Frank called Evangeline every night while he was away. She however, didn't want him to worry so she didn't mention at all her continuing headaches with pain that was so bad she could barely open her eyes. Instead, she talked about mundane life events like the dry cleaning. She confirmed the date of his dental appointment so he could add it to his calendar. She clenched her fists at times during the conversation, because the pain would come in waves, but she dare not say anything. She would wait until Frank came home and then they would address any issue she might be having together.

Frank attended the different seminars and panel discussions. He met with colleagues and opinion leaders. He visited the different vendors in the exhibit hall. His feet hurt, not used to all of the standing and walking around.

Several days into the conference, on a day when he was particularly tired and hungry, his pager went off. He stepped away to check his phone. He recognized the number as Dr. Bernstein's office.

"Hi Frank, This is Alice Jones. Evangeline didn't show up for work today. No answer either when I called her numbers. Is everything okay?"

Frank felt his stomach drop. He put on a brave face. "I think so Alice. I will check, thanks for letting me know. Say hello to Dr. Bernstein and tell him Mrs. Lomegistro will get a stern talking to when I get home."

Alice let out a slightly nervous laugh. She wasn't buying the fake jolliness. She knew Evangeline and she knew something was very wrong. But she didn't want to make things worse, so she went along with Dr. Lomegistro's awkward attempt at humor. "I sure will. Doctor's orders right?"

Frank hung up and immediately went into panic mode. That was not like Evangeline. She had never missed a day. He could barely get her to stay home sick when she had a fever. She always put the needs of others before her own. Her family, her husband, her friends and her patients all knew that she was the most giving person who walked the earth.

Frank left the conference the minute he could excuse himself and went up to his hotel room to pack. In between, he kept trying to reach his wife. He left her messages at home, on her cell, everywhere. He contacted her parents in Texas. Nothing. They begged him to let them know as soon as he had reached her. He promised to do so, but he was beside himself with worry.

Frank called Mike Ramsey. His voice on the phone was nearly unrecognizable.

"Frank is that you? What is wrong?"

"Mike, Mike, something is wrong with Evangeline. I just know it. Please go by the house as soon as you can. I'm on my way back from San Francisco. She didn't show up to work today. She's been feeling ill Mike. I'm scared. Please go by the house. Please Mike."

"Frank, calm down. I'm heading there now. It'll be ok. I'll let you know when I get there."

Frank raced to the airport and caught the next flight to LA. Luckily the flights were practically every half hour. The flight itself was the longest hour and a half of his life. He emerged into the chaos of LAX. He immediately checked his phone. Mike had called. He returned the call immediately as he ran to get his car.

"Frank, her car is in the driveway but I'm not getting a response when I ring the doorbell. Call me right away."

Frank's trembling hands dialed the number. "Mike, what am I going to do without her? She's the best thing that ever happened to me."

"Whoa, whoa, whoa, Frank. Come on. Don't talk that way. I'm here in the driveway. I'll be here when you get home. Maybe she went somewhere in someone else's car. Don't jump to conclusions." Mike was trying to be reassuring but he also had a sickening feeling in the pit of his stomach. He couldn't bear to break down the door of the Lomegistro residence without Frank there. He was afraid of what he would find.

Frank drove home as quickly as he could. He cursed LA traffic out loud in his car. He cried and he screamed. He finally pulled into his driveway where Mike was waiting for him. He ran to the front door leaving it thrown open as Mike followed him in. And then Mike heard Frank scream.

"Oh no, oh no, not Evangeline!"

Mike ran up the stairs to a horrible scene. Frank was

holding a very ashen, mortally limp Evangeline. The master bedroom reeked of vomit.

Mike called 911 as Frank commenced CPR on his wife although he already knew she had been gone for hours. She had probably passed during the night.

Frank wept falling into Mike's arms. He believed Evangeline had vomited in her sleep and drowned in her own vomit. The autopsy report confirmed the cause of death. She had died of an aneurysm at the base of her brain stem that had burst causing the massive brain bleed. Even if it had been caught earlier on an MRI or CAT scan, nothing much could have been done. It was inoperable.

Frank couldn't forgive himself even though none of it was his fault. He sank into a deep depression. He was so frustrated that he was a physician and couldn't have prevented his wife's death at age 36.

He threw himself into his work more than ever to try to keep his depression at bay. It was no use. He would see her dead body at every turn in their home. It was gut wrenching. He decided to put their house up for sale and move to a condo on the beach, hoping to find some solace. He and Evangeline had spent so many good times at the beach. Perhaps this would soothe his nerves and help mend his broken heart.

Mike tried his best to cheer Frank up. After several months, he set him up on dates, taking him to a new and awesome Karaoke bar knowing how Frank liked to dance and sing. It was hopeless. He couldn't get Frank out of his slump.

When Mike accepted the position of Warden at Lynchfield Women's Correctional Facility, he immediately thought of his friend Frank. The prison had a medical department that was barely used. It was exactly the type of environment Frank needed. Low stress but still something in the medical field. He could help the inmate patients with minor illnesses or injuries. If there was a fight or a stabbing,

Frank could bring his surgical skills to the table and save some lives. He could feel useful again, without the stress of a hospital emergency room. Frank had already cut his hours and was in virtual semi- retirement. He had invested the life insurance proceeds wisely and money wasn't an issue. Working at Regional Memorial reminded him of his dear deceased wife Evangeline. Three years had passed since her death and he was still haunted. When Mike suggested this work change, Frank accepted the position of Medical Director at Lynchfield. He felt he had nothing to lose.

The inmates at Lynchfield were nothing like Evangeline or any of the women he had ever known and his new job helped him refocus. It was a cushy position with mostly treating the flu or stomach aches. Occasionally someone overdosed on contraband drugs or was beaten up badly. Sometimes even a rape by a guard or another inmate's homemade dildo came through the doors. A few cases were serious, but nothing he couldn't handle with his eyes closed, and nothing close to the trauma he was used to at Regional Memorial.

Life settled down a bit and even bordered on mundane. Frank Lomegistro wasn't happy by any stretch of the imagination, but his condo on the beach became his sanctuary, and in a way, his salvation.

CHAPTER 12
THE ENCOUNTER

Why do people say, "Grow some balls?"
Balls are weak and sensitive. If you wanna be tough,
grow a vagina. Those things can take a pounding.
~ Betty White ~

George Ferguson was one of the most feared guards at Lynchfield, but he was also the sexiest. He was an Adonis and he knew it, tall, dark and handsome, with cut muscles that bulged through his perfectly pressed uniform shirt. On the bottom half, his huge dick protruded from his tight uniform pants. His face, if you could look up and take your eyes off the swell in his pants, did not disappoint either. George Ferguson was gorgeous. That cleft in his chin and sculpted cheekbones. He resembled a model on the cover of a men's fitness magazine. His strut made you think he should be walking down some catwalk at New York Fashion Week. When that ass moved down the hall, every woman, even the die-hard lesbians, turned their heads. Most of the women at Lynchfield craved him at the most primal level, even if they found him a bit intimidating.

Susan Chatham was no different. Roberta Jimenez had

warned Chatham to stay clear of Ferguson, but Susan was drawn to his sexual magnetism. After all she had been through during her first year of incarceration, she had now reached a new state of being. She had been through all the stages of grief and she was coming to acceptance. She would do her time, watch her back and survive. She had become used to the routines, knew who to steer clear of, and had tried to make herself invisible. She had succeeded for the most part, barring a few run-ins and general prison mishaps. She couldn't figure out why Bert was so repulsed by Ferguson. "Maybe the Puerto Rican isn't used to leading-man-type faces and body types," Susan rationalized. Yes he was intimidating, and often made her freeze in her tracks, but, so did that face, those dark eyes when they looked at you. There was something naughty about that man, and it made Susan desire him, now that desire was an emotion she was starting to feel after such a long time.

George was always coming on to her as well, which made it even more confusing for Susan. Her mind told her to say no, because he was a bully when it came to dealing with her and the others. Bert had told her to stay away, and she was legally still married to Dale, wasn't she? But that day when he grabbed her in the hall and put his fingers down her pants and into her, well, Susan was very curious where that would have gone.

There had been talk recently about a possible inmate reward program and furlough. Nothing was certain, but it sounded interesting and there was buzz all over the prison. If those rumors were true, Susan wanted that reward more than anyone. A chance to leave Lynchfield for a week or two was tantamount to going to Heaven.

She was a model and an actress and used to life's finest things. She missed her fancy home, cars, and parties. She missed healthy delicious food choices, and drinks that went down smooth. Susan missed her freedom and she missed having sex. Her life had been one of abundance. Lynchfield was the definition of scarcity. Was there any room for sexual gratification at Lynchfield? Could she find what she was looking for in Officer George Ferguson?

One quiet day as Susan was nearing the end of her work duty shift she thought she heard something. Susan went to put the mop away, but as she approached the utility closet she stopped. She did hear something, it was groaning and moaning. She knew what those sounds meant. Definitely a man's voice and a woman's and they sounded breathless. The man's groans were deep and thundering and made Susan feel wetness in her panties. The woman's voice came out in squeals and at one point she giggled, but at another she cried out as if in pain. Susan wanted to put the mop away quickly and run away and avoid whatever sex was going on in that closet and pretend she hadn't heard anything, another part of her wanted to stay and listen. She had been so horny recently.

There was no privacy anywhere at Lynchfield. Recently, Susan had tried to masturbate on several different occasions, late at night, in her bunk when mostly everyone was asleep. All of her attempts were a bust. Any orgasms she had were pitiful at best, even after her fingers had almost gone numb in trying. She tried to fantasize about Dale. But things had turned so sour in their marriage that thinking of Dilly now made Susan sad, not horny. She surprised herself one night when she accidentally began thinking of George Ferguson and she actually reached her first prison orgasm. So although she was a bit afraid of George, her naughty side craved him.

She chose to stay; paying heed to the wetness in her panties, and the horniness that had her spellbound. Before she could even ponder the consequences of her decision, the door to the utility closet flung open, under the weight of the two people fucking behind it.

Susan was now a witness to a sexual encounter. Hot, crazy, kinky sex between George Ferguson and another inmate, Susan recognized her from the day she went to the hair salon. It was inmate Hilary Dugan.

But Susan wasn't looking at Dugan. She couldn't take her eyes off of George. "Oh my," she thought. He was even a finer specimen now that he was naked and controlling that woman. His pants down by his ankles, he was so huge, even more than in her fantasies. "He must be 9 inches or more," she thought, "and thick, and his ass sure knows how to move. Oh my! Oh Dear God!" Susan knew she should run, but she couldn't help staying. Paralyzed. She was a voyeur. Susan not only wanted to watch, she wanted to be next in line.

But George was rough. Dugan was sweating, her face was red, and tearful, but the sounds she made sounded more like pleasure. It was hard to tell for sure. Wasn't there a very fine line between pleasure and pain?

Susan had always had what others might call vanilla sex, especially by Hollywood standards. She was into some kinky positions and using adult toys but she had never been part of the BDSM world. Was that what she was witnessing right now?

She wasn't sure. Was she willing to try it? Maybe. She sure was curious and her pussy was voting yes.

"He's a bad boy," she thought. "I don't usually go for that type. But, I am in prison now. Does that make me a bad girl? Don't bad boys and bad girls belong together?" Ferguson and Dugan were so busy doing the wild thing they were oblivious to Susan's presence, or to the conversation she was enthusiastically having in her mind.

He seemed a bit brutal, but not enough to scare Susan. She found herself drawn to him. That face, that body, that huge dick and the way he seemed to know how to use it! Hilary Dugan protested a bit but she also seemed to enjoy it. Susan could overhear during their brief pause George's words, similar to what he had promised her in the past.

"Dugan, stay, fuck with me again. I can make your life here at Lynchfield easier. What's your work duty? I can get you an easier detail. I am in good with the Warden. What do you want? Need contraband drugs? How about something else? I left a fresh Cobb salad and a Coca Cola in your bunk locker for you for fucking with me last week."

Damn! Now Susan's vagina, her stomach and her taste buds were all saying yes to a fuck with Ferguson. Screw Dilly and screw being a goody two shoes. This was survival of the fittest. At Lynchfield you needed to take what you could get. And if it meant fucking Ferguson, so be it.

Susan stopped her thinking and just watched, as they started up again. They had gone back into the utility closet but had not closed the door all the way.

Susan repositioned herself, ashamed that she had become a peeping tom in prison on top of everything else, but not being able to resist.

George Ferguson went down on Dugan and kissed and licked her clit relentlessly, Dugan continually moaned and squirmed. George was gorgeous, his ripped abs and his oblique's were clearly defined and looked hand sculpted and almost painted. His broad shoulders and muscular back glistened with moisture. His masculine sweat made his aftershave scent permeate the hallway. Even his armpits were sexy, his body hair all neatly "man-scaped" from his chest to his pubic area. His cock was thick and the veins twisted on it like vines. His erection was hard and strong and he began to thrust into Dugan making her whole body ride up and down with each deep push, pull and penetration. His hands were all over her breasts as was his mouth, and he alternated between kissing her mouth and working her tits.

It almost appeared like he was hurting her, but Dugan had gone for a second round so Susan thought not. Susan was left stunned when they went for round three.

At one point, Ferguson took Dugan over his knee and gave her a spank, and another, and another, and made her count with him as he did. Then he pressed his lips to her ass and circled her anus with his fingers, or something else? Susan couldn't see. It may have been something dark. His baton? Not that. Couldn't be. Could it?

He turned her around and used his tongue to kiss and suck and his teeth to gently nibble at her vaginal lips and her clit. Dugan had a grin from ear to ear. But then she yelped, "Ouch!"

"Your pussy is so wet," he said in response. "You taste so good." He used his hand to guide that nine-inch hard thick, veined cock, slick with juices into her again. He began to thrust in and out, and in and out, and Dugan matched his moves and rhythm, their asses moved like ships bouncing on a wavy sea. Dugan came first shuddering, and then George, groaning, "Dugan, oh fuck yes." He exploded in and around her. He pulled out squirting his hot thick cum, Jesus, how did he even still have any left? It went all over Dugan. He wiped it with his fingers on her lips, then on her knockers, and finally sticking his finger in her ass. "Tell me my cum tastes good."

They looked up and Susan was afraid they saw her and so she quickly ran away. She was breathless and it wasn't from running down the halls. She got back as quickly as possible to Cell Block D and tried to put it all out of her mind. She continued with her day.

That night, when she awoke as she did most every night, she masturbated to that vision in her mind and she climaxed as close to pre-Lynchfield as she ever had.

The next day she was happy as she took her usual cold shower in the shower room. Next to her was Hilary Dugan. It wasn't polite to stare at the other inmates while they showered due to the lack of privacy and the threat of violence, but Susan couldn't help it. Dugan didn't like her to begin with, so she took a big chance, but she was curious to see Dugan's body and the aftermath of her encounter with George. She wanted to see if Dugan looked happier. Susan did her best to look when Dugan wouldn't notice. What she saw worried her a bit. She saw bruises she hadn't noticed yesterday when she had been fixated on George's amazing body. She wondered how Dugan got those. George Ferguson?

After their shower, Dugan left without even so much as glancing at Susan. Her spying had gone totally undetected, both yesterday and today. Susan decided to explain away the bruises as understandable when fucking in a utility closet and on a cement floor. Collateral damage if you will. George was hot and Susan wanted privileges. It was as simple as that. She HAD changed since she entered Lynchfield. She was a survivor now.

The word came to her through Bert, later confirmed by Susan's meeting with Warden Ramsey. Furlough had been approved and they were sending one inmate to test it out. That inmate was Susan Chatham and George Ferguson would be her "host." Susan couldn't believe her luck. Finally something good had happened to her after the worst year ever. Bert didn't share her enthusiasm. "Don't go Chatty. I have a very bad feeling about this."

CHAPTER 13
REWARD OR TORTURE?

People cry, not because they are weak.
It is because they've been strong for too long.
~ Johnny Depp ~

Susan awoke two weeks into furlough, curled up and laying in a fetal position on the floor, quivering uncontrollably. She was cold, naked and afraid. The cold made her skin feel like pins and needles in some areas, and quite numb in others. Deep pain seared through her body from the last several days of experiencing beatings at the hands of her tormentor. What was wrong with him? Why did he take such pleasure in hurting her? Why was he such a loose cannon? Not even her first days at Lynchfield had been this miserable. Could she feel any hungrier? Feeling an unrelenting gnawing burn in her stomach, she wondered if this was pay back for all the times, as a child, that she had left her peas uneaten on her plate and her mom had sternly warned her that children were starving in Africa. Or was it China? Susan had entered delirium.

Why couldn't she think straight anymore? Was it because she had been physically, sexually, and verbally abused? Was it the lack of food, lack of clothing, lack of warmth? Her throbbing head spun, as she tried to make sense of it all. How could this be happening to her? Hadn't losing everything she had in life, and being sent to prison for a crime she didn't commit been enough suffering? She said a silent prayer. "Please dear God let this man let up on me before he kills me. Or if he's going to kill me, please make him do it swiftly." Then, trying to concentrate, "Please, dear God, forgive me for my sins. I must have done something horrible for you to send me this burden, this hell. I must have had this coming to me? Please forgive me for whatever it is I did to deserve this." Her prayers seemed to fall on deaf ears. All she was left with was her pain and a river of tears.

What a fool she had been, excited for the new furlough program. Inmates would benefit by getting to leave the walls of Lynchfield, the community would still be protected as these women would be with the guard at all times, plus be tracked by the GPS in the anklet. The anklet could also be programmed to induce a severe shock that could stop any inmate in her tracks. Guards would benefit from inmates doing housekeeping duties, cooking, laundry and such for them, as the inmates needed to continue some sort of job detail. They might also get laid. The warden hoped it would make the current rapes, and inappropriate sexual relations between guards and inmates more controllable.

Susan Chatham remembered the day the warden had called her into his office and given her the good news. She would be the first inmate to go on furlough and with none other than George Ferguson. It was exactly as Susan had hoped. She eagerly signed the consent form that released the prison of any liability and confirmed that she had been informed of all of the provisions of this new program. She signed her life away. Freedom smelled sweet and she couldn't wait to go home with George. In her mind she planned the delicious meals she would cook for him. She planned how she would clean the house and get the chores done efficiently. Her goal was to leave more time for playing and for sex. She planned how she would seduce him. Oh how she missed having sex. Her excitement filled her waking thoughts.

Susan regretted her decision deeply now. From the moment he picked her up, his icy stare intimidated her. She wondered what was wrong. Perhaps George Ferguson was equally nervous about the two of them being the guinea pigs for this novel inmate program. She climbed into his black SS Camaro bringing a bag with one change of clothes, her toothbrush and other personal items.

"Cool car, Officer Ferguson," she beamed at him.

No response. What happened to George telling her how hot she was and coming on to her at every opportunity? Susan looked down at her outfit. She was surprised by how much weight she had lost while at Lynchfield. She knew she was often hungry, but it was only when she put on her previous "street clothes" that she saw the real damage her year on the prison diet had done. Susan's once form fitting jeans and tight tee now appeared way too big and quite frumpy. She had wanted to look sexy for George. This was not the first impression she had wanted to make. Perhaps how she looked was his issue? Was George disappointed seeing her outside of the prison walls?

George yelled suddenly, "Get in," with a cruelness that sent a chill down Susan's spine. What was bugging him, she wondered?

"Thank you for taking me on Furlough, Officer Ferguson," Susan said in her sweetest voice, trying to cut through the frozen tundra. "I'm really looking forward to being with you, getting to know you. This is fantastic." Susan really tried. She couldn't believe his response.

"Look, let me set you straight you little fuck ass cock teaser. Don't get any fancy ideas about what this is and what it ain't. You do my shit, you know; clean, laundry, cook then fuck, nothing more and nothing less. Got that?" His hands banged on the steering wheel so hard his knuckles blanched, almost as much as Susan's face.

Susan felt a lump catch in her throat and a fear rising up in her gut. She had felt this fear before, during her first weeks at Lynchfield. What would become of her? What had she gotten herself into? She decided to remain optimistic, hoping her sweetness would perhaps calm him down. She hoped he would forgive her for being a "cock-teaser" or whatever else he was angry about. The old Susan Chatham naiveté was alive and well, even after a year in the penitentiary. She fastened her seatbelt and sat back in her seat and concentrated on trying to steady her breathing and fake a slight smile. George started the car, turned on the radio, blasted the a/c and sped off into hell.

It seemed to take forever to get to George's place. Susan finally felt the need to speak up, "George, please sir, if you don't mind, I really need to use a restroom."

George stared back. "It's still Officer Ferguson to you cunt. Why didn't you go before you left?"

"I did, Sir, but I have the urge to go again."

"Well I don't really give a rat's ass what you need Chatham. My urge, bitch, is to get you back to my place. Just hold it."

"Mr. Ferguson, please, I don't think I can hold it any longer."

"No!" He continued to pass at least two service plazas. Susan was counting.

Why? Susan realized he was doing this on purpose. He's using this to exercise control over me, shit! Susan felt her bladder cramping. She tried to wiggle in her seat, cross her legs, anything to help hold her pee in. She wished she hadn't taken that second drink of water while she dressed to leave on Furlough. Finally, in a cold nervous sweat and when she thought her bladder would burst, George pulled over and shouted at her again. "Get out now and take your leak over there by the tree."

How humiliating. She had no choice now, the pressure in her bladder was just all consuming. She barely got her panties off in time before the warm pee escaped. Before she could get her panties back up, George was behind her, picking her up with his strong arms and tossing her back into the back seat of the car. Right there, he ripped a condom packet with his teeth, and fucked her hard from behind before she could respond. This was not the sweet sexy seduction she had envisioned. This was like rape. Her blood ran cold.

"I've waited way too long for that Chatham! Your tits are mine, your mouth is mine, your cunt is mine, and your ass is mine. All mine now Chatham. I will control everything you are now, everything you do. What you eat, when and where you get to sleep, when you pee, when you take a shit or get to wash. I will pick what you wear and when we fuck! Got that?"

"So that's the deal for this furlough, Officer Ferguson?" Susan asked this rhetorical question with the breathiest voice she could muster. She hoped to seduce him into a hint of kindness.

George slapped her. His blow was hard enough to knock her off his lap and onto the floor of the back seat. Susan landed with a thud and hit near her eye, on an umbrella lying on the floor.

"Ouch," she yelped and struggled to get back up.

"Get up and get back in the front seat and buckle up. You shut the fuck up and don't think you can sweet talk your way with me you scumbag bitch." George was red faced.

Susan felt like a reprimanded child. She clamored back in the front seat, fastened her seat belt and turned to her right. The sting of her face caused tears to well in her now sad eyes. Susan stared blankly out the window, her eyelid swelling. The black Camaro sped towards George's place carrying two silent passengers, one was seething, and the other was terrified.

Today had only been the first day of the torturous two weeks that would follow. Reward? This was no reward. Susan was furious that she had allowed herself to agree to and look forward to anything that had to do with Lynchfield prison.

As the days went on, the more Susan Chatham tried to please Guard George Ferguson, the harsher her life became. There was just no pleasing Mr. Mercurial. He didn't like anything she cooked for him, even when she fixed her most gourmet recipes. It was strange, because his mouth looked more than pleased. He would clean his plate but take her plate away, after she had just taken a few bites. George complained that what she made was crap! One night he dipped several cotton balls in hot sauce and stuffed her mouth with them, as he screamed at her, "You feed me shit, this is what I'll feed you." Her mouth burned for hours afterwards. Her stomach hungrily grumbled.

Ferguson critiqued the job Chatham did with his laundry.

"You mixed the colors with the whites, and got ink on my shirts, idiot!" She hadn't of course, but Susan suspected George threw in an ink pen, which ruined the lot on purpose. Probably, just to get her into more trouble, and torment her. Susan had developed the habit of checking all pockets and turning them inside out when doing laundry. She remembered her former husband Dale had been terrible at leaving stuff in his pockets. She always double-checked. How did the pen get there? Sabotage? George approached her smoking a cigar. He threw the damaged laundry in the trash. He took the lit cigar, and with horror, Susan cried as George held it on her upper arm and waited until it thoroughly singed her skin.

Susan tried everything to make the torture stop. She sought to fix herself up to look good for him, but with every passing day, she grew more weary, more pale, hungrier and thinner. Dark circles formed under her eyes from the interrupted sleep. Her eyelid was now a healing black eye. It was nearly impossible for her to look or act sexy. He shot down every attempt at kindness.

If you looked up "abused" in the dictionary, you would have seen a picture of Susan Chatham. If you looked up "psychopath" in the dictionary, you would have seen a picture of George Ferguson.

One day, he fixated on her ironing skills. Susan was exhausted after ironing his shirts for the third time. "What the fuck is wrong with you? Why can't you get this right? Iron a fucking shirt Chatham? Do I need to teach you how?" And with that he picked up the iron, burning her foot with its steam on purpose.

George yelled, "What a shitty job with these floors, Chatham! I thought mop duty was your specialty?" He took a paper cup, scooped up the dirty pine scented wash water and forced Susan to drink it. Susan spends the next several hours vomiting and miserable.

Susan cleaned the bathroom and the toilet. "Can't you clean a fucking toilet merry fucking maid?" He dipped her toothbrush in the toilet and forced Susan to brush her teeth with it. Susan cried incessantly. Life was intolerable. She longed to go back to prison. She couldn't even believe she was thinking that, but this was too much.

One particular day, all hell broke loose. Susan noticed George was in one of his moods. She tried to steer clear by going into the kitchen and began to busy herself cleaning, even though every inch of her was sore, and she had previously rendered that kitchen spotless.

George entered the room. "What the fuck are you doing Chatham? You call this a clean kitchen? Do your hands work, Chatham? Are you trying to clean with a broken finger? Is that your problem?"

"Broken finger?" Susan blurted out the question before she realized what he meant. It was too late. She realized what he was about to do to her.

"Oh no Officer Ferguson. Oh please no. I will be good. I promise. Please, Sir, I will do everything you say, everything and anything you want." Susan pleaded and pleaded and got down on her hands and knees in front of him, but to no avail. George Ferguson was a merciless monster. He was as dark and evil on the inside as he was handsome on the outside. Why didn't she listen to Bert? Why was she so fucking stupid and naïve?

He yanked her up off her feet, and held her hand in the pantry doorway. He slammed the door on Susan's finger so hard that the hinge broke. The pain told Susan that her finger broke too. There was simply no relief. With every infraction, came the punishment. Oh the punishment. Pain on steroids!

Susan was always on edge. She never knew what would make him snap, and she felt helpless, and hopeless to help him or help herself.

Every night was the same. First came sex that was harsh and rough. Sex that was all about George finding his relief. There was no love, no romance, and no gentleness. Susan had so been looking forward to the sex. What an idiot she had been. Was all of this because she had chosen to refuse his earlier advances in Lynchfield? She would have been better off doing it in the utility closet with Ferguson like Dugan had. Her punishment would have only been a few bruises and as many orgasms. This was a fucking nightmare. After every fuck he would push her onto the floor. Susan became an object to be toyed with, then promptly discarded. He would force her to lie naked and sleep on the floor, no pillow, no blanket, not even a sheet. He would blast the air conditioner up extra cold on purpose. She would spend each night shivering and miserable.

Susan was starved, slapped, pinched, had her hair pulled, and worse. Pure agony.

One particular night after fellatio, George became livid.

"Officer Ferguson, please," Susan pleaded, "I will give you all the oral sex you like. I just don't like to swallow. I don't like the taste. I don't want to do that."

"Not your thing is it bitch? Well who gives a flying fuck? Not me! I've had it with you. Got that? You can eat dick and drink semen, it's full of protein you know." George Ferguson began to starve Susan Chatham.

Another day, shortly after, Susan lost her footing and toppled to the floor because of her weakened state. George lost it and began to kick her with his boots. Not just any boots. These were combat boots, with high hard heels and metal trim. They hurt like hell. With one blow to the head, Susan passed out. When she came to, he punished her for passing out.

Susan didn't know if she could live another day with this psychopath, never mind survive two weeks. Escape . . . she contemplated the ramifications of running away. She considered suicide for the first time since her trial. This was just too much. She knew that the GPS and TASER in the anklet would go off if she ran away, but she didn't care. The Warden would either throw her back into prison, sending her to the "Shoe" or she might be lucky enough to die from the shock. Death was better than this. Susan gave herself a pep talk. One of the many she had received from herself since her ordeal at Lynchfield started. She thought of Bert and the kindness of Officers Sterling, Somners and Gomez. She thought of Warden Ramsey and how he had also thought this was a good idea. He had done it with the right intentions in mind. Susan decided right then and there that she would survive this as well. No matter what, she wouldn't let George Ferguson be the cause of her demise. She braced herself for the last few days of furlough.

CHAPTER 14
A BROKEN WOMAN

There comes a point when you have to realize
that you'll never be good enough for some people.
The question is, is that your problem or theirs?
~ Unknown ~

The final 24 hours of furlough with George finally arrived and just in the knick of time. Susan was close to her breaking point. She decided to celebrate getting out of this colossal blunder by making a delicious meal. She even baked a pie. Psycho Officer George Ferguson enjoyed it thoroughly, eating and drinking in front of her, but refused to let her have so much as a morsel of it. Clearing the last dishes, she slowly reentered the living room where George was seated on the couch watching television.

As he had all the previous nights, he called out to her. "Come here!" But this night he didn't curse her or call her an obnoxious vulgar name. He used her name instead. "Susan, come sit with me." What the fuck was this all about?

"You look like hell," he stated matter-of-factly. "Turn around, oh my God, damn, awful, girl."

"How am I going to take you back to Lynchfield looking

like that?" he wondered out loud, as if suddenly realizing he was in a bit of a pickle.

Susan shrugged her shoulders, fearing how to respond. During her week at George's every word out of her mouth was taken in contempt, ending with punishment. Now she barely spoke at all.

"That my dear was a great meal," George said with a smile. "I knew you had it in you." Motherfucking psychopath. What the fuck was wrong with this guy? She didn't know how close she was to understanding when she muttered that vulgarity under her breath.

"Sit," he warned. Getting up from the couch, George walked over to the fridge, poured a glass of orange juice and spread some butter on two dinner rolls. He returned to the couch and handed them to Susan.

"Eat," he ordered. Susan was so famished she almost choked on the rolls and juice. Almost instantly she felt better, as if the OJ were a blood transfusion instead of just juice. "Thank you," was all she managed to whisper to George. He pulled her close and began to rub her back, but this time, tenderly like a dad would stroke a child.

Susan, exhausted, and finally satiated, fell asleep in his arms. George stared at her, and for the first time since she had arrived, wondered if perhaps he had taken his "game" too far. He remembered what a beauty she was the first time he laid eyes on her after her arrival at Lynchfield. He had heard that she had been a former model and actress before her arrest and her looks certainly didn't disappoint. He had approached her multiple times, but she always discarded his advances. Muttering something about her husband. But word was her husband had abandoned her and wanted a divorce. George had become angrier and angrier as each month passed and she refused to give in to him. He would not allow this piece of shit woman to dismiss him.

Susan reminded George of his mother, dark hair and blue eyes. Mrs. Bitch Troll from Hell. She was beautiful on the outside but wickedly hideous on the inside. His mother would starve him, make him pee and shit on himself, beat, pinch, and push him. His mother had broken his finger by slamming it in a door. His mother had sexually abused little George. His mother would turn down the a/c and make little George get out of his bed and sleep naked on the floor. George's mother would kick him with her stilettos.

George Evan Ferguson had learned from the best and he had sworn he would never allow another woman to ever treat him badly or dismiss him. If they did, they deserved every bit of hardship and pain that he could dish out. Susan had said no to him. That simply would not be tolerated. No, he hadn't gone too far with Susan. She deserved every bit of pain he inflicted on her, if he couldn't get revenge on his mom, punishing Susan was the next best thing. But she did look like hell. How was he going to have her look better in a mere 24 hours? He knew he had to try. His job might depend on it. He didn't want to lose his position at Lynchfield. He was Master of Fucking and Contraband. It was so satisfying. No, he had to do something. He had it too good. He would have to make something up as to what had happened. He would blame her for trying to run away, and he would put the task on her to explain her injuries away by threatening her further. In the meantime what could he do? He turned off the TV and scooped her up in his arms. He carried her into the bath. Susan awoke as he washed her, and tensed, eyes filling with fear. Earlier in the week, George had taken her into the bathroom, the water was too hot, scalding her, too cold, making her shiver uncontrollably. Once he had tried to drown her, letting her come up for air just when he thought she could not hold her breath another gasp. She had sputtered water out of her chest when he did.

Tonight was different and he let her know it was ok before she panicked. The water was just right and smelled of wonderful bubble bath. He disrobed her and soaked her in, caressing her in a tenderness that she hadn't suspected he possessed. After the bath he laid her in his bed and massaged her with Arnica and Calendula creams. "This minimizes bruising," he stated, as if there would be a quiz later.

He handed her some of his old sweat pants and shirt and socks. She felt warm and pampered, and surprised when he then handed her two Ibuprofen tablets and a warm cup of tea. "Take these," he ordered. "Get into bed, time to sleep, Princess." He laid next to her covering them both with the warm, soft down comforter. As she lay there, Susan sensed his panic. In less than 24 hours Guard George Evan Ferguson was to deliver a Ms. Susan Chatham back to Lynchfield. How were they going to explain the state this inmate was in physically, after just two weeks of furlough? With that thought on their minds, they both drifted off to sleep, together.

CHAPTER 15
BACK TO LYNCHFIELD

You are only as strong as you allow yourself to be;
never get discouraged, never give up because
consistency and dedication is the key to success.
~ Unknown ~

Jackie Somners was the guard on bathroom and shower duty
the day Chatham left for the new furlough program. She
hadn't thought much good would come of it. Ferguson was a
creep and all the guards knew it. The only one not wise to
him was Warden Ramsey. Jackie wished her luck.

Somners was also on duty the day Susan Chatham
returned. She was very interested to hear how it had gone.
She loved gossip. But as soon as she saw Chatham
approaching, her interest turned to horror. Jackie took one
look and knew something had gone very wrong. Susan had an
obviously healing black eye. Her entire face appeared swollen.
She watched wide-eyed as Susan disrobed out of the sweats in
order to be deloused before being handed her orange scrubs.
Her jaw dropped.

"Chatham, what the hell happened?"

"I fell down some steps," Susan whimpered.

"Chatham, what the fuck? How did you get so thin? Your finger appears broken. Tell me the truth! What the fuck happened to you?" Jackie was shrieking by this point. Susan shrugged her shoulders and struggled to maintain her composure as she opened her legs ready for her internal exam for contraband.

"There are burns on your buttocks, Chatham, and on your arm," Jackie exclaimed. Susan remained quiet. If she said anything to Officer Somners, George would come after her. He would kill her and deal with the consequences later. He had been very clear. She had made a decision to stay alive and she meant to see that through. She would not die at the hands of George Ferguson. She had survived two weeks of non-stop agony. She could keep her mouth shut now.

Susan listened, shocked as she heard Jackie's next words over the walkie-talkie, a call to the Medical Department at Lynchfield. "Medical, I need you to admit inmate Susan Chatham."

"What is the situation? Illness? Has she been jumped?" Being jumped was jailhouse lingo for having been attacked.

"No. She has been abused by Guard Ferguson while on furlough."

The silence that followed echoed.

"Shit!" Susan knew she was fucked, again. George Ferguson would kill her for sure. She had to figure something out. She had to make them believe she had really fallen, no matter how preposterous it seemed. But Susan was weak. Her body had suffered unimaginably during her torturous stay at Chez Ferguson. There was only so much she could hide or explain away. She stayed quiet as the Medical Department arrived with a stretcher to take her for examination and treatment.

CHAPTER 16
THE FIRST TIME EVER
I SAW YOUR FACE

There will be obstacles. There will be doubters.
There will be mistakes. But with hard work,
there will be no limits.
~ Zig Ziglar ~

Everything upon her return to Lynchfield after her furlough
with George was a blur. Nurse Practitioner Icasa was the first
to greet and treat Chatham. She recognized her from the time
she was there with the flu. She was dismayed by the state she
was in. Chatham was weighed first. Her weight from when
she first arrived to now was shocking. She had lost 20 lbs. off
of an already slender frame that had no weight to lose. It
seemed as though the Furlough Diet seemed to cause
dramatic weight loss.

Susan was stripped nude and Icasa and the second nurse
took pictures to document her injuries. In her mind, like
Jackie, she suspected severe abuse.

The Lynchfield staff physician would later join them and
perform his own examination. Many photos were taken.
Susan didn't know what was worse. Was it the actual abuse,

having these strangers examine her abused areas, or having her naked injuries photographed as a permanent record? She wanted to sob but felt her allotment of tears for a lifetime had been spent.

Even during a gynecologic exam, the camera snapped. Her vagina, her anus, her breasts, and face, her arms and back, her ribs, her hands, her feet, all fodder for the camera's lenses. She was given a sedative, which made her blissfully sleepy, and pain medication. Through her foggy haze she heard their comments.

"Cigarette burns to the buttocks, cigar burn on her left arm, left black eye in healing stage, bruised ribs, suspect broken ribs, flogger type welts on her back, steam burn on her right foot, bruises inside her anus and vaginal walls, smashed, broken ring finger." It all sounded surreal. Surely they were talking about someone else. Had she really endured all of this in two weeks? There was more. They continued. "Malnourished, dehydrated, severe weight loss."

Susan fought to keep her eyes and ears open so she could hear everything. She knew what the findings would be but she wanted to hear it spoken aloud. She had indeed survived all of this. It was unbelievable. There was that human resiliency again.

Susan awoke on what she assumed was the next day, only to find the Warden talking with the Lynchfield staff physician. Dr. Franklin Lawrence Lomegistro looked refined, and very muscular for his age. He had thick longer wavy hair with a hint of salt and pepper on his sideburns and mustache. His strong brows framed striking dark grey eyes. He was tall and strong. He was extremely handsome and debonair. Dr. Lomegistro fumbled with some medications, and peered over his broad shoulder at Susan. She overheard references being made about a guard in the prison, George Ferguson, and Susan barely made out words to the effect that he had been reprimanded and suspended without pay while an investigation took place.

Susan winced as she tried to sit up. She just couldn't.

Somehow knowing that she was now safe allowed her to let her own guard down. The adrenaline that had helped her keep her sanity in hell had faded. Every nerve ending that had been injured suddenly came alive and demanded to be heard. Her tears spilled out like a free flowing river. She sobbed into the sheets, she grabbed onto them, clinging to them trying to gain solace.

Warden Ramsey stepped over and whispered into her ear, "Chatham I am so terribly sorry. I would have never allowed George Ferguson to take you on Furlough had I known this would have been the result. This is Dr. Frank Lomegistro. He will take good care of you. You are safe now. Rest and get better quickly." He left, leaving her alone with the Doctor.

Susan glanced up at him, blinking her long wet lashes. He reminded her of those handsome physicians on TV, the ones that always came up with the most rare diagnosis and saved the day just before the patient was about to die in the final minutes of the show.

Frank moved towards the bed and grabbed her non-injured hand and gave it a gentle squeeze. "Where does it hurt?" Susan continued to sob. Her fear to speak up at George's because of the punishment that would follow had made her afraid to speak now as well. She was also just too hurt and too weak to speak. She moved her lips but nothing came out. She began to burn up with fever, drenched in sweat. Later on she would learn she had pneumonia from soapy bath water aspirated into her lungs, during her near drowning at the hands of Officer Ferguson.

She heard the Doctor's voice again. He had a lovely, strong, majestic voice, "I am going to give you an injection right here in your buttocks, Chatham. It will sting a bit, and then I will give you another shot in your IV with strong pain meds. We need you to sleep and get lots of rest. When you wake up, you will begin to feel better and stronger and we will get you something to eat okay? I know you are very hungry, but it will just be a little bit longer before we will feed you okay?" He gave Susan a small squeeze in her hand again, bent down and patted the top of her head as if she were a little girl. He got up to reach for the needle and syringe. The rest of the day melted into a sleepy blur.

A day earlier, Franklin Lomegistro had made his way to Lynchfield. Mike Ramsey had urgently phoned him. It seemed his new furlough program didn't go as smoothly as he had hoped. In fact, the situation had been a complete clusterfuck. Mike told him inmate Susan Chatham had gone on furlough with George Ferguson and returned in very bad shape. Ferguson had gone nuts on her. Mike was distraught. He told Frank that the nurse practitioner had already begun to examine Chatham and had taken the documentation photographs. Warden Ramsey was about to call Ferguson into his office to reprimand him, put him on suspension, and begin his investigation. He asked Frank to please get there as quickly as he could, and get the girl some pain medication. She really looked awful. Frank dressed quickly and drove as fast as he could.

Upon arriving, he clocked in and went straight to medical.

Sally Icasa handed Dr. Lomegistro the chart and began her report. Frank listened attentively, frowning as she proceeded with the details of Chatham's injuries. He felt angry inside. How could this corrections officer do this to this poor woman? What the hell was wrong with this Ferguson character? What could she have possibly done to bring such a wrath from this asshole? Fuming, he took a deep breath, calmed his head, and with his professional demeanor approached her bed.

Frank stared at Susan Chatham. Whoa . . . she was beautiful. He was drawn to her. Even with her healing black eye, pale, thin face, he could see her stunning features. That black hair, porcelain white skin. She reminded him of Snow White, albeit a worse for wear Snow White.

Now that she was awake, he could continue his exam. He picked up his stethoscope and listened to her heart, retook her blood pressure, pulse, respirations . . . all vitals good.

"Sit up for me please, if you can Chatham," he asked. He noted that caused her a lot of pain. He leaned over to try to help her, pulling up under her arms.

"Ouch," she grimaced.

Frank knew about her rib injuries. He would make sure she was given some strong pain medication when he was finished with his exam. Broken ribs hurt like hell. He listened to her lungs and chest through her back. He frowned again. Not good, sounded like she had fluid in her lungs. He doubled checked her temperature. Hmm, she felt a little warm to him, and her face looked flushed.

"Have you been sick Chatham?" he asked her. She stared at him with those sad deep blue eyes, as if he were speaking a language she didn't understand or was it she was afraid to answer. He asked her again.

"Have you been sick?"

She still took some time to answer, until finally in what seemed like slow motion she spoke softly, "No sir, I swallowed some water in the bathtub."

"What? What do you mean?" Frank was confused as to how an adult would swallow water in a tub.

"I swallowed dirty, um soapy, bath water when he tried to hold me down in the bathtub and drown me." She said it in a soft, scared voice, but matter of fact, as if it were just a normal daily occurrence that everyone experiences.

"Ferguson? He tried to drown you?"

"No. Maybe. Yes." Her eyes became teary and her breath turned to a pant.

"Jesus, Chatham!"

Frank decided this wasn't the time nor place to make her any more upset than she seemed already, more traumatized than she already was. He tried to smile at her and calm her down. She stared back at him, not quite able to focus, and not quite smiling, more like less of a frown.

Frank continued his exam following the same order of

his nurse practitioners exam.

He noted the cigar burn on her arm.

"Does this still hurt you? What about this?" He pointed to the steam burn on her foot. On the outside Dr. Lomegistro was cool and collected, inside he was screaming.

"What did Ferguson do to this chick? What? How? Why? Fuck!"

Susan looked down as if she was ashamed of her injuries. She was afraid of what Ferguson would do to her after he returned or after she was discharged from medical. She didn't know this doctor from Adam. She wasn't sure she could trust him. She had been fooled before.

"I can't help you if you don't tell me what is wrong. Where are you hurting? What did he do to you? Please Chatham, tell me everything. It's important."

Susan just looked at him. She was so exhausted. All the questions confused her. She was in pain, nauseous but hungry, and oh so tired. She wanted to scream, to cry, to reach out and hit George Ferguson back. She wanted to call her dad and be hugged by his strong arms. She wished she was still with Dale. She wanted to see Bert. Maybe Bert knew how to get her out of this mess. Instead she did none of the above and just looked blankly at this tall, handsome doctor, and said nothing. She shrugged her shoulders, closed her eyes and collapsed back onto the bed and immediately fell asleep.

Frank stared at her thinking, "Did she just fall asleep on me in the middle of my exam and questions? Poor beautiful girl. What she's been through. Unimaginable." He decided he would continue his exam while she slept. He noted the burns, he would dress and bandage those. Her smashed finger, he would have to splint that. So many bruises, he could apply Calendula and Arnica creams. He pulled down the covers and opened her medical gown and noted her naked body and all her "private area" injuries. Her bruised ribs stuck out. Way too skinny. She needed some food. Even after his exam was completed he stared at her and watched her sleep. She was so beautiful. Simply gorgeous.

He drew blood and started an IV. She winced at the pinch on her arm and then the prick in her hand but didn't open her eyes at either needle. Pain medication, antibiotics? Frank decided to wait on the stronger antibiotics, after all she didn't have a fever. Covering her with a thick warm blanket, he left for the evening.

Around 3:00 a.m. Frank's phone rang. He rubbed the sleep out of his eyes and climbed out of bed to check the number. Lynchfield. They never phoned after hours. Something must be very wrong.

"Doctor, sorry to bother you at this hour but I didn't think you would want us to wait until morning. It's Chatham, high fever, 103.5, burning up. What would you like us to do?"

"Begin IV antibiotics, I'm on my way." Frank dressed quickly, splashed cold water on his face, grabbed a quick espresso to wake up and headed out the door.

"Report?" Frank asked the night nurse on duty, grabbing his white coat.

"Started the IV antibiotics per your order Dr. Lomegistro."

"I think she developed pneumonia from aspirating soapy water into her lungs when Ferguson tried to drown her in a tub." He told the nurse. "Can you imagine that?" The nurse made a horrified face. "Did you administer her pain medication?"

"I gave her Tylenol, Doctor."

"No, no. Need to give her something stronger."

As the nurse stepped away to get the narcotics, Frank looked at Susan's bed.

"Where is she, the bed is empty?"

"What?" replied the surprised nurse.

They both went looking for Susan Chatham finally finding her half way down the hallway.

"Chatham what are you doing out of bed?"

It was obvious by then that Susan Chatham was delirious and sleep walking. Burning up with fever, she was having trouble breathing. Her mind was playing tricks on her. She thought she was back at George's and was looking for the bathroom to pee and for the kitchen to cook for Ferguson.

Frank would have found it funny if she wasn't so sick and if she didn't react the way she did when he grabbed her to put her back to bed. She completely freaked out.

"Don't . . . . Don't hit me! Stop! . . . I can't breathe! . . . You are drowning me! . . . Please, I haven't eaten in days, please give me something . . . I'll do anything you say. . . . Please sir." Susan broke down into convulsing sobs.

Frank and the nurse just stared at each other horrified. What had this girl been through? They both suspected it was a lot worse than even her serious physical injuries showed.

"Chatham, you are safe. No one here is going to hurt you. Come let's go to sleep." Frank led her back gently.

The nurse gave her a cool sponge bath to lower her temperature. She dressed her in a clean hospital gown, put clean linens on the bed and got her back into it.

"She is too sick to be getting out of bed like that, she'll hurt herself, and she's hurt enough already." He didn't want to cuff her but he did have a gentle restraint placed so they wouldn't have a repeat of a disappearing Chatham. It was for her own good, but Frank felt awful doing it. He gave her stronger pain medication and a sedative so she could get some real rest, and had the nurse insert a catheter. He finally fell asleep himself in a nearby chair.

The next morning was touch and go, but by afternoon the antibiotics were beginning to work. Although Susan was still flushed with fever, it was lower and she appeared to be breathing easier.

Frank found himself consumed by wanting to get this girl better. He felt she had him under a spell. He spent hours just watching her sleep. No one should look that good when they were that sick.

Slowly Susan began to improve. She began to wake up. The world began to make sense to her again. Hunger took over now.

She woke up one day and looking Frank straight in the

eyes, finally spoke to him. "Please, Sir, I am so hungry. Please can I have something to eat? Anything. I'll do anything for anything."

Frank just smiled and said, "All I need for you to do is get better and smile Susan Chatham." He went to fetch her some soup. He knew just the place for take-out.

After a nice warm jasmine smelling sponge bath, the wonderful aroma of piping hot chicken soup replaced the disinfectant smells of the medical ward.

"Ok, Sweet Pea, let's get you up and fed."

"Hmmm" was about all she could manage to whisper out. She wondered why this man was calling her Sweet Pea. He barely knew her. What the hell? That was a nickname for those close to her. For those who loved her. Since those people were few and far between, as in no one, Susan decided to let him call her Sweet Pea.

The creamy chicken soup tasted divine. Dr. Lomegistro spooned each mouthful carefully, slowly blowing on each so it wouldn't be too hot, wouldn't burn her mouth and tongue. She had been burned enough he knew by now.

"Slow Sweet Pea, slowly. Eating too quickly after a long fast will make your stomach hurt or you might vomit." Susan just nodded happily and smiled.

"Ah, so you do have a smile in there somewhere." The warmth of the bath and the soup had her thoroughly warmed inside and out and she soon drifted back to sleep.

"That's right, Sweet Pea, rest up, soon you'll be good as new."

The next few days followed suit. It seemed whenever she managed to open her eyes, or even just one eye, Dr. Franklin Lomegistro was somewhere nearby. He would be feeding her, making sure the nurse had washed her or changed the linens, or given her the right meds. Sometimes it was a look he gave her, or a gentle squeeze of her unhurt hand. Sometimes a gentle stroking of her back or a caress of her hair. Sometimes their eyes would meet and they would just stare as if two love birds on honeymoon.

Susan felt safe, and loved. It was a wonderful feeling she hadn't enjoyed since prior to her arrest. Susan wondered if he was an angel. Was she in Heaven? Had George Ferguson accomplished his goal of killing her?

After five days, she opened her heavy eyelids, blinked several times and cleared her blurry vision. She coughed repeatedly to loosen the phlegm from her chest. The excruciating pain she felt in her ribs and lower back reminded her that George Ferguson had beat and kicked the crap out of her. It was a memory that she hoped she would soon forget, but now tortured her nights.

A cup of hot tea with lemon and honey would taste delicious and would soothe her burning sore throat. Did they even have fresh lemons and honey at Lynchfield? She thought not. Susan dreamed of how good a steaming hot shower would feel, the steam would loosen her congestion and the water would run down her back and massage her aches away. She wished to shampoo her hair.

Susan felt so damn awful. A pity party seemed appropriate.

She lied to the medical staff about the amount of pain she suffered. A little white lie. She implied that she felt better than she really did. Why? She hated being sedated and the mental fogginess those medications caused. It was easy to become addicted to opioid type pain medications and the last thing Susan wanted was to become an addict like a lot of the other prisoners.

Did the Doctor believe her? Susan thought Dr. Lomegistro's dreamy eyes could see right through to her soul. Every time his eyes locked with hers, Susan felt she would melt. She loved those clear bright eyes, and the way his thick strong eyebrows played contrast with them. He was so handsome and smelled so good. She loved the way "Good morning Chatham" rolled off his tongue in his deep majestic voice. He was the one thing in her current life that brightened her day. She wanted to run her fingers through his wavy long locks and kiss those wonderful lips that uttered such kind and soothing words to her. Would his mustache tickle her lip? She wanted to find out. She also longed to be held in his muscular arms and lean against his strong chest and inhale his warm wonderful scent. As she felt better her thoughts turned naughty. She yearned to touch his muscles through his crisp dress shirts, loosen his expensive tie, grab his sexy ass and wrap her lips around that glorious bulge in the front of his pants. Was it love or lust she craved? Susan Chatham had a huge crush on her new physician but she believed this could only be a fantasy. She kept her feelings to herself.

"Ouch," she yelped, as she sat up in the bed.

"Good morning, Chatham. Are you in pain?" his deep majestic voice resonated.

"Good morning, Dr. Lomegistro, sir. I am good." She bit her lip.

He studied her face, surprised by her response.

Susan hoped her rapid, shallow breaths didn't betray the tingle she felt when his long strong fingers dusted across her breast as he held the stethoscope in the valley between her mounds and asked Susan to take a deep breath then cough. No he hadn't noticed. His frown told her she wasn't going to return back to her Cell Block D bunk to see Bert any time soon.

"Please turn over Chatham," he instructed her as he put some Vaseline on the thermometer. She wouldn't mind turning over for him for sex, but not this. She winced as she rolled over to expose her backside.

Other men had always desired her, would Dr. Lomegistro want her?

His cold hand against her warm ass startled Susan. "99.9, okay better almost," he said withdrawing the thermometer. "Turn over please."

Susan turned back around. "Ouch!" She closed her eyes to stop the room from spinning, but quickly opened them again. She wanted to see his handsome face. Mmm, she inhaled his divine aftershave scent.

"Are you hungry?" he asked her.

Susan just stared at him, not answering, lost in her playful thoughts.

"Do you like toast? Jelly okay?" But he didn't wait for her to answer.

"Take a bite." He held the toast to her mouth.

Susan would have sang and danced for him, cooked him one of her gourmet meals, and offered him mind blowing sex, if he would have asked her. Taking a bite was an easy to follow request. She leaned forward and crunched on the toast.

Susan smiled, "Mmmm, cherry preserves. So good."

Her raspy-ness made her voice deep and sexy.

He watched her full mouth as she chewed, her lips pink from the jelly, and he imagined kissing her and how that mouth might feel going down on him. "No, I am her doctor, I shouldn't be thinking of her this way," Frank reprimanded himself.

Even though he pushed those heathen thoughts away, he couldn't help but contemplate, "Would this gorgeous young woman be interested in an "older" man? In him?"

He looked into her eyes and her eyes locked back on his. So blue he thought, so dreamy she thought, and they just stared at each other, she munching on her toast, he holding the sandwich out for her, neither saying anything to the other, lost in their lusty thoughts.

"I am thirsty please," she finally spoke.

"Tea right?" he asked her.

"Yes, please sir, if you have some. Thank you."

But before he went to fetch Susan some tea, he turned and asked her, "I don't know your usual voice Chatham, but you sound hoarse. Is your throat sore?"

Susan shook her head no when she wanted to nod yes.

"Why do I think you aren't being truthful with me inmate Susan Chatham?" he said to her. "You have to understand that I cannot give you the best care if you aren't straight with me."

Susan's eyes widened. He read her like an open book.

"I get it. You don't like all the medication and you hate being sedated, and you don't like medical environments and want to get the hell out of here. So you are acting, right? Pretending that you are fine and that the world is terrific when you are feeling anything but and probably feel like shit! You are a very good actress then, because you are fooling all the nursing staff, but I am not sure you are fooling me."

Susan's blush told Frank what he wanted to know. He rose to fetch her cup of tea.

Susan felt sad. He was so wonderful and the last thing she wanted was to be a disappointment. He hadn't come back with the tea. Was he angry? She was thirsty and her water pitcher had long gone dry.

It had been a crazy busy day in Medical. By the time he went back to her bedside with the hot cup, he felt sorry that he had taken too long and she was now asleep.

He gently stroked her cheek with his long forefinger and smiled. So soft, so warm. He was smitten by her beautiful face. He rubbed his thumb pad along her full lower lip to wipe away a remnant of cherry. Susan felt his warm touch straight to her groin and squirmed. "Oh my," Frank thought, "so responsive." He imagined what being in bed with her would be like. "It must be incredible." He pictured her killer body and was glad his long white medical coat hid his growing hardness. He swallowed hard to push the lump in his throat away.

"Your tea Ms. Chatham." He handed Susan the cup, her hands holding the mug and his hands gently over hers, hand over hand.

They looked at another. Each wondered if the other had felt the spark that ignited them when their skin touched.

"Here is some Advil for your sore throat, and your ribs, and that broken finger."

Frank lifted her forward, and placed something warm and soothing on her back. "If the heating pad gets too hot, move it around, okay?"

Susan smiled, the heat felt so good on her sore back.

"Open up, Chatham," he spooned some cough medicine. "Drink your tea while it is hot then finish your nap. When you wake up we'll see about removing that catheter you hate so much. Would you be okay if I got your cellmate Jimenez in here to help you shower and wash your hair?"

"How did you know what I needed . . . what I wanted?" Susan batted her long eyelashes at him, her voice conveying much more meaning than she wanted to let on.

"Yes, I am a mind reader so don't think you can act your way with me."

Susan frowned, thinking he was annoyed, but he grinned from ear to ear, and bent down and grabbed her hand and pretended to kiss her knuckles in chivalry.

"Anything you want Chatham to help you get better my dear." He stepped away to make the arrangements, but first he picked up her water pitcher, scowled when he saw it was empty, and filled it with water.

Susan rolled over. "I think George Ferguson killed me and I am in Heaven. This must be my guardian angel, so of course he knows everything about me." And with those happy thoughts in her dizzy confused head, she promptly fell back asleep.

A heavy Latin accent awoke Susan.

"Chatty, Oh my God Chatty! What did that asshole Ferguson do to you?"

"Shhh, Bert. Are you crazy? They will hear you and throw us both in the Shoe."

"Chatty, you look like you went to a place that was a lot worse than the Shoe. All those burns, and broken shit! Did you see the devil in hell?"

Susan looked down. "Maybe," she said sadly, her tears returned.

"No, no Chatty, don't cry! Dr. L asked me to help you take a "Chower", wash your hair right?"

"Oh Bert that would be wonderful. I feel so gross. Sponge baths are not showers!"

"Oh Chatty, you're pretty no matter what, girlfriend."

They waited and waited but Medical was swamped that day and the nurse had not been by to remove Susan's catheter so that Bert could help her with that shower. Bert was bored. As Susan slept she helped herself to her lunch and joined her nap.

When Dr. Lomegistro returned he found the two women spooned together. He knew inmates were not supposed to touch nor be in bed together. "Would a guard really give inmates shots for that?" He thought Prison sucked. He figured Jimenez would have finished helping Chatham shower by now, instead he saw that no one had even been by to remove Chatham's catheter. "Jesus, I must speak with Mike about how we are just too understaffed to provide adequate care here."

"No one has been to see you Chatham?" His voice woke the two. "I see you ate your lunch."

Roberta looked away hiding her guilty blush.

"No, the nurse didn't come, Dr. Lomegistro, sir," Susan responded, her voice only a tiny bit stronger. The Advil and sleep had done her good, and seeing Roberta had lifted her mood. She realized Bert had helped herself to her lunch. She wasn't hungry anyway.

"Oh forget it, I just have to do things myself around here," said the frustrated physician.

"Roll on your back and open your legs," he instructed.

He lifted the covers off and slid her hospital gown out of the way, he removed the tape that had held the tubing to her thigh.

Susan was embarrassed. She imagined opening her legs for him for sex and thought that would be a lot more fun. When had she last had sex? Good sex so long ago with Dilly. George Ferguson? No, that hadn't been good sex. That was rape even though she had consented to furlough. Then Susan's fear took control.

"Relax, Chatham, don't be scared. This isn't going to

hurt."

He tried to reassure her but she had been hurt so often that everything now terrified her.

Susan couldn't hold her tears back.

"Chatham, please, Sweet Pea, don't cry, no one is going to hurt you. It's going to feel strange and tingly and cold, but that is all. Relax. Come on relax, I don't want to hurt you."

Susan opened her legs and felt shy about her sex being exposed. His words were calming in a fatherly way, and outwardly he was everything professional, but in his mind Frank was thinking wayward thoughts. "Oh my, her clit, that slit, so perfectly pink, framed by soft dark pubic curls." He lusted to insert his cock into her not pull a catheter tube out.

She felt his strong warm hand on her belly, well just below it and heard him count one, two, and three. And quickly, with his other hand, it was out and done.

"That's it?" she whimpered through her tears.

"Yes, I told you silly. Don't make such a big deal of things. You know that saying: Fear is False Evidence Appearing Real?" He helped her sit up, untied her hospital gown and letting it slink down around her as she sat on the bed naked. He swallowed hard, a lump in his throat and a throb in his groin.

He reprimanded himself again, "Lomegistro get a grip . . . this inmate needs a shower, not her physician lusting after her."

"Good girl," he said, lifting her chin up and smiling into her eyes.

He helped Roberta walk her over to the bathroom.

"Okay, I am turning the water on, there is soap and shampoo and a brush. Jimenez, don't leave her or let her do it by herself, no matter what she tells you."

He gave Susan a stern look.

"Don't even think about that Chatham. Jimenez, please help her shower and wash her hair, and get dry and dressed. Medical is just crazy busy today and it's great that you can help your cellmate. If you need anything, or she doesn't feel well, push the call button over there."

Roberta shampooed Susan's scalp and ran her fingers through her long black hair. It felt even more silky and softer than she had imagined it would. She hummed a Latin lullaby as she washed Susan and Susan began to relax and let Roberta touch her everywhere as she soaped her body up. Roberta had never seen tits that pretty except in magazine bra advertisements. They were so round and uniform. She washed them slowly circling those perfectly placed pink nipples. She watched them harden under her touch. It made Bert curious as she washed Susan's private areas.

Susan protested. "Bert stop that please, I think that's clean enough down there." Bert felt a bit ashamed, she loved her friend so much and she got carried away. "Sorry Chatty." She kissed the top of her head then gave her a quick kiss on the lips. Before Susan could protest once more, Roberta quickly finished washing Susan and helped her rinse off. Roberta quickly showered herself. The shampoo and soap were better in Medical and the shower was nice and hot. It was a welcomed luxury in prison.

Bert dried herself and her cellmate. They dressed in clean orange scrubs. They waited for the staff, but no one came. Susan was too wobbly on her feet and Roberta decided to push the call button. Dr. Lomegistro responded.

"I am sorry," Susan whispered. "I feel very dizzy." She was apologetic.

When he picked her up in his arms, Susan wrapped her arms around his neck, and without thinking, nuzzled her face into his chest as he carried her to the bed. Roberta was shocked.

He thought she weighed way too little, but smelled delightful.

Susan thought his arms felt as wonderful as she had imagined and his aftershave mixed with his own scent made her punch drunk.

He laid her down and tucked her into the nice clean sheets and quilt, and turned to Roberta.

"I'm going to bring her another hot tea. Would you like some? Sugar?"

Susan, sleepily opened her eyes, "Yes, please, Dr. Franklin, Bert and I would love some hot tea, I like mine plain but Bert would love hers sweet. Thank you."

Roberta was doubly stunned. As the Doctor left the room she burst out.

"Chatty, don't call him Dr. Franklin to his face girl. You will get a shot! Or thrown in the Shoe!" Roberta grinned, "Girl you touched him."

"I did, didn't I?"

"He's so hot!"

Susan laughed, she felt happy, and clean, and loved by her roommate and new best doctor ever.

"Chatty, you have a crush on the Doctor L."

Susan denied everything, but giggled.

As Frank rounded the corner into their room, he overheard their laughter. After hearing her painful sobs for days now, her laughter warmed his heart, and he couldn't help his grin as he handed them both their tea.

"Mmm, Maple Chamomile? This is really yummy, Thank you," she hummed.

He nodded in acknowledgement. "You are most welcome."

"Please stay and enjoy your tea, Jimenez and dry her hair for her. It shouldn't be left that wet when she has been this sick."

"Yes, Dr. Lo . . . meh . . . geeeestro, sir," Roberta agreed.

"Thanks for fixing my hair Bert."

"Chatty, you are a piece of work girl."

Bert gave Susan a hug before she said goodbye and returned to her bunk. "Feel better Chatty, come back quick."

Before leaving for home, Dr. Lomegistro checked on Susan. He couldn't stay away from her. He wasn't happy when he noted she hadn't eaten her dinner.

"Chatham you haven't touched your dinner. You must eat."

He removed his jacket, and rolled up his sleeves. Susan admired his arms.

He placed the meal tray on her lap after he had helped her sit up. He opened the cutlery packet and cut her meatloaf into small pieces for her, and sprinkled some salt and pepper on the whipped potatoes. He handed her the fork.

"Now eat." He sat there and stared.

Susan took the fork and put a bite on it, but just gazed back.

"I'm not leaving until you eat some dinner Chatham."

Susan would much rather have him hang around, and she thought for a moment it would be better not to eat this.

She noticed he looked tired. It was way past the end of his shift and it had been such a busy day.

She felt guilty taking up his time. Slowly she took a bite then another.

"It's so dry," she couldn't help commenting.

She watched him get up and leave, and he surprised her when he returned in several minutes with ketchup.

"Here Sweet Pea," he said as he squirted some ketchup, dipped a small bite into it and fed it to her.

"Tolerable?" he asked her.

Susan nodded.

"Thank you, sir."

"No problem Chatham. My pleasure."

She couldn't finish it all but ate more than half and he seemed to be okay with that.

He handed her a new toothbrush with minty toothpaste and a small spool of floss.

Susan smiled, her cheeks meeting her eyes.

"I heard you have a thing for dental floss." Then he laughed at her. "You have quite a reputation around here Chatham."

Susan wasn't sure if that was a good or a bad thing. Was he laughing AT her?

"I would rather have the admiration of my TV and movie fans, sir," she answered back.

Frank's thoughts turned mischievous again. In his mind he responded, "I would love to hold you in my arms, kiss that smart mouth of yours until your lips are pink and swollen in pleasure then fuck you until you cum smiling, while calling my name." Instead he smiled at her and said out loud, "You have a good night Chatham."

Susan looked at him, she wished she could reach up and give him a big hug and a huge kiss, and she wished she could wrap her legs around his waist and feel his hard cock filling her and making her wet, but instead she just smiled at him and said in a soft voice, "Thank you Dr. Lomegistro. Good night sir."

Susan brushed and flossed and rolled over, wincing, closed her eyes and fell asleep.

In her dreams she was a little girl and playing with Tommie, her twin. She told him, "I am going to grow up and be an actress and marry a Doctor."

Frank left in his white Mercedes convertible and put down the top. It was a warm night, and his mind soon turned to the furlough conversation he had had with Mike. He turned on the radio. He needed a distraction. The easy listening channel played George Michael, "The First Time Ever I Saw Her Face." He sang along, his mind soon again on Susan Chatham.

Once home, he fixed a turkey sandwich and downed another water, then brushed and flossed his teeth. "I need to floss more," he said out loud to himself as he stepped into his shower. He showered quickly, simply exhausted. PJ pants and shirtless he crawled into bed. He touched the empty pillow, on the spot next to him, "Evangeline, would you be upset with me if I brought inmate Susan Chatham home on furlough?" He paused as if to hear her answer, while he pictured his wife's beautiful blond hair and big saucer eyes, and remembered her wonderful massages. "I love you Evangeline, and I miss you so very much, every single day, but I am so lonely." He spoke into the night air. Then closed his eyes and drifted off to sleep.

That night Frank dreamt of a dark haired beauty, thin with porcelain skin and big blue eyes, and her soft warm tongue and pouty full lips were kissing him all over, and she approached his happy trail and erection, her pink nipples hardened as he tweaked them with his fingers, she tasted of cherry preserves when he kissed her, her pussy was soft, pink and tight and he heard himself cry out as he squirted hot cum all over her, "Oh my God, I love you Sweet Pea."

Frank awoke gasping for air, shocked that he had a wet dream at his age. Surprised he didn't remember what it was about.

The following day at Medical, Warden Ramsey came by to speak with Frank.

"George Ferguson was suspended without pay Frank. What the fuck was he thinking? The program which should have been a good one, was his own idea. His suggestion! Why sabotage it like he did and with Susan Chatham of all inmates? She consented to going with him. She was excited about it. What could have possibly changed? Did she piss him off?" He thought it all made no sense. Susan Chatham had been a model inmate. Why would George Ferguson be so angry with her? Why would he have wanted to hurt her so badly? Sick, just sick.

Frank answered sternly. "I have seen a lot of women that have been 'jumped' here Mike. These inmates are amateurs at abuse compared to George Ferguson. Did you see what he did to that poor girl? And that's just marks that we can physically see on her body. What else did she suffer? She's scared to death most of the time. Hallucinating. For God's sake Mike, how can you even think of bringing that SOB back after what he did to her? And how can you even suggest she did something to piss him off? That girl is so sweet, and polite. He's obviously a sick fucker and you've been in the dark this whole time about him."

"I know this is fucked up Frank, but I have protocol to follow. My hands are tied. I can only suspend him without pay, for a few weeks, and I can demote his position, but I have to give him some type of job back until the investigation is completed. It really sucks. I still think this program is a good one with promising potential despite what happened."

"Are you fucking crazy Mike? I'll admit I was intrigued when we first talked about it. But after what happened to Chatham, who the hell is going to sign your next consent contract for this program to even begin to have a chance? There are just too many unknown variables."

"Frank, I agree that we need the right people and to set up some more parameters and protocols to ensure safety. We need to find, eliminate, and exclude those that would exploit the situation like Ferguson did. I need to impose a minimum of two unannounced on site visits during the furlough, if we continue it. It could work but I need to be so much more careful. If I had gone to visit Ferguson and Chatham unannounced, I would have seen she wasn't well, or she would have had an opportunity to tell me. Trust me Frank when I say I feel absolutely awful, that I let this poor woman down, and I had promised her a reward, and instead delivered her into a living hell." Mike Ramsey sighed and looked over at Susan in her infirmary bed. "I need to fix this and get Chatham to do it again with another chaperone. It's got to be her if it's going to work."

"Oh Mike for Christ's sake! What the fuck are you talking about? How are you going to get her to consent to another round, threaten her with a trip to the 'Shoe' or extend her sentence into a life sentence with no opportunity for parole? And what guard in their right mind would take this risk?"

"You and Susan Chatham, Frank!"

"Come again? You are crazy!!!"

"No, I am not Frank. I see the way you have been so lonely since your wife Evangeline died. You haven't been yourself for years. I see the way you take care of that poor girl Frank. You have feelings for her, Frank I just sense it. And you will say yes, because you will want to do everything in your power to keep her safe and away from George Ferguson. And she in turn will want to be as far away from Ferguson as she can be. She relaxes around you too. If it weren't for your loving care, I don't think she would have made it. I have to bring Ferguson back to Lynchfield to work in two weeks, and two weeks will give us ample time to get the new protocols put into place and for you to request a furlough with Susan Chatham and for Chatham to be well enough to go and to consent Frank!"

"Mike this is totally insane. The stress of this mess has loosened one of your screws."

"Yes, it is totally crazy, but crazy times lead to taking drastic measures Frank. I won't take no for an answer. I know you want to keep Susan Chatham safe."

The Warden turned to exit then looked back and said, "I will talk to Susan Chatham as soon as she is better. Take 24 hours Frank. I will leave a copy of her inmate records on your desk so you can see for yourself. She's a good girl Frank. Have your brother Jimmie do a background check. Whatever you need to feel comfortable Frank. I know this much, I know you want to be with Susan Chatham." Frank stared at Mike, nodding his head as if to say no, but in his heart, he knew he had already been fantasizing about taking Susan Chatham on furlough.

CHAPTER 17
PR DISASTER

Don't be afraid to start over. It's a chance
to build something better this time.
~ SimpleReminders.com ~

As the days went by Susan began to feel better. Her pneumonia cleared up and she was able to breathe easier. Her ribs were healing, and she only had a little bit of discomfort when she first sat up. Once she was up, it was tolerable. Her eye healed as did her burns. She was beginning to put on weight and get her strength back.

The food they gave her in Medical was amazing. Well actually the prison food still sucked but Dr. Lomegistro was always sneaking in take-out or sharing his own breakfast or lunch with her. He would bring her soups, and sandwiches, and make her oatmeal in the morning with nuts and dried fruits in it. Early on he would feed it to her. Later on he would hand her a bowl and a spoon and sometimes even sit on the side of her bed and eat his while she ate hers. How come he was so good to her? What had she done? He was such a wonderful wonderful man. No edge to him at all. She knew she could trust him, and that wasn't just naïve Susan

133

Chatham falling for trickery again. She felt it in her very soul.

Susan had nothing to do in Medical but eat, sleep, and take short walks around the hallway. She began to sense that Dr. Lomegistro was keeping her there longer than necessary. Why? Finally one day came the conversation they were both dreading.

"Hey Sweet Pea, how's today finding you?" Susan had come to love his nickname for her.

"I am doing very well Dr. Lomegistro, sir."

"Chatham, I don't know how else to say it. I am getting some heat about discharging you. I wish I could keep you here forever, and keep you safe. I just can't. I need to send you back to your Cell Block."

"All good things must come to an end. Thank you for giving me my health and sanity back doctor."

"Sweet Pea, you won't be alone. If something is wrong, please reach out. Jackie Somners, Sally Icasa, Paul Sterling, Juan Carlos Gomez, Warden Ramsey. If you are in trouble, send word through them to me. I will fix it for you. Anything."

"That's a very generous offer, sir. Thank you."

"Well, okay then, that's that." With that he handed her a cup of hot lemon ginger tea. Her favorite. Then he bent down and kissed her cheek, and to his surprise, she reached up and kissed his cheek back.

Susan's transition back to her Cell Block was as smooth as possible. Bert greeted her with a warm embrace and a pained look. She thought Susan would be perfect by now and was surprised to see her still recovering. The few friends she had made at Lynchfield were supportive and sympathetic. Word of her nightmare had spread like wildfire through the prison grapevine. Susan confided in Bert all that she had suffered, and Bert listened with tears in her eyes. It was worse than even the physical injuries she had seen with her own eyes when she had helped Susan shower in Medical.

"Why didn't I stop you from going?"

"Bert you tried to warn me about Ferguson. I was hell

bent on going. I was the fool. I have no one to blame but myself."

"You are not to blame Chatty. That sick motherfucker is entirely to blame. He's on leave now and when he gets back, he'll be assigned to the Shoe. I don't know why they didn't fire his ass. Better yet, kill his psycho ass. That is some bullshit that he still has a job at this prison."

After a few weeks, Susan settled back into shitty prison life. She was watched carefully by the guards to make sure she wasn't bothered by anyone. It was kind of nice to be protected for a change, but she missed Dr. Lomegistro. She missed him so much.

When Warden Ramsey called her into his office, she wondered if everything was ok. She was apprehensive because she had been in Lynchfield long enough by now to know that getting called into the Warden's office was not a good thing.

"I am so happy you are well Chatham. Thanks for coming into my office. So after what you have been through, it's only right that I give you a head's up about the return of Officer George Ferguson. I have assigned him to the 'Shoe'. This will minimize the number of inmates he has access to. Still I thought you might want a chance to be away during those first two weeks of his return. I have another furlough proposition for you Chatham."

Susan nearly collapsed. Her eyes filled with tears. "Regretfully, Warden, sir, I cannot accept your proposal." Her voice betrayed her fear.

"Of course you can, Chatham and you will. I know you don't want to have to confront Officer Ferguson especially when he returns and he will be none too pleased with his new work duty. This program needs you in order to be a success. We have already discussed that, the first time we met, when you signed the first contract. But this furlough will be different. I suspect you are very happy to be well enough to be back in your old bunk, but most likely missing the likes of one very handsome physician who treated you with such tender loving care."

Susan looked at him suspiciously. Warden Ramsey continued. "Well this certain physician has put in a request for a two week furlough with a Ms. Susan Chatham. He will keep you safe Chatham, while I figure out what to do about Ferguson and the investigation. Think it over and let me know what you decide."

Susan knew she wouldn't need any time to think it over. Seeing Dr. Franklin Lomegistro was all she needed, all she wanted. He had consumed all of her thoughts while she was awake and in her dreams, ever since she had been well enough to leave medical.

"Where do I sign Warden?" she asked.

Warden Mike Ramsey smiled. He might just avert a complete and total PR disaster if this furlough was a success. He knew it would be. Lomegistro and Chatham were made for each other. This was a totally different animal than the Ferguson situation. That sick fucker would have to be dealt with carefully. Mike had to get rid of him by the book and that would take time. There could be no mistakes. In the meantime, he could keep Susan Chatham safe and facilitate her continued healing. It was the least he could do for her. His pal Frank wouldn't be so bad off either. He suspected he had fallen hard and fast for this girl, now he could see if it was real or just an illusion.

CHAPTER 18
A SECOND CHANCE

Everyday is Beautiful if you choose to see it.
~ Unknown ~

Dr. Franklin Lomegistro brought his car around. Nervous as shit. He was actually doing it. He was taking this inmate to his apartment for two weeks. This beautiful woman who had suffered so much and to whom he had felt so connected. What would happen? What did he know about her? What would she be like in the real world?

He only knew what she had told him and what Mike had said. She was a model inmate, considered polite, she was highly educated, a rule follower. Kept her nose clean. She had been a famous actress. Frank thought she was vaguely familiar, but he was way out of touch with pop culture.

Frank had read and reread her Lynchfield prison report, and he had spoken with his other correctional officer friends to see what their experiences around her had been.

His younger brother James, an attorney, had helped him by running a background check on Susan Jordyn Chatham. Frank was just as surprised as Jim was about his findings. Something didn't seem right about her trial and conviction.

Frank remembered Jim's face the day they met to discuss her.

"Christ Frankie, I don't think this chick did it. In fact, I am so convinced that something is up with the witness testimony and the evidence, I feel compelled to look into it further. If I find anything, I will let you know. I don't think you have anything to worry about with Susan Chatham. If you like her and want to do this, you have my legal blessing."

"Thanks Jimmie. That means a lot. I knew she was special and I couldn't figure out how she had ended up at Lynchfield. So bizarre. Please look into it further if you can. If there is something up, I want to help her clear her name." Frank felt like a teen. He was giddy thinking about Susan. He had planned what he would do, what he would say, where he would take her.

He imagined looking into her beautiful blue eyes and touching and smelling her silky hair and feeling her soft skin. He missed her every day. He had grown so accustomed to starting and ending his days with her while she was in Medical. Now that she was back in the general population, he never saw her anymore. He couldn't wait to see her again.

He pulled his white Mercedes around and there she was. She was still too skinny. Her tee shirt too big and jeans too loose. Her hair in a ponytail, no make-up. But at least, no orange scrubs either. He would have to feed her well when she came to stay. He wanted to treat her like a princess, and he planned on doing so.

She saw him and waved. The butterflies in her stomach danced. He offered her his passenger door.

"Get in Sweet Pea. Do you have an overnight bag?" he asked.

Susan looked embarrassed and shyly nodded no.

"Ok, not a problem, a shopping we will go." Leaning over he helped her with her seatbelt.

Susan, squirmed in the white Mercedes's seat. She seemed very nervous and looked frightened. Frank was not surprised. He assumed the trauma of her last furlough would take a very long time to heal.

Susan thought the Mercedes smelled of rich leather and of his comforting aftershave. She watched as he put the convertible top down and turned up the music. She eyed him suspiciously.

Frank smiled at her saying, "I figured after being in THERE, everything FREE might be welcome."

"Yes, thank you Dr. Lomegistro, sir." She addressed him so formally out of habit.

"Okay, we are no longer in Medical and not in Lynchfield, so less formal please . . . Franklin or Frank. What do the real people in your life call you Susan Chatham?"

"Real people?"

"Yes, you know, your family, your ex-husband, your best friend?"

"Susan, Susie, Suze."

"Seems so boring for such a lovely and special person. How about Sush, Sweet Pea? Can I call you Sush?"

"Sure, anything." She hadn't really understood the complement. The Mercedes zoomed away.

Susan didn't know why she was so nervous. Well maybe she did. Occasional thoughts of the Furlough From Hell with Ferguson crept uninvited into her head. She hoped that the good Doctor would be as nice to her on furlough as he had been in Medical. She trusted him. She had to be right this time.

She took a few deep calming breaths and forced herself to relax. She glanced over at Dr. Lomegistro, studying his handsome jaw line, his dark hair with just a hint of salt along the edges, those striking gorgeous eyes, and strong arms. Susan felt so serene, so safe and content, and the wind was so warm and breezy on her face. She felt herself getting sleepy. Susan quietly drifted off to sleep.

Frank glanced over at her every so often. So much for taking the scenic view home and having the top down. Poor exhausted Sush. Watching her sleep reminded him of their time together in Medical. How he loved to stare at those long lashes, touch her soft hair and skin. She looked fairly well.

Maybe not quite as skinny. Ok, still skinny but not deathly so. Less pale. Her face seemed more peaceful now and free from the painful grimaces he had witnessed.

When he got to "Janney's" he woke her up gently.

"Hey Sush, rise and shine. Time for lunch."

Hadn't he said these same words to her many times? But this time they were going in for burgers, fries and shakes. The best ever.

She opened her eyes, at first surprised at where she was. "Janney's! I used to come here all the time as a kid! This is the bomb!"

"Please, Sush, I am uptight enough about bringing an inmate home without talk of bombs," he joked.

They both laughed and began their first date at the well-known burger and shake joint. "Janney's has the best burgers Franklin." He liked how she said his name.

Frank opened the door to the restaurant for her.

Janney's had a Fifties diner feel with black and white vinyl tiled floors and silver aluminum pedestal tables. There were photos of Chevys and Fords framed in black. The booths featured red vinyl seats trimmed in grey.

Susan said she was going to use the restroom and excused herself. She seemed to take forever, and Frank was just about to ask another female patron to go in after her and check if she was alright, when he watched her come out. Her eyes revealed she had been crying. Susan felt the emotions of happy childhood days contrasted with how she felt now. Seeing her pale thin make-up free face reflected in the mirror brought out raw emotions.

She attempted a smile at Frank and picked up her menu after placing the napkin on her lap.

Frank smiled to himself. Nice manners he thought.

She stared at the menu for the longest time, and he found that odd since she had mentioned being there many times.

The waitress was dressed in a black and pink poodle skirt and white blouse with black horn rimmed glasses and took their order.

"The lady will have . . . " Frank allowed Susan to order first but seeing her stall, he piped in his order.

Frank ordered the bacon, Colby jack King Burger, well done with lettuce, tomatoes and pickles. "May I have a large chocolate malt, no whip cream and an order of curly fries and onion rings too please." He grinned. He eyed Susan suspiciously wondering what was wrong with her.

Finally, she spoke up quite meekly, "I'll have the junior burger, cooked medium, with cheddar, lettuce and tomatoes and may I please have Janney's special BBQ sauce with that? Oh, and a junior chocolate cherry shake and iced water please. Thank you."

The waitress turned on her heels to put in their order.

Frank looked at Susan, "So pretty, so polite," he thought.

But then he teased her.

"Sush, Are you a little kid? Junior? Do you want a toy with that kiddie meal?"

Susan looked embarrassed and he wished he could take it back almost as quickly as he had said it. He changed the subject.

They were sharing harmless small talk when their meal arrived.

Frank enjoyed his burger and watched her intently. When had she last had something to eat or drink?

Susan ate her food voraciously. She grabbed at the french fries and onion rings as if they were a life line to Heaven. She downed her water in a single gulp and then she dug into her burger.

"Don't eat so fast, Sush, I won't take it away." But then Frank frowned at the amount that she actually finished.

"Is that all you are going to eat?"

It seemed that her tummy had quite shrunk in prison and no matter how hungry or how good lunch tasted, very little left her satisfied and full.

Back in the car, it also didn't take much to have her fall asleep again. She felt full, and relaxed and soon grew quite sleepy again.

Frank pulled into the parking lot of a CVS drug and sundries store. He woke her up.

"I took the liberty of buying a few things I thought you might need for the week. Jackie Somners let me know your size. But I don't know shit about feminine products, Sush."

Embarrassingly, Susan replied, "I don't have my period, Franklin."

"No, Sweet Pea, I meant makeup, hair stuff, deodorant, you know personal stuff?"

"Really?"

"Yes, really."

"That's super cool Franklin. What's my budget?"

"No budget, Sush, get what you need. Two weeks together, you know dates? We will be going out. I am thinking dancing, Karaoke, picnic, beach? What do you need from a drug store? Oh and I know how much you like dental floss."

"Franklin, don't tease me." Her eyes welled up with tears again.

"Who is teasing you?"

"You can't be serious?"

"Furlough Susan Chatham, is supposed to be a reward."

"I never dreamed it would be, could be, and with you . . . "

"Yes, my dear, it will be, can be, with me; and the best part is I get to be with you . . . ." And with that and a sweet kiss planted on her cheek, he grabbed her hand and led her into the CVS.

"What a romantic." Susan thought.

Frank handed Susan a red plastic basket. "Don't just stand there, go get what you need girl." Susan grabbed her basket and started down the aisles.

"What the heck do I need? What did he say I would need?" Susan couldn't think straight. Beach: sunscreen, lip balm, aloe? Dancing: make-up, but what? Mascara, eyeliner, blush, lip-gloss, pink or red? Bath: bubble bath, soap, deodorant, ladies razor, shampoo, conditioner, leave-in conditioner? Perfume, no! Body spray? Yes! Would she be getting her period? No, thank God no! Moisturizer, ah yes. She had felt like a reptile while at Lynchfield. She was hoping he would apply it on her in that gentle way he had. Nail polish, a nail file, she hadn't done her own nails in forever, but then not at all in prison. Birth Control. Safe sex? Ah, yes. Condoms, lubricant, warming and sweet, yes.

As Susan turned into the personal or "safe sex aisle" as she liked to call it, she ran straight into Franklin. He looked more like a kid in a candy store than a surgeon, as he stared at the various types of lotions, potions, and condoms.

"What kind do you like?"

"Whichever you like."

Both smiled shyly.

The two of them acted like innocent teens wanting to do the "wild thing" for the first time.

"Oh, Jesus, just pick something."

At checkout, Frank added some Ibuprofen, massage oil, aftershave, and a feather duster.

"Yikes. What is he thinking?" Susan wondered.

"Grab some candy bars, Sush. Whatever kind you like, for watching movies!"

"Yep, a little boy in a candy shop," Susan smirked.

"You have a very smart look, Ms. Chatham. What are you thinking?"

"I haven't the foggiest notion of what you are asking of me, Dr. Lomegistro."

With their CVS purchases in tow, and two huge grins, they headed to Frank's condo.

"Wow! You live on the beach, Franklin?"

"Yes, yes I do. It's a great building Sush. You will love it. We have a gym, heated pool, BBQ grills, a bar area, tennis courts, beach volleyball, a sauna, billiards room, ping pong, party room, and of course the ocean. Do you swim Sush? Do you play games?"

"I was on the swim team in grade school. Does that count as knowing how to swim?" Susan said with a hint of sarcasm. "And to your second question, truth is, I don't play games, but I like to play, if you know what I mean." She winked at him.

"Ahh, why do I get the feeling this is going to be a very interesting week?" Frank grinned from ear to ear.

CHAPTER 19
BEACH GETAWAY

The beach is where our souls realign
with the universe. The horizon answers questions.
The surroundings give peace.
~ OceanSkinCare.com ~

"Come on in, Sweet Pea, let me show you around."

"Wow, you have a great place here Franklin. Is that the Pacific Ocean? Oh My God, what a spectacular view!"

Frank beamed, "I fell in love with this place as soon as I saw this view. 15th floor penthouse overlooking the ocean is not a bad place to be. Do you want to see the view from the balcony?"

"Absolutely," she shined.

"My oh my, seeing the beach and the ocean after staring at cream colored cinderblock walls and barbed wires gives me goose bumps, Franklin."

"It is my refuge and makes working at Lynchfield tolerable my dear. Come and see the rest of the apartment."

Susan followed Franklin around, like a puppy dog following her owner hoping to play fetch with the new toy. There was the living and dining room beautifully appointed.

The contemporary wood furniture had an almost Asian Fusion feel. The couch was soft leather, a sectional with reclining seats. Her inner chef marveled at his real chef's kitchen with granite counter tops, and stainless steel appliances, even a beverage fridge with wine racks. He showed her the in-apartment laundry, cleaning and storage closets, powder room, 2 guest rooms, one with a spa tower shower, his home office, and finally his master suite and spa bath. She loved the slate walls and pebbled floor, the frameless glass shower doors and the tub looked like it could easily fit the two of them. Her thoughts turned playful and naughty. "Maybe I am not ready to give up on men and sex," she smiled to herself.

Franks words snapped her out of her daydream.

"Here, you can keep your new things in this drawer, I made space for you."

"I bought you these as well, let me show you." He pulled out some clothing and accessories. Everything was beautiful. She couldn't believe the length he had gone to make this furlough so entirely different from her experience with George Ferguson. He handed her a pair of shorts, and a cute linen sleeveless collared blouse. She also noticed a soft nightshirt with leggings for sleeping, a bikini with a cover-up, and a floppy hat for the beach, a pair of flip-flops that could double for the beach or as slippers. Even a pair of designer sunglasses. She blushed when she noticed the pretty lace panties. It was everything she would need to be a "normal" woman visiting her "boyfriend" at the beach.

"Tomorrow we will go to the mall and get some 'evening out' clothes and anything else that you would like." Frank was thinking of their date nights.

"I don't know what to say. How can I possibly thank you? I really can't afford to pay you back for all these things Franklin." Her voice became shaky and apprehensive. "My ex-husband moved a lot of my money out of our joint account and into his account without my knowledge after I got arrested. My attorneys, although trying to recover a lot of what rightfully belongs to me, are having a hell of a time. My ex Dale is so well known, and so connected. My chances, especially after my sentencing, are slim to none. And now so much time has passed."

Her eyes welled up and her voice cracked. Unknowingly, she automatically sat on the edge of his bed and reached for his hands, holding them, pulling him down to sit next to her. She shared the details of the breakup of her once happy marriage. Frank listened attentively. Her physical pain had touched him in the medical ward. Now he was equally touched by her mental anguish.

"Sush, I don't expect for you to pay me back. These are gifts. Please stop. Please don't cry. Please just be."

He nuzzled up close to her and lifted her face in his hands until her chin looked up to meet his. He planted a kiss tender on her lips. She felt his caress down her face to the nape of her neck, and beyond. It was all encompassing. She opened up and kissed him back. At first very tender then their passion awakened. He tasted of chocolate and his tongue twirled around hers, his teeth were indeed as smooth as she had imagined. She tasted of chocolate cherries and her full lips were velvety smooth and her tongue, soft and warm. They fell back upon the bed, his bed, and kissed and made out for what seemed like an endless evening. The desire they had felt for each other came alive. There was no sex yet, but the blossoming of a beautiful relationship.

"OK, so here's a game." Frank teased her after their make-out session. "Your cellmate told me you love the cooking shows."

"Bert. I call Roberta Jimenez- Bert. She lied, and she is a pain in my ass! A lovely pain, but a pain no less. Yes, I happen to watch a lot of cooking shows, but it's really hard to love cooking shows when you are feeling hungry all the time. The food at Lynchfield is so awful Franklin. Everything is so over processed and there are so few salads and most veggies are either canned, overcooked, or just diced pieces in some too salty soup. Ugh! What I wouldn't do for some crispy green beans."

"Green beans turn you on Susan Chatham?"

"My favorite, Doctor."

"Well, when you finish ranting about food at Lynchfield, here are my rules for dinner preparation.

You have half an hour, which includes setting the table.

You can use anything in the fridge or freezer, and any spices in this spice drawer.

Surprise me. Your time begins now."

Susan momentarily panicked. Nothing she cooked for George had found favor and the punishments that followed left her drained and pained. What the fuck? Why would Franklin want to play THIS game?

Shit! She quickly opened up all the cabinets to see where the pots and pans were, the utensils, the silverware, plates, glasses, place mats. Then she eyed the fridge, freezer and spices all lined up neatly in a row. What would she do?

Frank heard her clamoring about in the kitchen and wondered what she was up to. He assumed she would grab some eggs and fix an omelet, or maybe make them some sandwiches. But all that noise and watching her scurrying around made him think that maybe this game hadn't been such a good idea. He hoped he hadn't polluted the beautiful connection they had begun to forge together. He nervously watched Susan as she nervously watched the clock.

Susan found a package of lobster ravioli. It was the pre-made type you would find in the refrigerator section of your supermarket. In the freezer, she located a package of frozen mussels in garlic sauce. In the veggie bin, she struck gold. There were pre-diced red, green, and yellow peppers, and in the second veggie bin a Vidalia onion. Yes, he had organic sweet butter in the butter tray. She pulled out an Italian spice grinder, and red pepper flakes from the spice drawer. She located an opened bottle of white wine. Yes, yes, she had a plan, this would do.

She quickly put a large pot of water to boil. She then ran to set the table. Then came time to dice the onion. She added it to the diced pepper mix and she began to sauté these in the butter in a large frying pan. Susan added the Italian seasonings, the wine and some of the red pepper flakes. She stirred her sauce creation. She knew when she added the sauce from the mussels that this would taste divine. She cooked the ravioli slightly more al dente than the package instructions and also cooked the mussels to package directions. Now she added everything together plating the ravioli first and spooning the sauce on top. Unable to find a cheese grater or parmesan cheese, she grabbed a citrus zester and used it to scrape some left over manchego cheese she found in the fridge. Sweat poured down her face and back, she ran to serve the meal with one minute to spare, and called Franklin to the table.

Frank could not believe his eyes. No omelet, no sandwiches. In a half hour, in a stranger's kitchen, Susan Chatham had managed to prepare a gourmet meal of lobster stuffed ravioli with mussels in a garlic wine pepper sauce, with a pairing of white wine. Plated like a five star restaurant!

Frank took the first bite. His lips melted to a smile. "Oh my God Sush, delicious. This is as good as it looks. How did you make this?"

Susan was overwhelmed by his kindness. She stared down at her dinner, trying to take in the magnificence of what she had prepared and accept the sincere compliments from Frank.

"Aren't you going to eat?" Frank stared at her full plate, even as he cleaned his. "Sush, great job, come on honey please eat too."

She looked at him and his smile and she began to relax. Yes, this furlough was very different than the one with George. She took a bite. It really was as yummy as it looked. With that she enjoyed her own plate.

After dinner, Frank rose. "That spontaneous meal was amazing! Now since you cooked, it's my turn, I'll clean up." Frank began to clean up the dishes and wipe down the kitchen. Susan felt guilty. She was supposed to do the chores.

Those were Furlough rules. She jumped up to help. The two of them worked with the efficiency of a couple that had been together for over ten years, not two people that had been together less than ten hours.

Soon the kitchen was back in order, Frank looked at her in appreciation and wanted to reciprocate and do something really nice for her.

"You treated me to something very special, and now it's my turn. I will run us a bath." He winked.

Hmmmm. What did Dr. Frank Lomegistro have in mind?

Frank disappeared into the master bath and sent Susan to fetch a bottle of Champagne from the fridge and two glass flutes.

Meanwhile he collected the bubble bath, the shampoo and conditioner and filled the tub with hot water making plenty of foam.

By the time Susan returned with the drinks, the bath smelled of lavender and sandalwood. Candles were burning and the lights were turned down. Yep, he sure was a romantic.

She didn't know why she felt shy to undress. He had seen her naked many times, and at her physical worst. But it still felt like the first time. Her last sexual experience had been so monstrous. Had it destroyed all of her confidence? Could she ever be normal and be with a man again? Frank took off his shirt then gently pulled off hers. He removed his trousers then freed her breasts from her bra. Slowly he pulled down her shorts and panties in one turn then quickly removed his own boxers. His long thick cock spilled out.

"You are so beautiful," he whispered as he moved toward her again, lifting her up and placing her into the tub before climbing in himself.

"You look pretty damn good yourself, Doctor." She smiled shyly at him.

He leaned her against his chest, wrapping his legs around hers and began to wet her hair. Pouring the shampoo into his hands, he worked up a lather and began to work the suds into her scalp then all the way to the ends of her long hair.

It felt so good. He soaped her up all over, from the top of her head, down her neck, her round soft shoulders, her back, her perfectly round breasts, her flat stomach, down her slender thighs and legs, her feet, then back up her buttocks to finally her apex. His long fingers had such a hypnotic touch, she molded like clay in a sculptor's hands. After he rinsed the suds away using a large sea sponge dipped in the water, he turned, kissed her tenderly, and then, handed her the sponge.

It was Susan's turn to wash Frank. She soaped him up all over as he had done for her. She began at the top of his scalp, playing with his long wavy locks. Her delicate fingers working her way down his neck, over his muscular shoulders, down his strong back, around to his stomach, tracing his sculptured abs, down his thighs and legs, around his feet, then back up his buttocks, finally reaching his manhood. She stroked his cock in the soapy water and her blue eyes absorbed him. It was obvious that he was turned on. He grew long and thick and that happy swell she had often imagined did not disappoint. Susan thought, "Oh, my dear God, he's better than as good as it gets." After delicately washing him with her fingers, she loosened up, and now hot and bothered and taking him by surprise, she bent down, and began to taste him.

"Whoa, you'll drown under water, might get pneumonia again," he exclaimed as he leaned over to lower the water level and let some of the suds drain out of the tub. He also knelt up to give her better access. Susan wasn't sure if she was being too bold. Her passionate desire had awakened and she wanted him like she needed him in order to breathe. Frank smiled broadly, only too willing to accept her advances. She began to caress the tip of his cock with the tip of her tongue. She took little nibbles barely touching him with her teeth, and stroked his scrotum with her free hand, sliding back and forth in the soapy water. She hollowed her cheeks and twirled her tongue and she had her way with him. It felt so damn good, sensations he had never experienced before. Frank used all his energy to hold back but resisting Susan was impossible, he exploded in passion and ecstasy.

"Ahhh, Sweet Pea," he moaned in his breathy voice, "that was great. Now I aim to please."

He wanted her so badly, more than he had wanted anything or anyone in a very long time.

With that he let the water drain out and grabbed two dry towels. He dried himself with one and wrapped her up in the other. He lifted her out of the tub and carried her into the bedroom.

He pulled the comforter from the bed and lay her down. He began kissing her lips and soon found himself tasting those beautiful tits he had been craving for what seemed like forever. He knelt down between her legs and began to work her over between her thighs. He gently sucked, and blew, and licked. Her labial lips were soft and pink and her clit was like a pink bud that perked up as he tweaked her. She squirmed responsively and seeing her turned on made his cock throb in delight.

"Ahh, you taste so good," he whispered, his voice deep. He teased her nipples with his thumb and forefinger as he continued to tease her clit with his tongue.

"Oh Franklin, that feels sooooo gooooood." Her voice was breathy and so very sexy. And just when she thought she couldn't take anymore, he tore open a foil packet and entered her sanctuary. She spread her legs to welcome him deeper and arched her back. They were lost in each other, meeting wave after wave, he thrust into her and she met him gyrating her hips, that lovely tight ass following his every move, a seductive dance between the sheets until they both climaxed together, hard, fast, their juices slick and slippery and fell exhausted, side by side, into post coital bliss.

"Oh my, where have you been all my life?" Frank asked.

"I don't know, passing the time away in jail." After a laugh, they cuddled together and fell asleep.

During the night Frank awoke. He turned and felt Susan

next to him. It was wonderful to feel someone on the other side of his bed once more. He snuggled with her. She was fast asleep. So tired, his Sweet Pea. She smelled so good, and her hair and naked skin were so soft. She was so lovely and warm, and lying next to her felt so great, true bliss. He had dreamed of and fantasized about this night with Susan, but reality exceeded all expectations. Frank smiled to himself. He couldn't wait to see what the rest of their time together would bring. He was excited about the thought of taking her shopping tomorrow. Snuggling and spooning next to her, he wrapped his arm around her waist resting his hand next to her soft breast, resting his head near that silky mane, and he drifted happily back to sleep.

CHAPTER 20
ESSENTIAL OILS

A gentleman will open doors, pull out chairs,
and carry things. Not because she's helpless
or unable, but because he wants to show
her that she is valuable and worthy of respect.
~ DigitalRomance ~

The sunlight peeked in through the wooden slats on the master blinds. Frank woke up alone in the bed. Where was she? But he soon smelled the wonderful aroma of fresh brewed coffee, and could it possibly be his favorite breakfast, French toast? The apartment smelled of vanilla, cinnamon, and of buttery maple syrup, with a hint of bacon.

Like a dream, Susan appeared in a soft yellow nightshirt, the one he had bought for her. She wasn't wearing the leggings though. Was she naked underneath, or had she put on the lacy panties he had bought for her? Either way the thought of whatever she had next to her apex was a sexy turn on. In the sunlight he could make out those perky beautiful tits through the delicate fabricate. He almost wanted to reach for them again, but hesitated. He must exercise patience.

She breezed through the door bringing him breakfast in

bed, flashing him her bright white Hollywood smile. Fresh squeezed orange juice, two thick slices of her vanilla, cinnamon French toast, crispy bacon, and fresh, hot coffee. She had even warmed the maple syrup.

"You are spoiling me! Thank you, I love this." Frank smiled appreciatively. "This French toast is delicious. How did you know this is my favorite breakfast? Aren't you going to join me?"

"I will after I clean up and do the next load of laundry and other chores I have planned for today."

"Too much, way too much, it's not right. You aren't here to be my slave Susan."

"It's my job Dr. Lomegistro."

"Stop it Sush, really, I don't like it and it doesn't become you. Go grab a plate of breakfast for yourself, or better yet grab a fork and I'll share mine with you. You are amazing Sweet Pea! Truly you are."

Susan and Frank enjoyed their breakfast, then went for a quick jog on the beach both wearing lots of coconut smelling sunscreen to protect them from the hot sun. Susan had quite a way of slathering on Waterproof Number 30.

"Jesus Sush, you are going to make me cum right here on this beach woman!" He wasn't sure which was sexier, watching her put sunscreen on herself, or feeling her hands caressing it onto him. Oh how he wanted to find a way to reciprocate. She would have no idea that his dear wife Evangeline had been a masseuse and taught Frank quite a few of her tricks and techniques. Frank planned how he would return the favor.

Back from the beach run, Susan finished cleaning and laundry. She had insisted against his protests. While she was preoccupied, Frank stepped into the bedroom and prepared the room. He turned the radio to the "spa" station. He set out towels, scrub, seaweed detox cream, massage oil, lavender eye sachet pillow, hair and scalp oil, aromatic oils, and lit the tea lights. He drew the curtains for privacy then went to find her.

"Hey gorgeous, what are you up to? You are working

way too hard. Do you think you are in prison?"

She smirked back sticking her tongue out at him. Susan was beginning to unwind and she felt safe around Frank. Her genuine personality was starting to emerge, her fears falling behind.

"Leave that! Enough! Come, m'lady."

He led Susan into the bedroom.

Susan looked around. "You want to make love again? Honestly Franklin I don't think I can. It's been wonderful really but I am almost sore and need some time to recover. You are just insatiable."

"No, I have had enough myself for now. This isn't about that."

"I don't understand." Susan looked surprised.

"Time for a massage. I will step out of the room, I don't even want to be tempted by your beautiful sexiness. Get undressed and lie face down first and cover yourself with the towel." With those words he stepped out.

Susan did as she was told, taking everything off and folding her things neatly and placing them on the chair. Face down she heard his footsteps. "Take a deep breath through your nose then exhale slowly through your mouth." Susan did as instructed. He held a cotton ball saturated with lavender and eucalyptus aromatics under her nose. It smelled lovely. "Take one more cleansing breath, nice and deep."

"Hmm, that smells so good, Franklin."

Frank folded the towel carefully so her buttock, thigh and leg only on one side were exposed and her privates totally covered. Although not sexual it felt totally sensual to her. First came an exfoliating scrub. He rubbed it over and into her skin and it felt gritty but wonderful. He removed the remaining scrub paste off her skin with a warm moist towel. He repeated on the other leg, covering up the previous. Susan began to relax. He moved up her leg, thigh, and buttock and then spent extra time on her feet, rubbing each individual toe and spending time in her arch, then heel.

"Franklin, this feels incredible."

Frank covered both legs and moved up to her arms. Again he focused one arm at a time moving from shoulder to arm to wrist to hand to each fingertip. Heavenly. Then her back. He rubbed her neck, kneading her shoulders again, upper back, middle back, sides and lower back. Susan hummed in enjoyment. He then held a towel up so he wouldn't see her nakedness while he had her flip over. It was so arousing. Again he repeated the process. First one leg, then the other leg, one arm then the other, her neck and décolletage. Even her abdomen received a rub with him carefully keeping her breasts and bikini area covered. By the time he stopped, he had rubbed the scrub over every part of her except for her breasts and private areas, and wiped the scrub off with the warm, moist towels.

Susan smiled broadly and said, "Thank you Franklin, this was wonderful."

"Oh and what makes you think we are finished here?"

"There's more?" She sounded surprised.

With that he applied a slathering of a citrus, seaweed body detox mask. It felt cool and creamy and smelled marvelously fruity. Again Frank carefully kept her privates covered, isolating one group at a time. "Please sit up and keep the towel over your breasts." He wet her back and neck with the creamy mixture, then the front and back of her arms. He bent her leg at the knee to slather the front and back of her leg and thigh and back of her knee. He reached up with the cream covering her buttocks. He repeated on the other side, equally efficiently. Soon she was entirely covered in the creamy, citrus mask. It felt wet and cool. He began to tuck all the towels around her then surrounding her in a plastic sheeting until only her face, head and hair were exposed.

"I now know how a mummy feels," she giggled.

"Are you warm enough?" he asked.

Softly she whispered, "Yes, very."

Frank began to massage her face with an oil that reminded her of sesame. He used his fingertips in circular and wave-like motions to massage her forehead, around her eyebrows, around the outskirts of her beautiful eyes, across the bridge of her nose, down the sides and tip of her nose, her high cheekbones, her now sun kissed cheeks from the run, her lovely chin, around her luscious lips. It felt smooth, velvety and had a hint of a nutty scent. Frank followed up with more pressure using a different oil for her hair and scalp. Susan recognized the familiar smell of Moroccan Argan oil. It smelled so delicious, like Salon Miku. Her tension melted into his capable hands.

Susan felt all the stress of her current life situation just dissolve away. It's as if he had turned back the clock on her arrest, Lynchfield, the humiliation, the psychological turmoil, the physical pain, all gone with his gentle strokes, pulsating kneading, use of his hands, his elbows, his fingertips.

After a predetermined amount of time, he nudged her gently. Was she in a meditative trance, or had she fallen asleep, she wasn't sure, but she just knew she felt so tranquil.

"Susan, I need you to get into the shower. Wash yourself off and use the liquid gel and wash cloth I left for you inside there, then towel dry."

"Should I do my face and hair too, Franklin?"

"No, Sush, just from your shoulders down. While you are in the shower, I will clean up in here. Make sure you return. We aren't finished."

Still not finished, there will be even more? She couldn't believe it.

The body wash smelled incredible. She washed quickly, not sure how long she was supposed to take and she didn't want to keep him waiting.

Toweling off, she returned to the bedroom and laid down on her front and covered herself once more with the towel as Frank had instructed her.

He began again, this time with a Heavenly smelling massage oil. "Hmmm, lavender and patchouli."

"Ahhh, so good Franklin."

"I know Sweet Pea. Enjoy."

When he reached her upper back, she guessed she must

have missed a spot in the shower as he stopped, grabbed another moist warm towel, wiped her upper back and neck off, then returned with the massage oil again.

By the time Frank had Susan turn over for the last pass, she was thoroughly relaxed, oily, smelling divine. Her breath was slow and she barely moved, her eyelids heavy and resting. Satiated indeed.

Frank gently planted a kiss on her lips.

"Franklin, you have turned me into Jello."

"That, my love, is payback for being the best thing to come into my life in a very long time."

CHAPTER 21
NAME THAT TUNE

I wish I could turn back the clock.
I'd find you sooner and love you longer.
~ ILoveMyLsi.com ~

Frank and Susan climbed into his Mercedes, top down, radio on, seat belts fastened.

"Hey Franklin, may I change the station to POP?"

Frank preferred Classic Rock or Easy Listening, but decided to let her amuse him.

"Sure, enlighten me."

The dial landed on "Outside" by Calvin Harris and Ellie Goulding. "I love this song!" she squealed.

Susan began to dance and sing in her seat, at the top of her lungs.

Frank stared at her in disbelief. Susan could really sing, and not like a mom singing a lullaby, or a child in a school choir. She sang like she could be on the radio herself.

"Susan you can really sing! Where did you learn to sing like that? Wow! What a voice you have."

"I was a theatre, drama and music major in college."

"Can you dance like you sing Sush?"

She replied with a saucy tone.

"Do you mean like 'Do the Mash Potato' or 'The Macarena?'

Do you mean like if I can dance the waltz, swing, or the samba? Or do you want me to tap dance and audition for a Broadway show?"

Frank pulled over into the next safe place to park the car, and glared down at Susan.

"What the fuck, Susan?" Sounding annoyed he said, "I have been talking about taking you dancing and to Karaoke and you tell me you sing and dance well enough for Broadway."

"Are you asking me if I could put on a one woman show? Well then yes, Franklin. Yes I can, yes I could."

Susan appeared worried. "Are you angry with me because I possess these talents or because I didn't think to tell you? Don't be angry with me Franklin, please."

Then sadly, her eyes tearing, "I couldn't do anything right for George. I can't face displeasing you too."

"Of course I'm not angry. Displeasing me? Are you crazy? I am thrilled, ecstatic! Oh Sweet Pea, please don't cry. When will you get it through that stubborn, beautiful, head of yours that I am not George and would never, ever treat you the way that asshole did. Never! We are going to the mall. I want you to buy anything you would normally want to get to go on a date, a real date, with someone you really wanted to date, with friends you want to impress. No questions asked, no budget. Do you understand?"

"Dress to impress, sing to impress, and dance to impress, Franklin."

"Yes!" Susan almost fainted when he explained that he had started a bank account in her name with $10,000 for clothes, attorney fees, and money for the Lynchfield commissary. Whatever she wanted, it was now her money.

"We are going to go out tonight to my favorite dancing, Karaoke, restaurant club. You, I mean we, are going to knock the socks off of everyone we know there and have a marvelous time. Susan Chatham, you my girl, are a gift from God!"

"No Franklin, I am an inmate on furlough from Lynchfield."

"Oh, no my dear. You are much, much more. Don't you see?" He pulled back onto the road, and joined her in the next song, Black Eyed Peas, "I Gotta Feeling."

When they got to the mall, Frank and Susan strolled through the various shops pausing here and there. Frank showed her styles he liked, she selected others, until finally they reach a consensus of the look desired. Truth be told, Frank quickly realized, Susan Chatham, a former model and actress would look just as amazing in a burlap sack, or wearing her Lynchfield oranges, as in any tight pants, well-fitting blouse or short mini dress.

On the way home, the two shared information about their past music and dance training. Susan explained were she went to school and productions she had starred in. Frank told her about how he danced after school at his mom's dance studio, the boys' choir he had a solo in and the men's glee club he had joined to relieve stress while in medical school. Susan and Frank sang songs they both knew and could do in a duet. They sang Pink's "Just Give Me a Reason" perfectly together and decided they would perform that at Karaoke.

Once back in the apartment they continued dancing together in his living room. Like the first night when they were so efficient cleaning the kitchen, they were effortless in their dancing and singing together. Natural and meant to be. Like they had been together doing this for years instead of just recent partners. Susan felt so alive . . . and free, she thought she had died and gone to Heaven.

When they arrived at the Karaoke bar, everyone was already there. The usual Lynchfield group of friends. Mike Ramsey, Jackie, Paul, Juan Carlos, and Sally. They had their usual drinks and appetizers on the table. Mike spoke up.

"Now, I am telling you all that Frank is bringing Susan Chatham, who is on furlough with him. Please folks. I need your cooperation. I haven't had much of a chance to talk to him and I don't know what to tell you other than I know he said he was coming and bringing her. Just give the girl the benefit of the doubt. Be nice."

"Well I spoke to Frank and he sounded like a mad man." Paul stated sounding worried about Frank.

"Spill it Paul," the group chimed in.

"Sounds like the Doc's in love! Fuck this furlough program. How can you have a doctor fucking an inmate and falling in love after a few days! Heck, how is that ever going to work? And tonight she will be here partying with us like she's one of us but next week we will be waiting for her to take off her oranges and looking up her asshole searching for contraband. Give me a fucking break!"

"Oh, come on now Paul!"

"No you come on!"

"Look it isn't the same with Chatham."

"Really? What makes her so special? Her pretty face?"

"She's been a model inmate. And what's more, I recently received a letter from the Governor's office regarding her conviction. There was mention of a possible future exoneration due to some new evidence that is being currently investigated. Her entire conviction may be thrown out the window."

"Sounds like Susan Chatham may not be that different from the rest of us."

"Fuck there's Frank."

"Holy shit, who's the beauty on his arm?"

"It can't be. Chatham?"

Frank led Susan towards the group. He was handsome in his grey trousers, blue shirt and grey tie, she was gorgeous in a black, skin tight, short dress, strappy stiletto heels, perfect makeup with smokey eyes, and her hair cascading around her shoulders.

"Sush, stop you will crush my fingers," he whispered in her ear.

She swallowed hard but her mouth was dry and raw. She

could barely utter a "hello", much less contemplate singing here, tonight, surrounded by the very guards who controlled her every move IN THERE. She started to sweat as she sensed an equal uneasiness from the group. Franklin, cool as a cucumber, ordered two Mojitos. He had asked her earlier what he should order for them.

"Ms. Chatham, you look lovely this evening," said Warden Ramsey. That broke the ice, and Susan began to relax.

"Call me Susan, please."

The song "Poison" by Bell Biv DeVoe comes on and Frank pulled Susan onto the dance floor.

Susan and Frank danced, sang and had a grand time. The Lynchfield friends were awe struck. These two sounded like professional singers and they danced so well together.

The two shared grilled calamari as an appetizer. The drinks flowed maybe too easily. By the third round of Mojitos even Juan Carlos had asked Susan to Latin dance with him to Enrique Iglesias' "Bailando." Juan led the way and she swayed her hips in her sexy way, her short, tight dress revealed all of her lovely, albeit, thin figure. Frank wasn't the only one working at cooling his hard on with Susan there.

Susan and Frank did their Pink's "Just Give Me a Reason" duet and Susan did her version of Ellie Goulding's "Outside" that Frank loved so much. By the time she sang some Kelly Clarkson, and some Taylor Swift, she had become a club favorite. The next request came from the club's owner. He suggested she do a Christina Aguilera number. The same owner came over to their table later and comped their entire bar tab. He then told them to all order dinner on him. He said it was the least he could do to pay Ms. Susan Chatham for providing the entertainment for his customers that evening. He stated she was so good that patrons that normally stopped by for one or two drinks, had decided to remain the entire evening, ordering drinks, appetizers, entrees, even coffee and dessert just to hear her sing.

Susan realized she had had a little too much to drink and

needed to use the restroom urgently. She excused herself and got up. The two shots had pushed her over the edge. She felt tipsy. Mike Ramsey had gotten up before her and headed to the Men's room. On her way to the Ladies' room, she noticed something on the floor. She picked it up and realized it was Mike Ramsey's wallet. No one seemed to notice it but her. No one was watching.

"Crap! Anyone could steal his money, they could steal his credit cards, could even steal his identity," Susan thought. "I wonder what a Warden's wallet would be worth at Lynchfield. This could be my ticket and insurance policy to help me get by, to avoid a beating, or a rape, or worse." Susan snapped out of it. How could she contemplate that even for a second? What had Lynchfield done to her? She knew she was not a criminal nor could she try to be one. She was an inmate by mistake. Stealing was not in her vocabulary and not something that someone of her integrity would or could do. After all, if Susan stole the Warden's wallet and any of its contents how would that make her any better than the jail house lot at Lynchfield? Upon her return from the bathroom, she approached the Warden.

"Please sir, you dropped your wallet. I saw it on the floor and picked it up. Here it is."

"What are you saying Chatham? Are you drunk girl? My wallet is right here in my back coat pocket." He reached for it, but nothing was there. "Hell, where is my wallet?"

"I am telling you, you dropped it sir. Here it is."

"Stop calling me sir, it's Mike, Chatham! And thank you."

"Then don't call me Chatham, it's Susan, Mike! And you're welcome. I'm glad I saw it before anyone else did."

Mike Ramsey excused himself discreetly and went to check the contents of his wallet. He smiled. It was all there. His ID, his credit cards, $850 in cash. Susan had taken none of it. As he walked back into the club, he knew there is no way in hell that Susan Chatham committed the crime she was accused of. No way in Hell.

By the time dinner arrived, the conversation was lively.

Susan and Frank shared tuna sliders and a kale salad with honey mustard dressing. He fed her, she fed him. Susan was surprisingly comfortable now. She joined in the conversation like she hadn't a care in the world. She was bright, and funny. Sarcastically witty. She shared great information and interesting stories. Everyone did their best to keep Lynchfield out of the conversation. It was stored away as if locked in a closet, out of sight, and out of mind.

These were not guards but a group of good friends. She was not an inmate but Frank's girl. He was not her doctor, but her boyfriend and lover. It was a magically fun night.

Ed Sheeran's song "Thinking Out Loud" played and Frank asked Susan to slow dance. Their dancing was so tantalizingly sensual that it was almost a sexual experience for those watching. Their bodies were close together and their hips swayed in an "S" like pattern. His hands moved up and down her tiny waist and grabbed that tight little ass. She lifted her legs up to grab him, and their lips came close, becoming a passionate kiss. They were oblivious to the world. Their chemistry palpable.

By the end of the evening, not one person, not even Paul Sterling doubted Susan's right to be there enjoying with them. As the evening progressed she became Frank's girl. When Paul noticed that Frank had had a bit too much to drink, he offered Susan and Frank a ride home. He asked if he could crash at Frank's pad and Frank agreed.

The car ride was quiet, both of Paul's passengers had fallen fast asleep, both more than drunk. Susan was asleep instantly and Frank joined her after muttering something about wanting to marry her. If Paul hadn't seen it with his own eyes he wouldn't have believed that evening. If Frank wasn't so hot for Susan, Paul would have considered her for himself. "This model of Susan Chatham was not the Lynchfield model that is for damn sure," he thought. "This babe was beautiful and sexy, and wow could she move that ass, and that voice was divine. She was bubbly, smart and witty, and seemed to be able to hold her liquor pretty well too. She seemed to be the complete package if only one didn't know about her Lynchfield Dirty Secret. Could Mike be right about her being innocent?"

When they reached Frank's apartment, Paul had to roust them and tell them they were home safe. It didn't take long for desire to take over. By the time they got into the elevator Frank and Susan were kissing passionately. Paul tried to look away but without much success. They seemed blind to his presence.

Paul unlocked the door, and Frank and Susan staggered into the apartment and before he could even get the door closed Frank had freed Susan's breasts from under her dress and bra, his pants hung low and his man weapon was more than armed and ready for her. She jumped on him, naked, only wearing a lacy black thong, locking her legs around his waist. Paul shook his head, mostly feeling a pang of jealousy, more so than disgust, and went into the guest room, leaving the two drunk lovebirds to fuck away. He could hear their passion clearly.

In the morning, Paul awoke first and moved quietly, not wanting to disturb what he was certain were two very hung over people. He couldn't help but wonder how all of this would play out when Frank had to return Susan to Lynchfield. He walked over to the dining room table and placed two tall glasses of orange juice and four Advil's on it. Still shaking his head, he headed into the kitchen to start the coffee.

Frank woke first and joined Paul in the kitchen. "Hey, Paul, I, we, Jesus, sorry man. About last night. Shit, man, I am so sorry."

"Hey, I'm cool, don't worry about it."

Then he grinned ear to ear. "Did you ever think about starring in a porno flick?" He saw Frank's embarrassment.

"I care about you, Bro. It's not sex that I am worried about for you man, it's the whole Furlough, Doctor, Guard, Inmate, Prison thing. How will it play out?"

"How can it play out?" Frank responded.

"What happens when you have to bring her back, Frank? How will you see her? What kind of life can you make together?"

"Never mind that, how will I keep her safe?"

"Can you keep her safe? Is that even possible? She's a great gal, I get it, but, if there isn't any hope isn't it best not to get too involved now?"

Before he could answer, Susan sleepily walked in. Softly she said, "I know, I am no good for you. Not good for anyone anymore. Not Dale, not George, and not you Franklin." She bursts into tears and stormed out of the room.

"Sush wait!" Frank called out and ran after her.

"Thanks a lot Paul."

He found her packing. She looked up at him with sad big eyes.

"Maybe, this isn't good Franklin, Paul is right. We are getting too connected here. Maybe you need to take me back before I fall anymore in love with you Franklin Lomegistro."

"I think it's too late for that Susan, don't you? I am already in too deep. I am already in love with you too."

"Where do you think you are going?" He put back her things and scooped her onto the bed. He caressed her face with his hands, using his thumbs to wipe away any remaining tears. She reached up to kiss him then began to plant wet kisses down his chest to his waist. She began to undo his pants. He reached up to undress her pulling on the hem of her nightshirt. He inserted his fingers into her, she felt wet and ready for his now hard and thick cock. She took the condom he handed her and quickly placed it on him. He entered her as they wrapped around each other, breathing heavy, hips gyrating, matching their pounding, in and out, in and out, in and out, at an increasing pace, until reaching a crescendo and finding their release. Their skin was moist and warm, and their breaths were hot and heavy.

Frank laid on his back and Susan was on top of him, with her legs and arms on the outside. They rolled over on their sides, and she left one of her legs underneath him with her other leg on top. This position allowed them to continue to kiss and Frank gazed into her beautiful blue sapphire eyes, she stared into his gorgeous gray ones and they continued their intimacy, bonding, colliding, and soon peaking yet again. Fulfilled.

They quickly dressed and walked back into the kitchen after their lovemaking and Frank looked directly at Paul. "We are going to need your help. We will need everyone's help, all the guards that we know well. The one's we can trust. We need to try to keep Susan safe in prison."

"Have your juices and pills first for your hangovers. Get hydrated too please." As he and Frank discussed a plan, Susan cooked breakfast.

"God, that girl can cook too," Paul thought, fully satisfied after a delicious breakfast of Western omelets and a side of crispy hash brown potatoes.

Frank had decided to invite everyone for a beach day, so he suggested Paul just stay and enjoy the sunny Saturday. There was no reason for him to rush home.

Frank asked Susan to put together a picnic lunch, which she did gladly. He grabbed the beach umbrellas and extra chairs with Paul as they all set out toward the warm sand. Susan, looked gorgeous in her lacy bikini and floppy sun hat, but she also looked too hot. She stared at the ocean, her cheeks flushed, wishing she could go for a swim. The GPS tracking anklets were safe for bath water and showers, but the TASER would go off in seawater, delivering a painful shock. So although Frank and Susan enjoyed the beach every day, she hadn't been able to go for a swim.

When Warden Ramsey arrived, he and Frank shared a few words.

Mike motioned to Susan to come sit by him.

"So are you enjoying your furlough?"

"Yes, sir. It's been quite wonderful."

"Remember, just Mike out here Susan, please."

"Yes Mike."

"It's awfully hot out here. Want to go for a swim?" He

said as he lifted up her ankle, pulled out a key and unlocked the GPS anklet.

Susan couldn't believe it. "What? Are you kidding me? Are you going to shoot me when I head for the ocean?"

Mike threw his head back and laughed, understanding why Frank loved her sense of humor.

"Go swim with Frank Susan, he's been asking me all week to come and do this and gave me quite an earful today. Now don't make me regret this."

"No regrets. Thank you Mike, really, thank you." She gave him a hug and planted a kiss on him, leaving him flushed. He quickly rustled for sunscreen and vigorously applied more to cover up his now blushing cheeks.

All of Frank's invited guests took full advantage of the stunning beachfront and warm ocean waves, Susan more than anyone. She swam and splashed for what seemed like forever, the taste of freedom mixing with the salt of the sea. After a few hours, she grew tired. It had been so long since she had gone swimming. Even her athleticism couldn't make up for the months of incarceration and deprivation. She was simply not used to all of this activity.

"Franklin, I am pruned out, look at my fingers. I need to sit out for a few." She slightly staggered over to one of the beachside lounge chairs and collapsed into it. The sun and her exhaustion put her right to sleep. The rest of the Lynchfield crew continued swimming and chatting. A few went for a walk on the beach. Some collected shells. Frank watched Susan sleep for a while, he felt powerless against her beautiful face and then headed over to speak with Mike.

Susan awoke to the overwhelming sensation that she had to use the bathroom. Without any thought of repercussions, she headed to the facility adjacent to the pool. She glanced at the food she had put out for their guests and noticed that the sandwich platter was empty and the chip bowls had only crumbs. She needed to make more sandwiches and put out more snacks. Changing course, she headed up to the apartment, running quickly. While she was up there, she would also get more beers for the gang. It had been such a great day. She felt so alive.

On the beach, everyone had started to come out of the water. Frank glanced over at the lounge chair where he had last seen Susan snoozing and noticed it was empty. She was nowhere to be found. In an instant, he felt anxiety in the pit of his stomach. "No, no, no Susan, please tell me you didn't do this. No, I know you wouldn't. You wouldn't do this to me."

After looking for her by the pool, on the beach, in the ocean, Frank realized he would have to let the others know. Everyone looked at him with suspicion and fear as they realized they had let a fugitive loose and had even removed her ankle bracelet.

Mike's face turned red again, but this time in anger. Why had he agreed to take off the GPS tracker? He raged at Frank, not thinking.

"I trusted you Frank, you guaranteed me she wouldn't run if I took that thing off her. Dammit! There goes furlough, hell there go our jobs! I need to contact Lynchfield immediately to put out a warrant for her arrest."

"No please, Mike, wait, I am sure there is an explanation," Frank pleaded.

Mike pulled out his cell phone and started to dial. He couldn't even have the prison command use the TASER function. He had removed the anklet. He couldn't believe how stupid he had been. Mike thought briefly about the night before at the bar. Susan had returned his wallet so sweetly. How could she do this? He looked up, the phone still at his ear.

Susan came bounding down with a big smile on her face, balancing two coolers jammed with more food and beer. Her smiled turned to panic as she saw the group staring at her and Paul facing her, his gun drawn. She dropped the coolers and put her arms above her head instinctively. "Don't shoot me please!" Frank saw her and ran as fast as he could. He scooped her up into his arms as she fainted.

When Susan came to, she found herself on a blanket in the sand. Frank was over her gently rubbing her face and offering her ice water and a sugary soda to give her energy. Tears welled in her eyes.

"I am sorry Franklin, I just wasn't thinking. These last few days have been so normal for me. I forgot I was a prisoner on furlough. All I thought about was getting to the bathroom and making more sandwiches. I know I shouldn't have left by myself like that. I should have said something. I am really, really sorry. Is my furlough over now?"

Everyone gathered around her and she looked suspiciously at each face. The party continued and everyone enjoyed the delicious sandwiches, as if nothing had happened. Susan couldn't. Paul was right. She was different. She was an inmate in a women's penitentiary. This was a rude awakening but she needed it. She was not one of them. These were her guards, her captors. She withdrew into herself.

Frank looked at her and sensed what she was feeling. He understood her pain exactly. He noticed her broad white Hollywood smile had faded and she had stopped eating. She insisted that Mike put her anklet back on and even though he hesitated, he agreed in order to calm her upset disposition.

Frank, Mike and even Paul, who was beginning to get to know Susan very well by now, noticed the change in her. They knew it wasn't the same Susan.

Earlier that week, Frank had asked Susan if there was anywhere she really missed going to and she had mentioned a Dim Sum restaurant where she had been a regular. She hadn't had Chinese, one of her favorite foods, in forever.

Frank suggested to everyone that they all shower and rest up and meet at the Dim Sum on Bloomers and Taft Street later that evening. He hoped that would cheer Susan up and put the events of the day behind them.

CHAPTER 22
JUST ANOTHER NIGHT
OUT WITH THE GANG

Love is not what you say. Love is what you do.
~ Power of Positivity ~

It was a testing situation for both Frank and Susan and she was still fairly subdued, as they got ready for their trip to the restaurant. Susan knew that she was doomed to return to Lynchfield at the end of two weeks and there was nothing Franklin could do about it. Her nightmare would continue at least another two years until she was eligible for parole. She tried to push it out of her mind and live in the moment, but feelings of dread would take control. She had fallen hard for Franklin and him for her. What would happen to her and how would she change after serving two more years of a prison sentence? It was a chilling thought. Prison changed people – guilty or innocent. She had already changed – she would never be the same Susan Chatham again. She brought herself back one more time to the present moment and focused on the evening ahead. She hoped, as did Frank, that some Dim Sum would cheer her up.

She put on a pair of tight jeans and her new pink Oxford

shirt looking very preppie and more like a Ralph Lauren model than a convicted felon on prison furlough. Her sun kissed skin looked radiant. If only her mood would match.

Frank had been disappointed, when after the beach that day, attempts to make love were less than satisfying. She seemed distant and he knew she was feeling conflicted with their situation. How could she not? He wanted to be as supportive as possible, but he also wanted to enjoy their remaining days. He hoped that dinner at a restaurant she had raved about would be just what the doctor ordered.

The Dim Sum was in a small place just on the first block of Chinatown. The group began to arrive and were chatting about the great day at the beach. They raved about the delicious lunch Susan had prepared. The missing Susan fiasco was now just a funny joke to them. But not to Susan. As soon as everyone had arrived, she led them into the restaurant. Susan and Dale had been regulars there. They were bonafide Hollywood celebrities. Mrs. Chen greeted her by name.

"Oh, Miss Susie! Where Mr. Dale at? You want your usual table?" The owner suggested the best seat in the house in her heavy Chinese accent. She was short and chubby, wearing a pale blue silk Chinese style blouse and black skirt. The salt and pepper hair curly around her face looked over-permed.

"Actually, no Mrs. Chen, thank you. I am here with some friends who are Dim Sum Virgins." Susan didn't want to even be near the table she had shared with Dale so many times.

Susan and Mrs. Chen laughed together at the "virgin" reference and it was clear that this was a familiar inside joke between them. Susan had brought the restaurant a lot of business over the years, especially welcomed celebrity business . . . other virgins to try Dim Sum.

Susan took charge as she appeared fully at ease here. "We need one of your large tables, and the menus with the photos of everything. And would you please start us off with several pots of your wonderful Jasmine Oolong tea. God how I have missed your tea! Oh and some plum wine for all the ladies and the guys will have your Chinese beer. You know, the one that Dale always liked."

Mrs. Chen led the way to a large table with a spinning family style server in the middle. A young handsome Chinese man with no accent arrived with their drinks. Serving all the beverages, he put down the tray, and gave Susan an embrace and kiss like a long lost lover. Frank felt a tinge of jealously and couldn't hide it. Paul noticed the way Frank glared at the server.

"Susan McCraven where have you been? What, no Dale? Then you must be mine, only mine, tonight!" he swooned.

"Oh Kai, you always were the flattering flirt! I don't know where Dale is. We had a falling out, and have divorced. I take it he hasn't been around either?"

"No, Susan. So sorry to hear. Mom will be devastated. You two were her favorite customers. She moved your picture see."

He pointed to the far wall by the entrance among photos of various well known celebrities that had visited the Dim Sum on Bloomers and Taft. There in the center was a stunning photo of a striking couple, Dale and Susan. The photo proudly autographed: "TO OUR FAVORITE DIM SUM FAMILY THE CHENS, ALL THE BEST, LOVE, SUSAN AND DALE McCRAVEN." It was an awkward moment tinged with sadness for Susan. Those were wonderful times, what the fuck had happened to her life? Susan quickly excused herself to the restroom. Overcome with emotion, she escaped to wipe away the tears before anyone saw them.

The Lynchfield group had studied the restaurant, and the owners and waiter's reaction to Susan Chatham. They couldn't believe the photo on the wall and the way she was treated here. Everyone started talking at once. Frank was the only one who stayed silent. They all wondered now how Susan had ended up in prison. What was her crime? Mike had mentioned that there might be new evidence that would clear her. What happened to Susan's husband, this Dale guy? How could this gorgeous celebrity be the same person who was now a convicted felon?

When it came time to order, the group consensus was, no one had a clue. They happily let Susan do the ordering. She didn't miss a beat. Grabbing the paper order form and the pen she began to bark off and explain the dishes, after asking if anyone had any food allergies, or had some food they were unwilling to try. "About two to three dishes per person," Susan suggested, "depending on how hungry everyone is. We will get some steamed, some fried, and a variety of veggie, pork, shrimp and chicken. I'm not crazy about the beef, or the chicken feet, but does anyone want to try those?" Her voice was confident. She was in her element. Anyone looking in on this scene would see a group of friends having dinner. "The house special soup is amazing here and so are the crispy green beans. Dale's favorite dish." She paused, realizing what she had just uttered. Frowning for just an instant, she quickly handed the order form to Mrs. Chen with a half-smile.

While waiting for the food she downed a glass of plum wine way too quickly almost choking on it. She was still coughing when Mr. Chen in his white chef's coat appeared, smelling like fried dumplings. He gave Susan a big hug lifting her out of her seat and off the floor.

"You too skinny now Ms. Susan. See what happens when you no eat my Mr. Chen food in long time? I make special for you tonight and you still bring many customers like always. I make special for them too!" He planted her back down, greeted everyone at the table, with a special focus on Frank, who had been introduced as her special guest. He then ran into the kitchen to cook.

Shortly after, the dishes began to flow out of the kitchen as quickly as Lynchfield processed new inmates. Susan explained each and helped serve. She was at ease with her chopsticks. If it weren't for her obviously looking Caucasian, you would have sworn she was Chinese. Mrs. Chen brought forks to the table for everyone else. Everything was as delicious as promised, especially the soup and the green beans.

The conversation turned lively and soon even Susan was back laughing and joking and sharing stories of funny things that had happened in this restaurant over the years and some gossip about some of the celebrities in the photos on the wall.

It was a magical night. By the time the bill came, everyone at the Lynchfield table was stuffed and content. They even smelled of fried dumplings. They were impressed with the restaurant and captivated with Susan Chatham. She was more than they ever imagined. They understood how Dr. Frank Lomegistro had fallen for her. They parted ways and Frank and Susan headed back to his place.

"Thank you for this evening Franklin. It was wonderful. You are wonderful. I'm in love with you." She looked at him nervously – should she have said that?

"I'm in love with you too Sush. You are the best thing that has ever happened to me. I never thought I could feel this way. After Evangeline died, I went into a tailspin. You've saved me. We're going to get through this. We're going to be together, I don't care what I have to do."

That night Susan and Frank reconnected. Their sex was hot and heavy, gentle yet rough and all levels in between. Their positions and strokes as varied as all the dishes at Dim Sum had been. And two to three orgasms per person felt about right. Was she missing her old life? Was she missing sex with her young, rich and gorgeous ex Dale? Frank didn't give a shit. He was enjoying her beauty, her passion, her energy, and her sex. He was smitten. Frank could never have imagined doing what he was doing even six months ago. A prison employee having the hots for an inmate was one thing. But falling in love?

Susan was different. She was beautiful, intelligent, witty, cultured. She was a gourmet cook who could shake up a killer martini or choose the best bottle of wine to go with dinner.

She could sing like a Broadway star and dance like a Rockette. And their sex life was out of this world. Frank had never felt like this before, not even with Evangeline. From the first time she sucked his cock and he tasted her, he knew he had to have her. He needed Susan. He wanted her in his life forever. He would be lying next to her and her scent alone would drive him wild. He would reach over to her and caress her velvety porcelain skin. He loved everything about Susan.

They had shared so much and even though it had only been a few days, he felt he had already known her for a lifetime. He recalled clothes shopping in preparation for the Karaoke bar. Susan had gone into Victoria's Secret and forbidden Frank to follow her. She said she was going to surprise him. Wow, she did indeed surprise him. One night she sashayed out in her purchase, a sheer crotchless full body stocking. Frank had never seen anything like it. Evangeline just wasn't that sort of woman. Frank had nearly come before even touching her. He loved every detail of her from head to toe, inside and out. She was teaching him so much. She was his world. Life without her would be impossible.

CHAPTER 23
LOVE IS IN THE AIR

She was beautiful, but not like those girls in the
magazines. She was beautiful, for the way she
thought. She was beautiful, for the sparkle in her
eyes when she talked about something she loved.
She was beautiful, for her ability to make other
people smile, even if she was sad. No, she
wasn't beautiful for something as temporary as her
looks. She was beautiful, deep down to her soul.
~ F. Scott Fitzgerald ~

Every day on furlough was better than the last. Frank
Lomegistro felt he had won the lottery or possibly died and
gone to Heaven. This was supposed to have been Susan's
reward, her freedom and fun, but it was Frank who had won
the prize. Susan Chatham freed him at last from his grief after
Evangeline's death. He felt he had been reborn.

Every night was full of different and passionate sex.
Sometimes they would go at it again in the morning. Frank
felt like a teen. He was learning about his body, new
sensations, what his body could feel, and what it could do,
and what stamina it had. Susan showed him things he had

previously only dreamed and fantasized about. He hadn't thought they were really possible.

Sometimes Frank would wake during the night, and stare down at this young beautiful girl, he loved everything about her, her looks, her energy, and her passion for life. She was funny, bright, and very playful. He loved the way she smelled of fresh soap and conditioners. Her skin was so soft and warm. Cuddling and snuggling with her, he slept like a baby, and woke up refreshed and ready to tackle the day.

Frank had never eaten better either. Susan insisted he take her to Fresh Market at the edge of town so she could pick up the best and freshest ingredients with which to prepare gourmet meals. She purchased meats, poultry and fish, lots of fresh veggies and fruits, and she transformed them.

He would have worried about his weight except that her energy was endless and she kept him on the move. They enjoyed running on the beach and rented some bikes and took a long ride enjoying a picnic in the park. Susan always seemed to know how to add a special touch to even the simplest of activities.

With Frank's convincing, Susan consented to letting Mike Ramsey remove the ankle bracelet again so that they could go swimming. On calm sea days they snorkeled. On high surf days, they boogie boarded. Frank put on a kite surfing demonstration while Susan watched. She never once ran away even though she could have with the bracelet off and no one guarding her. She wouldn't have dreamed of leaving her Franklin.

Frank loved to watch her swim laps in the pool. You could tell she had been a competitive swimmer, and he found it so sexy the way she would whip her head around to get the water and hair out of her eyes as she came out of the water. He thought he should buy her some goggles. She was like a fish the way she could turn at the walls. If he raced her, she would certainly win, so he didn't even try. They played a game where she swam laps in the various strokes and Frank had to guess which strokes she had excelled at as a girl and which she had won the most medals in.

Sometimes they would go down to the hot tub late in the evening, after one of her delicious dinners, when all the other building residents were almost asleep, with a bottle or two of wine. They would talk for hours about their childhoods, college days, and hobbies they had. Frank shared stories about his medical school days and interesting cases he had treated over the years. Susan shared about what it was like to model overseas, and about the differences between filming for television vs. movies.

Their intimacy in communication led to increased intimacy in the bedroom. Frank thought she was nirvana, and her response to him let him know she found him equally delicious and perfect.

Probably the only thing Susan wasn't good at was tennis. She spent more time running after the tennis balls than she did hitting them. Frank didn't mind. He enjoyed watching her running around the court and catching a glimpse of that wonderful ass of hers. Even her imperfections appeared perfect.

"Sush, you are such a spaz!" Frank laughed at her. "Is it the fuzz on the balls that gets to you?"

Susan just laughed back, turning red and sweaty as she ran around the court.

The simplest of activities became special around Susan Chatham. Frank had to admit one of his favorite times of the day was when she showered. He would time what he was doing to listen to when she would shut the water off, and he would be there waiting with a warm towel as she stepped out of the shower, dripping wet with that gorgeous body of hers, now wonderfully tanned, and he would wrap her up in the towel and begin to towel her off. It became a ritual, between them, so sensual. After he toweled her off he would scoop her up and carry her into the bedroom where they would make love, or she would allow him to dress her. He loved to feel how the fabric lay over her wonderful skin. It left him yearning and made the next time they connected sexually that much more intense.

"Phantom of the Opera" was playing at the City Center for Performing Arts, and Frank bought two concierge level tickets. They dressed up in their best and went out to Hugo's grill for a filet and lobster dinner before the show, and sipped on expensive Champagne as they enjoyed the performance. Susan appeared to be in Heaven, and on the way back to Frank's apartment, the two of them listened to the CD they had purchased as a souvenir and sang along with the score. It was another magical evening.

Some nights were just quietly spent at home, Frank's condo on the beach. The television might be on for background noise, Susan would have her book in hand, Frank surfing on his IPAD, or reading an article in his JAMA journal. Susan would be sipping on her favorite Lemon Ginger tea. It didn't bother Frank that her favorite porcelain teacup and saucer had been Evangeline's favorite as well. Frank might have a glass of wine, or a beer, or even a decaf cappuccino.

It would have been obvious to anyone walking in on the two of them, that Franklin and Susan were totally comfortable with each other and belonged together . . . relaxed, blissful, and in love.

CHAPTER 24
BACK IN ORANGE

Tact is the ability to tell someone to go to hell in
such a way that they look forward to the trip.
~ Winston Churchill ~

The morning Susan was scheduled to return to Lynchfield was devastating for both her and Frank. They were both so upset, they couldn't even enjoy their last lovemaking session. Their adventures between the sheets came to an abrupt halt. Frank had tried everything in his repertoire. Nothing seemed to be working. Susan was sad and anxious. She was heartbroken and fearful. Frank understood and decided to just let her be and be there for her.

He tried to offer her a massage, but Susan wasn't interested. She just had a far away look on her face. Watching her mope and move around strangely in the kitchen while preparing breakfast was too much for him to bear. She had taken ownership of that part of the house and now instead it seemed as though she was seeing it for the first time. Frank offered to make breakfast. Susan said nothing and merely walked to the breakfast table and sat down. She picked at her food, moving things around her plate. None of it making its way into her mouth.

"Hey, Sweet Pea, how about I feed you like old times?"

She just stared back, with her pouty lips and sad eyes as if shaking her head yes or no would be too much effort.

"I will keep all your things here Sush for when we are together again."

She gave him a slight smile, but she couldn't let herself believe it. It was too painful and she now had to shift back into survival mode. She was heading to prison again. There was no more lovemaking, no more gourmet food, no more walks on the beach, no more Franklin. The tears welled up.

Susan changed into her regular clothes, the ones she had worn when they took their first trip to CVS. She didn't take anything that Frank had gotten her, she couldn't. She would have no use for them at Lynchfield and if she had tried to bring them, they would be stolen or confiscated immediately.

Behind the scenes, Susan was also worried. Was all their talk about love just "talk"? Would Franklin go on to bring some other inmate home on furlough or meet another gal at the Karaoke bar? Would he leave her when she returned to Lynchfield the way Dale left her when she went there? She was beside herself in a downward spiral of emotions.

Frank was beside himself as well. He couldn't accept that this was how their last morning together would play out.

Before either was ready for goodbyes, the Mercedes pulled into the Lynchfield parking lot. Jackie Somners came to the car to escort "Chatham" back to inmate registration.

Jackie whispered to Susan in a low voice, "Susan Chatham it was really nice getting to know you. You are a lovely person with a fabulous voice. Stay safe and under the radar. You have some eyes and ears looking out for you now, but also jealous gang member inmates. Keep your guard up. Good luck."

With those last words of warning Susan had to strip and spread her legs and cough and have her mouth and privates checked for contraband even though Jackie knew she would have none.

Back in Cell Block D Susan put on a brave face and shared her furlough adventures with Bert. Bert could not believe her ears. Susan had lived the dream. She could see that her friend was deeply affected and had fallen madly in love with Doctor L. It was so sad to see her depressed – almost as depressed as she had been when she first arrived to Lynchfield. Bert also had some news for Susan. A certain Officer Paul Sterling had requested a two week furlough with a certain Roberta Jimenez.

Susan hugged Bert. "I knew he had the hots for you Bert! Paul's a great guy, you must say yes!"

Planning Bert's furlough helped Susan take her mind off her own sadness. In their giggly excitement, the two friends became careless. They failed to catch on to the fact that they had been enormously indiscreet. Their plans and laughter had been overhead by Beulah, the leader of the ruthless Bitch Warriors. She was furious and quickly made plans to have them "jumped" at the first opportunity. Who were they to have a good time while at Lynchfield? Their payback was overdue. Beulah had never been able to stand that college snot Susan Chatham anyway. Roberta Jimenez would be collateral damage.

After Susan's first week back passed, she was settled back into a routine. It was a shitty routine, but a routine nonetheless. She ate as much of the crappy food as she could choke down, but still started dropping weight almost immediately. The food and the conditions were just too fucking awful to be withstood. Bert tried to comfort her and keep her strong, as she had so many times before.

Susan never saw Frank. It just reinforced those worried thoughts that she had about him leaving her when she returned to her incarcerated status. Paul Sterling and Jackie Somners would once in a while give a slight nod with their eyes but otherwise none of her so called "new friends" acknowledged her in any way that was out of the ordinary.

Even the Warden hadn't asked for a meeting. Not even a debriefing. Susan hadn't seen him either since her return.

The only difference in Susan's prison life was the fact that when she went to buy a new toothbrush at the commissary, her balance was $600.00.

"Franklin," she said out loud without even realizing it.

Roughly ten days back, Susan and Bert were on their way back to their cell from the cafeteria when out of the corner of her eye, Susan registered a strange movement. Before she could react, they were upon them. She barely managed to scream out.

"Bert!"

The rest happened in slow motion. Susan felt a sharp pain in her abdomen and then a rush of warm oozing blood. It was her blood, there was no doubt. She had been stabbed. Susan fell to the floor and the kicks started. There were blows to her groin, her ribs and her head. Susan was unable to move and through her pain she tried to form a thought. Where was Bert? What was happening to her? Was she ok?? Then suddenly, everything went black.

CHAPTER 25
INPATIENT

Maybe the journey isn't so much about
becoming anything. Maybe it's about
unbecoming everything that
isn't you so you can be who you
were meant to be in the first place.
~ Unknown ~

Paul Sterling dialed Frank Lomegistro's number, but wasn't sure what he was going to say when the call was picked up. Frank had fallen into a deep depression, as had Susan and was beside himself since she returned to Lynchfield. Finally, Mike Ramsay had decided to give him time off.

"Get your shit together Frank. If something urgent comes up, I'll call you."

Both Paul and Mike had advised Frank not to see Susan at Lynchfield. It would be better for both of them to go back to their "normal" non-furlough lives. It was a body blow to Frank. When his phone rang several days into his "vacation," he almost didn't pick up. The thought of making small talk with anyone was nauseating. He slowly lifted the receiver.

"Frank, it's Paul. It's Susan, Frank! Bad, very bad! She got jumped and she is seriously hurt. She lost a lot of blood and she's been air lifted to Regional Memorial." The pause was palpable.

"I'm sorry Frank, I called as soon as I heard the news! We are all praying for her!"

"Oh my God!" Frank uttered what sounded almost like a primal scream and Paul heard the phone drop. He knew Frank was on his way to Regional Memorial.

Frank arrived at the hospital and rushed to Susan's side. His love was barely recognizable. She was pale with tubes everywhere. He wiped away his tears and read her chart with shaking hands. He joined the attending physicians in a status conference.

"You have her wrist and ankle handcuffed to the hospital bed? Really? You have her in a medically induced coma for Christ's sake! Where do you think she is going to go?"

"Following protocol Frank. You know that," his former colleague Dr. Graney responded.

But the doctors had much more serious issues to worry about than Susan's criminal history. Susan Chatham had a rare blood type and she required a blood transfusion immediately. The platelets they had on hand were keeping her alive, but she was not thriving. Their blood bank was empty of her type.

"Frank we have called her family and left several messages. I believe your Warden also left messages. But we haven't heard back from the Chatham family. We also have calls in to the nearby hospitals and blood banks to check for a match, but figured getting a family member would be the best bet, plus they will want to know she is here."

Frank gave a pained look and then recovered quickly and said he would take care of contacting Susan's family. He knew it would be a tall order, but he wouldn't dream of not trying his very best to convince them that it was a matter of life and death. Surely they would understand and put aside their contempt in order to save the life of their daughter and sister.

Mr. Richard Chatham was annoyed as he looked through some work papers on his desk. He stared at the phone. Even in a tizzy he was a striking figure, an extremely good looking man. He had been mistaken for Cary Grant in the past with his full head of pure white hair, blue eyes and fair skin. Susan was his female doppelganger, with a little bit of his stunning late wife Gloria Chatham thrown in. Richard Chatham had always been an upstanding citizen. He was a prominent businessman and a no nonsense individual for whom life was black and white and things were either right or wrong. When his beloved daughter Susan was charged with shoplifting, Mr. Chatham was destroyed. It took him back immediately to an unfortunate incident in Susan's early teen years when she was caught shoplifting with her best "friend" Jenny Cavilieri. Looking back on that time was painful. When Susan was convicted more than a year ago, Mr. Chatham made the difficult, but he believed correct, decision to have nothing further to do with her. He simply could not pretend that everything was ok. Life was about rules and they were to be followed. He would never stop loving his daughter, but he had to let her know with his silence that she had failed.

"Tommie, if I get one more call from Lynchfield I am going to lose it. Why can't they get it through their thick skulls that I, we want nothing to do with Susan anymore? That woman in there, the one that committed that crime is NOT my daughter Susan. The Susan I knew and loved is DEAD! I want nothing of the one still using MY NAME!"

"Dad, calm down. I understand how you feel, but let's see what is going on. Here, let me listen to the messages and I'll deal with this for you. Let me find out what they want."

Tommie Chatham headed into the kitchen to listen to the voicemail messages left by the staff at Lynchfield.

Even though Tommie Chatham was Susan's fraternal

twin, he and Susan only slightly resembled each other. Tommie was very handsome, but no one would have guessed he and Susan were born only three minutes apart. He had more of his mother's looks than Susan did. His mom had kept the family together and her death had been a huge blow. The family dynamics had changed. His father had changed. As Susan tried more and more to help her father cope, Tommie began to retreat. He began to do his own thing. He had been good friends with Susan's ex-husband Dale McCraven since high school, but their friendship ended when Susan was tried, convicted and sent to Lynchfield. As angry as Tommie had been at his sister for stealing, he was also angry at Dale for taking Susan's money. He had not been a good husband to her, never giving her the benefit of the doubt after she was charged. And he ran off not only with money Susan had earned during their seven year marriage, but also the money she had earned as a teen model and actress, which her father had put in trust for her. Susan had trusted Dale enough to transfer that money to their joint account and Dale had taken every penny of it. Something about that just didn't sit well with Tommie. Dale had been a dick and Tommie wouldn't soon forget it.

When Richard Chatham turned against his daughter Susan, Tommie couldn't understand that either. How could somebody love someone so much and then disown them? How could a parent disown a child? Would he be disowned too if he did something Dad didn't approve of? It left him feeling numb and sad, but his personality was not strong enough to fight against either of these potent male forces. Tommie had continued to play the dutiful son, but in the back of his mind he wondered what had really happened the day Susan was arrested. He had a twin's instinct that something was off, but he had never said anything.

Mr. Chatham went ballistic any time there was a phone call or letter from the prison. It was all too painful for him to face. Susan had gone from being Daddy's favorite, his sweet little girl to being nonexistent in one thought and breath.

Tommie walked over and played the messages. Three hang ups. One solicitation for what . . . cable television? Three more equivalent and disturbing calls, "Lynchfield Women's Correctional Center will you accept the charges?" Then a call from the Warden. "Hello this is Warden Michael Ramsey calling from Lynchfield Women's Correctional Center please call me at . . . ."

"Hello? This is Warden Mike Ramsey again. Please, it is urgent that you call me back. There has been an accident and it is imperative that we speak with someone from the Chatham family."

Tommie didn't bother to write any of these down, instead he pressed the Delete button. Click, Click, Click. Delete, delete, delete. Then three more almost identical messages. "This is Regional Memorial Hospital, please call us at . . . ." Click, delete times three. Finally, the last message left Tommie uneasy.

"Hello, this is an urgent, emergency call. This is Dr. Franklin Lomegistro calling from Regional Memorial Hospital. Please call me back at . . . ."

Hmm, isn't that or wasn't he the Chief of Emergency Medicine there?

Nah, maybe not . . .

Click, delete and then . . .

"Hello, Dr. Frank Lomegistro, Fuck HIPAA, I am in love with your daughter Susan, we are trying to save her life here. Please help! Please!"

Tommie ran into the study where Richard Chatham was working.

"Let's go Dad. NOW!"

"Where? What?"

"I'll explain in the car, let's go."

They grabbed their wallets and jackets and the two Chatham men climbed into Tommie's silver Land Rover. They sped off toward Regional Memorial Hospital.

Frank Lomegistro was pacing back and forth, with Dr. Stanley Graney trying to calm him down.

"Look Frank, thanks for calling the Chatham family. Let's think positive. Maybe they got the message you left and may be on their way here right now. Meanwhile, our blood bank is calling every blood bank within a flying radius of us. We will find her blood type. She will be okay, you will see."

"You have no clue Stan what it is like in a women's prison. They think nothing of beating each other up or worse over a peanut butter sandwich or because someone borrowed their mascara, or someone gave them a look they didn't like. They are animals."

"So how did you fall in love with this inmate Frank?"

"Oh, Stan, Susan is not like the others. You have no idea of her loveliness. She didn't commit any crime, I would bet my life on that. My brother Jim is researching that fact as we speak. She will be exonerated. I believe that wholeheartedly. But shit Stan! Lynchfield. Christ. They couldn't even keep her safe for a fucking week!"

In her medically induced coma, Susan's dreams came fast and furious. She saw herself sunbathing nude on her honeymoon with Dale. She saw herself romping on the beach with Frank. She saw herself being thrown in the Shoe naked and afraid and being beaten by George. The machines she was hooked up to started to beep. Frank and Stan ran in. Susan was coding. Stan threw Frank out of the room and yelled "Code Blue!" The team that specialized in just this kind of crisis came rushing down the hall, flying past Frank and letting nothing stand in their way of a patient in need.

When Tommie and Mr. Chatham arrived at Regional Memorial Hospital, they didn't know who to ask for or where to go.

"I am sorry dad, I should have listened to the messages more carefully, I should have written down the numbers. Lomegistro I think? Ask for a Dr. Lomegistro or I guess we could just ask for Susan."

The receptionist, an elderly woman who looked like she would be better suited working in the gift shop than being the gatekeeper at a busy teaching hospital glanced at a list in front of her with a puzzled look.

"I don't see Dr. Lomegistro listed here. He used to be Chief of Emergency here, but he is semi-retired and last I heard, he was working at some women's jail. Susan Chatham? Yes, I do see a Susan Chatham. But she's listed as no visitors allowed, high security risk. Sorry I can't help you more."

Tommie became livid. "Look, we had, I don't know how many messages from your Hospital. I fucked up and didn't write down the phone number or department. You have already admitted that she is here. We are her next of kin and heard she is dying! We want to see her now! Fuck your rules lady!"

"Security, security!" The security guard strolled over.

"Susan Chatham, is that who you are looking for?"

"Yes, please, I am sorry for losing it, she's my sister. This is her father. We are very distraught can you help us? We aren't looking to make trouble here."

Dr. Frank Lomegistro was getting off the elevator when he noticed a commotion at the front desk. Frank himself had just thrown a fit when Stan called a Code Blue on Susan. Frank no longer had hospital privileges at Regional Memorial, and was not allowed to be in the room during a called Code. In the middle of barking the orders for the Code, Stan told Frank to get out. Frank understood that he was too involved with this girl to be objective but he still became irate.

"Chatham? Are you two looking for Susan Chatham? Are you her brother and father?"

"Yes, I am Richard Chatham, and this is my son Tom Chatham. Who are you and do you know something about our Susan? Seems we got a call about a life and death situation?"

Frank introduced himself and the three went to grab coffee in a more private setting so Frank could explain everything.

For what seemed like an eternity, they waited for word about Susan's condition. Richard Chatham could not hide his concern. Finally, Dr. Stan Graney called Frank. It was the good news that they were hoping and praying for. Susan was better. She was in stable condition. Something had gotten kinked and the lack of oxygen, in her severely anemic state, had triggered the alarm, initiating a Code Blue. Now that she was back in stable condition, they could go up and see her.

Tom Chatham knew he was a match for Susan's blood type and within minutes, they were admitting Tom and he was quickly downstairs donating blood for his twin's transfusion.

Frank Lomegistro and Richard Chatham sat down together and began to speak. Frank shared stories of Susan's life in Lynchfield, how they met in medical and how he hosted her on furlough and had fallen in love. He didn't share too many details of why she was in medical or her experience with George Ferguson, reasoning that a father just didn't need to hear that about his daughter. He shared about how his brother, Jim Lomegistro had found inconsistencies in her trial and sentencing and how he was using his contacts to research her case. He strongly believed that when the details were re-evaluated a full exoneration might not only be possible, but probable. Frank shared how he and the Warden didn't think, for one second, that Susan had done the crime she was sent to Lynchfield for. Frank told Susan's dad that, worst-case scenario Warden Ramsey had already submitted paperwork for an early parole.

Richard Chatham listened attentively and in shock. He could not believe what he was hearing. Could his daughter have been framed and really not be guilty of her crime?

After hearing all Susan had been through, Richard Chatham had an epiphany. He realized his daughter wasn't a disappointment. She was a hero. He had made a terrible error turning his back on her. He hoped she could find it in her heart to forgive him.

Frank, Tom, and Mr. Chatham walked in to see Susan. The three men stared at her in silence. Susan had looked better, that was for sure. She was pale and gaunt, tubes everywhere, machines beeping. Her eyes were closed, sunken in, surrounded by dark circles. They watched as the transfusion was set up. Tom reached out to Susan while Richard Chatham just gently held his daughter's hand.

"Susie, it's me Tommie. Hey! Daddy and I are both here. Susie can you hear us? Hey met your new boy toy Frank. A doctor Suze, like you always wanted to date as a kid. Hey sis heard you are a hero now. Come on Susie, you've got to get better. To the moon and back, sis, remember that one?"

Susan dreamt she heard her brother Tommie's voice. But everything sounded weird and strange like she was in a tunnel. Everyone was muffled and muddy. Was this reality or another dream? She couldn't move, and couldn't think straight. To the moon and back, yes, that was their way (Tommie and Suzy Q's) of being with each other, especially as kids when they would get in trouble at school for talking too much. She remembered. He remembered. Her dad was there? How could that be possible? Her dad was having a conversation with Franklin? On what universe was this? Then she thought she heard Dale's voice. No not really? She heard Tommie asking Dad if they should call Dale and let him know. Would he visit her? Did Dilly still love her? What about Franklin? Does he love her? Is he here because he loves her? Is he here because he is her doctor? Why was she in jail? She couldn't move. Ouch! Pain, pain, pain, hard to breathe.

It was all too overwhelming. Too complicated, feeling too much pain, to make any sense of any of it. Her head was spinning around and around. She had heard them say she was in a medically induced coma. No, she screamed inside of herself. It's me. I am here. I can't move. I want to throw up. I want to pee. I want to suck my thumb. I want . . . I don't know what I want. Delirium. She groaned. Help me. Help me please. But there was no relief.

"Mike thanks for coming. Look at her Mike. She is so uncomfortable. Please for the love of God take those cuffs off her." Frank motioned to the Warden, who was equally disturbed by the grimaces on Susan's face.

"OK, alright, I'll take the cuffs off." Warden Mike Ramsey removed Susan's handcuffs and ankle cuffs.

Susan felt an instant sense of relief. It felt like freedom. It jolted her senses. She opened her eyes and mouthed the words "thank you" to no one in particular, rolled over and drifted back to sleep.

Frank and Mike yelled out simultaneously, "she's conscious!!!"

The next couple of weeks were a blur of activity. Slowly Susan spent more and more time awake and rehab started. First it was just getting her off the oxygen, then removing the catheter, then sitting up, eating and drinking by herself, then getting her up out of bed. She received physical therapy to work on some muscles that were beginning to atrophy.

She spent time with Frank, and reconnected with her Dad and her brother Tommie. Susan could not have been more pleased.

She continued to get stronger. As she improved physically, the Warden pressured her mentally.

"Chatham. Susan please don't make me do this to you. I have to follow the protocols in place at Lynchfield. If an inmate gets jumped and refuses to identify the perpetrator, the punishment is being thrown in the Shoe Chatham. I don't want to do that to you. Please, I know you know who did this to you. Who?"

"Warden, I can't tell you. I just can't, I won't. Trust me when I say the Shoe is less of a punishment to me than what can and will happen if I speak out. Throw me in the fucking Shoe Mike! I am not going to tell you anything. You do what you have to do but I need to do what I need to do."

"Damn you Susan, George is on duty there. Is that what and who you really want to face?"

"I won't tell, I just won't," Susan answered in despair.

At hearing this, Frank broke out in a cold sweat. Here he was getting her back to some semblance of decent health, and she was going to Solitary to lie naked in a 6 x 8 foot concrete cell with a metal toilet and sink to be guarded by the same guard, a Mr. George Ferguson, who had nearly killed her mere weeks ago.

"Please Sush. I beg of you. Tell Mike. Tell me. Tell your dad or your brother and have them tell so they don't know you lagged."

"Well, you must think that I and the other women in Lynchfield are just stupid, Franklin. You think that I can do that? You think I could tell you, Mike, Tommie, or my dad and then that would get me off the hook for lagging? Now that's stupid. Look at me Franklin. Just look at me. I know what I am doing."

"No, Susan you are a fool to think that you are keeping yourself safe."

"It isn't me that I am trying to keep safe!"

"What? Please Sweet Pea, Don't take the bait and go to Solitary. It's what they want. It's a set up by George. I just have a gut feeling."

"Well, if that is true, Franklin, then I suppose they got me. Because it's a risk I have to take."

Susan Chatham was released from the hospital when she was deemed well enough and sent directly to solitary confinement at Lynchfield, the infamous Shoe.

CHAPTER 26
THE PRISONER'S DILEMMA

You can't change someone who
doesn't see an issue in their actions.
~ WomenWorking.com ~

"OK Chatham, you know the drill," yelled the guard. "Strip down. Let me check your mouth. Let me check your privates, cough. Get in your cell."

Susan, humiliated and afraid, sat naked on the floor. There was nothing in that cell, only concrete walls. She looked around at the cold metal stainless steel toilet and matching metal sink. There was one half roll of toilet paper, and a sliver of soap. No toothbrush, no towel, no bed, no blanket, nothing. Not even a cup to get a drink of water. A camera rolled in the corner. She looked at the slot by the front door where meal trays would be delivered. The cell smelled of urine, feces, and body odor. She began to cry, having to use the back of her hands to wipe away her tears. What else could she have done? Did she really have a choice? Was she the stupid one? Was this really a set up? Lag on Beulah and the Bitch Warriors . . . now that would be suicide. They would kill Bert, and maim Susan. They would attack

Frank. At least that's what they had said after they stabbed her and while they were beating on her. Susan could survive the Shoe couldn't she? What about George Ferguson? Would she have to deal with him? She last saw him when he dropped her back after furlough. He had been reprimanded and suspended without pay. He would be furious with her. Has he returned to Lynchfield and reassigned to Solitary? What would he do to her? In those last 24 hours at his apartment during her first furlough, he had actually begun to show her some kindness. Maybe he had some remorse and accepted some responsibility for his actions? Or would he just pick up and continue to torture her here as he had in his apartment. Susan Chatham was naked, cold, and afraid again.

"Hah! Look who we have here, if it isn't Bitch Chatham joining me on furlough again, this time in the Shoe! Hey, Chatham! Missed sucking my dick? You couldn't come up with anything better than you fell down some stairs? You poor excuse for a bitch."

And on that note, began the physical, sexual, and mental abuse all over again. George Ferguson, Guard, Psychopath, the sequel. Susan was helpless. She had to protect Bert. She had to protect Franklin. She could survive anything that Ferguson dished out. She survived before.

"I don't understand it," Mike Ramsey told Frank. "I can't figure this out. It just doesn't add up. There are security cameras everywhere in Solitary. George enters her cell and that is to be expected, as he is the guard down there. But, he doesn't touch her. Damn it Frank. Look at the video footage. He doesn't go near her. But, at the same time, you don't see her injuring herself either."

He continued, "yet, the other guard, I don't think you know him, Rich Surzman, says she looks terrible. That she has bruising on her side, and seems hurt although he couldn't specify what was wrong with her. He also suspects that she's on a hunger strike. Because he says she barely eats any of her food. It all doesn't add up. Watch the video feed Frank, you know her better than anyone here. See if you see anything that would give us clues."

Frank painfully watched the videos per Mike's request. They were heart wrenching. He was furious with Mike for throwing Susan in the Shoe. He was angry with Susan for choosing to go in the Shoe. Livid that George Ferguson was back and a guard at the Shoe of all places. He was in such despair. Every day Susan appeared weaker and thinner. He noticed a lot of crying, and that she was not eating even though she seemed to be clutching her stomach and even sucking her thumb out of hunger. He could see that in the video footage George Ferguson enters then later leaves her cell, yet he never goes near Susan. Why is he in there then? What is he doing? She seems worse after his visit with her. What is going on? Is he hurting her, and it just isn't showing up on the cameras. How is this possible?

Mike decided to call for a sweep of Solitary. All the inmates in Solitary were taken for showers and a recess in the yard. Now that the inmates and all Solitary guards were out of the way, a full investigation could begin. It didn't take long to discover that all the cameras in Solitary had been messed with. Sabotage.

When Mike returned to his office he called the security camera company and ordered for additional cameras, installed at every conceivable angle. When the new footage came in and Mike asked Frank to watch with him, they were aghast. It was horrific. Frank began to weep.

Day one: George Ferguson is seen entering Susan's cell. He grabs her by her hair and throws her on her knees and has her give him a blowjob. He climaxes and comes all over her, then takes his cum and rubs it onto her body like sunscreen. He kicks her side and pushes her onto the floor. Spreading her legs wide, he takes his boot off and using the heel like a hammer, hits her between her legs. Susan screams out in pain but he uses his other hand to gag her mouth then quickly removes his sock and shoves it into her mouth. He flips her over and fucks her hard in her ass, no lubricant, nothing, then hits her again with the boot. Pulling the sock out of her mouth he quickly dresses himself. "You bitchy whore. Shut the fuck up." Leaving Susan collapsed and whimpering on the floor, he pulls out his dick once more and pees all over her. George tells her to sit up as if nothing happened, and makes sure she is positioned by the view the original security cameras would cover. He calmly walks out of the room.

Day two: George Ferguson is seen entering Susan's cell, grabs her by her hair and throws her on her knees and has her give him a blow job. This time he comes in her face, pushes her down on her back, makes her drink his urine. He stands her up and fucks her standing up, then pushes her down and shoves her face in the toilet water. He makes her sit up as if nothing happened, and makes sure she is positioned by the view the original security cameras would cover. He walks out of the room.

Day three: George Ferguson is seen entering Susan's cell, grabs her by her hair throws her on her knees and has her give him a blow job, makes her swallow all his cum, by holding her nose so she can't breathe, until she does so. He makes her lay on her back, takes his guard's baton stick and uses it as a dildo to masturbate her hard, then makes her get on all fours and fucks her ass with the same guard's baton stick. When done, he kicks her in her lower back, and when she falls on the floor, he pulls his pants down, and squats over her defecating on her and making her use her own hands to rub his feces over herself.

After viewing the unbearable torture, Frank has to sit down. Warden Mike Ramsey makes arrangements for Officer George Ferguson to be arrested immediately.

A team is dispatched to get Susan Chatham out of her cell and into treatment. She is inconsolable. Warden Ramsey, personally, takes a blanket and wraps her up in it.

"Chatham you are finished being in Solitary." He ordered the team leader to get her bathed, dressed, fed and to Medical. When Susan is bathed and treated and fed, she falls asleep exhausted.

Frank couldn't find the words to say to his beloved Sush

when she awoke a few hours later. He just stared at her speechless. How could he offer any comfort? He slowly and methodically began feeding her hot creamy chicken soup, her favorite. He blew on every mouthful so she wouldn't burn her tongue. After what she had been through, a burn on the tongue would go unnoticed.

Susan said nothing either. She just opened her mouth and accepted the soup.

Finally she spoke when Mike Ramsey came into the room. "How did you figure it out? He would mess with the cameras and position me in a certain way to avoid detection." Her voice was still soft and shaky.

"Yes, we figured out he was messing with the cameras. Thank God for Officer Surzman, Susan. It was Surzman who told us he was noticing injuries on your body. He thought you were on a hunger strike because you weren't eating."

"I know," she said softly, in almost a whisper now, as if George would hear her and come after her again. "Surzman would try to get me to eat. He would ask me if I was hurt, if I was sick. And he would stare at me as if he was making a mental note of my condition on a daily basis. Ferguson threatened me. He said if I ate he would kill me and he would kill you Franklin. He even threatened to hurt Mike. He was forcing me, black mailing me to starve myself." She swallowed hard, took a deep breath and said, "I need you to please go now and save my friend Roberta Jimenez. Beulah and the Bitch Warrior gang are going to jump Bert. Please hurry. They'll know I lagged. I don't care anymore. Just keep me safe. I never did anything illegal. I don't belong here. I have been humiliated, fucked, beaten, and starved. Fuck this shit, I am done playing nice."

"OK, all right! We got it. And we have devised a plan. We will keep you safe, for real this time. Frank's brother Jim has made progress on a full exoneration as well. In the meantime, Susan, you are going to do a one-woman show for Lynchfield. Raising money will be the excuse. You will practice for your show in the chapel/auditorium. I will have

Paul, Jackie, and Juan Carlos guard you there so you will be safe. You will recruit others to help. You start as soon as you are better and out of Medical. What will you need?"

"Really, Mike?"

"Yes, Really! Are you game Susan?"

"Okay. I'll do it. I will need fabric and tap shoes, dance shoes, dance clothes, costume jewelry, makeup, an iPod and an account to download music and speakers."

"You got it. Anything else?"

"Yes, better food, this processed Lynchfield diet is crap! I will be burning a lot of calories dancing and rehearsing, I am already too thin. I want salads and veggies, especially crispy green beans. Franklin knows how I love my green beans. You got that?"

"Yes, ma'am, and what else?"

Susan looked at Frank with that naughty I want to fuck you now look.

CHAPTER 27
THE SHOW MUST GO ON

Be Bad Ass with a Good Ass.
~ Unknown ~

Susan had a lot of work ahead of her but it sure beat mopping and cleaning shitty toilets. She had fabrics to order, costume props, shoes, she needed to make posters to promote her upcoming auditions. She looked for a couple of backup singers and dancers. Could she teach them and get everything completed in time? Dottie, a seamstress, doing time for petty theft of tips, had already signed on to sew the costumes. Bert was in of course. They found a few other inmates who had some high school drama/musical experience. Frank was on part time medical duty, so he could spend a few hours helping choreograph. Focusing on the show turned out to be therapeutic. Things were coming along quickly, and Susan selected music which Frank uploaded on an iPod, and figured out how to get to play through the auditorium sound system.

"Susan, it's too much Sweet Pea. Too many hours, too much dancing. You keep losing more weight and you can't afford to."

"Franklin, I need the practice. It makes me feel better, I promise. It's been so long since I did this for more than my hobby. Plus, I would think about eating more but, I'm sorry. I just can't force down the food here."

"What if I send you in some Boost drinks or yogurts with Paul?"

"Are you sure Mike "the Warden" Ramsey won't throw me in the "Shoe" for contraband?"

"Funny, Sush! Very funny! Look just don't over do it."

She did a high kick and pirouette in front of him and stepped away, blowing him a kiss and giving him a wink.

Paul stared at Susan's beautiful body dancing and singing for hours. But he preferred more curvy voluptuous types and his eyes fell on Roberta Jimenez. He waited for his own turn as furlough host with her.

Dance rehearsal clothes still hadn't arrived and Susan had everyone dancing in their orange tops and their panties complaining that the orange scrub pants would get caught in the tap shoes. All those gals dancing in their panties. Paul had had it, and went to the Warden to remind him of their demand.

"Mike, uh, Warden Ramsey, sir." The friends tried to remember conventions during work hours.

"Please get these women some dance clothes. If I catch one more glimpse of a hoochi coochie while they spin around and high kick in their panties like that, I will be following George Ferguson to the Klink."

"Ah, right fine, but this production is way over budget already. She better be able to pull in an audience and make this fundraiser count."

"Mike, have you heard her sing and dance?"

"Of course, we all have at the Karaoke bar."

"Oh, No Mike, you have no idea. This is professional tap dancing, high kicks and gyrating asses to Broadway tunes. "Anything Goes", "All That Jazz", what is this talented woman doing in our auditorium at Lynchfield? She's trying to train a bunch of cons into being her chorus and supporting cast."

Paul shook his head, "And furthermore, Frank should be practicing medicine in an ER but instead he's here singing a rendition of "The Impossible Dream (The Quest) from Man of La Mancha" that will knock your socks off."

Mike's brows furrow, "He's in her show?"

"Absolutely, she recruited him, said something about her costume change and needing time off the stage and Frank is the diversion."

Mike stood up, furious, "This is getting out of control, and I wish you had told me earlier. I think it's time I visit a Chatham rehearsal and see what the fuck is going on in my auditorium."

Frank found Susan. "Sush, we got problems. Mike wants to see a sample of your show. He became concerned after Paul's panty complaint and may shut this all down."

"What? No fucking way. Do you know how hard we have worked?"

"Then save it! Use your talents. Raise the bar Susan. You gals better kill it."

"Don't say kill in prison Franklin. Not everyone here is as harmless as your new girlfriend."

Then Susan had an epiphany, "Can I pretend to kill you in "All That Jazz"? You can play Fred. And can I strip from my formal gown in the 'I Dreamed a Dream' from 'Les Miserables' and get into my oranges and have a guard cuff and shackle me? Maybe Paul would be in the show. I am going for full shock value here Franklin."

"You are one, brave, crazy, muse Susan Chatham! My incredible sage! Love, love, love your ideas."

A few weeks into rehearsal, Mike Ramsey decided to check on rehearsals. He arrived unannounced. Jackie Somners was on duty and gave him a quick nod. The music was blaring so loud it felt as though the floor was moving. Mike spotted Dottie, in the corner, fabric everywhere, sewing sequined costumes at a feverish pace. In the other corner there was a cooler filled with ice and cold wet wash cloths. Was that beer? No, Boost supplement drinks, and yogurts with plastic spoons. Roberta Jimenez and the other recruited performing inmates were tapping, yes really tapping. Damn good too. Mike was pleasantly surprised.

All of a sudden, out came Susan Chatham in the shortest shorts with the tiniest, tightest, sexiest ass on the planet gyrating to "All That Jazz". She turned and belted out some notes her face red and sweaty and her voice breathy and oh so very sexy and then she hit the high note with both voice and pelvis. Mike opened his mouth to say something official sounding. But, all that escaped was "WOW!"

Susan froze.

"Wait, what," the Warden responded. "Hey don't stop on my account."

Susan asked if he wanted to see one of the ballad numbers. The warden agreed. She excused herself, put on her orange pants, wiped herself with one of the cold wash cloths, grabbed a Boost, and drank about half of it and then about a third of a bottle of water.

"Warden Ramsey, sir, your best friend, a Dr. Franklin Lomegistro instructed me to include in my Lynchfield show one of your all-time favorite songs. May I sing "Over the Rainbow?"

With that Susan began to belt out a version of "Over the Rainbow" that left Warden Mike Ramsey astounded in appreciation. Mike had intended to reprimand her but now . . . he couldn't believe how professional everything was. Susan was marvelous.

"You will have a full dress rehearsal for all the prison, inmates, and any of their family members that wish to attend right here. I will make arrangements to invite the Governor and his wife to your official fundraising performance and we will move the venue to the City Center for Performing Arts.

We will have a cocktail reception for the audience afterwards which only you, not the rest of your "cast", other than Dr. Lomegistro, will attend. I will personally escort you. You will sign autographs there. Am I being clear on my instructions Chatham?"

"Yes, sir!"

Susan jumped for joy. She felt alive again performing. It was exactly what she needed.

Susan's weeks flew by quickly. She was safe and spending her days dancing and singing. The food still sucked, but she kept Franklin at bay by downing a few Boosts here and there and the yogurts were pretty good too. She slept like a baby each night. Her body was better than ever, as was Bert's. Frank and Paul just smiled at each other, looking forward to their next furloughs.

Susan managed to be alone with Frank once a week for about an hour, thanks to Mike Ramsey. He would take an extended lunch and use the extra half hour to make his prison rounds. He would leave Frank the key and invite Susan into the office just before Frank arrived. Sometimes the two lovers would just talk or hug or make out. Occasionally Frank would sneak her a burger. Frequently they would make love. It was as good a life as possible in prison. Before she knew it, the day of the full dress rehearsal at Lynchfield arrived.

Warden Ramsey came early to wish her luck. "Break a leg Chatham."

"Please sir call me Susan."

"Susan, please call me Mike."

With a smile and an appreciative nod she left to go fetch her costuming.

The show was a mega hit. The warden, guards, inmates, and family members couldn't believe their eyes and ears. This wasn't a prison talent show. This was about as close to a Broadway production as one could get without scenery and a live orchestra. The supporting cast held their own. Franklin Lomegistro's rendition of "Man of La Mancha-Impossible Dream" was remarkable, and watching him get shot as Fred in "All That Jazz" with Susan spinning the prop gun, had all the inmates cheering.

When the finale was sung and the "cast" all got introduced and took their bows, they received a standing ovation.

When it came time for Susan to perform at the City Center for Performing Arts, she knew she was ready, but was still nervous. Her brother Tommie had told her that her dad, Richard Chatham and ex, Dale McCraven were coming. She had almost fainted. Dale had been feeling really guilty about not coming to the hospital to see Susan, after learning about her stabbing. The jury was still out on how Susan felt about seeing Dale again. Was he still seeing Allison Cray? Would he be bringing that "throw your ass in jail, steal your husband troll?" It didn't matter anyway, the divorce was final and Susan was in love with Franklin now. Members from the parole board would be in attendance. Also the Governor and his beautiful wife Carmen would be there too. They would be seated right up front in the special mezzanine seats.

Susan reminded herself to breathe and when Frank arrived, Bert went and got the others along with the rest of the costumes and props. Paul and Juan Carlos arrived on time and within a few minutes the costumed Lynchfield show cast was cuffed and shackled for the drive over to City Center. Sequins and cuffs and shackles were indeed quite a sight. It was show time.

The theatre was full to capacity. The fundraiser, in terms of ticket sales was a huge success. The audience this year had heard that Lynchfield actually had a professional singer and actress starring in their show. A few had even recognized her name, Susan Chatham. They spoke about her amongst themselves. "Wasn't she that teen child star on that family show?" "Wasn't she nominated for an Emmy for CSI?" "I didn't know she could dance?" "I heard she's very pretty." "I heard she has a killer body, that's the only reason I let my wife drag me here to this prison show." "Can you imagine being an actress and ending up in jail?"

The audience came for many reasons that evening. Some out of obligation, some out of curiosity, some because they loved musical shows, and some to support the charity. Very few came because they were fans of Susan Chatham, or because they gave a shit about her.

City Center was a gorgeous theatre. It had rich red plush overstuffed seating, deep cherry wood walls, red and gold thick carpeting in an ornate pattern, with that extra thick padding that made your heels feel squishy as you walked on it. The acoustics in this theatre had been well designed and they made the music from the iPod sound like a live orchestra on its digital sound system. The lights went down, spotlights and lighting came on and the show began . . .

Backstage the cast was fidgety, fussing with their costumes, hair and makeup. Warming up for the tap number. Susan was gargling with tequila.

"Thanks for sneaking in the tequila Franklin." She gave him a kiss. "In college, we had gotten in the habit of doing tequila shots before and after a performance. It was just our thing. We used to sneak it in, so our professors didn't know. It was part of the fun, and a way to relieve stress and nervous energy before and after a show. I am good to go now!"

"First number is up! 'Anything Goes'."

"Break a leg," Frank whispered in her ear. "I love you."

The audience clapped as Susan Chatham took the stage.

Susan was dressed in a sequined red, white, silver and blue ensemble. Her short shorts revealed a hint of her tight ass. Her legs looked endless and her perky tits peeked from the sequined vest. A bow tie accented her long neck and a tiny hat balanced on her head, her shiny hair framed her perfectly made up face. She looked like a sexy cross between Uncle Sam and a sailor for "Anything Goes". Her voice rang out and her feet and legs began to tap at a lightning speed. She spun, tapped, danced and sang, joined by her magnificent cast on stage. Their energy was contagious. The audience now squirmed in their seats. They clapped and foot tapped along.

The once apprehensive star was now confident, poised, singing and dancing. Every cell in her body committed to entertaining her audience. And wow, were they being entertained! The audience had been expecting something along the lines of a school play. At least this is what previous fundraising Lynchfield talent shows were like year after year. This year the production was over the top. Professional. Bold. They were pleasantly surprised. They were stunned.

The audience roared and clapped at the end of her number, but Susan didn't hear them. She was in her own zone, concentrating on her costume changes, the lyrics, the music, the dance steps and timing in the dance numbers, the details of her body and her voice.

She ran off the stage to change into her sequined gown in preparation for "Over the Rainbow". Roberta helped her zip up her gown and change into silver stilettos and put on lots of diamonds. All the jewelry was costume of course, but they sparkled on stage. It didn't matter that they weren't real. Susan took a swig of ice water, wiped her brow and checked her makeup, just as Franklin was finishing his final chorus from "Man of La Mancha" so debonair in his black tuxedo, his voice majestic and deep.

Susan went back on stage, truly looking like she belonged back on the red carpet. She dedicated her next song in thanks to Warden Michael Ramsey. She belted out "Over the Rainbow." She killed it!

The show continued with Susan singing various songs, all from well-loved Broadway hits. She featured songs from "Annie," "Cats," "South Pacific," "Cabaret," "King and I," and "My Fair Lady." All were crowd favorites. Finally it was time for "All That Jazz."

This was their planned show-stopper. Frank donned his trench coat looking very Mafioso. His white fedora in place. Bert and the girls changed into their "flapper" short dresses. But Susan, oh Susan . . .

in her Victorian lace bustier, red and black, all lacy and

sequined at once, with panties that fit like a thong; her tight, smooth, backside almost entirely exposed. Her breasts propped up by the push up bra.

Frank was aghast!

"Susan, you had Dottie redesign your costume since the dress rehearsal. That is over the top sexy Ms. Chatham."

"Is it now Dr. Lomegistro, like you would know?"

"Always the flirt!" He winked at her.

The music began and Susan danced and sang her way on stage toward Frank. Their chemistry and energy undeniable.

Susan shimmied and shook, first towards her audience then turned 180 degrees towards her chorus, which provided a perfect view of her exposed derriere twerking. She turned and her pelvis rocked back and forth, her hips swayed side to side in a way that made the men in the audience want cold showers. It was a real toe tapper.

Susan belted out, "Where the gin is cold . . . but the piano is hot . . . ."

"Oh Fred . . . nobody walks out on me! Bang! Bang! Bang!"

Frank, as Fred, dropped to the ground as rehearsed, dead. Susan twirled the prop gun around her forefinger like a cowboy in a western movie, and continued to sing, swinging those salacious hips and well-toned arms, "Allll . . . Thattt . . . . Jazzzz!" When the number was done, the audience went wild.

The Governor leaned over, turned and asked his aide,"I forget what crime was this woman convicted of? What a show!"

The energy in the theatre during intermission was palpable.

They came expecting a charity snoozer, instead Susan Chatham had knocked the socks off the gentlemen and heels off the ladies in the audience. The bar had a record sell out of cold drinks as the men try to cool off from Chatham's hotness!

Backstage the cast is just as excited. Bert and the girls are giddy with happiness. They have done an awesome job and for many it was the first time they were ever in a theatre, never mind starring on stage. Everyone was high on endorphins. No one more than Frank who beamed at Susan. This girl had stolen his heart through her cooking, cleaning, her intelligence and wit, her incredible good looks, her hot sex, and now her amazing dedication and talent. And the way she looked in that bustier. He was high on Susan!

After intermission the show continued. Susan was back in her zone. For a brief moment in time, she wasn't an inmate, wasn't a divorcee, wasn't anything other than her original, real authentic self. She was Susan Chatham, a beautiful, sexy, talented singer, dancer, and actress who knocked performances out of the park! It was exhilarating.

When Susan returned to the stage, she was dressed back in her sequined gown and stilettos and did a few more Broadway songs, even her personal favorite, from "Phantom of the Opera," before it was time for her second act showstopper, "I Dreamed a Dream" from "Les Miserables."

Susan took a few deep breaths, and was almost tempted to take her second shot of tequila early but decided against it. No need to go against custom.

Susan began the song in her full makeup, lovely cascading hair with her jewelry, sequined gown and stilettos. As she sang the lines, her beautiful voice echoed through the theater. Swallowing hard during the pause in the music and lyrics, she commenced her physically gutsy and shocking transformation. On stage, a small makeup table had been set up. On it was a package of eye makeup remover wipes, cleansing cream and a moist wash cloth and towel. A small dish in which she could place the jewelry and containing her hair ties. To the side there was a coat stand and on it a hanger on which was hanging prison issue orange scrubs. Nearby, backstage, Paul Sterling, dressed in his official guard's uniform, had excused himself and was ready, holding full handcuffs and shackles, and carrying Susan Chatham's prison name badge/lanyard.

While singing the song Susan first pulled her hair back into a pony tail, using her hair ties. She slowly and methodically took the jewelry off. First the earrings, then the necklaces, then the bracelets and rings. She wiped off her eye makeup with the eye makeup remover wipes, then applied the thick creamy cleanser on her face and wiped that off with the moist, wet washcloth. She dried her face with the towel. All of her movements were perfectly timed to the lyrics in the song.

Finally, as the song was approaching its "fourth quarter," Susan stood up as the music and song reached their crescendo.

"But the tigers come at night . . . ," she unzipped her gown and let it drop to the floor by her feet, "as they tear your hope apart as they turn your dream to shame . . . " standing there in just her plain bra and underpants. The undergarments were nude in color to simulate the nakedness of prison life. The spotlights through the shear fabric, revealed a hint of her true nudity. With great sadness in her eyes, her voice perfectly timed with the lyrics expounded as she removed the stilettos, pulled on her prison issued oranges, first just the scrub top, and later the pants, tying them at her waist, and finally donning her prison loafers. As the audience sat stunned, the piece de resistance was when Paul, the prison guard approached. He handcuffed and shackled her while putting on her prison name badge/lanyard. Everyone in the audience, especially her father and brother, were deeply moved by this performance. There wasn't a dry eye in the audience as she sang, "I had a dream my life would be . . . so different from this hell I'm living . . . "

After the number, Susan quickly ran off stage. Well, as quickly as she could in full shackles. It was very effective and very moving. Backstage she took her celebratory second shot of tequila. The show had been an incredible success.

The audience clapped and cheered as Roberta, Frank and the other supporting cast members took their bows.

Susan's eyes teared with joy as she received a standing ovation and pleas for an encore.

She nervously glanced at the parole board members and the Governor and his Argentinian wife. They clapped as hard as anyone and also called for an encore.

Susan hadn't practiced the song, but knew that an actress never forgot her first starring role. She had anticipated an encore and decided on a song from "Evita."

After Susan's encore rendition of "Don't Cry for Me Argentina," the Governor glanced at his Argentinian wife, who was touched and teary eyed. He turned to his aide and whispered, "Tell me again where that paperwork is that we were examining in the office, to get this woman exonerated."

"Yes, Sir, I will have it on your desk first thing Monday morning."

"Thank you for looking this over and considering her case," Mr. James Lomegistro, Esq. said as he shook the aide's and Governor's hands.

Susan hugged Bert and the others, but the feeling of stardom was fleeting for them as they were soon cuffed and shackled and ready to travel back by prison van to Lynchfield, escorted by Officers Stirling, Gomez and Somners. Susan would be attending the after-show cocktail reception with Frank and the Warden as she was promised.

Most of the dignitaries in attendance were looking ever so smart in their suits and the ladies equally stunning in their evening gowns . . . . Chatham went in her oranges, as is. Her fall from grace now apparent. The cuffs and shackles had been removed though, as had her badge. The Warden put her badge inside his suit pocket. He was determined to escort Susan. He was hoping she would enjoy herself, and sign autographs. He was hoping to introduce her to the parole board members and the Governor and his entourage. He was hoping to make himself look good and important and promotion worthy and improve her chances for an early parole or for a full exoneration. He was proud of his "star" inmate.

At the after-party, the caterer had prepared a stellar spread. There was a wonderful assortment of hot and cold hor d'oeuvres that were passed around by waiters in black tuxedos with white gloves. Some were passing trays of Champagne, and for those preferring their drinks stronger, a full cash bar in the corner. For those wishing to satisfy their sweet tooth: petite fours, and mini crème brulees, coffee and tea.

Susan had only a few minutes in which to say hello and good bye to her dad and Tommie. Quick kisses and hugs were exchanged. Susan could see they were emotional and she was so happy they had reconnected, albeit under unfortunate circumstances. It didn't matter, she had her family back.

Dale and Susan even shared a brief glance and quick nod. Susan wondered why that fucker even came. Possibly he was just curious. She never noticed if he had brought bitch troll Allison. She didn't have the nerve to ask either.

Frank leaned over and gave her a quick kiss, then excused himself. His role was to mingle as the show's choreographer. He was also on an early shift at Lynchfield tomorrow, and the Warden had planned to be the one to escort Susan Chatham and return her to prison.

"What would you like to drink Susan? You did a fabulous job! You earned it," Mike said.

"Actually I am quite exhausted and thirsty, may I have some sparkling water with lime please?" Susan's voice sounded tired.

"Not even one for the Champagne toast?"

"Ok, just a sip of Champagne for the toast."

Secretly Susan knew she had already downed two shots of tequila and she thought a tipsy inmate would not serve her cause.

The Warden thanked everyone for coming and for their generosity. He gave a brief speech on how important this fundraiser was every year and how their donations helped rehabilitate the incarcerated women of Lynchfield.

"Your financial support is much appreciated and helps our women in their rehabilitation. It allows us to purchase more equipment and supplies. It helps us improve our library program. It helps us hire better teachers for our educational programs and in our workshops. Your donations help our psychology department to help our inmates with their issues and teach them better coping strategies so they make better choices in their lives." Warden Michael Ramsey was a convincing orator.

Susan couldn't help but think what a load of crap that was. Most women learned how to commit more violent crimes, and actually became more delinquent in prison. Many learned how to make weapons. Some learned how to make lesbian love and turned to lesbian sex. Some learned how to fight, cheat, and steal. Prison was a training ground for the wicked. What had Susan learned? She stopped to think about that. She had learned about being sexually, physically, and emotionally abused. She lamented how Lynchfield had left her with permanent lower back pain, flogger scar on her back, burn scar on her arm, a stabbing scar on her abdomen and night terrors in her dreams. Susan frowned while everyone else was laughing, networking and mingling.

Mike Ramsey grabbed Susan's hand and began to introduce her to key people there. All were very interested and curious to meet this beautiful, shameless, brave girl who should be performing on Broadway but instead was in prison.

She was terrified. She shook hands, said hello, and conveyed autographs for people who held her freedom in their hands. The Governor, his wife, his aides and parole board members. She thought about how to sign and decided on Susan Chatham, exaggerated S, exaggerated C.

After fulfilling her duty with Mike, Susan wanted to go back to Lynchfield, brush and floss her teeth and sob in exhaustion into her pillow. She was too nervous and too tired to eat or drink anything more than sparkling water and a few bites of cheese. She knew that prison was her new normal and the inevitable end.

Back in his car, Mike leaned over and returned Susan's badge to her orange uniform.

Mike Ramsey smiled at her and said, "You were incredible tonight, Susan. Wonderful performance. Your contribution has helped raise a generous amount of money for Lynchfield. Thank you."

"You are welcome Mike," she replied softly and fell fast asleep before he had even pulled out of the parking garage.

Back at Lynchfield, Mike turned Susan Chatham over to the guard working inmate registration. He felt terrible and embarrassed for her, she was the returning star. He voiced his concern.

"This inmate has been with me, this isn't necessary. I'm the Warden, for Christ's sake."

But the guard on duty responded, "Sorry, sir, protocol. Following orders."

Susan looked up at Mike with an appreciative understanding of his compassion, and gently squeezed his hand, "It is okay Sir, I am used to this by now, my new normal, my new life." She stripped out of her oranges exposing her full nakedness in front of both of them.

CHAPTER 28
THE ROAD TO FREEDOM

Notice:
You are hereby allowed to be happy,
to love yourself, to realize your worth,
to believe in great things, and to be
treated with love and respect.
www.facebook.com/dailyfeelgood

In the weeks after Susan's one woman show, things went back to "normal." She was back on her old job detail and back in survival mode. She wondered if Frank would be telling her how lovely she smelled if he caught wind of her Eau de Pine Cleaner and Eau de Wet Mop.

On a happier note for Susan and the other inmates, the money from the fundraiser began to appear in Lynchfield's budget. Warden Ramsey, wanting to make an improvement that he felt would directly reward Chatham, had approved a new fresh veggie and fruit salad bar in the dining hall. Frank was much happier that Susan was keeping her weight more stable now that she had fresher food choices. He still had Paul sneaking Chatham and Jimenez yogurts. It was a "contraband" that the Warden and other "friendly" guards were now willing to overlook.

The Bitch Warriors were leaving Bert and Susan alone for now. They had moved on to "fresh" blood at the prison, and Susan and Roberta and some of the other "nice" girls had earned a lot of respect with their talent when they put on the inmate show.

Prison life had become rather mundane. Susan would wake, stand at attention for roll call, wash down breakfast of rubbery eggs or wallpaper paste oatmeal with dishwater-like coffee,or tea, take a cold shower, choke down salty cold cuts for lunch, canned spaghetti for dinner, and do lots and lots of mopping and shitty toilet cleaning for her job duty. Evenings were also much the same. There was evening countdown with the occasional contraband check and time spent card playing, or reading. Occasional cooking TV shows still left Susan drooling for a better menu. What was new for Susan was the constant horniness now that her weekly visits with Frank had ended. But despite the relative calm, there were still reports of lesbian gang rapes or jumps, overdoses or other such traumas that rocked her world and reminded her that there was no real safety at Lynchfield. The sobs of new inmates made sleeping through the night difficult. She remembered when she had first arrived – she had sobbed as well.

Susan was surprised one morning when she received notice that she had an urgent meeting with the Warden. This threw her for a loop. Susan immediately broke out in a cold moist sweat, her heartbeat pounding in her chest. Prison had a way of making you expect the worst outcome from the most innocuous news or schedule change. She stored her mopping supplies and equipment and tried to wash away the pine scent, with little success. She quickly brushed her hair, pulling it into a quick braid and tucked in her orange scrub top and rushed down the hallway.

When she entered the Warden's office, she was surprised to find the atmosphere very stuffy and formal. Susan stood at attention, feeling very insignificant and very vulnerable. She found three men in suits, two of them Lomegistros. The Warden, Franklin, and an attorney introduced as Mr. James Lomegistro. This was the brother Franklin had spoken of who he called Jimmie.

James Lomegistro was even more handsome than Franklin. Even balding, with a shaved head, he bore a definite resemblance to Franklin, but looked younger. Susan thought he looked familiar. She had seen this face before, and realized she had noticed him sitting in the audience at City Center. He had appeared to be part of the Governor's entourage. She now recalled that Franklin had said something about introducing her to someone important at the after-party, but that he had to leave early. Why was Jim here, in the Warden's office, with Franklin, and now?

Frank had been very busy in Medical that week. The flu was going around and many of the women were ill. Two inmates had been jumped during the last three days and he had to treat their injuries as well, some of which were severe. He hadn't met or seen Susan, at all. He was delighted to see her today. She looked a bit tired, but otherwise looked well. He simply adored her. As soon as he caught sight of her, he wanted to grab her arm, pull her towards him and kiss her passionately. Instead he just gave her a smile and a wink. They had hurdles to cross before they could be together, but cross them they would. He was a bit surprised when she didn't register a response.

"Have a seat Chatham." The warden motioned to a seat in the middle of the room which was facing a computer monitor.
"Mr. Lomegistro would like to show you several security video feeds, and ask you several questions. He also needs a handwriting sample from you."

Susan felt herself tensing up. She knew this was for a good reason, but it just brought back memories of her fate being in someone else's hands. At times she just wanted to be left alone to do her time.

The Warden was so formal. Calling her Chatham again. "What did that mean?" she pondered.

"What have I done now? What accusations are being made about me?" She couldn't help injecting sarcasm into the meeting.

"Quite the contrary, my dear girl. We are all hoping the exact opposite of what you are fearing will result from your answers." The Warden gave her a reassuring smile.

Susan wasn't buying it. Her arrest, her being sent to Lynchfield, the breakup of her marriage, her horrific abuse by George Ferguson, did enough damage to her psyche. At this point, the only person she trusted was Franklin, and she even eyed him with hesitation.

"Would you like some tea?" the warden offered. Frank had shared with him that hot tea was always a comfort to Susan and Mike Ramsey could sense her fear. She graciously accepted the Styrofoam cup of hot lemon ginger tea. Susan could sense she was about to be worked over. Her trust had been betrayed so many times, by those she had loved and trusted that now everyone felt like an enemy, and anxiety rose inside of her. She hugged the warm cup with both hands as if that would bring her comfort. Peace.

After what felt like an eternity but probably only a few seconds the questioning and showing of the videos began. Lomegistro the attorney and interrogator not Lomegistro the doctor and her lover, began. He handed her a form and black pen.

"Please sign your name here." He pointed to a specific line on the form. "Sign it with the name you would have used if you were going to the bank to make a withdrawal while you were still married, prior to your arrest." Susan studied the form. It was for handwriting analysis. She then turned her eyes toward Mr. Lomegistro.

"I would have used the name Susan McCraven," Susan said quietly.

"All right then sign that."

Frank was surprised by her nervousness. He couldn't

comprehend why she was so scared. He watched her clutching her tea as if it were a life preserver, and she had fallen overboard into an angry sea.

"Sush, relax Sweet Pea. There are no right or wrong answers here."

Susan looked up at him and tried to smile. For such a talented actress, she failed miserably.

"Okay."

She put the cup down after taking a sip.

"Mmmm," the tea was indeed comforting.

"This tea is so good." But, it was too hot and she burnt her tongue.

The Warden tried to lighten her mood but also rush her.

"I am glad you like your tea. Sign."

She picked up the black pen, rolled it around in her delicate fingers. Finally she said, "I'll sign."

The men stared at the form on the Warden's desk as she did so as if every letter she formed with the ink would subtract a month from her sentence.

Susan wrote in cursive, signing an exaggerated S, equally exaggerated M and exaggerated second C . . . . Susan McCraven.

The minute she wrote the first S, James Lomegistro smiled in his head. He already knew the answer his handwriting expert would confirm.

Jim Lomegistro pulled out another form and laid it next to the form Susan had just signed.

The signatures on both forms were practically identical. Even to an untrained eye it was obvious to all that this was definitely Susan's handwriting.

The three men reacted as if each had just won the lottery, or that she had just provided each of them with the most orgasmic blowjob of their lives.

Susan stared at both forms now lying side by side on the Warden's office desk. "Holy shit," Susan thought. That was a copy of one of her bank withdrawal slips. It was dated the same day that Allison Cray had testified she had seen Susan at the scene of the crime.

Susan's brain went crazy with thoughts: "Where did they get this? How did they get this? Who gave them access to my bank account and deposit slip? Why did they want her to sign today? Why were they so happily surprised? Were they making fun of her?"

She felt her breaths getting quicker and shallow. She swallowed hard. "Breathe, Chatham, breathe," she told herself, trying to remain calm. She picked up her cup and began to sip, blowing at the too hot tea. She watched anxiously as Mr. Lomegistro played the first video.

"This bank video shows a young woman with long cascading black hair wearing a white Oxford blouse and white shorts getting out of a navy blue Porsche, and going into the south location of First National Bank. She withdraws $975.50."

"Yes, I can see that," said Susan.

"Does this look familiar to you?"

"Yes," Susan replied.

"Do you know her? Do you recognize the car and whose car it is?"

"Yes, it's me!" Susan exclaimed. "That is, uhh . . . , was my car."

"Great," said Jim Lomegistro, "now watch the second video. Same questions."

Jim Lomegistro played the second video. Mike, Frank, and Susan were all staring at the screen.

"This security video shows a young woman with long cascading black hair wearing a white blouse and white shorts leaving the suspected location of the alleged crime. Later she is seen getting into a red Corvette. This was taken by the security cameras at the north branch of First National Bank."

"Yes, I can see that," Susan stated.

"Does this look familiar to you?"

"Yes," Susan replied. "I watched this video before at my trial."

Frank and Mike appeared sad all of a sudden, almost

afraid of what she would say next. Jim Lomegistro seemed unconcerned, and continued to ask questions.

"Do you know her? Do you recognize the car and whose car it is?"

"Well she looks like me and I would often visit that establishment. Holy Shit! That is Allison Cray's red Corvette." She was unable to contain her scream or hold on to her Styrofoam cup. Hot tea spilled all over as the cup hit the floor and exploded.

"Jesus," yelled Frank. "Are you okay? Did you burn yourself, Susan?"

"Fuck the tea Franklin!" Susan stood up and began to rant. She had to get it all out. "Allison Cray said she saw me at the scene of the crime. She testified that she saw me through the windows of the L bus. Why would she be dressed like me? Why would she say that? Shit, she knew what I was wearing that day, because we had met for coffee earlier, to discuss how we would coordinate a scene in the CSI episode we were filming. Allison Cray was my body double, stunt. You know? Shit of course she looks like me! Shit! Shit! Shit! At my trial they showed that video. Everyone thought it was me. Hell, I even thought it was me as first. But then no, I knew it wasn't or couldn't be me, because I knew that after coffee with Allison, I went shopping, then went to the bank. But it sure looked like me on that video! And the jury could see the lady in white shorts leaving the scene of the crime, Kane's Jewelers, looked like me. And everyone believed I was at the scene of the crime, because it looked like me in the video, and because Allison Cray testified that she saw me there because she was on the L bus that passed by that location at that time and that she saw me out of the window. And I was convicted, and my own family didn't believe me, not my dad, nor my brother! And even my husband Dale didn't believe me. And now I am here with you questioning me in Lynchfield. But they never showed this additional part of the video, that you are showing me today. No one got to see the rest . . . about Allison getting into the red Corvette. If she was in the red Corvette then she couldn't have been on the bus to see me. And she was at the scene of the crime then in the north. I was at the bank in the south." Susan's face was now red with rage. "I will tell you, as I told others before, I didn't do anything. I went for coffee, shopping, to the bank. But they said I did this crime. And they sent me to prison for it." With that, Susan burst into tears. The Warden handed her a tissue. Frank tried to comfort her but Susan was lost in the wretchedness of her emotions and of all that had transpired over the last 18 months.

Jim Lomegistro walked over to Susan and gave her a small pat on her shoulder to steady her. She stopped sobbing and turned towards him, realizing what this meant. He spoke clearly and in a tone showing his profound disappointment in Susan's attorneys and the justice system. Susan had been given a raw deal.

"Susan you were not shown this video in its entirety. It was edited by the prosecutor to prove their case. On top of that, neither the prosecutors nor your defense attorneys bothered to check the bus company. They didn't try to find witnesses who may have been on the L bus. They didn't pay attention to the fact that Allison was seen getting into a red Corvette, which in fact was not your car. You would have gotten into a blue Porsche or maybe a black Jaguar if you had taken Dale's car. Isn't that right?"

But, James Lomegistro didn't wait for Susan to respond because he already knew the answer. He continued.

"The red Corvette was registered to Allison Cray, but the plot thickens because I found out with further research, that the red Corvette was purchased for Allison Cray as a gift by a Mr. Dale McCraven."

"What?!" Susan cried out and her face grew pale. "Dilly bought her that car? What? Why?"

Susan began to tremble. She was overcome with fear, hurt, rage, anger, disappointment, all rolled into one overwhelming mix of emotions. Her mental pain was worse than the physical pain she had felt at the hands of George

Ferguson.

"And that white outfit, the one I wore that day, was a gift from Dilly. Shit! Did he buy her the same outfit? On purpose? Was Dilly part of this plan? That bitch troll stole my career, stole my husband, and stole my freedom!"

"I know it is a lot of information to take in and to confront all at once. I don't know about that, possibly. I can't say for sure if Dale McCraven was a part of this frame up Susan, but certainly the actions of Allison Cray are very suspect. Sorry, let me continue here Susan . . . ," said Jim Lomegistro.

"The attorneys in this case, in your trial, both sides, the plaintiff and defense failed to mention the existence of the south branch video. They should have verified everything you said you did that day. If they did know about it and had mentioned it, then was it the Judge who did not allow this video to be shown. And if that is the case, why? Why would a Judge not allow all the evidence to be shown? Yet, it is quite clear that the video shows Susan McCraven at the south branch, and, along with her signature on a bank deposit slip, confirm she was at the south branch at a verified time. It also proves that Susan couldn't have been at the north end location of the same bank because it is physically impossible to get from south to north in that amount of time. There is the time on the bank deposit slip, the time the crime is suspected to have been committed, the time the woman dressed in white was at the scene of the crime at the north end location. It doesn't add up. It is physically impossible to be at south end at the verified time and get to north end at the verified time. Which proves beyond a reasonable doubt that Susan Chatham McCraven, formerly and now, Susan Chatham is and always was NOT GUILTY. And further a Ms. Allison Cray, is at the very least, in contempt of court for lying on the witness stand. At most, she may have committed the crime. There is evidence since the red Corvette places her at the scene. It will be easy to check bus records, possibly less easy to see if there are any eye witnesses to confirm whether she was on that L bus at that time that day, but still possible. There certainly was suspicious activity between Allison Cray and Dale McCraven. Possibly even suspicious activity with the representing attorneys, and even possibly the Judge. I am not saying they are guilty mind you. They may have been victims here too."

"Shit! Shit! Shit!" Susan was beside herself. "What now?" She seemed to regain her composure and was coming to grips with the overwhelming if not harrowing news.

Jim Lomegistro responded, "Nothing, you sit and wait and do your time. I've got this. I have my law firm working on this. The Governor is waiting to exonerate you, as he is already aware of this information. He personally asked me to get a handwriting analysis. The Governor already knows in his heart it's you Susan, from the autograph you gave him after your show. But because you signed Chatham and not McCraven, well that's why I am here today."

Susan looked up at the ceiling and prayed aloud, "thank you God. Thank you." Susan walked right over to James Lomegistro and gave him her biggest bear hug. Mike Ramsey looked at Susan and said, "Go pack anything you need. You are leaving here right now for another week's furlough with Frank. This news must be overwhelming. Take the week to chill. Then you'll come back here and we will figure out how to keep you safe until the exoneration paperwork goes through and we can set you free once and for all."

With that Susan lit up. She went over to Warden Ramsey and planted a huge kiss, right on his lips and right in front of Frank.

CHAPTER 29
REFUGE

Sometimes we need someone to simply be there.
Not to fix anything, or to do anything in particular, but
just to let us feel that we are cared for and supported.
~ SteveMaraboli.com ~

"Franklin, let me say goodbye to Bert. I must tell her this news."

"No Sush, we need to get the hell out of here. Right now, let's go."

Susan was packing up her stuff, because during her prior furloughs her things suspiciously disappeared. Everything unattended walks.

"If anything is gone I'll replace it for you. Please Susan this is all crap!" Susan flashed him a condescending look. These were all of her belongings now. How dare he call "her life" replaceable crap?

In the car, she sat quietly, filled with conflicting emotions and a tad moody. As they neared "Janney's" she blurted out, "Franklin, I'm really hungry. Can we stop at Janney's again?"

"I was just going to suggest that my love."

They pulled up to Janney's and went inside.

"SURPRISE!" She turned toward the voices and came face to face with Roberta and Paul.

"What? How?" Susan was stunned and excited at the same time.

"Bert is on furlough with Paul. We are all staying together. It will be easier for the Warden to monitor. I wanted to surprise you. Close your mouth Susan, you'll swallow a fly," teased Frank.

The four friends enjoyed their burgers, and shakes, shared onion rings, fries and spirited conversation.

Frank told Paul and Bert all about what transpired in the Warden's office and about the handwriting analysis, about the bank security videos, about what his brother Jimmie had been able to research and learn about Susan's trial, her innocence, the Governor's involvement in her case. As he was speaking, Susan sat munching on her fries, remembering earlier days spent at "Janney's" carefree, staring at these new friends. One, a prison guard equally at ease driving her home when she's drunk or sneaking her "contraband" yogurts in prison. The other, her current best friend, her cellmate, who taught her everything she knew about how to survive in prison. And finally the third, her prison physician and lover, who looked out for her, provided the best orgasms, and had his brother figure out how to set her free. She heard Franklin telling "her" story, as if she were listening to a heroine in a romance novel.

Paul and Bert stared in disbelief at what they learned about Susan. The group also seemed dumbfounded at how she was just sitting there eating her lunch as if nothing ever happened. They couldn't know that she was lost in her own thoughts. Lost in her own disbelief. Bewildered.

After lunch, Paul picked up the tab. He thanked Frank for letting them all stay at his place for furlough. They left and drove back to Frank's beach apartment.

Frank had moved all of Susan's things into his bedroom. The guest room had been set up for Bert and Paul complete with red candles, and an iPod loaded up with Latin romantic music. It was just as Bert would have wanted. The two couples separated for some mutually desired afternoon delight.

CHAPTER 30
AFTERNOON DELIGHT

Remember, no storm lasts forever.
Hold on. Be brave. Have faith. Every storm is
temporary and we're never alone.
~ QuotesGate.com~

Frank had noticed a change in Susan for some time. He understood the stress she had been under with prison, rehearsals, the one woman show, the recent overwhelming news. He couldn't understand though what it had to do with him. Hadn't he always been there for her? Had she been burned so many times that she now felt that all men were trash? He felt it was now or never to win her back. He was in love with her, but had he told her, really shown her?

Frank helped her put away the things she brought over from Lynchfield, even though deep inside, he really did feel that it was all crap and he would have preferred to take her shopping again to purchase new things. She deserved better. He kept his feelings to himself and asked her to sit on his bed with him.

"What's wrong Sweet Pea? What would you like to do? I know what I would love to do. I would like nothing better than to make love to you, right here, right now. But, I get the feeling that . . . " Frank didn't know how to finish his sentence.

Susan looked at Franklin. She didn't know what to say, or how she felt. Her state of mind was biased by thoughts of betrayal by her body double, and her ex-husband. She was still stunned over the news about Allison and Dale. Susan thought Dilly and she had it all. She thought they were in love and had the perfect marriage. She thought they had trust. Now she questioned her feelings and understanding about Daleth Scott McCraven. This doubt spilled over onto her new lover, Franklin Lomegistro. Could she be wrong about Franklin? Maybe she was a fool to trust men. Would, could, or should she trust Dr. Lomegistro? She felt a new unfounded apprehension about Franklin. What did he really want from her? Was she just HIS new sex toy? If prison freed her early, where would she go? How would she rebuild? If she didn't get her money back from Dale, she was broke. She had lost her career. What would she do? She wanted to hide and cry, not have sex, not now. Still she was happy about being let out of Lynchfield again. It was so great to have Bert here too. She thought about how she had such a great time with Franklin before. This refuge was her sanctuary. She made up her mind right then that she would try to release her fears and make an effort to enjoy her furlough.

Susan turned on the music, slowly she began to dance provocatively and began her impromptu plan to seduce Frank. She turned with her back to him and undid her top. She peeled it off and let it fall to the floor. Then she turned to face him and slowly unfastened her bra, freeing her breasts and throwing her bra at him. He caught it with one hand, staring at her tits while he tossed it behind him. She reached down and pulled off his trousers so he was sitting on the bed in just his boxers, shirt and tie. She then loosened his tie and tied it around her neck instead. Then she removed his boxers. She lowered her own pants and turning away from him shimmied out of them so he could have a good view of her tight ass still wearing her panties. She spun around and swooped her panties off so that she was facing him now, continuing her erotic dance, swaying her pelvis and hips. Susan danced enticingly naked wearing only his tie, Franklin with his shirt and socks on but otherwise still naked from the waist down sitting on his bed.

Susan straddled him and commenced with a lap dance. His cock was growing hard. She continued her assault, rubbing against him with her thighs, her buttocks, the lips between her legs, her clit. Her increasing wetness caressed him almost to the brink. He reached down past her to get out a foil packet out of his trousers. She allowed him to get it but then just as quickly grabbed it out of his hand, and shocking him, discarded it. Unabated, she rubbed her now quite wet and sticky self around and around his growing erection. Frank could hold back no more, and exploded in ecstasy over the edge, yelling her name.

"Your turn," Frank cajoled.

But she wanted nothing from him at this moment, instead, Susan grabbed a night shirt and underpants from a drawer and hoped into the shower, leaving Franklin standing there, post orgasm, half naked, staring at the closed bathroom door and wondering . . . what the hell happened here?

Once in the privacy of the shower, Susan broke down in sobs until she could barely breathe. All of her emotions from that day, spilled out of every pore, being rinsed away by the streaming, steaming water. She watched the suds spinning down the drain. She imagined the videos, the bank deposit slip, that form, the one with her signature, Susan McCraven, all going down that drain too. She pictured Dale and Allison hand in hand sitting in a red Corvette, drowning, then spinning down that same drain. Only when she felt her pulse returning to her body, she searched to find her own pleasure spot, then rubbed herself quickly. Masturbating with her fingers, she ached to find her own release. Susan closed her eyes and held her breath and shuddered as she reached her own relief. She dried herself off and got dressed.

She padded out to the balcony, making sure to avoid Frank, and the others, and sat in her favorite chair overlooking the ocean. She allowed the sound of the ocean to enter her very soul. With exhaustion setting in, before she knew it, she was fast asleep.

CHAPTER 31
LATIN LOVE

There is a lot that is good in your life.
Don't take it for granted.
~ Joel Osteen ~

Paul Sterling beheld Roberta Jimenez and led her over to the bed. He lit the candles, red, just like Susan had shared with him about what Bert would like. He turned on the romantic Latin music.

"May I?" he asked softly and politely, waiting for her consent.

"In the Barrio, men I knew they didn't ask, only took," she said. "Chatty says you are a good man Paul."

"Chatty?" Paul questioned.

"Susan. It's hard for me to pronounce her last name with my accent."

"Oh, you mean, Chatham? You are so cute Bert and I love your sense of humor, your Latin accent, and your sexy dancing. When I saw you rehearsing for Susan's show, and got to know you better, I knew I wanted you Roberta. I've adored you for so long. Please, I so need you Bert. I want to have all of you." Paul confessed his feelings for her.

"Ok, what are you waiting for? Yes, touch me now, Gringo." Roberta responded in a matter of fact, yet sexy voice.

With that consent, Paul strode over to Roberta and began to undo her top. Her caramel colored, large breasts spilled out, her chocolate elevator button nipples already hard and erect. They succumbed to Paul's lips and caress. He kissed and suckled her nipples before he bussed her lips. While his hands delectably caressed those large tits, his smile happily betrayed his thoughts that there was a lot more than a handful to play with and to love. She meanwhile unbuttoned his shirt, unbuckled his belt, unzipped his trousers and opened his fly. His glorious manhood spilled out ready and willing. She broadly grinned and took the foil packet he was holding away from him and without using her hands, opened it just with her lips, tongue and teeth. He looked at her stunned. "Impressive!" his voice now deep and husky. She turned around, lowered her pants and panties in one swoop and bent down on all fours, revealing her large round voluptuous behind. She then lifted the lips between her legs up towards him and welcomed him deep into herself. He pounded in and out, in and out, thrusting with a fervor he didn't know he possessed. She met him all the way and felt his hammering in so deep, her belly and ass tightened around him, her mind lost in an ecstasy she hadn't felt in forever. Quickening their already rapid pace, they were now both gasping for air, their skin moist and tingling, their sex slick and pulsating, and it didn't take too much time before they too could be heard.

"Aye, aye, aye Papi!" she cried out.

"Agggh, damn good fuck girl!" Paul countered, his face red and his heart pounding.

They climaxed together to the tune of "Besame."

CHAPTER 32

GAMES PEOPLE PLAY

Change your thinking to what you
want and shout to the Universe:
LIFE IS SO EASY FOR ME!
LIFE IS SO GOOD TO ME!
LIFE IS WORKING OUT BRILLIANTLY
FOR ME EVERYDAY!
~ Sabine Hauser ~

The friends from Lynchfield all came over to Frank's apartment for their monthly game night. This month the guest list included two new participants: Mike Ramsey, Frank, Paul, Juan Carlos, Jackie, Sally, along with the two inmates on furlough - Chatham and Jimenez. The "jailbirds" offered to make dinner. Their "work detail."

Normally game night consisted of subs or ordering pizza. Tonight all would be treated to a plated dinner. Susan the gourmet cook had planned the menu. Roberta helped and took charge of making dessert.

Freedom had a way of bringing out the best in people. Freedom had restored Susan to her normal cheerful self. Frank earned Susan back after he treated her to another one of his famous massages. He gave her space and didn't pressure her for sex. Finally when she began to relax and seemed a bit more like her happy self, he followed up with a different kind of massage the next night. Frank gave Susan a clitoral massage that had Susan enjoying multiple orgasms until she begged that she couldn't take anymore. She tingled for hours afterwards and she was pretty much jelly in his hands after that.

Great sex always motivated Susan to go gourmet in the kitchen. Tonight Susan planned a menu of hearts of palm salad with fennel and jicama followed by Chateaubriand with crispy green beans in garlic sauce. Dessert was Roberta's flan with coco.

Susan and Bert had set the table quite formally. Frank and Paul had bought the wine and some flowers.

The friends arrived on time. Frank poured everyone a glass of wine. Usually it was beer and pop. Interesting that the inmates had raised the sophistication bar for the guards.

The meal, like Susan's one woman show was a triumph. They didn't know what anything in the salad was but found the salad delicious. Crunchy veggies, semi-sweet and sour vinaigrette. There were "oohs" and "ahhs". Then came the Chateaubriand. The meat was moist, with hints of savory spices and fresh black pepper. The beef melted in their mouths, and was simply delicious and wholly complemented the crispy green beans. Finally, dessert was served. Perfectly set egg custard swimming in a melted sugar caramel and dusted with fresh, unsweetened, grated coconut. Superb!

Frank made espressos and cappuccinos with his Tassimo. Susan offered up different liqueurs. After dinner the women cleared the table. Susan and Roberta insisted on cleaning up while the others reset the dining room for game night.

Paul commented, "Susan and Roberta are amazing cooks as you can see, or rather taste! I must have gained five pounds this week. Susan should have been a chef, she uses all these ingredients and creates gourmet flavors. Roberta has a simpler style, but her Latin influences make everything so tasty."

Paul continued, unable to contain himself. "We know Susan is innocent. Roberta did some stuff she shouldn't have. But given those same life experiences and choices, would we have fared better? Who can say or judge. The world assumes the guards are the "good guys" but we all know that isn't always the case. Look at that asshole dick!" Everyone knew he was talking about George Ferguson.

"The world also assumes the inmates are the "bad guys" or in Lynchfield, the "bad gals." And yes some are like the "bitch warriors" gang and they deserve to be incarcerated," said Mike Ramsey.

"But what about Susan Chatham and Roberta Jimenez?" asked Frank. "These women are attractive, book smart in Susan's case, street clever in Roberta's, both amusing, both sexy, both great cooks, good dancers. Susan has amazing talent. These are good women and neither deserves the raw deal she has received in life."

All agreed about Chatham and Jimenez. They were committed to showing Susan and Roberta a good time and truly treat them as friends and one of the gang. And they did.

After dinner, the friends played "Balderdash." Susan won with her intelligence and wit. No one even came in a close second. Bert just laughed at all the hilarious wacko answers that Susan came up with especially when the others thought that they were the correct ones. Then they played "Yamado." The object of the game was to draw and begin the saying, then the next person added to it and the third added to that. Juan Carlos was the funniest, and had the women in stitches.

Lastly they played the game "Dirty Minds." The dirtier your mind was, the worse your score. Everything was a double entendre. Paul won to Bert's amusement. She had begun to call him "Pablito" and he loved it.

At the end of the evening, Frank turned on his own Karaoke machine. He and Susan entertained their guests with romantic duets and everyone watched and listened to them, in awe of their talent and chemistry. Finally they enjoy a late night movie. Susan, exhausted, fell asleep on Frank's lap and he excused himself, scooping her up in his arms and carrying her to his bedroom.

Paul and Roberta let everyone out, and when the last guest had left, Roberta finished the last clean up.

"Great night. Fun. Good night." They all waved.

CHAPTER 33
PORNOGATE

Be fucking brave! Say how you feel.
Leave the job you hate. Find your passion.
Love with every ounce of your bones.
Stand up for what you believe in.
Don't settle and never apologize for who you are.
~ Unknown ~

The media coverage surrounding George Ferguson's trial had gone viral. A reporter who had gone to high school with Susan Chatham recognized her name, researched the case and began reporting on it. It quickly turned into a media frenzy. They ate it up. It was a truth is stranger than fiction scenario and everyone wanted to know every detail. Susan Chatham, all American girl from a good family, teen star, married Hollywood producer, commits crime and goes to prison, gets raped, sodomized, abused physically and mentally by a gorgeous guard, that anyone would want to bed, and now he's the one arrested. She called it rape and abuse. He called it consensual BDSM sex. He claimed it was something they were both into. It was fun between a dominant and his submissive. The video evidence set to appear in the courtroom was rumored to be so hot and racy, it would receive a XXX rating if shown in a theater. The abuse was said to be so chilling, it would put a Hollywood horror film to shame. Everything was just a rumor at this point, but the proceedings soon earned the moniker "Pornogate."

As Frank led Susan up the stairs to his brother's James Lomegistro's office, he could feel her palms were cold, damp, and shaky. He swallowed hard, knowing that the next few months would be a living hell, especially for Susan, who must go through all of this, including reliving her abuse through video testimony at trial, then waiting for the outcome. He would have to be strong for her. He would be the one who would need to be there to pick up the pieces both during and after. He was committed to Susan 100%, the good, the bad, and the ugly.

Lomegistro, Holmes, Pagan, and Bradley was one of the top law firms in the area and the reception salon and conference room left no doubt about this fact. The plush carpet was thickly padded in rich hunter green, the walls paneled in rich mahogany wood. The opulent chairs were soft leather and oversized, pulled up to a beautifully carved leg table that expanded into infinity, with a glass top protecting the rich wood overlays. On the granite topped credenza there were multiple coffee and tea selections as well as trays of finger sandwiches, fruit, veggie bites, and cheeses. But today, Susan had no appetite. Frank handed her a cup of her favorite Twinning's lemon ginger tea. But this time Susan realized she was moving up in the world, no Styrofoam, instead fine porcelain china and a saucer, with a gold plated teaspoon, and lavender honey to sweeten her tea. She graciously smiled accepting the hot cup.

Jim began. "Hello, Susan, good to see you again. Okay, are you ready? Here's the team of attorneys that I have put together on your behalf." He introduced each one and their qualifications, specialties, and what specifically they were responsible for in her case. "So our side is proposing that George Ferguson, without your consent, raped you, sodomized you, physically and mentally abused you while you were in solitary confinement at Lynchfield prison. It was all premeditated as he sabotaged the camera security system, and tried to cover up his actions by always carefully and meticulously positioning you back in the original location and calmly stepping out of the cell as if nothing had happened. We have the testimony of Guard Rich Surzman. We have the video footage of the original security cameras, and of the secondary ones that the Warden had installed. And hopefully we have your testimony, if you are willing to face him and take the stand. In addition to the issues with Ferguson, we have additional complaints against Lynchfield, for failure to keep you safe, keep you properly clothed, properly fed, provide proper bedding and monitor temperatures. As you requested the last time we spoke, we will make sure this is against the general prison system and not against Warden Michael Ramsey, nor any of the guards that directly guarded you and that you consider your friends, Dr. Franklin Lomegistro and the medical staff, Paul Sterling, Juan Carlos Gomez, Sally Icasa, Jackie Somners, nor the guard that helped call attention to your abuse in the Shoe. We will make sure they are excluded and that their jobs are protected with our lawsuit when we move forward."

He continued. "Here's what we anticipate their side to say in the defense. You consented to have sex and wanted to be with George Ferguson. They have your signature on the furlough consent form. They could say that consent continues even after your return to Lynchfield. They could say you liked it rough and that you asked for that. They could say it was a Sadist/Masochist relationship with George being the Dominant and you being the Submissive. They could say you were into and enjoyed kink. They could say your weight loss was your own doing . . . that you don't like the food at Lynchfield, and that you were on a hunger strike or even accuse you of being anorexic. Our team totally believes in you

Susan, mind you, but this is what the other side will both say and believe about how this went down. Are you prepared to face this, because once we go ahead, there is no turning back? The videos we are going to show will be very graphic. The media will have a field day, of that we can be assured. Have you seen the videos? We are prepared to show them to you today. You must be strong enough to be able to watch them without too much emotion and be brave enough to face the world, knowing that people you meet throughout your life will have seen this; your nakedness, your body being physically beaten, kicked, pushed, prodded, and fairly graphic images of you having vaginal, and anal intercourse with George Ferguson. Are you game Susan Chatham?"

With that speech he passed her a form and a black pen. "Sign here if it's a go."

Susan was breathing hard, and felt like the room had grown colder like the thermostat was turned to its lowest setting. The air felt suffocating, as if it has been sucked out of the room. She felt like she was in a vacuum flask. What was it with Jim Lomegistro passing her white scary looking forms to sign?

"Do you want to watch the videos again, Susan?"

Frank cut in, "Do you want to take some time to think this over, Sush?"

Susan glanced up from the form she had been staring at to make eye contact with both Lomegistros.

"No, that won't be necessary. I know what the videos will show. I lived it. I have nightmares about it almost every night. My time in both the Shoe and my fucking furlough fortnight with HIM! I won't let him get away with it. I won't let him hurt other women like he hurt me. He deserves what he is going to get." Her voice turned from fear, to anger, to strength as she spoke. Susan held the pen in her hand, swallowed hard, said a silent prayer in her head, and signed.

After they had left the office, Jim Lomegistro called Frank.

"Shit, Frankie, the Judge is having doubts about admitting the graphic video into the trial. If it's excluded, we are sunk! It isn't fair. She got screwed in her first trial with them excluding all of the video footage and if this Judge does it too, ugh, where is the justice in this life! But listen I'm on it, still fighting for this to be shown. Just let Susan know. This will drag out another couple of weeks while I fight for this. Okay. Give her a hug. I've got her back. Don't worry."

After several weeks, the trial was finally set to start. Just as predicted, the paparazzi were everywhere and now the media had begun to swarm like bees. Susan and Frank couldn't go anywhere. George Ferguson, out on bond, had been equally in the news, Mr. GQ, sexiest man alive! Susan was being made out to be the villain. How dare she complain about getting to have sex with this Adonis? It made Susan sick. Oh if they only knew. Will they feel the same way after this trial is over? Or will they then believe her and be on her side? Will she just bring more doom and gloom on herself with this? No turning back, Jim had clearly said. Thank God for Franklin. Thank God the Judge approved all videos, and was even allowing parts of the information of what happened during her furlough with Ferguson in. Jim Lomegistro had won the first battle. He was stoked with the results so far. Why didn't Susan feel the same enthusiasm?

Susan dressed smartly in a dark grey pin striped pencil skirt, white collared blouse, and grey vest. She had gray pumps on. Her hair pulled back in a ponytail but curled at the ends. Frank looked handsome in his dark navy suit, charcoal gray tie, crisp white shirt and black shoes. She took a deep breath, holding his hand trying not to crush his fingers as she did so, and stepped out of the limo to walk up the steps to the courthouse. The photographers were everywhere, running up, pushing microphones into her face. But, she and Franklin were now accustomed to this and they smiled politely without comment and walked briskly and confidently as if they were Moses and the Israelites walking through the parted Red Sea.

They walked up the steps that seemed endless, and into

the doorways to go through security and up into the courtroom.

Susan felt her heartbeat increasing. It would be a few more minutes and she would be entering the courtroom and seeing him again, George Ferguson. "He must be furious with me. I can't imagine the wrath he would lay on me." Frank tried to shield her from the paparazzi, the would-be spectators, the others walking by, a premature sighting of George Ferguson, or of his supporters. He stood close to Susan, and faced her with his back to the hallway. Soon Tommie and her dad, Richard Chatham arrived. They surrounded Susan. She felt like a heavyweight boxer, in "this" corner, surrounded by trainer and team. If only they would wipe her brow, and squirt water into her dry parched mouth as they would for the "champ."

This was just day one, and she couldn't imagine what weeks of this would feel like for her or what toll it will take. She had been reviewing questions and her testimony over and over again with Lomegistro and his team/her team by now. How well rehearsed would Ferguson be, she wondered?

She knew she was as prepared and ready as she would ever be. Oh how she prayed that it would go well. When time was called, she smiled and walked confidently into the courtroom.

"All rise, the honorable Judge Dallas Matthews presiding."

Susan thanked God for Judge Matthews in her mind. He allowed the videos. Yes, each and every one! Even videos recovered from the sabotaged ones. There was justice, Jim Lomegistro had assured Susan. Jim had been very happy to learn that Judge Dallas Matthews was presiding. He was a tough, no nonsense Judge, but always fair, Jim had said.

Susan knew she had a fair Judge, a great legal team, family that loved and supported her now, and a great boyfriend, her personal physician. How lucky can a girl get? And then she saw George Ferguson, looking handsome as ever. How could a daydream be such a nightmare?

Susan wasn't afraid of George right now. "You are going down, George." She truly believed that now, and she was willing to risk it all. Her pride, her humility, her life . . . knowing that the videos would show her naked, vulnerable, and afraid, having intercourse, giving him a blowjob, him ejaculating on her, him urinating on her, defecating on her, and all the other vile things he had done to her, and forced her to do to him. Her dad was there, her brother, and the whole world via the media would see and know that about Susan. Her stomach turned . . . her appetite left her . . . her insomnia returned . . . but she would not surrender her right to find her justice and to take George Ferguson down.

And that's how "Pornogate" began.

Her lawyer took charge from the opening statement.

"This man, George Ferguson, took his revenge on this inmate when she was in solitary confinement. Not because she had done anything wrong, but just because she didn't want to name who had stabbed her to protect herself, her cellmate, and her physician. She was not armed. She wasn't even clothed in Solitary. He was supposed to just look in on her, serve her a meal tray at mealtime, walk her for a shower or out to recess. That was it. That was his job duty assignment. Yes, she had consented to go with him on furlough, but she never gave consent for what took place in Solitary. He abused her on furlough, and after being suspended without pay, and being demoted in having his job duty changed to Solitary, Ferguson premeditated his revenge on her. This was his motivation, his hate for her and what she had done to his career. He sabotaged security cameras in the prison. Not just in her cell, but in all the cells in his section. He took advantage, he forced oral sex, intercourse, he physically beat, kicked, pushed, and he urinated and defecated, and did other vile things to Susan Chatham, the inmate in his care. He refused to feed her, and threatened her not to eat when the other guard, Rich Surzman, was on duty, and all these facts will come out in this trial. You will hear Officer Rich Surzman's testimony and you will see video footage that will prove that George Ferguson did all of this to Susan Jordyn Chatham, and is guilty of these charges, beyond a reasonable doubt."

The defense, as predicted, threw the book at Chatham and made George out to be as beautiful and innocent, as he appeared physically.

"This trial is an injustice to Mr. George Evan Ferguson, a long time guard at Lynchfield Prison who truly believes in the care and rehabilitation of incarcerated women. He even came up with the furlough program to promote hope and reward the well-behaved inmates who played by the rules. Susan Chatham gave her consent. In this trial you will see her signature, confirmed by the Warden, and handwriting analysis experts to be her own, wanting to go on furlough with George Ferguson. And if furlough with Ferguson was so bad, why would she have consented yet again to go on furlough with Franklin Lomegistro? Not once, but several times. She's even on furlough with him during this trial. Susan Chatham is a slut. She has sex wherever and with whomever. And she likes it rough, although she tries to play Ms. Innocent. Don't be fooled by her acting skills. She fell for Franklin Lomegistro and wanted George Ferguson out of the picture and that is her motive for these terrible and false accusations against our defendant. We trust that the facts will show this to be true and George Ferguson will be acquitted."

And so the trial commenced and resumed.

By lunchtime, Susan had a knot in her stomach that was growing like an aggressive cancer. She stared at the sandwich Franklin ordered for her. All conversed at the table, her legal team, her dad and brother, unaware of her feelings, all eating their delicious lunches, drinking soft drinks, confident that the trial was proceeding as expected.

Was she invisible and invincible? She thought not. Even this early on, she was beginning to be recognized and stared down by the public. If they stared any harder at her and her lunch, they would pull the nutrients out of her sandwich.

Franklin nudged her, "You haven't touched your sandwich Susan. Eat. We only have an hour." As if it were lunchtime at school. How could he be so nonchalant? Then angry with herself, and her inner Diva, for wanting to give up this early on, she scolded herself and took a bite of her sandwich.

As the days went by and the testimony proceeded, it became increasingly difficult for Susan to stay positive. Her team was fantastic, but so was George's, meeting blow for blow, heavy weight fight tied. George, arrogant as ever, sat proudly at his seat, glaring at Susan in a way that he knew would intimidate her, with a smirk that only she understood. It looked kind and gentle to the unsuspecting, but evil lurked behind it.

As Susan anticipated, her nightmares worsened, causing her terrible night terrors and insomnia, she began to look paler with dark circles developing under her eyes. Susan's appetite left and she began to lose weight. Frank got on her case, very angry about her eating habits.

"Are you crazy to lose weight now, Sush? You are giving HIS team, ammunition; to believe that you ARE responsible for your own weight loss, and NOT that HE starved you out! Don't you GET that?"

Yes, Susan got it, but how and what could she eat? Not at a time like this. She didn't feel hungry, and the knot in her stomach was all consuming. When she did eat, her stomach was so upset that everything gave her diarrhea. Frank pushed Boost shakes on her again. The same shakes she so loved while rehearsing for her show now made her want to throw up.

"Leave me alone Franklin," she yelled at him as she locked herself in the bathroom to sob, and have another "Poop" attack. Frank knew it would get rough, and it had.

Frank couldn't sleep either. He tried to sleep in the guest room some nights, but Susan's night terror screams awoke him even there. He tried to crawl back into bed with her, stroke her back gently, in his special way, kiss her cheek and cuddle with her. Susan just pushed him away. There was no way to comfort her. No way to feed her, no way to kiss her, no way to snuggle with her, no way to fuck her, no way to love her! Oh, but he did love her, and wanted to erase all of her pain away.

"I know this is so difficult, Sush. We knew this was coming. You can do it. You are stronger than this. He will go down! We must trust the legal system. This time around will be different Sush. Hang in there. Let me help you. Let me love you. Why won't you let me in? You aren't alone, Susan, please, Sweet Pea."

The trial finally reached the point when the videos were introduced. As suspected the media went wild, "Pornogate" began.

Judge Dallas Matthews gave a strict warning, like the disclaimers on television or in the movies.

"Members of the Jury, and any spectators in the courtroom, I must preface that the next phase of this trial will feature some video footage of the most graphic nature. I must caution you all to maintain proper decorum at all times. I have seen the images, and know them to be quite disturbing. I will be willing to call for more frequent recess breaks as necessary. I will not tolerate any emotional outbursts and request that if you cannot contain yourselves to please exit the courtroom quietly as to not disturb our process. Am I being very clear?"

What George Ferguson couldn't know, was that the security camera team was able to recover the original footage too, those video feeds that Ferguson assumed were lost that George trusted he sabotaged.

Mr. Mercurial appeared in all his handsome evil glory. His voice clearly recognizable on the video screen. Exhibit A.

"Hah! Look who we have here, if it isn't Sue Chatham joining me on furlough again, this time in the Shoe! Hey,

Chatham! Missed sucking my dick? You couldn't come up
with anything better than that you fell down some stairs? You
poor excuse for a bitch?"

And on that note, distinct and discernible on the screen
the physical, sexual, and mental attacks on a naked Susan
Chatham, in her Shoe cell by Guard George Ferguson
commenced on the courtroom screen.

As Susan always knew . . . it was never about the sex was
it? It was about violence, humiliation, aggression, revenge.
George was a psychopath who wanted to hurt her. She didn't
know the details, that in hurting her, he vicariously hurt his
mother. It was his revenge to free himself from his own
abuse . . . and end a little boy's Hell.

Susan sat in the courtroom, stunned. Where did they get
this footage, which she believed he had sabotaged? She felt
like she was having an out of body experience. She saw
herself as if that Susan was just a character role she was
playing, just another acting job. She couldn't really have lived
through that? Had she? Staring at the screen emotionless she
found it actually much easier to do than she previously
thought. But, she looked over at her dad and brother and
noticed that they were both crying. And she saw her pain in
the jurors' eyes too.

She looked over at George Ferguson, who for the first
time looked pained too. Pained because he knew he was
busted.

"Gotcha!" she screamed in her mind.

The Judge called for a recess. You could have heard a
pin drop as everyone exited the courtroom. It was a dramatic
scene.

Even the media was stunned. Graphic was too kind a
description, and like Susan said all along, the sex wasn't the
disturbing part, although there was little to the imagination
here, it was the physical abuse, it was George's voice when he
did speak, belittling her, condemning her, and her voice
shaky, hearing her cries, her sobs, her whimpers of
discomfort, her pleading for his mercy, which tugged at the

viewer's heart in ways no one could have or would have imagined. This was not about pornography. It was about violence of one human being against another. It was about inexcusable pain.

After the recess, Exhibit B was played. Just as strong, if not more so. The courtroom was aghast. Even members of the media were almost quiet and speechless.

Video two, Day one: George Ferguson enters Susan's cell, grabs her by her hair and throws her on her knees and he forces her to give him fellatio. He climaxes and comes all over her, then takes his cum and rubs it onto her body like sunscreen. He kicks her side and pushes her onto the floor. Her grunts are now audible. Spreading her legs wide, he takes his boot off and using the heel like a hammer, hits her between her legs in the sweet spot. Susan winces and screams out in pain but he uses his other hand to gag her mouth then quickly removes his sock and shoves it into her mouth. He flips her over. The thump of her body hitting the concrete floor echoes in the courtroom, and on the video he fucks her hard in her ass, no lubricant, nothing, he is seen forcing himself hard onto her, pinching her buttocks harshly in order to gain his entry into her, then he hits her again with the leather boot. Pulling the sock out of her mouth, he quickly dresses himself. He is overheard to say "You bitchy whore. Shut the fuck up, stop crying." Leaving Susan collapsed and whimpering on the floor, he pulls out his penis once more and urinates all over her. George tells her to sit up as if nothing happened, and makes sure she is positioned by the view the original security cameras would cover. And calmly walks out of the room.

Lunchtime that day was different. Susan sat quietly, still feeling like she was having an out of body experience. She noticed others that were there in that courtroom staring at her, but differently. Even media celebrities covering the trial, eating their lunch, looked on with varying expressions. What were they thinking? She herself thought she would be embarrassed. They had seen her naked, doing things that should be done only in private between a man and a woman who felt love, but what they had seen was harsh, rough and full of violence, and they had witnessed pain, and raw emotion . . . HIS ANGER, HER CRYING and COLLAPSE, and they had witnessed things that were simply REPULSIVE.

Susan was tired, and not very hungry, and Franklin agreed to just let her order a soup. She sipped at her soup, now emotionless. A part of her wished she could just shrink, and drown in that bowl of broth.

Upon returning from the courtroom that night, Frank offered to fix dinner. He made something light, seeing that she still wasn't very hungry and that she looked exhausted. After dinner, he gave her a light foot massage, and put her to bed, in his bed. He retired to the guest room himself.

That night, for the first time, in weeks, Susan actually slept well. No nightmares. Although seeing the video was so disturbing, she realized that they were a way for the truth to finally get out. Every graphic scene that showed the monstrous things that George did to her, scored points for her side of the equation. People would realize what she had said all along. She felt a glimpse of hope. She wasn't a slut. She was a victim. Well, maybe she was just a little bit of a slut. For the first time in weeks, she felt a little horny too. She went to where Franklin was sleeping in the guest room, climbed into bed with him, and began to seduce him.

"Whoa, hey," Frank smiled, "so 'Pornogate' videos make you horny?"

Susan just laughed and winked at him.

"I'm sorry, I have been so withdrawn."

"I get it, it's okay. You are entitled. You are one very brave and gutsy woman, Susan Chatham."

With that they made beautiful love and certainly not of the 'Pornogate' flavor. They both exploded and climaxed in each other with pleasure.

The next day in the courtroom it seemed the tides were turning. The evidence on those tapes was overwhelming and persuasive. The old adage that "seeing is believing" held true.

Susan appeared more lighthearted and peaceful, happier. George appeared more concerned, more troubled, more stressed, especially when the day's video started.

Exhibit C

Video Three Day Two: George Ferguson enters Susan's cell, pulls her by her hair and throws her on her knees and again makes her give him fellatio. This time he ejaculates in her face. He is seen grabbing his organ as he pushes her down on her back, and forces her to swallow his urine as he relieves himself in her mouth. He slaps her as she protests, and tears are seen to be running down her face. His face is harsh, red, and angry. He stands her up, yanking hard on her arms, she winces and then he assaults her, forcing intercourse on her upright. Her face confirms that there is a fine line between pleasure and pain, and hers is the face of pain devoid of pleasure. Then he pushes her down hard, and again her thump against the concrete of the cell echoes and shockingly he shoves her face in the toilet water, almost chipping her beautiful teeth, swelling her lip. The splash is heard and then a gurgling noise, and her gasping as she struggles to breathe.

Someone in the courtroom, actually one of the media reporters gasped themselves, and blurted out, "She can't breathe, he's drowning her."

Judge Dallas Matthews had to call a halt, and asked this individual to leave the courtroom immediately. He requested that the remark be stricken from the record, and cautioned the Jury to ignore it. Susan and George both looked intently. They both knew the memory of this wasn't likely to be ignored, and they both realized what that could mean. Then the video resumed.

On the video, they replayed that same dramatic and disturbing scene . . . he fucks her standing up, then pushes her down, again her thump against the concrete of the cell is heard and he shoves her face in the toilet water. The splash, a gurgling noise, her gasping. He then wipes her face with the back of his shirt, and makes her sit up as if nothing happened, and makes sure she is positioned by the view the original security cameras would cover. And he tucks his shirt back in to hide the wetness, and he glares at her as if his look could kill her, and walks out of the room.

The courtroom was silent after the video ended. Susan quickly wiped a tear out of her eye, and rubbed her nose hoping no one had seen. George looked down, ever so briefly. His mouth appeared dry.

The trial day concluded and the Judge called a recess until the next morning.

George Ferguson went into a meeting with his legal counsel. His attorney was livid, "George, this isn't looking good. You had her drink urine? How are we going to put this into a dominant submissive theme? Did you make a contract with her? Did you have any safe words? There isn't any mention of any of it either in evidence nor seen in the videos shown thus far. You shoved her rather hard. Her face clearly doesn't appear like she wants to have intercourse with you, George. Why would you stick her face in the toilet? For what purpose? What do you want us to say?"

George looked at them with venom. "Fuck you! You are the legal team and you want me to give you the answers. Fuck you. Fuck you all, I pay you enough money. Get that bitch! She had it coming. She hurt me."

"How? How did she hurt you? Damn it George, not one video shows her doing anything to you other than what you are seen forcing her to do to you."

George screamed, "She hurt me when I was a boy, she

pushed me, she pinched me, she pulled my hair, she said no one would love me, she told me I was no good. Everything I did was never good enough for her. Not my grades, not how I danced, or how I looked, how I smelled, or how I cleaned, or how I cooked!"

"Snap out of it! Susan Chatham did and said that to you?"

"Yes, Susan Chatham, my mother."

"But, she's not your mother George. Does Susan look like your mom, George?"

"Yes, and she turned me down at Lynchfield. No one turns me down. No one! Not that fucking whore, that College Snot! Sanctimonious cunt! Get her."

The attorneys fell silent and shook their heads. They dismissed George and tried to figure out what they could do. They needed serious damage control for their sick bastard client.

The next day's scheduled video was the most repugnant.

Susan skipped breakfast that morning. Frank was appalled.

Susan was livid. She realized what would be shown on today's video in the courtroom and she was afraid of her own reaction.

"Ferguson is going to use me like I'm his fucking toilet, and you want me to eat? If I eat and I watch him do that, I will puke in the courtroom Franklin. Is that what you want? It isn't enough for everyone there to watch me soiling myself on video, you want me messing myself in real time, in real life in the courtroom?"

Frank was shocked by her reaction, but saw her point.

He felt helpless. He made her a cup of tea. Susan's nerves got the best of her. She picked up the teacup and hurled it at the sink where it shattered into a thousand pieces. She began to cry, "I'm sorry Franklin. I just can't."

He ran over to her. "Leave it, I'll get it later. Stop! You

will cut yourself. You are too upset to do that now."

Susan wiped at her tears, "I don't know how much more I can take. To sit there and appear calm, I should get an Academy Award for my acting skills, Franklin. That was the worst day of my life. He's so disgusting. Who does that? He's an animal! Maybe we shouldn't show it."

"Is that what you really want Susan? Do you want to stop this now, when we are so close? Think of your reaction to how GROSS Ferguson is, and that yes he is an animal."

"Don't you think the Jury may have the same exact reaction?"

"Yes," she said.

"And when the Jury learns Ferguson is a disgusting animal, and they realize he IS a monster, they will be more likely to empathize with your side, and convict him Susan."

"I must go through with this now Franklin, I have no choice, just like I had no choice on that day." Susan looked down as if she wanted the ground to swallow her up.

"No Susan, we all have choices. You could have fought back, but an inmate attacking a guard would have brought you more time. You did the right thing. You did nothing then but are fighting back now via the proper channels. You are protecting yourself and helping other women, so that this jerk, this monster, doesn't hurt anyone else again. You will see. The Jury will convict him. The truth will set you free, my love."

And with that he grabbed her purse and held it out to her, grabbing his own jacket and motioning toward the door.

Exhibit D

Video Four, Day Three: George Ferguson enters Susan's cell, grabs her by her hair, and throws her on her knees against the bare concrete. She is swollen and covered in black and blues and scrapes. His erect organ is seen being forced into her mouth as he uses his hands to pry her jaw open. He holds her nose closed with his fingers, so she can't breathe and has no option but to swallow all his cum. The downward frown of her lips makes it very clear on video that this is not something that she wanted to do nor something that she enjoys. She gasps for air as he shoves her down and throws her on her back. He is seen using his strong muscular arms to pin her down below him. You can count all her ribs as she lays down giving proof to how thin she has become by now. He takes his guard's baton stick and uses it as a dildo to masturbate her hard, and her whimpers and grimaces are heard, and it is very obvious to all in the courtroom that this is not a gentle use of a "sex toy" but battery of a woman's private area in a way that is causing pain. He commands her to get on all fours (hands and knees) and sodomizes her with the same baton. No lubricant is used. This isn't an anal sex toy. He rams her with that big stick and pulls it in and out, relentless in his assault until her blood drips. Rising, he kicks her lower back, leaving his boot imprint on her delicate skin. Screaming out she falls onto the floor. Ferguson stares at her for a minute, then tugs his pants down, squats over her, defecates on her and forces her to use her own hands to rub his feces over herself.

The Judge takes stock of Ferguson, who was gazing straight ahead in disbelief. Then he scans Chatham. She was sitting straight up in her seat, her face pale, and a tear in her left eye. Only one.

He admired her strength and decided not to stop the trial or interrupt this intense scene.

Back on the video: Prison guards are seen entering and arresting Ferguson, and others are seen lifting a very pained and weak Susan Chatham up and the Warden is seen covering her with a blanket, and giving orders to get her cleaned up, fed, and medical attention. Warden Ramsey is overheard to say, "Susan Chatham your solitary confinement is over."

Susan Chatham took the stand. She was wearing her grey pin stripe suit again, the one with the pencil skirt and vest and white blouse. Her hair was loose but with the center pulled back in a Swarovski crystal barrette. Her hands manicured in a French traditional style. She looked at the courtroom spectators and the Jury who looked so different from the witness stand. She glared at George Ferguson. She wanted to spit in his face, kick him where it hurt him most. Instead, she just stared him down blankly and concentrated on what Jim Lomegistro had instructed her to do.

"Susan Jordyn Chatham, do you swear to tell the truth, the whole truth and nothing but the truth, so help you God."

"Yes."

"Remember that you are under oath."

"Yes."

"Did you sign this Furlough agreement?"

"Yes."

"Did you consent to having sex with George Ferguson on Furlough?"

"Yes."

"Were you in the Shoe at Lynchfield with a Guard named George Ferguson?"

"Yes."

"Did you consent to having sex with George Ferguson in the Shoe?"

"No."

"Did George Ferguson make you perform fellatio on him?"

"Yes."

"Did you want to?"

"No."

"Were you and George Ferguson in a Dominant/ Submissive relationship?"

"No."

"Did George Ferguson offer you a contract? Did you negotiate the terms? Did you have any safe words?"

"No. No. No."

"Did George Ferguson ever hurt you, humiliate you, or do anything against your will?"

"Yes."

"What did George Ferguson do? Remember that you are under oath."

"He forced me to have oral sex with him, and intercourse, and anal sex. He hit, pushed and kicked me. He withdrew food from me. He threatened me not to eat from the other guards too. He forced me to swallow his semen and his urine. He urinated on me and defecated on me and forced me to rub my body with his excrement. He held my head, uh, my face under water in the toilet. I couldn't breathe, no, yes I was hungry, yes it hurt, no I don't remember, I passed out. Yes, I was bleeding. No, I didn't hurt myself. No I wasn't on a hunger strike. Yes, I saw him interfering with the security cameras. No I didn't tell anyone. Why? He threatened me. He threatened my friend Roberta. He threatened my boyfriend Franklin, and he threatened the Warden."

Susan was matter of fact as she had been instructed by her legal team to be.

At home she would sob, and shake and scream. But in the courtroom she was quiet and still and put together, although every so often a crack in her voice, or a tear in her eye, gave her feelings away. Twice the Judge called a recess so Susan could compose herself.

Once he called her into his chambers himself.

"Susan Chatham, are you all right?"

Susan nodded, "Yes, sir Judge Matthews."

"This is hard, hard for everyone, the Jury, Ferguson, you, me."

"If you can't proceed, then that is an option for you. I want to make sure you understand that. You don't have to take the stand anymore, we can pull the rest of the videos."

"No, no, I'm fine, really I am." Susan wiped her sniffles with a tissue he handed her and stood up tall, trying to smile. She knew she had gone too far to have this not go her way now.

She had to be steadfast, show her perseverance and be resilient.

"Thank you for the recess and for speaking with me Judge Matthews. Much appreciated, but I am fine and want to continue."

"Okay then Ms. Chatham. Keep it together."

George Ferguson testified.

"George Evan Ferguson, Do you swear to tell the truth, the whole truth and nothing but the truth, so help you God."

"Yes."

"Remember that you are under oath."

"Yes."

"Did you sign this furlough agreement?"

"Yes."

"Did Susan Chatham sign this furlough agreement?"

"Yes."

"Did you consent to having sex with Susan Chatham, and did she consent to have sex with you on furlough?"

"Yes."

"Were you on duty in the Shoe at Lynchfield when an inmate named Susan Chatham was admitted?"

"Yes."

"Did inmate Chatham consent to having sex with you George Ferguson in the Shoe?"

"Well, I thought I already had her consent, you know she signed the furlough form."

"Did Ms. Chatham perform fellatio on you?"

"Yes."

"Did she want to?"

"No. But, yes, she really did, you know how women can be."

"Were you and Susan Chatham in a Dominant/Submissive relationship?"

"Yes, she's the biggest fucking liar, it's just her way, a game she likes to play. She's an actress you know. Never know when they are acting."

Judge Dallas Matthews cautioned him.

"Please, just a yes and no answer Mr. Ferguson. I don't want to have to caution you again."

"Did you ever hurt, humiliate, or do anything against Susan Chatham's will?"

"Yes. Um, no, no. She was cool. We had an understanding. Susan, tell them." He stood up and looked at her.

Judge Matthews intervened again. This time he addressed Ferguson's legal team.

"Mr. Dupree, please control your client. I will not have these outbursts in my courtroom."

"What did you do? Remember that you are under oath."

"Susan and I had an understanding. We had a Dominant/Submissive relationship. We had agreed to be rough, to kinky sex. We were both into that bodily function shit. You know . . . Urolagnia,Coprophilia etc. She liked it. See she rubs it on herself. She wanted to. No, I didn't starve her. She wanted to lose weight. She's anorexic. Did you see her? She even lost weight here. She's a slut, goes from one man to another. Even took her clothes off in front of the Governor with the excuse of putting on a show."

"Objection your honor," Jim Lomegistro called out after each and every one of George Ferguson's accusations.

"Mr. Ferguson, please." Judge Dallas Matthews responded.

The Judge called another emergency recess. He was compelled to address the jurors. The Jury members were distraught. Between the videos, and the testimony, most were overwhelmed. Many were also tearing up. One had asked to be excused, and sought psychological counseling and treatment. One of the alternates had to be called in to service. Everyone understood the Judge's initial orders but no one could have comprehended the graphic nature or how abhorrent the video footage was and no one could have predicted how they would be touched, by this beautiful, well spoken, gentle appearing young woman who had testified in such a calm, quiet, reserved voice, and the confident handsome looking guard, who so convincingly told them of their consensual but unconventional and certainly unpalatable relationship. How could they? How could he do those things to her? She didn't appear to want or like it. How could he? How could she? It was all so emotional and so overwhelming. And they were just witnessing the video footage . . . but these two people sitting at courtroom tables with their legal teams, they lived through this. Horrific!

Finally came the photos. Close up and graphic, still pictures took the emotions out of it. They didn't leave much to the imagination. Rough fetish sex? Hardly.

Exhibit E
    Documentation photos from the Shoe taken after Susan Chatham was removed from Solitary confinement. The photos documented injuries to her arms, legs, back, ribs, vagina, buttocks and rectum. Semen samples, urine samples, and feces samples genetically linked to George Ferguson. Boot prints linked to George Ferguson's boots.

Exhibit F
    Documentation photos from Medical taken after Susan Chatham returned from Furlough with George Ferguson. Photos documenting burn injuries to her arm, foot steam burn, smashed, broken finger, black eye, swollen face, rib injuries, flogging injury to her back, burns to her mouth, anal area, miscellaneous contusions. Severe weight loss with dehydration.

Susan's father stood to exit the courtroom, unable to stand it anymore, unable to see his "baby girl" treated like that, abused like that, hurt like that. On his way out he collapsed. Medics were called. Frank ran over to him in the meantime to render any care he could. The Judge called for another recess. An ambulance came and they evaluated Richard Chatham. He was stabilized and fine, but sobbing hysterically. He wanted to see his daughter.

The Judge lent his office quarters to Chatham and Chatham.

Richard Chatham wept, "Susie, Sweet Pea, please forgive me honey. I am so very sorry. I should have been there. I am your father. I should have protected you. Instead I just gave up on you. When you were arrested, when you went to jail, I didn't want to believe that my baby girl was a bad girl. I couldn't accept that. I turned my back on you. Out of sight out of mind. I didn't have to deal with you, or your antics. I had no idea that prison could be like it is, or that stuff like that could have ever happened to you. And now I am powerless to help you. I sat there like a stranger, like all those other strangers in there watching you, watching that animal. Why did you go with him? Why did you not fight him? Why was I not there for you? But I get it, that in prison you just have to accept everything that happens. This trial, everyone seeing you like this. My God Susan, I can't take it. I don't know what to say to people when they ask me. I don't know what to say to you Susie. I don't know how to show you that I love you and I am so very sorry."

Susan had tears streaming down her face. She walked over to her dad, gave him a warm embrace and said, "You just did Daddy. You just did."

Finally the day of closing arguments arrived.

George's team began, "And Susan Chatham consented when she went on furlough with George Ferguson, and she went on furlough with Franklin Lomegistro, she's healthy, now, she wasn't permanently hurt. She wanted and liked rough sex. She had a Dominant/Submissive relationship with our client. She's an actress that can twist things to her advantage. She was the inmate, convicted of a crime in another trial. Our client is innocent, beyond a reasonable doubt. We ask that you move for an acquittal of all counts and charges. Thank you."

Susan's team gave the real version, "Susan Chatham is a victim here. She went on furlough with George Ferguson and came back abused, so much so as the photos have shown, that she ended up in Medical. Yes, she enjoys sex but not rough and did not consent to a Dominant/Submissive relationship, nor did she consent to Urolagnia and Coprophalia. She has never had that type of sexual relations with any of her other sexual partners. Yes she is an actress but that has nothing to do with any of this. Yes there was some nudity in her one-woman show but that had nothing to do with this trial either. Video footage clearly shows how George Ferguson spoke to her and how he treated her. Testimony from the other guard confirms her injuries. At first Ferguson's team tried to explain her injuries by stating she was abusing herself by throwing her body against the walls and metal sink and toilet, but there is no video showing that, no evidence, but then there is video showing him abusing her, and now with that footage they say she consented to and liked it rough. Which was it? Don't believe them. The video footage of their interactions in the Shoe and the photos from Medical of her don't lie. The Warden and security camera experts have testified and confirmed the cameras were sabotaged. Her injuries were well documented in her medical records too. Dr. Lomegistro wrote these records, before any relationship developed."

"George Ferguson physically, sexually, and emotionally abused inmate Susan Chatham. He did so when taking her on furlough and continued further when he guarded her in solitary confinement. The testimony, video footage, and photos all document this beyond a reasonable doubt. Susan Chatham was raped, sodomized, abused physically and mentally by George Ferguson, who is a handsome, but psychopathic sadist who feels it is his duty to punish the women of Lynchfield. Mr. Ferguson sabotaged the security cameras in the "Shoe" to cover his tracks, but the Warden suspicious of injuries on Ms. Chatham's body when the security tapes do not show Susan Chatham injuring herself, caused him to install additional secret cameras. These cameras clearly show George Ferguson in the act of attacking Susan Chatham repeatedly. We ask that you move for a Guilty verdict for all counts. Thank you."

That night was a tranquil evening. Frank and Susan shared a quiet dinner. They decided to stop at the market on their way home and picked up something to grill together. They selected some rib eye steaks, fresh greens and arugula for a salad, and a bottle of Merlot wine.

Susan seasoned the steaks and fixed the salad. Frank gathered together a basket and they headed downstairs to the BBQ grills in the building.

Frank poured two glasses of wine and began to grill. Susan came up behind him and hugged his waist as he cooked. Neither one of them said too much. Both felt like the trial had said more than either of them could say and both were exhausted, physically and emotionally spent.

Frank had kept his feelings in, not wanting to upset her further, but he was deeply affected by the proceedings. Seeing the woman he loved in those videos, and photographs, seeing her abused repeatedly and remembering what it was like caring for her injuries, her pain and suffering, his rage at George Ferguson, his jealousy at seeing her having sex with George, or giving George oral sex, even though he knew it was forced. All of this was too much to bear. Then there was her moodiness at home, her erratic eating and sleeping habits, and her night terrors with her shrieks to wake them both from any slumber, and her pushing him away one minute and coming on to him the next. Who was being mercurial now?

Wasn't that the word she liked to use to describe George? All he could think about now was cook the damn steaks, eat, then bed.

"What's wrong Franklin? You seem very strange?" She poured him a second glass of wine, and another for herself.

"Everything Susan really, everything. I don't want to talk about it. I don't know what to say."

"Look we both knew it would be a rough road, and it certainly has been. We have both had to elevate our game. There was so much for us to have to remember, to take in, and to withstand. Now we wait and see, Franklin, there is nothing more for us to do."

"Oh but Susan there is a lot for us to do, how do we repair what we had? I mean separate beds now, we hardly eat or bathe together, and sex is erratic at best. What do you want Susan? Do you want me? Will you go back to Dale? Has he asked for you? I heard he had. Will you move back home now that you and your dad have reconciled? You won't need me Susan."

"How can you say these things Franklin? What do you mean? You can't. You don't feel like this, do you? We are both just exhausted and consumed. We don't mean this Franklin we don't, we can't!"

They sat down, breathing in the fresh, salty ocean air, and ate their medium rare Montreal seasoned steaks and their greens salads with her sweet and sour vinaigrette dressing, and finished their wine.

Somehow the repetitive sound of the ocean surf soothed their souls as they dined quietly and soon they were more relaxed, their heartbeats in sync with the ocean.

"Let's take a walk on the beach, Sweet Pea. We haven't done that in ages."

They walked hand in hand in silence until the sun went down and then they made their way back by the moonlight. Reaching the dunes, Frank bent down and kissed her.

"I'm sorry Susan. Truly I am. You have been through so much and it isn't fair for me to dump on you further."

"I'm sorry too Franklin. You have been there for me through all of it, and more than supportive. If it weren't for your brother, I would never have gotten this chance for justice. I have been taking my frustrations out on you and that wasn't fair for me to do that to you. Please forgive me, Franklin. I love you."

"I love you too Susan."

"I really don't want to live anywhere else, or be with anyone other than you my love."

Suddenly, the dunes become an inviting love shack. Frank lifted her face up to his and began to kiss her. She nibbled back at his lips. She tasted of red wine and of Susan. He pulled off her sundress, and unfastened her bra from behind and removed her panties. She unbuttoned his shirt and unzipped his shorts, smiling as his long and thick length spilled out. They lay down on the sand, lips locked, his hands now enjoying the feel of her breasts, teasing her nipples into submission. She squeezed his tight strong ass, and reached around his thighs, searching for what she wanted. She found and felt his hardness, her treasure, and began to rub herself around his now hard thick cock.

"You feel so wet, ah, that feels so good Sweet Pea." She just hummed, happily. They rolled in the sand and Susan was now on top and began to ride Frank. She rode him up and down slowly at first and then began to pick up her pace. Frank arched his back to meet her, pushing deeper. Her throaty moans between her gasps for breath were such a turn on. She felt so wet, and tight, and she was riding him fast and taking all of him deep inside of her. Nirvana. She leaned forward and intertwined her warm wet tongue, deep inside of his mouth and they kissed passionately, and when she resumed riding him, Frank thought she would blow his mind. They had felt each other's pain and now felt each other's ecstasy.

"Oh God, Oh God, Sush!"

"I am going to cum. Oh My God Franklin!"

They released into the night, like confetti shooting

towards the stars.

She lay warm and moist, on top of him, her belly quivering, he held her tight against his chest, kissing her neck and then her lips. She grinned.

"You find my love making funny, Ms. Chatham?"

"That was amazing Franklin." She thanked him with another kiss.

Now sated, they returned upstairs, taking the dishes and the cooking supplies, and the empty wine bottle up for recycling. They decided to shower together before hitting the sack.

"I even have sand up my butt, Franklin."

"Well I have sand up my balls, Sush."

They both laughed, deciding that next time they have sex on the beach they would bring a blanket. They continued their lovemaking in the shower, and climaxed together one more time in the bed.

"Three times the charm Chatham."

"I suppose Dr. Lomegistro."

Making up for lost time, satiated and spent, they fell into the abyss of a deep contented sleep.

The next morning, Susan felt the stress of the trial had been lifted off her. The Jury was deliberating, but she felt a freedom she hadn't felt since before she went to prison. She felt reborn.

Franklin woke up first, and snuggled next to her. She felt warm, and soft, and so inviting. He kissed the back of her neck as she slept. Repeating his approach, ever so gently. He planted tiny kisses up and down her back. She rolled around, opened her eyes and batted her long eyelashes.

"That tickles," she giggled.

She cuddled back at him and said with a twinkle in her eyes, "Do you want to play with me Franklin?"

"What?" Frank responded, confused. "I thought you told me once you don't play games, Ms. Chatham."

"No, well yes, I said I don't play games, but I like to play. I ordered some things on line, play with me?"

Frank didn't know what to say. He trusted her for sure. But let's play? It was so cryptic. He hadn't a clue what she meant but knew he was about to find out.

Susan got out of bed and fetched a draw string satin bag out of the bottom drawer. And she took out a bunch of colored "toys."

"Holy shit, Sush, you bought kinky sex toys?"

"They are adult toys, Franklin. Grow up."

"Maybe George was right about you, you like it rough and kinky?"

She gave him a "play" pretend slap and got up and left the bedroom. Frank stayed in bed studying her quirky collection, wondering what the fuck she had in mind.

She returned with a cup of hot tea!

"Okay, now you really have me stumped. First I thought you wanted to have sex again, not like we didn't do it enough last night. Then I thought you wanted to play. Now you are going to drink a cup of tea?"

"No, Franklin, we are going to do all three, sort of . . . "

She handed him a bottle of lubricant and a pink looking rubbery thing. "That's a butt plug. Spread the lube on it."

"It smells like cherry," Frank commented.

"Taste it Franklin."

"It tastes like cherry too with just a hint of sweetness."

"It's my favorite, I hope you like it too, there did you spread it on the pink, silicone, butt plug."

"Yes." Frank's breath caught in his throat, as she took off her pajama pants and panties, still in her pajama top, and turned around with her cute ass facing him.

"Put it in my butt. Don't look so surprised Franklin, it feels good, it's not a stick, and you aren't going to hurt me with it." She knew Frank had images of George with that baton, hurting her.

Susan asked him to lie down and pulled down his pajama pants snickering to herself at his absence of underwear. He still had his pajama top on, and she leaned over and just unbuttoned the buttons.

Frank smiled broadly very curious as she leaned over and took a sip of her tea, and it appeared like she drank some. While she held the hot tea in her mouth, not swallowing, she poured just a little of the cherry lube in her hand and began to stroke his now semi hard organ and scrotum with it. She used her hand and her fingers delicately, moving them round and round, and it wasn't very long before any traces of cool limpness disappeared, replaced by hardness, erectness and warmth. Taking another sip of the tea and holding it for less time, this time, again in her mouth, she swallowed quickly and took his hard cock into her mouth.

"Oh my God. That feels so good. Oh, God, Oh God. Oh my God Sush!"

"You have a fine-looking cock, the most handsome I have ever seen. You taste so good too. Of cherry and my favorite Doctor." She winked at him.

"Well you can drink tea, every time we have sex if you want to Sush."

Then she stopped briefly just to take another hot sip and turned to straddle him from the other side. Her hot tea warmed mouth fucking his cock as her ass with the pink plug now faced his eyes. Her slit was dripping wet. The sight of her was all encompassing. Frank ogled her bobbing up and down as she sucked hard and fast on his dick.

Frank tried to last, to hold out, but her "sensual assault" was too much, the warmth he felt and the way she moved her tongue and lips. Her smooth teeth nibbled in a light teasing dance and her hollowed cheeks sucked until he throbbed. Even though his eyes now closed in pleasure, the thought of her having that butt plug in that cute naked little ass of hers. It was overpowering. His fighting his urge to spill his cum was hopeless and he came quickly and powerfully, surprised at how much energy he still had and how much juice he still had left to squirt. "You will do me in woman!"

She smiled at him quite naughtily. She waited as his

quivering waves subsided. Only when he was fulfilled did she instruct him on how to use the toys on her.

"I guess you can teach an old dog new tricks," thought Frank.

She handed him a silver bullet, an egg looking thing and had him cover it with a rubbery cover that had fingered tentacles on it so that it resembled a jellyfish. "Put lubricant on that," she motioned.

It had an attached cord connected to a remote control.

She instructed him to insert it into her and turn it on.

"This is a bullet vibrator Franklin. It feels real good, trust me."

"I do trust you Susan, really I do. It's just that this is all new to me."

"You never experimented with toys?"

"No, not really, I thought maybe they were dirty or too rough." Frank looked a bit embarrassed.

"Do you think that now?"

"No, not really, they are fine, I'm very curious, they are turning me on, and I see they turn you on."

"I like them Franklin, sometimes, not all the time. Sometimes I can use them on you."

"I am not interested in any anal play Sush. The thought of that grosses me out."

"That's fine, I like it for me but we won't use that on you. But, like if I held this vibrator especially with the jelly silicone cover on it lightly on your balls while I sucked on you, your orgasm would be so much more intense. I almost did that today but I thought you had enough new stuff to get use to."

"Oh My God Susan, where did you come from?"

"From Lynchfield!"

Frank laughed at her, "okay, enough tutoring, let's use this stuff on you, before you decide you don't want to play anymore."

"Oh, I always want to play, especially with you Franklin."

With that she had him use one type of vibrator on her

273

clit, while the bullet was inside of her and the butt plug was in, and when she came, her quivering went on and on for what seemed like forever. She was so wet of lubricant, of his cum, of her own stimulation. As she came she motioned to Franklin to turn the vibrators off quickly. "When I come like this, it's just way too intense for me, I need you to turn the vibrators off, as soon as you see me come okay."

"That was quite a sex education, Ms.Chatham." She ran to the bathroom and he heard her cleaning the toys. She came back and snuggled back close to him. He felt her body still warm from the sex, and still quivering.

"My God are you still having an orgasm? Why get up and clean the toys like that? Why not just lie here and enjoy the moment?"

"I don't know Franklin, I just always like to clean them right away, and this is still very nice for me, lying here with you. I had a great time, a really great time."

He loved to cuddle with her. He felt his warm still semi hard cock leaning against her warm thigh, the quivering still in her belly, the softness and nice smell of her hair, the smoothness of her skin and neck. He could lay with her, intertwined in her scent, nuzzled like that for hours. Along with the quavering he felt, he heard her quickened short breaths, still sex like. Soon the quivering dissipated, her breathing slowed, and those long eyelashes closed. Frank stared at her beautiful face, and thanked God he found this incredible woman, always full of surprises. He drifted off to sleep as well.

CHAPTER 34
ANOTHER VERDICT

I will breathe. I will think of solutions.
I will not let my worry control me.
I will not let my stress break me.
I. Will. Simply. Breathe. And it will be okay . . .
because I don't quit.
~ Shayne McClendon, The Good Girl ~

The phone rang. It was James Lomegistro.

"Frankie, it's time, the Jury is in with their verdict. Get dressed and meet me in the courthouse by 10:30 at the latest. Make sure she eats something. The emotions can be quite intense. Okay, see you then."

Susan was so tense in the car on the drive over. Frank tried to distract her.

"So Sush, how come you always call me Franklin?"

"I don't know. You like to call me Sush, or Sweet Pea a lot. I like Franklin. It's different and you are different. Frank seems too plain for such a special man."

"Is that what you really think?"

"Yes, why do you doubt what I say?"

"I don't."

"Well then."

He turned on the radio and played one of their favorite duets, the one by Pink that they sang at Karaoke on their first evening date. Frank smiled, thinking of all the fun times and of all the good memories they had created together. He trusted the verdict would be positive.

They arrived at the courtroom early and sat on a bench outside. Frank brought Susan a cup of tea. He drank his coffee.

Frank didn't pretend to protect her anymore. Susan was strong and confident, everything had been disclosed, and she was still here. Now the verdict would be read.

A woman approached, one who was in the courtroom for most of the trial. Part of the media, or just a curious spectator, they didn't know and didn't really care. She leaned towards Susan and said, "Susan Chatham you are the bravest woman I have ever met. I just needed to tell you that."

Susan smiled at her and replied, "Thank you, and thank you for saying that and for coming."

Susan realizes IT wasn't about her nakedness, not about her abuse, not about rape and sodomy. All of her fears about what people would see when they looked at her dissipated. What they would remember was her bravery, and that was a comforting thought.

James arrived and hugged his brother. He leaned over to give Susan's hand a squeeze and planted a friendly brotherly kiss on her cheek.

They entered the courtroom and took their places.

Susan wore a smart suit, navy blue pencil skirt with matching jacket, light blue blouse, simple pearl earrings and necklace, beige pumps. Her heartbeat began to quicken. She looked over at George Ferguson, no longer as angry. She almost felt sorry for him. She realized that he was a very sick man. She decided to focus on the fact that because of his behavior, she was sent to medical and met the love of her life, Franklin Lomegistro.

Susan knew firsthand what it felt like to be standing there waiting for a verdict and hearing that word. "Guilty." It was excruciating.

They all sat at their places when the Judge arrived.

"All rise as the Honorable Judge Dallas Matthews enters the courtroom."

"Has the Jury reached their verdict?"

"Yes, Your Honor."

"George Evan Ferguson, please rise."

"We the Jury in the above entitled action find the Defendant George Evan Ferguson . . . Guilty."

"George Evan Ferguson, you have been found Guilty on all charges and are sentenced to 25 years in prison without the possibility of parole."

"Mr. Ferguson, you took an oath to uphold the law. To protect and rehabilitate the women in a correctional institution, under your care, and instead you chose to usurp that power and did unconscionable things to an innocent woman."

And with that George Ferguson was led away in cuffs and shackles.

Susan just stared at him, happy and sad all at once. She was happy that he would pay for what he had done to her and others. She was sad at the memory of herself having been in that position. Hold up, had the Judge used the word innocent to describe her?

Then the Judge did something utterly unexpected, calling her to rise too!

Susan froze. "What the fuck?" Her blood turned cold, and her feet felt numb in her heels.

"Quiet in the courtroom please, I am not finished. Susan Jordyn Chatham please rise. I want to read this in a United States Courtroom to make it all the more official, and while the media is still here to capture this moment."

Richard Chatham stared at his daughter. Tommie looked at his sister. Dale McCraven was there by himself, eyeing his ex-wife. Franklin Lomegistro observed his new girlfriend.

James Lomegistro smiled. All eyes were on Susan as she stood before the Judge.

"Susan Jordyn Chatham, I hold in my hands a letter from the Governor, upon a review of the case for which you were previously convicted and sentenced to five years at Lynchfield Women's Correctional Facility, new evidence has surfaced which completely exonerates you from all charges. You my dear are to be immediately set free."

A hush of sighs echoed through the courtroom.

Susan stood there in disbelief. Taking a quick glance at her Dad, brother, Dale, and staring at Frank, she mouthed the words, "Thank you."

"Furthermore," the Judge continued. "There's more?" Susan couldn't believe it.

"The Prison system has failed you. It was supposed to protect, to rehabilitate, it was supposed to provide edible food and nutrition, decent clothing and warmth, a suitable place to sleep, and a proper place to shower and wash. The prison system should have kept you safe. You should not have been physically or mentally abused. You should not have been raped, nor sodomized. You should not have been subject to having a guard urinate, defecate, and do otherwise unconscionable things to you."

Susan stood there, still shaking. She couldn't believe what he was saying. She couldn't believe that she lived through all these things. She was now standing in this courtroom and was free. It was overwhelming. She swallowed hard, not knowing how she could listen to any more of this while standing there, while everyone in that courtroom had their eyes on her. And just when she thought she couldn't listen to another damn thing, Judge Matthews said, "and for your pain and suffering, Susan Chatham, the court awards you, $2.8 million dollars! To be paid out . . . "

But Susan didn't hear the pay out information. Amid the gasps from everyone in the courtroom, Susan Jordyn Chatham fainted.

"Jesus Christ! Susan!"

Frank was the first to run over to her. Jim Lomegistro ran to the Judge. "Call 911, she split her head open. She's bleeding profusely from her scalp, and she's unconscious."

All hell broke loose in the courtroom that day. Susan was exonerated. She was awarded a huge sum of money. And now she was flat on her back on the floor, blood everywhere, paramedics called.

Frank pulled off her jacket and used it to apply pressure to where she had cut her scalp, trying to stop the bleeding, and calling her name but she doesn't open her eyes. His eyes filled with fear.

The ambulance arrived and paramedics quickly put her on a stretcher and carried her off, all the while the media was having a field day filming her being taken by ambulance to Regional Memorial Hospital.

Susan woke up in the hospital with a massive headache.

"Ouch." She grabbed at her head, and tried to sit up, but it hurt too badly.

"What happened? I remember the Judge . . . Franklin?" She saw his face close to hers. "The Judge said I'm free right Franklin? Where am I, why does my head hurt so much?"

"Jesus, Susan, you don't remember anything do you?"

"No, Franklin, ouch! Don't make me think . . . it hurts too much."

"Sush, you are not just free, my girl, you are a very wealthy woman. The court awarded you 2.8 million dollars from the State for your pain and suffering. You heard that and passed out, and you hit your head on the wood chair on your way down splitting your scalp open."

"Fuck Franklin, how embarrassing. Do I always have to be so dramatic?"

"Oh you were dramatic all right, it was plastered all over the news . . . television, radio, newspaper, social media . . . you are the talk of the town. 'Convicted felon featured in Pornogate given freedom, becomes a millionaire, ends up in the hospital.' That about sums it up."

"Fuck Franklin, fuck, ouch!" She lay back down, tears in her eyes.

Before she got a chance to digest any of it, she was shocked to see the Judge in her hospital room. He walked over to her bed, sat down in a chair next to her bed, and grabbed her hand in his. Jim Lomegistro was there too, and the Governor! Susan was overwhelmed.

What? How? Why were they all here? For a brief minute she thought it was a dream, a hallucination from a mildly concussed brain.

Frank spoke first. "Susan, you will be fine, you have several stitches. They will keep you here 24 hours just for observation, because you did suffer a mild concussion, and then we will go home. You don't have to report back to Lynchfield. I told Roberta she could have all your things, and that if you wanted anything, we will get it next week when I take you to visit her. The Judge has something he wants to read to you. You passed out in his courtroom and he isn't sure you heard him, and because it is recorded in the courtroom log, he wants to make sure you are aware. And the Governor is so smitten with you, ever since your show, that he wanted to see your face when you heard the good news, but he was late to the courtroom, but now that you are here, he was able to attend."

"Franklin, I am dreaming."

"No Susan, this is not a dream. This is for real Sweet Pea. You are FREE and you are RICH, very, very RICH!"

Judge Matthews began, "I need to repeat myself Susan, because dear girl, are you all right? Wait let me read this again to you. Susan Jordyn Chatham, the prison system has failed you. It was supposed to protect, to rehabilitate, it was supposed to provide edible food and nutrition, decent clothing and warmth, a suitable place to sleep, and a proper place to shower and wash. The prison system should have kept you safe. You should not have been physically nor mentally abused, you should not be raped, nor sodomized.

You should not have been subject to having a guard urinate, defecate, and do otherwise unconscionable things to you."

Susan listened attentively. Hearing it again as if it was a scene from a television biography.

"And for your pain and suffering, Susan Chatham, the court awards you, $2.8 million dollars! To be paid out . . . "

She still couldn't comprehend the pay out, and it didn't even matter to her. It was all so very shocking.

CHAPTER 35
FREEDOM AND FRANKLIN

We must be willing to let go of the life we have planned,
so as to have the life that is waiting for us.
~ Joseph Campbell ~

Life at Frank's had a totally different feel now. She wasn't there in his care as an inmate on furlough. Susan Chatham was free.

Frank appeared worried, "So what now Sush?"

She winked back at him happily, "What do you mean my love?"

"Well, now you are free, to come and go as you please. You are at liberty to live where you want, love who you want, work where you want. Jesus, Sush, you don't even have to work, you have enough wealth. Damn Susan, you will be so busy. Jimmie and his team still want a meeting with you. He thinks you can negotiate for up to 3.5 million. He hasn't been wrong about anything concerning your affairs thus far. And you still need to meet with that screenplay writer and producer about doing the movie about your life and experiences at Lynchfield, and then there's that lady that is writing your biography. Have you called her back yet? You probably want to move to your own place, you can own quite a penthouse if you want."

"Franklin, stop, just stop." She walked over to him, planted a kiss on his lips and gave him a big hug. "You are a buffoon! Why would I want to live anywhere but here? This apartment of yours was my refuge, my sanctuary, during my darkest days. I don't ever want to live anywhere else. Oh, yes, I could go stay at some very nice high-end places with all my money, and spare no expense, but I would still want to come home to you. Are you afraid that I will get back together with Dale is that it? You know he has been calling me. He's a dick Franklin. Why would I want Dilly back? Yes, I loved him, and yes, I would be lying if I said I didn't have feelings for him, I suppose in some ways I still do . . . but Franklin . . . he didn't believe me, he didn't trust me. He had an affair with Allison Cray, he may have been involved in me being set up and framed for a crime I didn't commit, and he dumped me like a hot potato when I was imprisoned and wasn't there for me. He stole my money, my trust, and my love. You Franklin were and are my savior, my guardian angel. You went above and beyond in taking care of me when I ended up in your Medical Department after George nearly killed me during my furlough. When I went on furlough with you, you bought me things and "dated" me and made me forget I was still an inmate. I had the best of times. "Janney's," shopping, "Karaoke Bar" dancing, singing, and dining, you even took me to my favorite place in the world, Mrs. Chen's "Dim Sum." We went to the beach, and made love, and you gave me the world's most incredible massage. But most importantly Franklin, you gave me back my dignity."

Susan kissed him and hugged him again even tighter and more passionately.

"Franklin, you came up with that brilliant idea about the one woman show. That kept my friends and me safe for a very long time while we rehearsed. You also made sure we had enough to eat and arranged for the yogurts and Boost. You have no clue, when you are in prison and hungry, what something that simple means. In our minds that was lobster, filet mignons and truffles. Well for Bert it might have been Mofongo and Alcapurias." Frank laughed.

"And Franklin, because of the success of that show and all the fundraising money we raised, things did improve for all the women at Lynchfield. And the Governor being there, that led to my exoneration, I know that moved him into action. I am just the puppet here. You are the puppeteer. You are the genius behind what will be our success."

Susan grew more serious and she beheld Franklin with a longing, with an appreciation, and a love that Franklin felt she was reaching his inner soul with those deep blue eyes of hers.

"Franklin, if it wasn't for you doing the background check on me and your brother Jimmie's discoveries . . . I would not be free now, and wouldn't have won this major lawsuit and have all this money. I owe you everything Franklin, my trust, my wealth, my love. There isn't anything I wouldn't do for you and no one I would ever want to be with but you my love."

They embraced each other and kissed. Their kiss turned to passion, a roaring river of emotions between them. All else seemed to disappear. She allowed him to pick her up and carry her into the bedroom, and there with closed doors, they had sex now on a different plane of consciousness, a deeper level altogether.

This time it was about more than the bodily pleasures, this was between two people who had a deep trust, appreciation, and love for each other. Two souls that were connected in a way most people only dream about.

He caressed her hair, and ran his fingers down her forehead, her cute little nose, around those perfectly high cheekbones, and luscious soft lips, and down that sensuous chin. He kissed her neck and down her collar bones and her sternum, over her breasts, and spent time sucking those deliciously soft yet erect nipples, and stroking those lovely soft creamy skinned, perky, perfect mounds, those squishy tits of hers. He licked down her flat tummy and around her belly button, down just to her pubic hair. He played with the soft dark curls then stroked her lower lips with his fingers feeling her begin to get wet under his touch. He continued down her thighs, to the back of her knees, those beautiful dancer's legs of hers. He bent down and suckled on every cute little toe, seeing her begin to squirm from the stimulation of it all. She was hot for him and more than ready.

He pulled out a foil packet, and smiled remembering that first day in CVS. He put the condom on and entered her, as if she were the Taj Mahal. They made love in a way that left them speechless, satisfied, and spent.

Just when he thought that would have been enough, she rolled over and began on him. But she then stopped abruptly and got up and fetched her bag of toys.

"Oh my, what do you have in mind?"

"Shhh." She put her finger on his lips.

Susan took out a lavender filled eye sachet pillow and placed it over Frank's eyes and turned on the Bose sound system to some romantic music, with erotic undertones.

She warmed some lavender sandalwood oil in her hands and massaged his scalp.

"MMMM" Frank murmured sleepily.

Then she massaged his forehead, his cheeks, his mustache and beard areas, his lips, she bent down and began to kiss him, moving her tongue over his, biting and sucking on his lips. Then she turned and did the same to his ears, first the right then the left.

Frank felt he had died and reached Heaven.

"Is it my birthday?" he asked.

"Everyday," she answered.

Then she massaged his neck, shoulders, arms, chest; she bent down and began to suckle his nipples like he did hers. It was a new sensation for Frank. He loved his Evangeline, but their lovemaking had been very traditional and not bold and adventurous like with Susan.

Susan continued now kissing him on his stomach and sculpted abdomen, moving down to his pubic hair. He felt her stroking his scrotum and manhood with the lubricant oil, it was warming and he smelled the cherry scent. She bent down and kissed his tip. He was fully erect and ready again. His cock throbbed to feel her tight pussy around him again. But she didn't continue. She went down to his feet, massaging the heels, his arches, ankles, legs, thighs, then went back down and suckled on his toes, like he did hers. It was all so sensual and he was just lost in the thought of her beauty, and her sexiness. He almost felt like he would orgasm even without her touching him where it counts, but just as he thought this, he felt her back there. She stroked his balls and cock again with the cherry lubricant with her delicate fingers, then she continued with her lips and tongue and cheeks and those teeth with that nibbling that she did that drove him to the brink. Just when he thought the sensations were just too much and he couldn't hold still any longer, somehow, she was holding that damn vibrator bullet with the jelly tentacles on his perineal area, that delicate area between his testicles and his penis. Frank had never experienced anything like it. His balls tingled and his cock pulsated.

She sucked with fervor. He came hard gasping, as if releasing an energy, passion, and love pent up for an eternity.

He heard his voice yell although he didn't feel his lips move.

"Oh My God, Susan Chatham. You are going to kill me!"

He heard her giggle. "That good huh, Dr. Lomegistro?"

Paul Sterling and Susan had been scheming to plan a surprise party for Frank for his birthday. Reservations, music, food, beverages, decorations, invitations, every detail was perfectly executed.

They were all going to the Karaoke Bar Lounge for an evening of dancing, singing, and dining, but Susan had planned quite a bash for Frank.

Paul agreed to pick Frank up, and he was supposed to drive Frank there. He knew everyone including Susan would already be in attendance. Mike Ramsey would be bringing Roberta Jimenez to be with Paul on furlough, so she would enjoy the party too. This way Paul would drive them all back, so Susan and Frank could get drunk again. He was destined to be their permanent designated driver.

Paul suspected Susan had been teaching his Bert a few tricks and treats too, because she kept getting hotter and hotter every time he saw her. Or was her inner Latina coming out? Warden Ramsey, now that Susan was free, had been concentrating on getting Roberta Sanchez Jimenez an early parole. Paul couldn't wait, and hoped she would move in with him, like Susan did with Frank.

Paul knew how over the top the bash was that Susan had planned. He had also seen the ring that Frank bought for Susan. Frank had shared that he just didn't know how or when to propose? Paul thought, "If a woman I loved planned a party like this for me, I would want to propose right then and there."

Paul snuck into Frank's bedroom while he was in the bathroom changing to leave, and he popped the ring Frank bought for Susan in his pocket. Paul thought Frank might want to propose to Susan tonight. Frank's birthday and Susan's proposal; double surprise!

Paul and Frank arrived at Karaoke. Frank was wearing black trousers and a black collared shirt and his black blazer, looking much younger than his 45 years.

"SURPRISE!!!"

Frank couldn't believe it. He noticed Susan standing in the corner and knew immediately it was her doing. Always full of surprises this love of his, in the bedroom and out on the town.

She looked amazing. She was wearing a short skin-tight turquoise dress. Her legs appeared endless. Her hair was cascading around her naked shoulders and she had some highlights put in. Her makeup was spot on with those long eyelashes of hers and those deep blue eyes and those red luscious lips. Frank smiled and she winked back. He almost wished everyone would go home and he could TAP her right then.

And what song should come on? The first song they had danced to at that same bar, during her first furlough, Bell Biv DeVoe's "Poison!"

Frank grabbed her waist and pulled her to the dance floor.

The night was a blur of boogying, feasting, and imbibing. Instead of just Karaoke, there was also a full live band. Dinner consisted of oysters on the half shell with fresh squeezed lemon and hot sauce, there was surf and turf with the most succulent lobsters all pre-shelled for the guests with lovely drawn butter, and there was tender well-seasoned filet mignon. Crispy Green Beans arrived fresh from Mrs. Chen's and other sides included Mofongo and Alcapurias. Roberta was in her glory. The open bar served top shelf liquor. Susan had spared no expense. When it came time for dessert, a special cake arrived on a moving dolly.

It was a multilayered sheet cake, with a cherry preserves swirl, with a picture of Lynchfield prison printed on the fondant icing, and on it was a big "Get Out of Jail Free" card and a replica of Frank in his medical white coat, and a reproduction of Susan in her orange scrubs, but wearing her showgirl hat from the "Anything Goes" show number. Frank saw the cake and broke out laughing. Susan did as well. Everyone else cheered and sang "Happy Birthday" to Frank. Susan sang him "Have I Told You Lately" one of her favorite songs by Rod Stewart and Frank serenaded her with, "The First Time Ever I Saw Your Face."

They embraced and kissed. Everyone blushed thinking they were going to tear each other's clothes off and have a go at it right there, right then.

But instead, Paul approached the lovebirds. He tapped Frank on the shoulder and showed him the tiny box with the ring. Frank, when seeing the ring, gave his friend a bear hug.

Frank took the box, grabbed the microphone from Susan, and got down on bended knee.

"Susan Jordyn Chatham, you are the love of my life. I can't imagine a day without you my love. Will you marry me? Please say yes!" Frank opened the tiny box, the diamond sparkled.

"Yes of course!" Susan burst into joyful tears.

Everyone cheered as Susan and Franklin kissed passionately.

The band played Jason Derulo's "Marry Me."

That night the drinking and dancing and singing continued until the wee hours and everyone was exhausted and said their goodbyes.

Paul drove Roberta, Susan and Frank home to Frank's place.

Fireworks shot out of both bedrooms.

EPILOGUE

Susan woke up curled up in their bed, Franklin's arms around her waist, his face close to the nape of her neck, his nose nuzzled her long dark hair. Spooned together, their warm bodies intertwined, her breath slow and soft, he ran his big toe lengthwise along the bottom arch of her foot.

"Sweet Pea, ahh, you are so soft, so warm, so lovely, my love. Are you up?"

"Are you hot for me again, my husband?"

"Always for you."

She rolled over with a smile, and a naughty twinkle in her deep blue eyes, and takes in her muscular, handsome husband. She ran her hands through his wavy tousled hair, ending on his salt and pepper sideburns.

She inhaled his amazing aftershave scent. How can he smell this good, even this early in the morning?

She leaned forward planting her tender, luscious lips on his. Kissing him, his trademark mustache tickling her upper lip. He took her lips suckling them, nipping at them, running his tongue inside, and finding hers. She followed back, rolling her tongue around his, tasting each other.

She felt him hardening and rising near her thighs, his fingers ran down her thighs feeling her increasing wetness.

Tasting his finger, "You are so wet, and taste so very yummy."

She laughed, "Oh you will flatter me to get what you want, you sweet talker."

"No more talking, I just want you, here, now, I want your poison."

She responded, opening up to him, splaying her legs, receiving his gift, his hard cock throbbing, giving him herself in return.

Their passion was endless, a frenzy between the sheets. Their deep love for each other overflowing, and their sex driving each other to unsurpassed heights and then cascading into ecstasy.

"Whoa, you are going to kill me woman!"

"Ahhhhh, the pleasure is all mine, my guardian angel!"

After amazing sex, the husband and wife sat at their kitchen table, the wonderful smell of her delicious vanilla, cinnamon, French toast, warm buttery maple syrup, and crispy bacon filling the air. She knew it was his favorite breakfast. It was a gorgeous kitchen, almost as beautiful as the couple living there. White contemporary cabinets, granite countertops, a sub zero refrigerator freezer, wine cellar, wet bar, butler's pantry, the best money could buy. Silver and crystal chandeliers hung from the ceiling. The seats were white leather with a silvery trim. Franklin spared no expense in remodeling his kitchen to accommodate his new wife Susan's gourmet cooking, and he enjoyed every morsel she prepared for him in that exquisite kitchen.

"May I pour you a cup of coffee Mrs. Lomegistro?" he asked as he fixed his own cappuccino.

"No, thanks, Dr. Lomegistro," she responded. "I'd rather have a cup of my favorite lemon ginger tea."

"How about some orange juice, Sush?"

"I'd love some Franklin."

They sat to enjoy their breakfast, smiling at each other, still feeling that wonderful post coital bliss, relaxed feeling. They conversed happily about mundane things like their plans to take some friends to Dim Sum that evening. "Mr. and Mrs. Chen will love meeting our Dim Sum Virgins!" They laughed out loud.

"I have had such cravings for crispy green beans. I may not share with you tonight Franklin."

"Oh, really Sweet Pea? Deny your magnificent husband crispy green beans? That's almost abusive."

"Speaking of abusive, Franklin, I just read in the paper that George Ferguson's appeal was denied."

"He got what he deserved Sush. How he could have taken such a wonderful woman and treated her so poorly, and done those awful things to you, he had it coming."

"Oh, Franklin, you are just jealous that he had his way with me. By the way, I was offered a new role. I just finished reading the script. It involves dancing, nudity, and sex. How will you feel about that?"

"Of course, I don't like it when others get to see and taste my wine, but I suppose that's the price I have to pay, to be married to my gorgeous and smoking hot, actress wife."

"Oh, Franklin, you sure know how to flatter me and get what you want."

"Always, Sush, always."

"Well, I do love this story. It's brilliant. I have so many great ideas for this role, but I suppose as the leading lady, I will need to lose a lot of weight, and get in super shape, as this character is very thin, and has a tight ass and killer legs."

"Ah, Susan, you have an amazing body already. You are perfect just the way you are."

"This project may have to wait until after the baby though."

"What? Baby? Mrs. Lomegistro, OUR baby?"

They hugged and kissed, and he lifted her up off the ground, spinning her around and jumping for joy.

"Ahh, Susan Chatham-Lomegistro, I am so lucky. You make me so very happy."

"No, Franklin, I'm the lucky one. You are so smart and handsome. You have the hottest body, are the best prison physician and my guardian angel. I just know you will make the greatest most loving dad ever."

The End

ABOUT THE AUTHOR

Doris Vilk was born in Havana, Cuba and has lived in Nassau, Bahamas; Milan, Italy and Madrid, Spain. She currently lives in South Florida where she loves the beach. She is happily married and has one son.